Sea Holly

Sea Holly

Robert Minhinnick

seren

Seren is the book imprint of
Poetry Wales Press Ltd
57 Nolton Street, Bridgend, Wales, CF31 3AE
www.seren-books.com

ISBN 978-1-85411-435-8

Cover photograph © Barry Needle
www.southwalesinfocus.com

Inner design and typesetting by books@lloydrobson.com

Printed by Creative Print and Design, Wales

The publisher works with the financial assistance of
the Welsh Books Council.

Monday

Vine

He lay propped against cushions, his arms folded on his chest. What was important was to be ready for it. So he stayed still and listened to the sand that brushed against the caravan in the darkness. And the sea like something electric left on overnight, so familiar as to be unnoticed until the rest of life ceased. Somewhere, a car horn. Last week he remembered a thrush. He knew it was a thrush because it repeated itself three times, a thrush out on the avenue, nesting over, its young gone or dead, a thrush singing in a world where there were no trees and sand was master and mistress and the skin of that world disintegrated when the wind blew. A thrush, singing for him. Its voice out of the dune like something lost, returning. Whether it wanted to or not.

And then it had happened. The seizure, the ripping of his breath from his body. As if somebody else had needed it. Somebody stronger. It had happened last week and last night. As it would happen tonight, soon. To defy the moment he did what he always did. He thought of the day that had passed. He held it in his mind as a DVD, the images coming as they would, editing themselves, unbidden, sacred.

Yes, thought Vine, sacred. Because who else would say it if he did not, the memories erupting, refashioning themselves. Memory like the stained glass above the chancel in St John's. So he lay with his arms together and if it looked like prayer, he thought, then maybe prayer it was, this being perhaps his last night, his last minute. He who was fit and fifty and dying. And thrush or no thrush, his requiem would be the music of sand, as it retreated, as it advanced.

When Vine closed his eyes he saw first a memory from another day. It was the typewritten card in the girl's glass case. Her body had been burned. But nobody could say why.

Child A.

One name as good as another. Only a painting now but there she was, Child A, holding a gull's wing, looking out to sea. The exhibit Child A. A for Anonymous, but he would call her *Arianwen*. He would call her that.

Arianwen. For the splinters that were left of her, polished by the sand. For the bones in their case in the museum where she lay under the painting that was her proxy, a girl on a hillside scanning the horizon. But he stood a mile away at her grave, at least the place they had found her, a cleft in the limestone above a pool that leaked into the dune. And he remembered her skull as an oyster shell and the thighbone that spoke her sex. As to the rest of her, the imagination must decide. He, like any other, was free to put language into her mouth, to pierce the meat of her and claim a kinship with her clan, those first people.

Vine lay still and allowed the day to remake itself. Had these things happened? It was the dream of the past. But his past. This was what he had done that day. Or was it? He came down the slope and followed the stream bed out on to the beach. Its sand was pale as stubble and skeletons of sea holly stood between the traffic bollards that the tide had brought in. There was something dark on the sea. Vine thought it was driftwood. But it moved differently from the current. It was a cormorant. The bird's wings were spread on the water in a black cross. Then it lifted them. Vine had seen cormorants stay that way for minutes at a time. There it was, an M on the swell, the cormorant's wings raised like two black mattocks.

He walked this way deliberately because it was exercise like no other, each step a challenge. For what reason there was no need to ask, the effort to keep moving requiring all his concentration. He wore seawater-bleached plimsolls and jeans with a shirt tied around his waist, the way he'd dressed all summer, and now despite the onshore breeze he kept it that way, aware that his body was leaner than it had been for years, and darker too, maybe as dark as Arianwen's, after her mortification.

It took half an hour to reach the slipway. Five minutes later he was amidst the caravans, ranks of them spread between the shore and the resort. His own caravan was on Avenue J, an address that still felt foreign, but he ignored that turning and carried on past the leisure park's arcades. It was 6 pm and few machines were occupied, children feeding copper to the Colossos, the familiar loners in the over-eighteen sections working the Excalibur.

Spellman was there with his saddlebags of change and in the next unit he could see Vanno thumbing a slot, Vanno who gambled like a nun prayed, gambled small, her prayers being humble ones, platinum Vanno in her Top Shop denim and FCUK tee, Vanno with a tanning studio shadow over her arcade pallor, stick-thin Vanno with her yin and yang tattoos, Vanno whom he would always call Myfanwy so that he could see her light up with that nicorette smile and say hiya luv, how's tricks then?

But he walked on into the desert before the funfair. This was a quarter mile of blown sand where shops and fish restaurants had once stood. But they had been cleared years earlier in advance of the regeneration that was coming. The road was drifted over, a three foot high dune having appeared in the last week. On his left, concrete steps emerged from the drift and led down to the beach. This week there had been a market here every day and now the traders were packing up. Two men were rolling bolts of cloth and loading saris into the back of a van. How long the material was, thought Vine, glancing at the red silk, the blue. How strange it must be to feel it wind endlessly around the body. The men whispered together, their arms full. But the tide was coming in, the breeze keening. He put on his shirt and turned in at The Cat.

Clint, the landlord's son, stood in the entrance, smoking, holding his Nokia. He'd dyed his hair blonde. It stood up in thorns. Clint smiled because he always smiled but they didn't speak.

Usual? asked somebody, as Vine walked to the bar.

The room was a negative of itself: a curved counter, a few tables, a television mounted in the ceiling. Ahead was the black space of the back room.

The usual, he thought to himself. That was the first time anyone had ever said that to him.

Thanks.

The cider was already pulled. Pale, ferocious. So he was a cider drinker now. He pushed the pound coins into the darkness.

How's life? the landlord asked.

A landlord who talked. Who asked questions. But he shouldn't be surprised. He'd been coming here most days for three months. That made him a regular. Suspicious, maybe, but still a regular.

Vine looked around. The open door was the only light, apart from the television. That music video channel was on again, but with the sound turned off. And there was Tania introducing the next three minutes, Downtown Tania Brown, local girl made good, Tania who'd somehow escaped to become a satellite siren speaking from Helsinki or Amsterdam or wherever Snow TV was based. Tania who owned the screen until the next Tania pushed to the front. Then Downtown Tania winked and the video started. Men in furs, women in rags, together in a burned out street, pointing at themselves. Look at us. Yeah look at us.

Could have been a boast. Or a warning. Then their gold roared, their gladiators' skins turned radioactive. But Snow was usually on. Out of two hundred channels the drinkers preferred Snow. Their patriotic duty, the young ones said. So tonight Downtown Tania was a star. With the sound off.

Fine, thanks George.

Vine took the glass to a corner table. The place was long and narrow. There were no windows, the bar being reached by a corridor usually covered with sand. It stood in a 1960s terrace of arcades and chip counters, the whole lot for sale, having been years on the market. A stranger would have walked past, the hidden-away pub advertising itself only with an aluminium keg and a blown-over blackboard announcing happy hour and the house doubles. Vine had passed a hundred times before even considering a visit.

And now he was a regular, a summer drink before him as the season changed, as the wind lifted the grains on the moraine in the corridor, as the glaciers advanced and retreated, shape-shifting by the moment, as sand arrived and sand fled, polishing, burying and offering its music as a farewell to warmth and a prelude to the cold.

As usual there was sand in his shoes and in his hair. Surely that was its dust upon his tabletop. Sand was a swarm and an army. At night he would listen to sand hissing against gas cylinders and caravan windows. Chorus upon chorus. And he had come to love its restlessness. What was good about sand was it did not cease. Nothing new could resist its attrition. Yet nothing lost in sand was lost forever.

The only other drinkers in were Hal and The Fish. Someone said that Hal was short for Hallelujah but Vine had never been inclined to ask. It seemed early for Hal. And surely The Fish should have been at The Kingdom, selling rides. But it was only Monday. Quiet night. Vine looked at The Fish. He was a five-foot forty year old with a shrivelled arm. On the counter before him it looked like a fin. Or perhaps he was younger. If you stared at him closely, he didn't seem forty at all. Sort of baby-faced.

Sometimes The Fish glanced around but most of the time they sat at the bar with their backs to Vine, not talking, because this was happy hour which meant it was the desultory hour that separated day from night, an hour to kill on a barstool under an unwatched television, a difficult hour Vine usually found, empty now of what once had been all consuming.

At this hour Nia would be cooking the evening meal, it being Monday so her turn. Siân, her mother, would be coming back from choir practice, getting ready for an evening's marking, and fourteen-year-old Brychan in his room with the PC on and the web at his fingertips. Family life. Beyond the sand's reach, Vine would have said once. But this peninsula was sand's empire, he now knew.

Then Donal came in and all was different. He greeted the room and came to sit by Vine. Sandals, Bermudas, washed out singlet advertising some marlin fishing club. Even in the bar's twilight his tan was noticeable, a deliberate and prized adobe, cultivated, shed and restored over a decade in the Med, and now back home on Avenue A in a silver Arizona with a windmill on the roof and a garden devoted to *lollo rosso* and the poppies that grew in the gravel of this coast.

Com est as, brawd?

All right, Donal, said Vine. How's the Portuguese man o' war?

Over Pwll Du way, this morning, but it was getting lumpy. Lovely screed on the water though. Some bastards had a net out quarter mile long. Such a fine mesh it would take anything. All the schoolies.

They'll give it to the French, said Vine.

Who can teach us how to eat it too. There's things around here we don't even have names for. But they've built a living from it all. Fancy another?

No, I'll be late. Any plans?

Donal spat dryly.

Quiet week. Looking down the telescope at what's going by.

You're washed up.

Aren't we all?

Donal was drinking cola. He rationed alcohol to the weekend, as doctor and bank balance instructed. To John Vine he seemed in good shape. Hair silvering, yolk of dark muscle not too thick. Maybe the eyes a thyroidal yellow, and his liver, okay, a sea cucumber, but he was wearing well, a surfer still, a longboard artist the youngsters had once craned to watch.

Got to keep the summer alive.

How long you been in that van? asked Vine.

Three years in January.

Ever get cabin fever?

Donal spat again.

It's not so bad. As you're finding out.

He tasted his cola.

Nobody bothers you. Much. In fact, you could die in one of those mousetraps and it would take weeks till they found out. I comfort myself with that thought when the fret's in and you can't see ten feet.

Same as anywhere.

I'm a gypsy now. But you've got family here. All your life.

Vine's cider was the colour of a pound coin. He had a last pull.

Life changes, he said. You especially must know that.

Hey, no inquisition from me. Donal held his hands up.

Listen, we'll go swimming one night.

You're the tide master, smiled Vine. But make it soon.

Bit of a fire, nice side of bass. A good white.

Some kind of sauvignon, laughed Vine.

And a full moon red as coral. We'll put some Brian Wilson on.

No way. I want the curlews.

Not as good as *Pet Sounds*.

I want the waves.

This Saturday might work, said Donal. Forecast is good.

Hey, the last night.

Yeah. Big night. See you on the beach.

A life of ease, said Vine. And walked out.

In the corridor Clint was holding a takeaway kebab tray, dropping iceberg on the floor. The twilight surprised Vine. He hurried on. Behind him, in the last week of the season, the funfair pumped out its music, the Firewheel flickering as it spun two riders above the town.

There were more people about now, the atmosphere tightening, special offers everywhere and eagerness at last masking the exhaustion in the faces of the arcade managers and stall-holders. A breeze was up and the sand spiralling off the beach. Vine could already feel it in the air. Above him, the flags were flying in their tatters, Old Glory a striped rag, the gold stars of the EU already burned through.

And everywhere there were voices.

Tainted love, came the words through the techno in the arcades where the children stood at their machines.

I, sang Shirley Bassey.

I who have

And if you should survive all of these the hounds of hell will surely, repeated the tape loop of the Kingdom of Evil.

Will surely

Will surely

And that's not really
That's not really
All
Nothing

He walked past the tattoo studio and the dinky rink. It was close to supper time at The Ritzy where the karaoke would start in an hour. Posters advertised The Dorrs, a Doors tribute band due Saturday night. He remembered the first time he had heard the organ on *Light My Fire*, Ray Manzarek's masterpiece.

And *The End* of course. Always *The End*. *The End* playing at 2 am in a million bedrooms, the end of everything because nothing was as sweet or as desperate or as long as *The End*, the final full stop. Until you woke in the morning with ashes in your throat and reached over and put the needle on *Light My Fire* again because that was better than daylight's amphetamine in the blood. But the tribute band was a circuit legend. The singer had been impersonating Jim Morrison for fifteen years. He'd been Jim Morrison longer than Jim Morrison. His angle was if people wanted to know what Morrison would have been like at forty five, then come to the show.

The sand in the carpark was blue under the security lights. Coming up the steps off the beach was Davy Dumma with his metal detector.

Any luck? asked Vine.

Davy was dressed in a brown mac and wellingtons.

Nah, he said.

Vine grinned. He knew that would have been the response if Davy had discovered a Bronze Age hoard. He was there every day, depending on the tide. Once Vine had seen him in the dunes.

You never know what those rabbits dig up, he'd said, which was Davy Dumma's longest answer to anything, in Vine's experience.

One day, eh? said Vine, but the man pushed past.

Now it was colder and there was no-one about when he crossed the desert and climbed the brackets on the breeze block wall and lowered himself into caravan city.

Here there were children, their parents scrubbed up in teeshirts and halternecks that looked transparent in the ultra-violet dusk, the men muscled, heads shaved, already holding the night's first cans, the women's backsides painted with dolphins and butterflies, and older couples, and loners, and teenagers clinging to one another, the cocklegirl with them on her way to work, her blue bandanna with moons upon it, and everyone gradually migrating east with the sand that stopped and swirled and moved in its dust devils, moved away from the sunset that was massing in reefs behind them, moved through the evening towards The Ritzy and The Salamander and the arcades that were full of seagull voices.

On his right was a breeze block building. Flat roof, aerial, line of wheelies at the rear. There was no window but a security guard stood at the entrance, mic'ed up, talking on a mobile, ignoring the occasional couple who passed in. In the darkness at the back Vine noted a shadow. He walked on for ten yards, paused, then returned. The shadow was still there, opening one of the bins. Vine observed it. Approached.

Lol?

I saw you first, said the shadow. Get over here.

Vine screened himself from the avenue. The second man was sorting scraps into a bag.

They don't chuck much here. Bit of pizza with pineapple. An abomination that. Couple of half bottles of wine. Valpolicella with the fizz gone.

How you keeping, Lol?

The figure put down the bag, ran a hand through the coalsmoke-coloured hair that hung over his collar.

Not so bad.

Look, said Vine, I can't stop. But I'll call round, okay?

Bring a bottle.

Surely. And you're okay?

As always. Just doing a little foraging.

Well don't let those goons see you.

Nobody sees me.

I saw you.

You know what to look for.

Vine pushed on into the site. On the corner of Avenue J a man was watering the marigolds in his garden. The flowers were black. His wife sat on a canvas chair, listening to a hymn. Their caravan was a big Brisbane. They'd called it 'Noddfa'.

Wel shwt ych chi eno? the woman called.

Weddol a bit.

Gwitho nawr?

Mewn munud, yn anffodus.

Vine took out his key but the door was unlocked. He brushed the mobile that Karoona had made from pieces of slate. The light was off but there was music playing, a sea holly music, prickly and bleached. Karoona had lit candles.

This is nice.

You're late again.

And I'm back out in ten minutes. But it'll be over by eleven.

So what do I do?

Good question, thought Vine. He wasn't sure what Karoona did with her time. But what did anybody do but waste it. Karoona played music. Sometimes she practised the songs she'd written. Karoona took showers and danced in her kimono and here she was now in her robe with her hair wet and smelling of mock orange.

Rehearse, he said.

Yes, like you rehearse. Rehearse for what?

Gigs.

There aren't any.

Put yourself about more. Be seen.

You should do that for me. I'm the singer. You should take my poster around the clubs.

But Vine was already stripped off and in the bathroom. He came out in a towel and opened the wardrobe. The dark suit, the blue shirt, the spivvy silver tie. Amazing, they were all there. Not clean of course, but they were there.

I saw Donal.

Old fart.

Hey, said Vine. Language. Where did you pick that up?

Karoona had lit incense and she sat near him on the bed while he filled the mirror.

Donal's okay, said Vine, getting the tie right. The Sun King's had a full life.

Wouldn't it be nice if we were… older, sang Karoona.

Whew. Your English is amazing, said Vine. Irony yet.

He was telling me how he can't afford to get his teeth fixed. Sad old man.

Vine smiled into the mirror.

What about mine? There's tectonic forces pushing mine apart.

He looked around.

Any food?

Skinny Karoona shrugged. She didn't cook because she rarely ate.

Look, I'll drop the flyers off in The Ritzy on the way up. Have you written your mobile number on them?

No.

Well how do you expect…?

Vine took a cloth and ran it over his Clarks. In the living room he found a black banana which had to do. Squashing a handful of pub-licity pictures into his case, he was back out in the darkness.

And then he was counting. Then he was calling.

Thirty seven of them in, which wasn't good or bad. It was the last Monday of the last week and you made of it what you made. Thirty seven players for the first round, which was always the best round early in the week, thirty women, seven men, a few of them in their twenties, most greyhaired. He looked down from the platform.

Four and three. Faw-Haw-Tee Three.

And he coughed. He knew he had to cough and he caught it before it exploded. But he coughed.

Vine had learned to call the numbers as they called the darts on television. To hold the word as long as possible. To tease them with it. Celebrate its power. Which was difficult with what possessed him.

Perhaps that walk had been too far. He looked down. How seriously the crowd was taking it, his thirty seven, heads bowed over the cards, pens poised. He could feel them concentrating. A good class. But here money was the teacher. Because money made things serious. He reached out and took the next ball, spinning in its perspex globe. It was cold from the jet in which it swam, a pebble out of the wave.

Reach out and I'll be there says number Faw-Orr.

He didn't cough again but he knew it was in him. The cough's white flower. On a vine. The vine in Vine. Hundreds of flowers on their vines. Opening in the darkness.

At the interval Vanno came up and said she felt lucky, a tenner's worth tonight if he could arrange it, which was lucky enough, because it had been a bad day so far, though twenty odd quid down wasn't that bad, can't grumble can you, not with the floods out in India, up to the domes of the mosques, a tenner's worth for a fish supper, maybe a nightcap in The Cat, which would leave two over to start tomorrow with a smile not that there was any fish left in the sea like. Course it was the children she felt sorry for.

Get your friend Mr Spellman to help out.

Norman? Tight as a cod's arsehole. Wears his moneybelt to bed. As I live and. Don't ask how I know but I know. Hasn't thrown a newspaper away for thirty years. And skimmed milk. Photocopies his bills too I've seen him down the Spar, he could get half a million for that house, lovely apartments, sea views to die for and the state of his trousers on a clear day mind.

How's the cats?

Vanno started to tell and Vine looked round, sipping his tea. They were in the Plaza that everyone called The Shed. Twenty red formica tables, one hundred white plastic chairs, a bar, a stage, toilets. Id came over in his smoking jacket, ruffled shirt. Id was old school.

Not exactly last night of the proms is it?

Vine laughed.

I've never done end of season before.

Nor might you again. It's all change.

Id looked around.

Once there'd have been a couple of hundred in. No danger.

Then he shrugged.

Liked the Four Tops thingy. Saw them in the Top Rank in the seventies. Build me up buttercup and all that stuff.

Id looked at Vine.

Don't get better do it?

Just a bit tight.

Try more antibiotics.

Vine had stopped tablets after the third course.

Needs time.

Yeah, yeah. Any plans yet?

For what?

Wakey wakey, said Idwal. After Saturday. When the curtain comes down whether we like it or not.

I'm sound, said Vine, and then they were starting on a new card, and he had a glass of water to hand, and Spellman won ten pounds and wanted it in coins and someone that Vine thought he recognised picked up a voucher, but then he recognised lots of people in the park but they were never the people from town or school because the park and the fair and the caravans were their own world. Oil and water. Still, the woman had stared hard. For a second too long to be comfortable. Vine looked into himself, trying to place her.

And that was the film. It went past in seconds. His day. Or all he remembered. All he had dreamed. Now as usual he lay on the sitting room couch because he didn't want his coughing to disturb Karoona. She was in the bedroom with her tapes and her headphones and the digital on, while he lay naked under a sheet propped against cushions. Arms crossed. His water and towel in reach, and the window open because the wind had dropped.

He could hear the sand settling in the avenue. There was nothing to listen to in the fair and even the sea was silent. One thought comforted. That, atom by atom, the dunes advanced. By morning the street would be buried a fraction deeper, the caravans settled further into their sites. Vine could see Vanno waving goodbye and Donal sitting with his cola and Id standing on the door as the thirty seven filed out. He could see the high tide that had passed and would return in the small hours. He remembered a child's plimsoll it had left behind.

And he could smell something. In that moment, something that was not a memory, but part of the midnight he now inhabited. It was a perfume, light, almost infinitesimal, gone and then there again. Something that came in the darkness. Black dew on his forehead. Black pollen on his lips. Perhaps it was Karoona, but he didn't think so. It was a musk that might have always been there which he noticed only at night. So he lay and let the sand cover his tracks. And waited for the vine to tighten in his chest and its flower to open as he opened his mouth to make his silent scream.

Donal

When I let the sand run through my fingers it looked brown and red. But the beach was black. It was black sand. Or maybe a very dark blue, the colour of the bougainvillaea that grew all the way down the cliff to the beach. You had to walk through those flowers down the steps cut into the cliff. And those flowers, they hung all over the iron rail. The iron rail that led you down. But that was the easy part. Coming back you'd have to stop at least twice for your breath. Near vertical it was. Great for the kids but not the people with the money.

We brought the supplies down the track from town. It was pretty lumpy, all stone and gravel. And the *arroyo* next to it, dry six months a year, that way was no rougher. But when it was in spate the current came over the edge and flooded our road. The only road. Brought a dead goat down once from the mountains. Brought orange trees with the oranges still on them like little brown purses. Brought one hell of a lot of crap down too, hundreds of plastic bottles and cartons. And nappies. Fucking disposable nappies. Like I say, that track was the only road in. And that's what I liked about it. You had to discover us. You had to be an adventurer to even get there because we were not on any tourist map. And the sea was amazing. Big waves, big blue waves on the black sand, breaking white. Breaking and stopping dead. You could draw a line in the sand and predict where the waves would stop. And they did. Always.

Except for that one in a thousand, one in a million wave that never stopped anywhere until it had taken a child off the beach, or a fisherman or a tourist rubbing cream into herself. Picked them off and gobbled them up. *El Zorro* they called that wave.

Locals told stories about it, scared the kids that the Zorro was coming if they didn't behave. So take my advice because it's good advice and served me well. Never turn your back on an ocean. And it doesn't matter where you are, crabbing on the Caib or diving in the Caribbean. The sea's the sea and if you don't respect it you're going to pay. Eventually.

But that beach was special. And the bar that was there already seemed a bargain, the bloke who owned it glad to be gone, he was going to Malaga he said, to live with his daughter. Eat watermelon and watch TV. But boy was it run down. The roof nearest the beach was just reeds and had nearly collapsed. So we asked around and some locals cut rushes from round the *arroyo* and we remade that roof, and we changed the furniture, cleaned up because it was a health hazard in the kitchen, and we took it from there.

And we changed the name too. *El Zorro*. One in a million. Which was risking it because of the local culture, but it seemed to work. And everything we served was local. All the wines, some of it from the Alpujarras and not even bottled. We went to the mountains for it and brought it back in plastic barrels. Some of it was rough but it was authentically rough. Or rustic, as they say. And some of the reds were not bad in a sherry-like way. One from Polopos I remember. I discovered it in Fransisco's, one of the traditional bars in the town. He had a barrel on the counter and it was an oily red.

What's this piss? I said.

Polopo he called it, because you don't pronounce the last 's' down there. I liked it. It was primitive. It was what I wanted at that time. It was real. But you got to have good beers and especially good food.

Local wine is scenic. But for beer you need a brand. And good tapas, that was the key. Do good tapas and the Germans arrive and then the Brits and then the Dutch. Big sardines with the heads and tails still on, the skin a bit hairy. Yeah, sardines, their brains so sweet. All together like ice in an ice bucket. And the little black eyes still in the head. Just eat it all, shut your eyes, stop being refined, stop pretending to be civilised and bite in and suck it all out. Sardine shit and all.

Maybe a few quail eggs, calamares of course and a little dish, my own speciality which I picked up in the Adriatic. Stewed aubergines with pimentos, a bit mushy but as fiery as you want. Serve it with toast and yes, it works. Easy. Comes from the Marines I suppose and learning to fend for yourself, because I've always loved food and respected it. To this day there's not a leaf I see I take for granted. Not a piece of scrag. As to the rest, we did a few simple things but did them well. Some locals were bringing us fish, dorado and such, but neither Marty nor me had the time to do them justice. So we served fish stew as our house speciality. We weren't chefs then and I'm not now. But I'm a cook all right, with an eye for the right ingredient.

Sopa del Zorro was a big bloody fish stew of our own devising. But based on local prejudice. After a while we made it as we wanted, and yeah, word got round. People came and we were busy. Closed Mondays to start with but there was pressure to open. And we knew the winter would be almost impossible and it was Marty's idea, Marty's dream, to shut up shop for four months and travel. She wanted to go everywhere. Most Australians do. Wanted me to take her up to Croatia, she wanted to hear people speaking Catalan, she wanted to come here to The Caib, she said I talked so much about it. And you know? We never did any of it.

We kept open Mondays instead and pulled the shells off shrimps and the skin off garlic cloves and put all of ourselves into that stew. Which I can smell to this day, as rich a broth as I'm ever going to serve. And we stayed open until the last customers left. Which is dangerous. Never make friends with your customers. We learned that fast. There's a lot of interesting people out there. A lot of lonely people.

Sipping that black Polopos wine at 3 am when you got to be up by seven is hard work. With hindsight we should have been tougher.

But it was often the couples who wanted to stay, or groups coming down that iron rail way past midnight expecting us to be open, coming through the bougainvillaea already tipsy, hurrying along the path between the cliff and the sea, where you had to time your run properly or get soaked. Those black waves were coming across the black beach. Can you blame them for wanting to lie out under the stars? To watch big old Orion rising over Morocco?

So night after night we sat out. Flaked out, deadbeat, but still taking cash for the drinks. And we'd all look south into that warm black wind coming up from Africa. Talking about the World Cup or local recipes from all over. A thousand things to do with a herring. But we were always facing that way. Out to sea. Sipping our Cruz-campos and looking out towards the next continent, because we were at the end of ours, our feet were in the black surf where Europe drowned. Where it had to end.

And yeah, it wasn't difficult to meet people who knew how to make money ferrying Africans. Arabs. Bringing them where they most wanted to go. What's wrong with that? It's natural, it's like the sea. And what did I tell you? Never turn your back on an ocean. It's good advice, my friend. And then early in the morning picking up the empties, driving up that track in the Toyota which already had busted shocks, limping into town, going to the wholesaler or maybe Lidl where you could get it almost as cheap. And Marty still in bed, she could never get up, curled up like a dark little prawn. Sucking her thumb. Christ.

By then the fishermen would already be on the beach, their lines right out, nets strung with silver floats like faces in the water, the sun hardly up and the sky red, the long African sky. And even in that town there were traces everywhere of their history. Of the Moors. That town was one place where there hadn't been a mosque. But there were walls, *murra islamica*, up on the hill in the old town. Where the fortress was. The Phoenicians had built that fortress three thousand years ago. Then, after the Romans, the Moors were there. All that territory used to be something else. These websites now, Al Quaida and suchlike, they say it's land to be taken back. And maybe they're right. I don't know.

But what I do know is that nobody ever said we were going to be able to stop it. There in the dark on the black beach, the cauldron still going if anyone was hungry, the bits of bread under the chairs, the winestains on the table, the drinkers' kids asleep in the sand on towels Marty'd brought out, and a group sitting there listening to the tide and knowing exactly where it would break. And smelling that sea which was always strong in the dark, the Moroccan sea, and all of us looking south. Where there were no lights ever. Because the sea's too wide. So you could always see the constellations you never do otherwise. All those strange stars. And the night nearly done.

And that's my story. Or part of my story. But this isn't my story, is it? I'm talking about John here. And John Vine's a good man. John Vine's done things to be proud of and we should admire him. We should all admire John.

But the problem for John is his faithfulness. I suppose you'd say it was diligence. No, not faithfulness to Siân, though I know for a fact there's few as faithful as John Vine, but faithfulness to an idea. To teaching. To giving people chances. To improving people. Because for the last twenty-five years John has sweated his guts out. I've seen that man so tired I feared for his life. For his sanity. And I can tell you, I know what tiredness is.

But that faithfulness became a habit. And the habit concealed a failure of nerve. Because that's what happened to John. His nerve failed him. He never squeezed up his toes in the black sand and said, yeah, this is mine. From now on this is mine. He just kept clocking on. And Christ, this is years ago he used to tell me about his acting plans. That's right. John Vine was going to be an actor. John Vine was going to be in a group. He was writing then, songs, the lot. With that Gil. Who's another one. Who was going to do this, do that. Oh yeah. But with John I really thought he'd make it work.

Christ, I used to tell him, bring Siân out to *El Zorro*. All you need is a teeshirt and shorts. The kids just play on the beach. Run the bar while Marty and I go up to Barcelona. And wow, yes, he promised. Great idea, he said. Time after time he promised. Spanish? I said. You pick it up. The cooking? You can cook, Siân can cook. It's fun. You just do it, you don't think about it. It's a stage, John, I used to say. Just get up there. But never think about it or you'll freeze. Dice the dorado and drop it in the stock. Sing your song. But that's what he did. He froze. John Vine froze and now if he's unfreezing I say that's good. I say that's very good.

But maybe it's too late. Maybe the consequences are too heavy. And when I think about John that way, it's crazy but I think about bananas. We ran that bar for two years. And about every six months I'd ring up John and say when are you coming? And he'd say yeah, yeah, we're looking at flights, we'll drive down, we'll be there. And I'd say, remember, the bananas are waiting. Because it was so hot down there that local people grew their own bananas. Weird looking things, kind of thick oblong skins, with a skinny fruit inside. Sometimes only as big as a pencil.

It was that hot, these bananas were growing everywhere. The local flora. And there's not many parts of Europe you can say that. The old man who sold us the bar, he had them in the garden there, behind the room where we lived. Marty loved that garden. She grew all the avocados we used, hundreds of the things. Couldn't give them away sometimes because we had avocados like people have blackberries. She'd use the dirty water from the washing up to irrigate that plot. And she brought those banana trees on pretty well. Three trees, that's all we had, and sickly things they were to start off with. But Marty was a genius with plants and soon she had decent crops on all of them.

And yeah, we had barbecued bananas and banana milkshakes and bananas with all the usual sweets. Yeah, those bananas. Green bananas in skins like pencil boxes. And I'd say, John, we need recipes for all these fucking bananas. What can you and Siân come up with? And boy, I thought, if that doesn't bring him out here nothing will. Your own bananas in the garden outside your window, and sometimes a couple of hoopoes, that's right, very early in the mornings, on the biggest of those trees.

I used to look at them out there at first light. Just me with a coffee and a brandy, yeah a Soberano, I'm the one who turned John on to that, blame me. Just me at dawn with Marty asleep in the other room and those hoopoes calling from the tree or swooping around, vanishing, coming back, and their crests up, pink and black. But Jesus Christ I heard something one morning. A cat had got the male hoopoe and finished him off pretty quick. So the missus is flying around, all bloody distraught, wailing, yeah, really wailing for her mate. Not something I thought I'd hear, a sound like that. A bird weeping for its mate. And I went out and I got the hoopoe off that cat and I spread its wings and looked at it and messed up as it was I thought that bird was a miracle. As it was a miracle that I owned the trees where they sang.

Or kind of chuckled. Because hoopoes laugh, sort of. Laughing in my trees. Yes, they were my trees. Or so I thought. But thinking you own land down there and actually owning it are different things. Everyone told me there were no deeds, that the bill of sale would be enough, and the affidavits. That the Spanish property deeds were lost in the Civil War. Well now I know better.

But looking back, that was the omen. The hoopoe was dead and John never came and the bananas were growing and we kept pouring the dishwater over the garden. And they used to love those bananas did all the northerners. We gave them as presents, a proprietor's thank you. But there's a time for everything and you've got to take it. Those hoopoes were with us a whole year and raised a brood. Well, one younker. But the female never came back. And I stopped calling John. Maybe it's bad luck. Maybe it's a curse to have a hoopoe die on your doorstep. But I'd still get up in the dark and sit with a brandy and get myself sorted.

John Vine? He has it all. Home, family, career. You can't knock that. You can never underestimate that. But he has this worm inside him, this dissatisfaction. He's a dreamer, is John. Did his job of course, but he was still dreaming. A boy of twenty, that's okay. He's going to dream. But a man of fifty? With a young piece who thinks he's not half bad? Well maybe that was the dream all along. Or so mixed up in the dream that you can't separate it. But believe me, that's when everything is going to come loose. That's when it's going to get dangerous.

The Fish

Let's get this over, if not out of the way because as far as you're concerned it will never be out of the way.

I drink. I drink like a fish. But that's not why they call me what they call me. This is my left arm but it's not an arm. It's a flipper. A withered limb, though really one that never sprouted properly. It never turned into a branch. Older people think it's thalidomide and maybe it looks like that, but it wasn't drugs my mother took, prescribed or otherwise. It was drink. That's why I'm small, apparently. That's why I look up to people I look down on.

Mam liked considerably more than a drop and yes I've inherited that too. Call it what you want, bad luck, foetal alcohol syndrome, holy retribution, I was born small and talking dirty. But people like my voice. They say it's sexy. Gruff, they say. Gravelly. Hoarse, I've heard. Surprising even. Women especially look surprised when I start talking because they never expect a voice like mine from a body like this. Notice that, please. It's my voice, although I've always thought of it as someone else's body. Where's it coming from, that voice, they wonder, my red voice, because voices for me are colours and my voice is red. Dark red. Very dark red. Red as a garnet, I'd say if anybody asked. Red as the Vermilion Hills of Dakota with the sun going down behind and the sky red and purple and purple-black as chillies. So yes, I like my voice. In fact I love my voice. Sometimes I feel it pour out of my mouth like smoke. Smoke with sparks in it, those gobbets of flame.

Note that. Gobbets. I fancy words, see. When I speak I feel the shapes of the words in my throat inside the colours of my voice.

Vermilion too. I can feel the shape of vermilion coming out of my throat. A demon out of its pit. But possibly a good demon, a very good demon. So yes, I like speaking. Which means I'm a good listener. Oh all through my life a very good listener and an observer too, I'd have to say. Matchless, maybe. No, matchless certainly. At least around here. Not quite all seeing because there are times when I'm indisposed. Not asleep, you understand, because I never sleep. But sometimes I'm indisposed. Though there's still not much that I don't see. So, yes, I'm The Fish. Whose left arm's good for more than you'd imagine and whose left hand, this claw, yes, I say it so you can absolve yourselves, this claw that's white and stronger than an adjustable spanner, has its advantages.

But I'll use the right to raise a glass to absent family and friends. Which includes mother, of course. The dear departed. Thanks Mam. I could have been a basket case. I could have been one of those triangular-faced botched jobs they push around in tartan blankets on the prom. You know, the wild eyes, the nappy under the chin. There for the grace of. And they're always taken to the edge of the esp to look at the waves. Which must terrify the poor bastards. Surely it must. Because it terrifies me. High tide, low tide. Who moved the sea, Daddy? It's gone. Who stole the ocean?

Anyway, I said we'd get this over but it's not over yet. I promised but I've disappointed you. For which I apologise, although you're going to have to get used to it. Not getting the full story. Or the correct story. You know I nearly said the true story there, but that would be absurd. Because there is no true story. So the story you're going to get from me is only part of the story. And you're going to have to work out the other bits for yourself. While the smoke comes out of my throat. With the sparks in it, the sparks red as grenadine.

Yes, that's it. *Sirop de Grenadine.* There's a bottle of it on the shelf behind me. I don't think anyone's touched it in years. A sediment at the bottom and a crust on the top. But it's pomegranate juice. Isn't that incredible? A soup of pomegranates on the shelf behind me in The Caterina. Made in France, I believe, by Lejay-Lagoute of Dijon. You see, I know every bottle off by heart here. But better than that, there's a fish on the label, the *amphiprion hercule* no less, a red and yellow fellow who must belong in the Caribbean or the Med.

What a world it is when you can create an identity from a booze label. That fish is my body. The grenadine's my soul. And I'm keeping my eye on that bottle for the rainy day that's coming. For that rainy day at the end of all the other rainy days when it's me in a room with the rain on the glass and the bed unmade and a thousand pomegranates distilled in a litre-sized test tube before me on the table. No food in the fridge. I don't eat either, you're going to find. But some of my drawings and a line of postcards are bluetacked to the attic walls because it's an attic room with a view across the badlands and then over the sea. On a good day. A room that holds two survivors from all this faff and fiddle. This palaver. Yes, pardon that. As the man said, so many words, so little time. Two survivors: myself and the bottle of grenadine. Which yes, of course, you're getting there, is vermilion. Is my Dakota horizon and my sweet chilli sky. My last moments spent with an exotic friend. And we all seem to need an exotic friend these days. Just like Mr Vine.

Not that we'll be totally alone. There'll be the site of course. Thank Christ for the net. Because all this will be on the site, with every word and picture listed. A life uploaded. Who'd have thought I had that talent? Or who wouldn't? But now, as I promised, let's get this over. So here you are listening to The Fish who might very well have been a basket case. Unlike his mother who was a chicken in the basket case. Sorry Mam. The Fish who copped ten thousand quid when he turned twenty one. Thanks Dad. The greatest thing you ever did. Want to know about my dad? Won't take long. Daddy's sixty two or sixty five or seventy three. Can never remember. He plays crown green bowls. Wears a white cap. And white shoes. And maybe that's all you need to know about daddy.

So, I'm indebted to dad. But I work for Hal. Want to know about Hal? Hal's the business. Hal looks after us. Out here on The Caib, our little peninsula. Hal makes it work. Just don't ask why, that's all, because there's no answer I can give.

I could love that man. Yet he's entirely unloveable, is Hal. Here he is at the bar. Lord of all he surveys. An hour ago he was burning the midnight in the office, making it work, making it all work. Well, with his accountant, with his lawyer. A bit sketchy those two. Manners is the one I know. A strange one, Manners. A bit like dad in a way because you don't see him much. Not a big player, see. But Hal? Most nights he's there above the fair in that lit window. In the office above The Kingdom where the children are poking at the waxworks and a pushchair's abandoned beside the hound of hell. That's Hal, calculating what's coming in against what's going out. Because everything here is tidal. With a swell and a current whose grip you'd better believe. Or in here at The Cat. Hal owns it so you see him in here a lot. One of his bases. Home from home.

It was three years ago that dad stumped up. Out of the blue, really. Guilt, I suppose. Or feeling his mortality. Make it work for you, he said. Showing the cheque. And he squeezed my arm. My other arm. And that, as far as dad goes, was incredible. Oh boy, that squeeze, that was orgasmic. So The Fish was flush. And you know what I did with the ten thousand? Or was it twenty? Not sure now.

Yes it's what you suspected, isn't it. Or rather, what I told you. Sorry, I'm losing it again. Yeah, I drank it. Want to know how to drink ten thousand quid? Try ten thousand cans of Stella. Or five thousand bottles of Asda special offer screwtop Pays d'Oc. Or one thousand litres of Bombay Sapphire. Maybe go for two thousand litres of Tesco Red Square instead. And that was on top of everything else. Because you've got to remember everything else.

And although I can't remember it, there must have been a hell of a lot of everything else. I drank it with the help of friends who will not figure in that ultimate scene featuring myself in a room with the glass of grenadine. But Hal drank it too. And Clint. And Tentpeg. And Mr Sun King, old Donal O'Connell, although he always insisted he'd had enough, he drank it too. Because that man will never have enough. And a crowd of others. All on the pish. An irrefragable fact, darlinks. With the belly-up Fish.

But fair play, looking at myself now in that mirror behind the grenadine and the bottles of Bols and peppermint schnapps, that broken soda siphon which has been there years, I don't seem too bad. Not a trace of the yellows. A little puffy maybe, because I'm no walker, but better than might have been expected. Mam of course, wasn't so lucky. At the end she was the colour of a glass of Advocaat. Which I always thought a shame because the old girl hated the stuff. A snowball in hell, so to speak. But the blissful, yes blissful thing is I cannot remember any of it. Not a session, not a weekend, not a lock-in, not an all dayer or all nighter or any of the girls who would have been with us in The Ritzy or The Cat. Just the black honey of amnesia, something I can recommend. Which is a painful admission for a listener. And for an observer.

So I'm sure you'll understand when I say that to colour in the spaces I assume certain things. I pull the rumours together with the hearsay and my own permissible prejudices and weave a narrative. A little DVD for you. From the site, of which you'll know more. Maybe you'll find my story unreliable but I promise I'll tell the truth as far as I can see it. But yes, I'll be colouring the vacant parts. Those empty spaces when I'm indisposed, or when I'm absent from the crowd and from myself and when my voice, this grenadine voice that women love, is missing from the scene.

Of the crime. Uh oh. Got to go now. Looks like business. We're on our way upstairs. But whatever happens don't make your mind up too soon. And keep listening. It's been a little complicated around here lately and you're bound to feel confused. Just be alert. And stay tuned in for the man with the smoke in his throat and the specklings of fire in it like the crystals you needle out of a pomegranate.

Hey, by the way. I've been meaning to ask. Because I don't think you know this. Did you ever hear, or did you ever read, or could you ever guess how much gold there is in a mouthful of sea water? Did you? Could you? No? Well you're going to find out.

Tuesday

Vine

Vine sat on the bed. There was nowhere else. It was littered with jeans and tops and dresses, some still on hangers, others discarded. The only chair in the room was piled with papers and magazines. Similar piles spilled over the floor and under the bed. He could see dog-eared school copies of *Romeo and Juliet* and *Ariel* and Christina Rossetti in the litter, with school folders and an I Ching and *Rock n Roll's Greatest Deaths,* with Vicious and Cobain and Jones on the cover.

Everywhere there were stuffed toys, most of them owls. There were china owls and a Tampax box on the dressing table, and an illuminated owl with fiery eyes hung from the ceiling. In a corner was a tiny desk where two candles burned, one red, one purple. Other candles were scattered over every surface and a string of purple lights hung around the bedhead. Rachel had draped a patterned scarf over the bedside light. There was incense burning. Cinnamon, thought Vine. The room was acrid with it. He blinked at the owls.

Rachel stood looking at herself in the mirror, fixing the equipment. That was what she called it. First the black studs that went into her ears. Then a red stud for her nose. Now it was the ring for her right eyebrow. Soon she'd fix the ring with its serpent motif into her navel. On its hook.

Where did you say they were? asked Vine.

Mum's out with the Tesco posse. Down The Lily probably, so it's lager and lime heaven. And Jess won't be back tonight, she's on that trip. Outward bound or something, with the sexually ambiguous Miss Rhiannon Esyllt Protheroe.

You think Rhi's gay?

Doesn't bother me. Sir. She's great. In fact, I think I fancy her.

And Rachel had pursed her lips in an extravagant kiss and squinted back at him through the mirror and the candle flame.

You know I don't really need to be here.

Course you do, she smiled, turning round. She was wearing Levis and a black bra.

Pour me that drink now.

Vine got up and gave her the can of Red Bull.

No, no, no. The Vlad, darling. The Vladivar. I want to be impaled.

This? hissed Vine. It's like lighter fuel.

All I want is a cap full. Not a cup, a cap. Just to get up as far as the others will be up. So they're not ahead.

But you can have a drink with me.

And you have to be home by nine, sneered Rachel. Some Friday night. Some Saturday morning.

She fixed the serpent and turned round to show him. Her belly was a golden dish. She gave a little shimmy.

What about that then!

Great.

Vine poured her the supermarket vodka. Rachel sniffed, winked, knocked it back in one. And stood there grimacing. She almost staggered.

Your turn.

I'm driving.

Your turn. Sir. Take it like a man. Sir. Straight up the arse. Sir.

Rachel.

But Vine had poured himself a shot. A vile and oily adulteration that tasted as if it was made from distilled cat litter.

Cheers, she said.

Vine looked around the room. Aerosols and pots of nail varnish on the CD player. Knickers on the floor. She'd tried three different pairs while he read the sleevenotes to Marianne Faithfull's *Greatest Hits* and a Destiny's Child compilation.

Look, I shouldn't be here.

Relax, can't you? No-one will come in, if that's what you're so scared of. It's not like we're doing anything.

You're unbelievable, madam.

You'd better believe I'm unbelievable.

So where will you go when I push off?

Oh, everyone's out tonight. The big ritual.

But she considered.

The Lily, Bloggsy's. Maybe even The Cat. Some of the girls said we should try it.

Jesus, said Vine. Why the hell would you go to The Caterina?

Rachel preened. Every time she moved she nudged a mobile of hollow steel tubes bluetacked to the ceiling. It was a constant accompaniment to everything they said. That and The Cure tracks she was playing. Vine had brought round a few things of his own – Jeff Buckley, some David Gray. Both got the thumbs down.

Dreary, Rachel had said. Fuck king dreary. It's Friday night, Sir. Remember those?

D'you ever see Nia out? he asked.

Rachel paused.

Your Nia you mean? Sometimes. Yeah.

She works too hard, I think, said Vine.

He thought of his daughter. She would be in front of her computer now, one of the three languages she was studying coming through headphones. God she was diligent. Sometimes painfully so. But she had learned that from Siân, learned the value of work. The problem for Vine was, he wasn't sure whether his daughter understood how to stop pushing herself. She'd always been a pale child.

Saw her a fortnight ago in fact, mused Rachel. Down The Lily.

Vine was pleased.

It's good to know she's not a slave to revision.

Nia! laughed Rachel. Oh she has her moments.

What d'you mean?

Well none of us are exactly bluestocking virgins, are we, though I hear they're making a comeback. Blue stockings that is.

You what?

Relax, Daddy, laughed Rachel. Relax Sir.

She hardly goes out, said Vine.

Yeah, yeah. Whatever.

Now she was looking for another bra. All the drawers of her dressing table were thrown open and all were stuffed. Rachel's wardrobe, Vine had noted, seemed filled equally with Army & Navy and Kathmandu kitsch. There was a small television set in the room stained with paint or powder, and a computer printer. But no computer.

Vine knew Rachel's assignments were all produced on a PC. Perhaps it was downstairs. He wasn't sure whether he'd seen her with a laptop. They were obligatory now. Or she probably shared one with Jess. Nia seemed inseparable from hers.

You never said about The Cat. Why go there?

Oh, I don't know, she smirked. A sense of adventure perhaps.

And perhaps that was when Vine had picked up his phone and filmed her. Only for a few seconds, he told her. It felt completely spontaneous. Anyway, she was forever filming him. Even once in school at a rehearsal with that little Nokia she carried.

But it was crazy in school with those things, thought Vine. It was getting out of hand. Phones ringing, images flitting from screen to screen. The new commerce. The digital invasion. But in the bedroom she screamed at first, then posed, as she fitted the new brassiere. Her breasts were little more than buds. Small and hard as tulip bulbs, he thought. A coppery dust on them in that dim light.

Such a dirty old man, she laughed.

Which had stopped him dead.

Okay, he said, jumping off the bed. It's time to go. Time to bloody go. I only have an hour, you know that. Now shift yourself. Shift that bloody arse.

But it didn't work. It never worked like that with Rachel. She had raised an eyebrow and snapped a strap.

Pass the Red Bull, darling.

Jesus, Rach.

As I said, I want to be where the others will be. Not ahead, mind you, just where they'll be. But if I get there first, then so much the better.

The Cure clicked off. The mobile sounded like rain.

Five minutes, she said. Smiling.

But first of all these bloody jeans have got to go, and she had started to wriggle out of the denim.

Then she turned.

Sir?

What?

You'll have to help.

They had sat in one of the private boxes in The Sea View Hotel. Dark wood, stained glass above their heads, and a table between. Vine had insisted on that, wanting space between them in case someone recognised him. Which was unlikely. The hotel drew a much older crowd, largely from the villas at the west end of town. It was discreet and expensive. He knew Rachel found it boring.

He watched her as she finished the baguette. Prawns, lettuce and mayonnaise in a foot-long stick of soft white bread.

Okay?

Mmm...

Have some water?

Water! Na, Stella. Our lady of the stars.

You'll be seeing bloody stars.

Half.

And he had bought it.

Half a lager.

Vine took one swallow before Rachel grabbed it.

Greedy.

Well go easy. It's only nine now. And time I was off.

But he waited fifteen minutes while she talked of Year Twelves and Thirteens they both knew, and then they were out in the car park. The lights weren't working and it was completely dark.

See you sometime, she'd said.

When?

And he remembered the syllable. The ridiculous question. The little boy pleading that must have surprised her. How she would have despised it.

As if she had any need to answer. In school of course. In the drama studio or the corridor to E block when she'd come past with whatever crew she had decided to grace with her presence, sometimes the surfers, sometimes the geeks, often the musos, the longhaired boys and henna-headed black-skirted girls with their Nepalese bags, all swirling around with their folders and guitar cases and laptops and coffee mugs.

And he'd wave hello to the whole gang and look for humour in their eyes. For the knowing expressions. For the sneers. Yes that's when he'd see her.

His top English set had to move rooms. The quickest way to E Block was through the Drama studio. When they pushed in, there was a rehearsal going on with Year Twelve. Vine's group decided to spend a few minutes watching.

Bowen, Head of Drama, was on stage with a group of three girls. Rachel lay on a blanket mimicking what she imagined to be birth pangs.

Too posh to push are you? shouted Bowen. Come on, woman. It should feel like you're being split in half. There's another human being about to appear from your nether regions. From your fanny, love. It's a miracle.

Rachel gave a whelp.

Come on.

She let out a strangled cry which became a laugh she couldn't stop. Soon the other girls were laughing and Bowen called a halt.

I can't, she wheezed.

You can.

I can't with an audience here.

There'll be a bigger crowd than this next Thursday. You're supposed to be an actress.

Rachel sat up and wiped what looked like tears from her eyes.

Vine could see the dust on her black jersey and trousers. For some reason Rachel was one of the few girls who wore the school badge. It had been sewn into the pullover: a red heart with an anchor within it. A black anchor draped with what looked like ivy. Perhaps it was a chain. Or a rope of flowers. There was no motto.

It'll be all right on the night, she said when she could speak. But it's just so, so…

And she spluttered again.

Ridiculous.

And laughed.

So… bloody… ridiculous.

And all the girls then shrieked together, with Bowen standing up front with one hand on his hip. Gorwel Bowen, whom everyone called Lost Horizon, though few knew why.

Okay, take five, he called. Get me a coffee, Sue. And one for our incorrigible heroine here.

Vine and his pupils had left slowly, trekking to E. So it hadn't been then that Rachel had given him the envelope. She was on stage, she never spoke to him, she couldn't have passed him anything. So when had it happened?

Vine took another swig from his coffee mug. It was 7 am and he was in the Seagull Room at the edge of the site. The only place open. He sat outside at one of the plastic tables and looked over the dunes to the north, the sea to the south. The tide was neither in nor out, but the reef was half exposed. A white stave becoming a black line. Soon it would be clear, a limestone atoll with its saltwater lagoon, one mile into the ocean. How clear it was. How well he remembered some of what had happened.

Vine came there most mornings. Karoona thought he was mad and would not have dreamed of sitting outside, wrapped up against the early chill, watching the sand migrate. Because that's what Vine did in that place. Consider sand. He knew that sand took its colour from the iron attached to the grains. Gold? Sand was iron. Every beach an iron quilt. And sand was a restless beast. What was hidden by sand would be revealed and the familiar lost. Sometimes overnight.

Out on the shore he'd identified the ironwork of a buried deck, chainlink and hawser indistinguishable from the rim of a barnacled pool. Everywhere were two-metre-high honeycombs that marine worms had built over the rocks. Golden, oozing salt, they hissed like something electric.

Vine stared at the land coming into view. He had known it all his life. And yet never bothered to hire a boat and explore. Or simply sail out and scramble up from the shallows. A castaway on his own island. To Vine it always seemed volcanic in the way it appeared so abruptly, extruding into daylight, clinkered with mussel shells, black with wrack. It was a reef like the roof of a submerged citadel.

Further out in the bay the dredger was taking its tithe. Because sand too must pay. Sand and gravel. Every day, night, the dredger was there. Sometimes invisible, but it was there, sometimes a ghost ship, a blur hardly noticeable. But still there. And sometimes a perfect imprint, its winding gear visible or a crew member in a yellow oilskin. Sometimes even its rust. The dredger at work with its claws on the seabed. The dredger's mite streaming into the hold – sand and gravel and starfish and the sluice of iron-coloured water that has to be pumped out.

So not in the drama studio. Surely not at her place. Not in a pub. It had to be in school, in E Block or the corridor. How many times had he passed her, both of them weighed down with paper. Always paper. And how easily he could see her waving it at him, waving the white envelope, coming through the press in the corridor with the white envelope held before her. Like a baton. Passing it on. And his own hand. Reaching out to take it. Through the scrum of bodies. Past all the other hands that held envelopes and essays and paper for him to take. His own hand accepting the envelope. The white envelope. Or was it manilla? Rachel releasing it. Her smile in slow motion. Her hand with its messages in blue biro. Her hand always tattooed that way.

He could see the scene clearly. Yes, he was imagining it, but surely that's how it happened. It was fantasy but it was plausible. A white envelope. A brown. A poem for the competition he had been told to judge. As if he didn't have enough other things to do. As if the Deputy Head of English in a school of twelve hundred pupils had a spare moment to judge a creative writing competition. But that's what the headmaster wanted. Big Guy the big guy. Yet what if it wasn't a poem. Or a story. What if it was a letter? What if it was a real letter instead of a text? A letter in Rachel's handwriting.

Vine huddled into his fleece. One day soon at this hour he would see the sun rising over the cliffs to the south-east. Out of the black bay. If he was still around. It was the last week of the season and he had much to decide.

The next rent instalment on the caravan was coming up. Karoona was tense as a hawk. Her time was coming, she told him most days. She could feel it was her time. And Hal was late in producing her passport. Hal had promised over the months that it was no problem but still there was no little red book for Karoona. Her book of spells.

How old do you want to be? Hal had asked that night. Five months ago. It felt like years.

Karoona laughed.

Twenty two, she said.

Vine couldn't tell. She might have been anything from eighteen to twenty eight.

Place of birth? asked Hal.

The fucking Sahara desert, said Clint.

All the men had laughed then. Except Vine.

Cueta, Spain, she'd said. It has to be in the EU.

Why not London?

Yes, she had said. Why not?

Or maybe thirty. Thirty five even. Not that Hal was writing anything down. Just sitting there looking at the brown girl in her red dress. Her hair an explosion. Looking at her thin legs crossed on The Caterina's worn seat. At the ankle bracelet. Despite her bravado she was shivering. It had been cold in the pub. Looking at the girl whose father had provided seventeen thousand pounds for a new life for his daughter. Well, that's what she said. Wherever it came from, the money had been paid.

And now she was asleep in his caravan. A black cat under his duvet. These mornings he slipped out for space as much as anything else. Life in a caravan was impossibly cramped. And there had to be space to think. To remember.

Vine sipped.

Rachel had given him an envelope. He remembered that. So it was either at home in his study or in his old room at school. He thought of both places. Two perplexing universes. His problem was he had never thrown anything away. And knowing school, nothing would be changed in the English department, despite the fact that he had left over five months previously. He should have gone back. Searched and made certain.

But after everything that had happened, Vine wasn't sure why it was now he remembered the envelope.

Donal

They sat on canvas chairs in the caravan garden. Donal's lettuce was well gone, but he'd kept one plant for seed. In the gravel he grew yellow-horned poppies, but again these were failing. One bloom was hanging on. Donal was proud of these poppies, a local rarity which had responded to cultivation.

Any weather, he said. Force eights can't kill them. Bloody little miracles growing straight out of the stones.

He looked at Karoona and smiled.

Straight out of the desert, he said.

She sipped her tea.

From here they could look over the bay. The tide was out, the sand olive. Beyond the beach the dunes rose and fell, empty and grey-green.

What I would really like, said Karoona, almost to herself, is an apartment. No bigger than the caravan, it doesn't have to be big. But all to myself. All my own. Where I can go and be myself. Where I can sleep or sing or drink tea all day and no-one is telling me what to do.

In London?

Of course. That's what you all promised.

There's more to this world than London.

I think I know that, smiled Karoona. But just to be where everything is happening. To go to the clubs. To listen to the singers. To compare.

There are clubs here.

But it's not the same.

You could vanish, said Donal. Look, I'll give you the bus fare. Get off in Victoria and start busking.

What?

Singing in the street. The biggest club of all. Wardour Street, Greek Street, go to Hampstead or over to the Irish pubs in Camden. Ask if there's a spot.

He grinned.

There's always a spot.

Karoona hesitated.

I want it to be...

Planned out, he said. Yeah, I know. Organised. But that's the hard work. That's what you didn't pay for.

Donal poured himself more tea. They were drinking from six-ounce, gold-painted tumblers with Arabic script on the sides. On each glass was the black silhouette of a minaret.

Or maybe you've caught it, he said.

What?

What everybody gets here. Finally. In this place.

What's that?

Oh, he murmured, sipping. A kind of belonging.

I don't belong here.

Look at the map, said Donal. Ever done that? Do you actually know where you are?

I don't have a map.

We're at the end of the road. Everything ends here. If you're here it can't be a mistake. You intended to come. All the way down the peninsula until if you go any further you're out there.

He gestured at the waves, their white staves, far off.

Just because you've come back, sneered Karoona.

Hey, I'll be frank.

Donal held his gold glass to the sky and looked through it.

This van? It's not mine. I rent it.

Like John.

Yeah. We're in the same boat, so to speak, but I'm ten years older. And that's the crucial ten years.

I thought you had money.

So did I.

But you use that boat, you…

Yeah, I use the boat and we know what for. S'funny though. The more work you do for some people, the more you end up owing them.

Hal…

It's more than Hal. Hal's way down the food chain. Okay, for around here you can't ignore him. He's got a grip. But this is a small town.

Karoona brightened.

I'm singing in the club again on Saturday. He asked me. Clint's getting the posters printed, he says. He scanned my picture in.

There you are then, said Donal.

Karoona looked out to sea. There was no-one on the beach. Nothing stirred behind them on the avenue. Some of the caravans were shuttered, their gas bottles removed, windmills taken down. She looked at her red tea.

Here's something I never told you, she said. Yes, yes, life is a story, I know. My father always said that. You say that. What stories do you have to tell? Here's one, a tiny one I'm writing my song about.

She composed herself, crossed her legs. Donal looked at the ankle bracelet.

Okay. I was walking down the New Binnenweg, past that

smokehouse we went once. Yes, Sky High was its name and you were, you were… contaminated just passing the door.

Karoona paused. And continued.

Contaminated? Yes. Exactly yes. A woman came up to me on the street there. At least I think it was a woman. She started speaking Dutch to me and I said no, I don't get it. Talk in English to me. The big language. So she doesn't even blink, she starts talking in English and says her magazines have been stolen. And she doesn't want to beg. So she asks if she can read me one of her poems. So I say yes and she speaks it in English.

Karoona narrowed her eyes.

But how could she do that? How could she translate them so quickly? The poem she spoke was called 'The Point of Life'. I looked at her face as she spoke it and there was blood coming down her forehead. As she was speaking her poem to me. In a foreign language. With blood on her face.

Yeah. That's the Dutch.

Karoona bridled.

No. That's not the Dutch. Do you know the trouble with people round here?

She gestured at the avenue.

You're all the same tribe. You all know what's going to happen and what's not going to happen. You're all the same and it suffocates you. So I gave her all my change – two euros sixty. I remember that. I had nothing else.

That was a strange time, said Donal.

Christ, he thought. What the hell had he been doing? That was more than close to the mark. Calling in favours from old contacts, using the flotsam that washed up in that Rodos bar. Jesus, The Rodos. And the Sweet Wok next to it. Noodles with a plastic fork. And those bicycles going past with hissing tyres and at the end of the road people coming out of the Metro, or disappearing into its hole in the ground. A few would walk towards the end of the street and its corner bar. His perch had been the window and he would look at them through the rain walking under that thirty-foot-high piece of public sculpture, a figure made of wire, a wire man, black wire wound again and again around a heart, a brain, a wire man above the tramlines like some forgotten gantry in the docks, its hawsers cut, a piece of the old dockland marooned uptown.

Meet under the wire man was what you said. Under the wire man. So he would sit in his corner and watch the people approaching but nobody ever came within a hundred yards, all the secretaries and computer fodder clutching their *Telegraafs* and umbrellas and vanishing into thin air before his part of town. Into the better lit streets where there was no bar like The Rodos.

Jesus. The Rodos. Where the tram bell sounded and the gulls hunched on the roofs outside and the sea's black neon broke behind your eyes.

The Rodos. Where you held your seaweedy beer, your coffee, your tea that girl would never make correctly, a bag poked into hot water already poured. Such terrible tea. Bitter and violet. Or the wine from Turkey, the Turkish red wine served in a tumbler almost square, thick hulled like a whisky glass and the port's coat of arms upon the glass worn away by the thumbs of sailors and drifters and men like himself waiting for the right moment. The exact moment.

Yes. The Rodos. Once it might have been a taverna. In alcoves in the walls was an assortment of torsos – no heads or thighs but breasts and orchid-like genitalia. A real palm grew in The Rodos, a purple-leafed palm whose purple was blackening, a purple that had once been red. The few customers brought the sea with them on their clothes, tobacco smoke and seasalt rubbed into wet wool. The smell had seeped into the walls.

Yes. The Rodos. The dark girl pouring the Turkish wine. But it was always the blonde woman he recalled. Lean she was. A spruce-white lath. And tall. And always in those green and yellow striped hipsters worn so low she'd show the gold stubble in the cleft of her arse and the arcana of tattoos above the sharp end of her arsebone. What were they? An angel's wings? A devil's? Maybe they were cult insignia. What was she anyway but the woman who spoke every language on God's earth.

How carefully he'd listen from his corner as the sailors came in or the bikers in their spurs or the tourists who didn't linger. Or the men with time on their hands doing deals. And she'd go Dutch with them and go German and sometimes Swedish because she was surely a Swede herself. She also spoke some Slavic-sounding lingo. Might have been Russian but what language was *pivo* then because it clearly meant beer as she flipped the tap and shaved the foam with that paddle they all used and stood looking with her grey lips and her pale hair up or down or in pigtails like some Dutch schoolgirl but with a face of cracked and aching alabaster.

Yes. The Rodos. And its mistress. Working mornings, presiding nights. For some she would have a smile. For others her adamantine deathmask. And for a few she'd nod the way downstairs.

It had taken him a long time to venture below. The *toiletten* were up a flight, whilst access to downstairs was through a door marked *ausgang verboten*. The eurodisco was an ache behind the eye that matched the pulse of his hangover. A computer voice was saying 'love your soul' again and again, a thousand times over, and he had listened and not listened because he had waited so long that the music occupied him like his Camel smoke and the raw Anatolian red. Love your soul. He was implored. He was commanded. Maybe the singer was giving advice but how could you tell when the singer was a piece of software. And then the beat had jumped with a sickening fairground lurch into a key impossibly remote and the blonde woman was looking at him from the bar. Time to go.

Behind the sign he discovered a stairwell. He descended to a passage painted black. At the end of the passage was another stair. At its foot was another black corridor and at its end a black door without a handle. This corridor had looked empty at first. He had thought it a dead end. To those who knew, there was a door. For those who did not, there was no recourse but to turn around. If the way still remained open. Love your soul, he had said to himself as he passed down. Maybe good advice.

But then the blonde woman had appeared behind him and tapped him forward and knocked and listened at the black door and it had opened for her and she had beckoned him in and everything had been revealed.

Because there sat Karoona who it transpired would not be visiting Felixstowe in the container ship after all. She would be accompanying Donal on his journey home. In Donal's boat.

Hiya kid, he'd said. Looking.

Good evening, sir, Karoona had replied, standing up with her bag at her feet. Like something out of Jane Eyre, he'd thought then. The heroine abroad. Ringed round by miscreants, yet spunky in that bedlam.

Relax, he'd smiled. We're not going yet.

Oh yes you are, said the man behind Karoona. Goodbye.

Yeah, The Rodos. And there he was on the pavement outside with a girl and her suitcase and guitar. He knew then she was different. There was nothing abject about her. She didn't plead then and she didn't plead now. Karoona stood beside him in her black hoodie and filthy black jeans like some hustler off the New Binnenweg.

So he'd led his charge towards town and they'd stopped in the Sky High and sat in the back room. An enormous black man had looked a long time at them and then stopped looking. They drank coffee and breathed the skunk smoke. Some human wreckage with a Glaswegian accent was getting his marching orders. Sky High staff had gone through his pockets and confiscated something, Donal couldn't see what, and now the boy was being ejected. Not a place to take the piss.

There was no-one else in but two shaven-headed types and an older woman in leather trousers, smoking, laughing together, glancing at the new couple. He had avoided their eyes.

Karoona had sat in an enormous armchair. He had watched her rip the end off every sugar sachet in the bowl at their table. Every white sachet emptied into her untouched cup.

Hey, said Donal looking round. I'll put some music on. And he went into the caravan.

What about this? he called.

Karoona listened.

It's old, she said finally.

Timeless love. *Sunflower* by you know who.

It's cold out here, she complained.

Well come in. I'll put more tea on.

They sat together on the narrow box of the sofa under the window. Karoona looked round.

I always tell you, this is bigger than John's.

Yeah. It was top of the range. Ten years ago.

I could have stayed here instead.

No way. You're a stranger to me remember and we have no ties. We shouldn't have sat outside anyway.

Nobody cares, said Karoona.

She looked around.

Maybe I should have stayed in Rotterdam?

And have your magazines stolen?

She stared at the minaret on the glass.

Yes. Strange days. We came away so quick I left my guitar behind. My guitar. This is no place.

She gestured.

Caravan city, she said. For the people afraid to be Roma.

Don't judge it. If you do you'll be wrong.

Listen. I saw the others. The Chinese boys. The girls from Russia. You get told to wait and you wait. We were waiting together. But I'm different because I'm what's coming. I'm what happens next.

Clint got you a guitar. A good one.

Karoona squirmed on what was only a padded bench.

So you sit and you sit. It could be in the Timmer in the Oude Binnenweg or you go over the Erasmusbrug and smell that air, that air after all that smoke, and you sit in the lobby of the Hotel New York and feel the eyes on you and you wait under those gold letters for something. With the eyes on you. Until it gets too much.

So you go out and wait in the rain and watch the people on the top deck of the Spido. With their white wine. Going somewhere. Somewhere they know. And you see the ferries coming in and going out and you know the police are watching you but they don't care any more. And those big boxes on the ferries, coming in, going out.

What is in those metal boxes? You should ask me because I can tell you. But not me in those boxes. I would die in a box like that. So I stood by the statue of who, who the…

Peter the Great.

Peter the Great's statue and looked across the water and knew I did have something to lose. I wasn't like those people in the boxes. They didn't know where they were going. I did have something. I had my songs. But I didn't have the papers.

Karoona stood up and touched the television screen. Donal kept a fifteen inch Sanyo portable.

Remember sitting in the Sky High and watching MTV? We didn't know what to do so we watched MTV. All the girls, all the girls. Well they can put me on an aeroplane and fly me to Algeria but if I live I'll come back. I swear I'll come back. But maybe not here.

One place is as good as another.

Karoona turned scornfully.

No. Never. You know that's wrong. You've been places. You know. Maybe John'll go with you.

Maybe…

Karoona paused. There had been a knock on the door. So soft she had hardly heard it. She waited until Donal came back.

Guess who that was? he asked.

MI5.

Little Nia. A librarian in waiting. She's looking for John. Said she has something for him. Said she'd called around on you but there was no answer. No housey on now is there? Bingo?

Karoona shrugged.

He says she never talks to him, she laughed. That she's always studying. And I agree with him. She's studying to go away. Away from here.

I thought you and John were together.

Oh we were, we were. In a way. Not like you mean though. I was not brought up to go with men.

John's been good to you, said Donal.

She laughed angrily.

The first time I met him, I knew. In that bar. He was all eyes. And he was drinking too much. Flirting I suppose and being a fool. But what choice did I have, there was nowhere to go and he was renting the caravan. Yes, you're right. I didn't know where I was or who he was. I thought he was somebody. A teacher. But he's lost, he's just... lost. You wait. He'll go back to his wife if she'll have him. Men like John always do.

It was Donal's turn to shrug.

We're on for a swim, I think. Saturday night weather seems to be okay. Fancy a skinny dip?

What's that?

Ah, just fun. A kind of tradition we have around here.

Karoona had noticed the longboard lashed under the caravan.

Do you surf in the dark?

Well it has been known. At least in my more relaxed moments. But you've got to know the coast like the back of your hand.

Donal turned round on the bench and looked out to sea.

I was out there this morning. There was mullet in, a big shoal. You could tell because the sand was creamy with mullet shit. Like a great big frothy coffee. Mullet's a kind of fish. Hundreds, maybe thousands of them. I could see them, a brown patch twenty yards out, all shivering and shiggly. Go swimming then, you'd know about it soon enough. As bad as years ago when everybody's waste went straight in. Or like now when the storm sewer's running. Those people in the hotels? Take a crap at ten, a dip at eleven and they were swimming in their own mess. Which is a nice concept. Or conceit, I suppose. A certain justice to it. But all that's mostly cleaned up now.

She looked at him hard then. Bare feet, khaki shorts, dirty singlet. The Sun King's skin was as dark as her own.

I could have stayed here instead. I could have.

No, smiled Donal. I like my space.

You don't beg, said Karoona. John begs.

You learn to live alone and then it's hard to change. John's never done that. He's used to a house full of noise.

Karoona held out her glass and Donal poured.

What's that? she asked.

She was pointing at a case on the wall. It held a dark beret with silver insignia.

Special Boat Squadron, said Donal.

You were a soldier?

Oh yes. In the SBS you're a special kind of soldier.

He lifted the perspex box from the wall. Under the beret was a framed photograph of three men and a knife as long as Karoona's forearm.

There was a time when this was never out of my hand.

He kissed the twisted blade and laughed at her, putting it back in the box.

Belonged to a Gurkha friend of mine. Beautiful piece of work. Like a viper in steel.

Were you married? she asked.

Of course. But I was too young and away on tours of duty. And yes, there were two kids and no, I don't see them. Ever.

Donal looked at her hard.

Don't even know where they are.

And anyone else?

The anyone was the usual mistake.

Yes?

Older man, younger girl.

Donal scratched a dark patch below his knee.

That was down towards your part of the world. You know I was running a bar near Tarifa, almost on the beach. And I liked it there. It used to feel a bit like this place, sand dunes and sand blowing, down at the ends of things. Far flung if you like. Except that was the end of Europe. Where the continent drowns.

And you can wave to all the people like me waiting on the other shore.

Yeah, I know, nodded Donal. They're coming, I don't doubt it. And you're in the advance party. Hey, listen to this.

Sunflower had finished. The Sun King replaced it with a Youssou N'Dour song.

You know, I play this in the dark. Maybe just a candle burning. All those crickets and frogs at the beginning, that's Tarifa, that's Africa. And yeah, I bloody cry when I hear that voice. My little tea candles like Tarifa fireflies. That voice in the dark, those verses. Honey on a razor. What's he say? Africa dream again, Africa live again, I cry like a baby when I hear that. What's he saying, 'the dawn, the dawn'? Sounds like he's crying too. And yeah, I watch the dawn come up here and the whole sky out front is one big rose petal. And the sky in Tarifa. Like the dawn anywhere. But I know what you're saying and you're right. We can't chain the gate.

They gave you money for taking me, said Karoona.

Donal laughed.

I told you. It's gone. It was gone before I got it.

So you bring other people too.

He stood up then.

They wanted me to, yes. It's big business now and getting bigger. Your new import and export. But I say no. When they ask I turn them down. So far. When they insist I just laugh. Of course, a boat has plenty of uses.

He looked hard at her.

You can bring things in. Or take them away. Whatever, nobody's much bothered here. Quiet little harbour, there's no hassle.

I want to go, said Karoona. Before winter.

You probably will. The big steps have been made. And maybe John'll go too.

She grimaced and Donal laughed.

Yeah, I know, he said. It's all mullet shit.

Vine

What are you doing here?

Vine looked at Siân framed in the study door. She was surprised and now he was waiting for her anger. Siân had never been a woman to hold back. In school her temper was notorious, and she'd been known to push six-foot Year Elevens around a classroom. She stood there in her gardening clothes, hands on hips, pale in the face.

John Vine had been sure his house would be empty. He'd rung the land line without answer. Brychan, he knew, was away all day with a friend and his parents. Nia, he was certain would be at county library headquarters using the reference section. Or cleaning at Clwb y Môr after one of its riotous nights. The language was going down gloriously in an all day happy hour and Nia was dutiful about her rota.

But Siân? She should have been at Tesco. It was her day for the big shop and during half term it was always a morning chore. Or she might have been gardening. Maybe talking with other singers in her choir. Even probably marking. But holidays were for work other than school.

So Vine had walked the mile from the site and slipped into the house. Siân's car wasn't in the street. The *For Sale* sign wired to the wall had been there for three months. No interest at all. He knew they were asking too much but Siân was determined to get what she felt the house was worth. It would be disastrous to sell at a loss. After everything else that had happened.

Siân hadn't changed the locks and Vine had stood in the hall and closed his eyes and breathed in the smell that he had helped create. Cooking and paint thinners and cats' piss and cat food and polish and flowers and incense and his own flayed skin which was still part of the dust on the hall table and on the frames of the pictures of his children in that house and in foreign places and in the sea of their home town, up to their waists in a wave with the sky behind them a furnace that Vine had watched cool from orange to grey in the minute he had taken to line up the shot.

On the table was a stack of letters addressed to himself. Siân was supposed to send them on but she made it plain it was of little priority. Most of the letters were junk. What the others were he couldn't be bothered to imagine. They were written to a different man.

Nothing had changed in the kitchen. That had been the room where everything had happened. Meals, arguments, the scheduling of work. Vine had often sat reading essays at the kitchen table when everyone else was in bed. Siân used it for her own marking while Brychan often struggled there with homework. Only Nia preferred her own room and her own music, quiet with her headphones and computer. Sometimes Vine had tapped the door to ensure she was there.

Then he had gone upstairs to his study.

What he had to do was search through the desk and his boxes of school papers. He hadn't been in the room for nearly three months but little seemed changed. A broken chair and bags of old clothes had been pushed in, and there were piles of newspapers, due for recycling, which didn't belong. But that was all.

It had to be found. Possibly it was in school but he had searched there. Now Vine pulled out bales of bills and letters and leafed through. In the desk drawers were reams of papers from the English department, edicts from the government, discussion papers from the Assembly, instructions from the union. He must have read some of them but could not remember a word. That's what life had been then. A paper chase. A silent storm. Bloody emails too with their attachments he never opened, whole books arriving on his school computer. Then the publishers' catalogues. He'd always laughed at those. As if he had time to open the catalogue let alone scan it let alone order a book let alone read a book on someone else's wish list.

Christ, he had thought. If he piled them up they'd reach the ceiling. In his boxes were the hundreds of poems he had collected for the last two school competitions, plus the short stories and plays. Everybody writing. No-one reading. The classes had been told to keep copies of their work, but Vine had always meant to get rid of the stuff. To slide armful after armful into the slot of the paper bank. That comforting maw. How often he had stood in the car park behind The Clwb with his bags of papers and felt that release. Gone. For good or bad. Thrown in error, terror or disgust. But gone out of his life.

How he loved that power – the power of banishment, of rejection. The sense of cleansing that a paper-chuck could provide. The slide into the dark. It was almost as good as his incinerator. This was an oildrum he had kept at the allotment. It was pierced at the sides and fitted with a grille and a lid. Siân needed it to burn garden waste she couldn't compost. Vine had used it three times in recent years for burning sessions. He carried his boxes of files down the allotment paths and started slowly. Usually this meant burning some local authority missive on health and safety, or government instructions on pastoral care. Thick, bilingual text with instructions emboldened. There were always instructions. He had ripped the papers apart and watched them grow silver and black. When the fire was established he had piled on the rest of the rubbish. The white smoke soon rose in a signal.

Freedom, that's what the smoke said, Vine thought. Holiday freedom. Teaching should be simple but it had become alien to him. There had never been a discipline problem in his classes. Unlike Siân, Vine knew instinctively how to keep order. Or perhaps the children thought him tougher than he imagined himself. But while Siân struggled and shouted, threatening and cajoling her classes into work, Vine had possessed a natural authority.

The kids like you, don't they?

That's what Siân had often said to him. As if it surprised her.

And he picked up the resentment in her voice.

So he never agreed with that. But there were wonderful moments he experienced in class. Sitting on a Friday afternoon with an already written-off group of thirteen year olds, Vine knew exactly what to do. He told them stories. Or rather, he read the class poems that told stories.

They had been enthralled. And especially when Vine had read D.H. Lawrence's 'The Mountain Lion'.

How they had listened then, those ugly, niffy kids. How they had looked delighted at that line about the lion's face as beautiful as frost.

How can a face be like frost? he had asked.

There were lots of answers.

And what an uproar when they realised the lion was dead. Everyone agreed with David Herbert Lawrence. That the world could spare a few million people. But it could not afford to lose a mountain lion. Which was rare. With its face of frost.

Everyone that is, but little Keeley.

Some people are beautiful too, she had said. As well as yellow lions in the Lobo Canyon.

Keeley had said that. Keeley who never spoke but sat in the corner, all drab hair and unwashed tights. Keeley the little dwt. Keeley whom Vine knew was one of Siân's unbeautiful girls.

For Siân, life wasn't fair and she told him as much. Her classes were laborious affairs. Vine had always understood that, and he had done his best to help her.

In the past he had told jokes that she must try out; prompted her with news stories to introduce. She was a language teacher, after all, he thought. It wasn't algebra she was scrawling over the board.

Vine knew his wife was unpopular with the children and at one time this had hurt him grievously. But he had grown used to it. Vine understood Siân's classes were difficult. The language was too important to her for irony. But her zeal was as intimidating as it was futile. Or so Vine told himself. Theirs was a bilingual home, but often he had felt himself wretchedly out in the cold as Siân had talked to Nia and Brychan. Vine, with his smattering, could only try to make out a word here or there. But Siân sometimes raced her words. They were all joined together in one untranslatable sound. She zoomed ahead into the undergrowth regardless, expecting to be accompanied.

You're lazy, she often laughed.

My head's too full of B minuses.

Well, I learned.

You're a genius.

No, I'm a worker. You're a dreamer.

And that irritated him. Was Siân dreamless?

He thought of her in the choir, in that high-necked blouse the women wore. Dark and almost severe. Siân with thirty other women in dark blouses buttoned to the throat. Their eyes become one eye on the conductor, and his baton that Vine found ludicrous, Vine who could remember the school cane on his twelve-year-old hand and the sting of his reprimand.

John Vine. Dreaming in class.

Yes, Siân was right. But how he had once craved to understand her own dreams.

So, yes, he tried to help his wife with her classes.

You have to tell them stories, he'd urged her.

Teaching isn't story-telling.

Oh but it is, he'd said. And how it is! If life is story-telling, teaching has to be the same.

And he remembered Keeley with the others in the Friday afternoon darkness with the rain outside and the poem's firelight flickering over their faces. They had walked together up the Lobo Canyon and come to the lair that the lion would never visit again.

Looking for something, he said.

Now she blazed.

You're not supposed to be here.

All my papers are.

You should have moved them weeks ago.

I know. I'm sorry. I did ring.

You never said you were coming. Creeping about...

Don't be silly.

Creeping about with your guilty secrets.

Half my life is here, for God's sake.

Yes. Where you left it. Your abandoned life. And that life's over. Siân?

I don't want to know. Go back to your gypsy.

She's not…

Your girlfriend, then.

Siân's eyes blazed. She came towards him through the clutter, treading over papers and files.

Do you know how absurd that word sounds? Girlfriend? Do you? A man with two teenaged children. With a *girlfriend*. Brychan might have a girlfriend. But Jesus Christ, his father? So go back to your pathetic whatever it is on the site.

She was close now and her mouth was wet with spittle.

Yes, bingo. Calling bingo numbers. Well you really hit the jackpot there. What's the word? House. That's it. Well what about this house? What about that payment every month? What about the insurance and the electric?

That's sorted. It's taken care of.

We're selling up, or hadn't you noticed?

The plan was that Siân and the children would move in with her parents. They lived in a villa at the resort's west end.

What guilty secrets?

Siân spat at him then. Her saliva lay on his cheek. There was triumph in her face.

Everybody knows. You fool. I always knew.

Vine stood with paper up to his knees.

Come here, she said, and grabbed his arm. She led him to the computer.

We'll use this one, she gestured.

Siân left to go downstairs. He could hear her opening drawers in the kitchen. She came back with a CD.

Here we go, she said. And slipped it in.

Christ, breathed Vine.

Yes here we go.

What's this all about?

Exactly as if you wanted people to know, she said.

Know what?

All about this.

And Siân clicked to start.

There was Rachel. She was on stage in school. While good old Gorwel was calling for quiet, Rachel stood in her black uniform, patient, waiting for her turn. That was when she had red in her hair, Vine remembered. Crimson highlights amongst the black.

Then she took her cue and began her recitation.

'Cousin Kate', by Christina Rossetti, she said. And her smile was huge.

There was a stirring from a largely unseen audience.

> *I was a cottage maiden*
> *Hardened by sun and air,*
> *Contented with my cottage mates,*
> *Not mindful I was fair.*
> *Why did a great lord find me out*
> *To fill my heart with care?*
>
> *He lured me to his palace home –*
> *Woe's me for joy thereof –*
> *To lead a shameless shameful life,*
> *His plaything and his love.*
> *He wore me like a silken knot,*
> *He changed me like a glove;*
> *So now I moan, an unclean thing,*
> *Who might have been a dove.*

Vine remembered filming at a school concert. Occasionally Rachel was obscured by the heads of others in the audience. Not knowing the poem by heart, she occasionally consulted the book. Vine had bought the Phoenix *Selected* for her as a present. Christina was cool and Italian, Rachel had said, rewarding him with a kiss. What a role model.

> *O Lady Kate, my cousin Kate,*
> *You grew more fair than I:*
> *He saw you at you father's gate,*

Chose you, and cast me by.
He watched your steps along the lane,
Your work among the rye;
He lifted you from mean estate
To sit with him on high.

When the poem was finished Rachel looked at the audience for a serious second. Then she had exited stage right to protracted applause. The film showed various Year Twelves laughing and Lost Horizon again calling order. It clicked off.

Vine looked at Siân. Her arms were crossed. He could remember filming Rachel but not transferring the film to CD.

What's the big deal? he asked.

Siân smirked.

You crashed and burned.

There was lots of filming going on that night. You can see those people holding up their phones.

You crashed and burned.

Cool down. Can't we talk?

And the amazing thing is, said Siân under her breath, that I haven't told the police.

Why should you?

Now Siân sneered in exasperation.

The girl's been missing for three months for Christ's sake. Or don't you read the papers? And there she is. On *your* film.

Vine cupped his face in his hands and rubbed his eyes. He looked old.

Listen, he said. You know school's full of things like that. Every computer up there is like a cinema these days.

Oh no. You've got a history.

Siân knew this was her time. Her words were full of cold fury.

Haven't you? A history. Look who you're with now. Some piece from nowhere. Shacked up with someone you hardly know the name of. But it was every year wasn't it? The brightest girl. Or the brightest girl who happened to be a bit of a looker. Every year for as long as I can remember. And Nia's age. The age she is now. Can't you imagine the shame she feels?

Vine sat down on the paper-strewn desk.

Do you want me to tell you some of the jokes they make about you in that place?

Staffroom crap. Everyone cops it eventually.

And how do you think I feel?

That's the job, shouted Vine. It comes with the job.

All those hours after hours?

Yes. If you're a good teacher. If you care, yes. Concerts, films, it's part of it. You above all know that.

Siân was scornful.

Don't make me laugh. Who else is out so far beyond the call of duty? Mr Vine, they say. Yes him. Old Vine. Look out or he'll be all over you. Ha ha. All over you like a creeping old Vine. Why could you never act your age?

Vine picked up a bundle of poems and put them down again.

So why not tell the police? That there's a film of her here?

Siân was calmer now but her cheeks were ashen and her voice was ugly.

Because you're weak all right. But that's all. Nothing more than that.

She ejected the CD.

Yes. A weak man who gave it all away. Who gave everything away.

Vine was silent in the room that had once been his. A box filled with his own life. He looked at the postcards and theatre posters on the walls, the restaurant cards pinned to an exposed beam.

You crashed and burned. You wanted a life without your family. And now look at you.

Siân seemed to shrink into herself.

Now go before Nia gets home. Get out.

I'd come back, he whispered.

Siân was startled.

You what?

I'd come back. If you let me.

There was silence in the room. Vine could hear himself breathe.

Christ, she whispered. You idiot.

She whispered again.

Christ.

Then spat. Caravan life not all it's cracked up to be?

Vine coughed. At first he was clearing his throat, but the cough persisted.

And wait till it's cold, said Siân. See how you and your dark little friend like it then. Yes see how you like it then with the rain horizontal off the sea.

I'd had enough of school, persisted Vine. I know you understand that.

Yes, she shouted. I've had enough of school. We've all had enough of school. But you could have done anything. You could have had respect. But you meet this girl from God knows where and the next thing all of us here know is that you're moving out, you can't stand it, you can't stand your old life so you have to make a new one. That's what you said wasn't it? I can't stand it.

Siân looked at the desk and Vine looked at the room. At the chaos of it. Once it had made sense. Now it bewildered him.

It was the wife moved first.

Whatever you wanted isn't here. Whatever it was. Now go. Please go. Nia's coming.

He waited in a phone box at the end of the road and watched Nia come from the opposite direction. Eyes down, plugged in. She turned in at the gate.

It wasn't at home. He was sure of that now. But he had already tried school. The previous month he had taken an enormous risk and searched his old room and store cupboards.

Getting in had been simple. He owned a side entrance key he had copied ten years earlier. Those were the days when he went in as early as 7 am. For marking, he told himself, but sometimes he knew it was to escape the mornings of half-dressed children and a blitzed kitchen and bathroom. Sometimes he had also used it to go in on holidays.

To read. He knew it was pathetic, or imagined others might find it so, but often school was the only place where he would be undisturbed.

So he sat at his desk before thirty empty chairs and consumed a chapter of *Bleak House* or *The Brothers Karamazov*. Each page a chocolate. No, better, a Kalamata olive. A sip of a decent shiraz. And what made it delicious was the knowledge there were hundreds of other pages to come in an almost endless succession.

Vine's reading was a vision of eternity. How he had savoured those moments in the empty classroom. And how he had anticipated them during the rush of a school day or the non-stop activity at home. The Saturday sun streaming in, the illiterate chalk scrawl behind his head. And the book in his hand a miracle.

But last month he had broken in. Vine knew the department would not have changed the locks. Why should it? The cleaners and last staff would be gone by six o'clock, and the head, Big Guy the big guy rarely hung about. He would have long since fled to a gravy dinner and the rugby club. Big Guy who had grubbed up the school garden and installed the car maintenance bay. Big Guy who had proposed training for pupils who wanted to work in call centres. Their lives in his hands.

It was dark when Vine had slipped into school. There was one interior light burning but the cleaner often left it on as a deterrent. He had come down the back path and turned up the alley between the old school and its extension. That took him into the middle of the campus where he reached E Block. Drizzle had been falling and Vine doubted whether he would meet any children larking after hours.

E Block was a prefabricated section of three classrooms, a store cupboard and what had been Vine's study. This room was the centre of the block and had no windows. In truth it was a glorified cubbyhole, but Vine had spent hours there, marking, assessing, and when he needed to, hiding. He had turned the key, twisted the handle and the door had opened.

He pressed a switch and after a few seconds the strip light pinged on. The room had looked the same but everything was different. His poster-poems and theatre bills had been taken down and not replaced. There were piles of books everywhere and the cupboards were overflowing.

Vine had brought his desk keys but there was no need. All the drawers were open and stuffed with files. Two brown-ringed china mugs had stood amongst papers on the desk top, and a plate with a congealed mess of chips and ketchup topped the filing cabinet.

It was Middleton's room now, Simon Middleton who was going places. The lean, the mean, the hard as nails Simon Middleton. The young Simon Middleton.

You're welcome to it, Simon Middleton, Vine had thought, looking at the man's squalor. The room had been a shrine. It was a pit stop now.

He spent an hour and found many things he had thought lost from his life forever. Names, photographs, histories. Middleton had simply added his papers to the stratum Vine had abandoned. There had been no effort to clear the disorder. Yes, there were envelopes here addressed to Vine from parents and the union and the local authority. But nothing in Rachel's painstaking longhand. No white envelope. No brown.

Combing the filing cabinet drawers he had despaired. So much of what he had called work seemed a waste of his time. Vine could not remember writing those reports or reading the projects that spawned them. He must have been dreaming. He must have been sleepwalking through his time away from the classroom, hunkered down in a condemned portakabin, dreaming, hiding, awarding B minus to the silence.

Then he had looked at the computer.

It frightened him.

Vine had been given the computer a year previously and it looked new compared with the battered PCs most of the staff used.

He wore me like a silken knot, said Rachel's voice in his head. How astonishing he had always thought that line. What did Rossetti mean?

Unbelievable, thought Vine. The screensaver was a picture of Middleton himself, taken in the staffroom. Middleton with his wolfish smile. Middleton in a suit too expensive for school. Not that his smile was a sneer or that the new man was disdainful. Nothing so obvious. But Simon Middleton was a man who anticipated success. Whatever that was.

Lazy bastard, breathed Vine.

You cocky, lazy bastard.

He listened to the school exhale.

A noise? Maybe there had been a door shutting. Or perhaps it was a car.

Then he had heard it again. Definitely a door, and emphatically closed.

Vine had frozen, trapped in the windowless room.

He had locked the door from the inside and snapped off the light, then crossed to the desk and crouched behind it.

Christ. He hadn't turned the computer off. There was Middleton's long face and charcoal Jaeger jacket against the staff lockers. Middleton like a lantern in the dark. His inheritor's smile.

Vine had never thought computers were so bright.

Someone came into the block. Vine could see the light outside his door in the entrance hall was switched on. A crack of white. A classroom door was opened and slammed shut. This happened three times.

Then the study door handle rattled.

He didn't breathe.

His hand was cupped over his own mouth.

What was that in his throat? It had felt like a seed. He wanted to cough it out but was petrified in the darkness.

Vine waited for the door to be thrown open but nothing happened.

Then he heard the door into the block slammed shut and footsteps moving off towards the old school.

Caretaker.

The man lived in the same street as the school but this late checking was unusual. Vine waited ten minutes and, when he heard nothing else, turned on the study light. In his throat the seed was smaller now, but still there.

He had been sure nothing was left on the computer. Nothing left of Rachel that is. The school computers might already have been checked, which seemed an arduous job. How could anyone keep track these days of that kind of commerce? Vine knew that floating around the internet were innumerable pictures of himself taken by pupils: Vine arriving one morning in the snow; Vine reading Macbeth to class, his ironic teacher's take on 'tomorrow and tomorrow and...' Vine in last year's staff play, a truncated and much ad-libbed *Waiting for Godot* that had sprawled out of the black cube of the drama studio into a seafront pub, with Siân there, merry on barley wine of all things.

Watch it, he'd said. It's not barley sugar. But she'd knocked it back and demanded another. That had been Siân enjoying herself. Siân with the kids and choir forgotten, her tight-lipped smile a triumph. And Middleton was there too, complaining about the lack of real ale, Middleton in his mohair overcoat with the little dark probationary biology girl almost under his arm, Middleton who'd made a decent Act One Estragon, Vine had to say it himself, and Gorwel with his white wine toasting the Year Thirteen producers, and yes, incredibly, Big Guy, the big guy himself buying the round. The Head who hadn't exactly sat through the performance but come in clapping at the end, his hands like a second row forward's, his bald head shining under the studio lights.

So try stopping it, thought Vine. It's like the sea. As for the chat rooms, they were predictable hotbeds of slander. Some teachers he knew had officially complained, but not Vine. Nor Siân, who received her share of malice. Long-suffering Siân. Or the Poisoned Dwarf, as she was characterised on one site. Some of them were like soap operas. Nothing you could do about that, was there? Oh no. Nothing to be done.

Hal

Remind you of anywhere? asked Hal.

They were on board The Bona Ventura. Despite the beards of rust, the ship's white paint dazzled Karoona in the afternoon light. The tide was out but the hull was sunk deep in the mud of the inlet. It would take a storm surge to move it.

Because of the list, Karoona held on to the aft starboard rail. She looked down at the bollards and crates in the inlet, the lagoon with its frosting of polystyrene and plastics, the moraines of driftwood, the driftwood in the shoals, and down at the quicksand where The Bona Ventura had come to rest. Half a mile away she could see the caravans and then the fairground. Beyond them was the town with its pier and harbour. The rides in the fair were all in action, enticing anyone who would dare. The Firewheel had paused in its rotation and from the highest car she could hear a girl's screams.

Not Rotterdam, she said.

Karoona looked along the beach and into the dunes. Behind them the hills waited, the hills she would never visit and which were not part of her calculation.

Maybe places I don't know the names of. Places that aren't places to me.

The deck was a slippery mess of oil and sand. There was a gull's wing swept into a corner with cigarette packets and beer cans.

The kids get up here, smiled Hal. Can't blame the kids. Then he looked harder.

But nobody else. Off limits.

Trespassers will be prosecuted, said Clint.

Oh that's right, smiled Hal thinly. Ask Jozz here.

He turned to the woman with cropped hair.

Trespassers will be prosecuted won't they, Jozz?

Civil offence, the woman said. Courts wouldn't touch it.

She was heavily built but muscular. Her sleeveless vest revealed a weight-trainer.

So we have to do our own prosecution, said Clint. If you know what I mean.

Hal brightened and held out his arms.

Okay, it's the captain speaking. So welcome aboard. I know you haven't been here before. Have you Karoona?

No.

So let's go for a stroll.

Slowly the group walked along the starboard deck, the stained bulk of the focsle above them. There were lengths of chainlink underfoot, fused to the metal deck.

Now before we go below for our treat, said Hal, I want you all to look over there.

And he pointed to the north west, over the town.

Just ten miles up the road. Think of it. Ten little miles. That's where he came from. The greatest genius I'm ever going to meet. Or you. Or you. And certainly you.

Karoona held on to the rail. The deck was slick with seawater and dead leaves. There was a lifebelt on the floor, the name of the ship worn away. Jozz in her shades followed, then The Fish, then Clint.

Our Richey, said Hal. Our very own Richard.

Who is he? asked Karoona.

Your ignorance is entirely forgiveable, beamed Hal. Considering. And there's so much to consider, of course. Although it still disappoints.

Richard Burton, said Clint, behind.

Sir Richard to you, said Hal, stopping so suddenly they all stopped. Il Generalissimo. Lord Burton. King Richard. The Emperor.

I have never heard of him, frowned Karoona.

My dear. The greatest actor this world has ever seen. And from up the road, just up the road.

Hal paused.

Here we are.

Out of his bag he carried he produced a torch and a bunch of keys.

Karoona had not noticed a door. There seemed only white paint beneath the oxides and algae. But it opened easily and Hal stepped in over the metal threshold.

Careful, ladies, called Hal. And Jozz too.

He led them down a ladder into a passageway. Everything was damp here and Karoona felt water immediately soak through her espadrilles. Hal's beam picked out blistered white walls. In places the paint was worn back to the metal. Above their heads the steel was a fur of rust. There was pipework leading in every direction, some of it wrenched away from the bulkhead.

Sorry about the damp, called out Hal.

After ten yards they came to a second door. Hal opened it with another key and fumbled in the dark. Karoona heard a low humming sound, then nothing.

Hal pulled the door shut and advanced another ten yards. His torch played deliberately on the sign immediately ahead.

Captain.

Even with the generator on, the cabin was barely illuminated.

Mr Fish, commanded Hal, you know your duties.

The Fish handed round cans of lager and cider he took from a metal cupboard.

Good God, lighten up, make yourselves comfortable, laughed Hal, gesturing at the chairs. Karoona manoeuvred herself into a bursting leather sofa that instantly felt damp. Jozz joined her, while Clint started to fiddle with a television set.

Little treat for us all now, announced Hal. A real little treat.

I don't drink, said Karoona, refusing The Fish's proffered Grolsch.

You should, darling, he said. You'd be better for it.

Just the one for me, said Jozz. I'm on tonight at eight. Twelve hours.

Then she turned to Karoona.

Muslim are you?

Karoona hesitated.

Maybe. Maybe not.

Jozz leaned closer.

Hey, you know those London suicide bombers?

Karoona shrugged.

My mate in the Met in London's got pictures. After the event, like.

She inched closer.

Not a pretty sight.

Karoona shrugged again.

Those Muslim virgins must be pretty special, said Jozz. Under all that black.

She licked her lips.

I love your colour, she whispered.

Karoona crossed her bare legs.

I was born with it, she said.

She was wearing pink espadrilles, with a bracelet on her left ankle.

You know London? asked Karoona.

You want to go there, don't you? smiled Jozz.

And leave us behind, said Clint.

Jesus, said The Fish. It's like a meeting of the AA down here. Hence, and I mean hence, all the more for me.

And he peeled back the ring pull on a can of cider.

Good God, he said. Read this. Eleven per cent. Daddy'll kill me. Pale gold pavement sherry. Shouldn't be allowed. But here's a toast anyway.

He waggled his fin.

To our livers.

Come on Clint, stop fussing, ordered Hal.

The captain had placed himself in a rancid leatherette armchair directly in front of the television. This looked brand new, being a four feet wide plasma screen, hung on the far wall. Apart from this, Hal's cabin held a DVD player, with a desk and double bunk both littered with video cartridges and CD cases. Everywhere there were crushed and empty lager cans, beer bottles, pizza boxes and the wrappings of takeway Indian food. Apart from the screen, the walls were covered in charts patched with damp and curling blackly at the edges. From the metal ceiling, the colour of cistern iron, Karoona noted tiny stalactites, each lit with a drop of moisture.

I think the sea's coming in, she pointed.

No chance, laughed Clint.

She's totally sound, shouted Hal, his voice metallic. His eyes were the colour of seawater.

Christ, all over the Med as far as Cyprus, the bloody Adriatic, the Aegean, then all those British cruises, North Sea, Irish Sea, Isle of fucking Man, The Bona Ventura's been everywhere. And still tight as a...

Which one? interrupted Clint.

Ah ha, said Hal. Let's have a little guessing game.

He stood up, but the cabin ceiling was too low for him to stand erect.

Ladies and gentlemen, who was, and is the best actor in the world?

Richey! cackled Jozz.

A drop of water fell on to Karoona's hand. She stared at it.

Yes. Sir Richard Burton. And knight or no knight, the greatest talent of stage and screen ever produced.

Karoona looked the other way from Jozz whose thigh was touching hers.

And eight Oscar nominations for our man. Eight! And yet no award.

Hal looked around.

Jealousy. Pure stinking jealousy.

Then he brightened.

And as befits present company, I'd like to introduce that greatest talent's greatest film.

Hal sat down.

So what is it then?

Who's Afraid of Virginia Wolf, volunteered Jozz.

Not quite, said Hal scornfully.

Anthony and Cleopatra.

Too foreign.

1984 then.

A good choice. How our man bewildered that skinny little sod John Hurt. Acted him out the door. But wrong.

The Sand Pebbles, shouted The Fish.

That was his missus.

Wild Geese, then?

One of my favourites, yes, said Hal. A masterpiece. But wrong again.

I have not a clue, whispered Karoona.

Then here it is, smiled Hal. And from his bag he took a silver disc. Clint, do the honours.

What is it? asked Jozz.

What could it possibly be? sneered Hal. You bunch of losers.

He paused.

Perhaps you'd like to look at this.

From inside his jacket Hal produced a book. Carefully he opened its cellophaned pages.

Here, he exclaimed. You can pass it round, but be very careful indeed.

That's beautiful, said The Fish.

Priceless, breathed Clint.

Every time I see it I want to cry, said Jozz, who hadn't bothered to look.

Karoona took the autograph book. A beer mat advertising Allbright Bitter was tucked inside a plastic envelope. There was blue ink over it. She tried to read the scrawl.

I can't, she said.

Hal grabbed the book back but then hesitated.

To Hal. Best wishes from Richard Burton.

We were in The Five Bells, he said. The fucking Five Bells. And do you know who walks in? Can you even bloody guess? Not in a million years can you guess. Because we're at the bar and there's a commotion and I turn around and there they are. Richard Burton. And Elizabeth Taylor. In a fucking fur coat. In The Five Bells. Ordering a drink each in The Five Bells with one for the chauffeur. The fucking chauffeur. Style? Don't talk to me about style. That man was born with it.

Unbelievable, said Clint.

Beautiful, said The Fish.

And nobody there says a word.

Hal's grey eyes were alight.

Not a word. So Richey's got his pint, sinks half of it, and looks round. Then he introduces Elizabeth to every fucker at the bar. In The Five Bells. We're just driving down, he says. To see the family, he says. Thought we'd call in for refreshment, he says. And still nobody says a word.

Respect, nodded Jozz.

Karoona watched a black drop run the length of the plasma screen.

Hello boys, says Elizabeth. She's got half a bitter in her hand. The pearls on her you wouldn't believe. As to the chauffeur, he's got a fucking pint down him already. In The Five Bells. Thirsty work, driving, says Richey. Anybody want another?

By which he means anyone at the bar. But still nobody says anything. Like they're all petrified. And boy, he's put his own glass down, and I remember as if it was yesterday, him wiping the froth off his mouth. And looking around. With those eyes. Those killing eyes.

So yes, I say. Yes please Mr Burton.

Richey, he says. Call me Richey.

Okay Richey, I say. Walking over. Thanks very much. I'll have another Allbright if that's okay.

And yeah, it's okay, and Richey puts his own cash down and the landlord is pulling it and they're leaving, they're at the door, it's like a dream and the dream's about to end and I call Mr Burton, Richey? And he smiles at me and I say will you sign this please Richey, and it's that beer mat here, the only piece of paper I could get my hand on, and of course, he says, of course, who's it for and I say Hal, for Hal please Richey and he took it and signed it and gave it back. In The Five Bells. And here it is today. And I tell you what. They should have put a plaque up in that pub to Richard Burton. And Elizabeth Taylor in her white fur stole. And the fucking chauffeur in his peaked cap and britches because he had the full gear on. Immaculate he was. Like a fucking guardsman with a stripe round his cap. I can see that stripe today. But did they put up a plaque? Did they fuck. There's nothing to this day to tell the tale. In The Five Bells. Only this piece of paper here, which is unique and therefore a priceless document.

Yeah, priceless, said Clint.

Hal looked round.

Now, the film. Please don't call it movie. Movies I hate. Because this is The Film. It's *Villain* of course. We're going to see *Villain*.

The Fish gave Clint a pained look.

Villain? asked Jozz. Never heard of it.

But Hal held up his hand and waved for silence. It was the hand that held the remote control.

Karoona glanced up at the ceiling. Every rivet was a raindrop. The sea was coming through the sofa.

The Fish

It was a big evening. At sea the light fell like knives, the sky was crowned with cumulus. On the other side the field shapes were visible with hedge lines distinct, the darker moorland etched above. A windscreen twenty miles away sparked like flint. In the fair the sirens were sounding and each ride cranking out its classic. The Firewheel was playing *Suspicious Minds*, the SkyMaster repeating *Tainted Love*. On the breeze the music tangled into one plume and blew across town.

Sometimes one word was clear, sometimes a chorus. For The Fish it was like listening to short wave radio. Occasionally he'd play the soundtrack to The Kingdom of the Damned, out of date because it didn't mention the newer attractions brought in last season. Because there were more than the demon king, the hounds of hell, the living skeleton now. They'd added a wax museum of contemporary monsters. In this annexe were the Yorkshire Ripper in a dinner suit and the man who'd murdered two schoolgirls. So there sits The Fish in his perspex cubicle, The Fish taking the public's money, sliding tokens and change back under his window. And for once, because it's been a poor year, he's doing good business. The Fish looks up.

Well would you? Pay money for this? I didn't think so. But plenty do, considering. The girls of course. They like to be scared. And the young couples walking round together, hugging each other, the pushchair rolling ahead. And the families posing in front of the mirrors, looking at themselves as they've never been before. Like they never imagined themselves. As if they weren't obese in the first place. Yes, fat. But no, it's not much. That nutter, Huntley, what's to see. Deadly ordinary. You wouldn't pick him out in a crowd. I've told Hal it's crap, and so have his, er, associates. Okay, not crap, but improveable. Because really there's not much money in a place like this. Fair enough, the good day, the good week. But how often is that? You see, Hal thinks we've modernised. That we're up to date and that'll be okay for the next ten years. Tradition, he calls it. That's his big word. Tradition. Last of the line, last old fashioned fair. You see, he's proud of it.

And where is he now but upstairs in the office looking down at the trogs coming through the gates, all the blokes pumped up, the girls with their bellies on display, all that gooseflesh straight out of the tanning studio. Jesus, those girls screaming. Ah, the vicarious life. What would they do if they walked in and there was a starving African kid with flies on its eyes? Or some Jewish pensioner stripped off waiting for a shower? Ask for their money back probably. Not scary enough.

Of course, it's all on the site. The Archive. The whole of this atrocity alley put up so you don't need to leave the comfort of your own home. Through the squeaking door, under the cobwebs, past some neanderthal peering out of the banana leaves, Attila the Hun, how did he get there? Frankenstein's monster, the Wolfman, those blobs from *Ghostbusters*, Freddie off Elm Street, some zomboid homicidal courtesy of Sam Rami, bloody *Alien* and all the rest of it. Even the siren that says 'do not touch' and which everybody touches, it's traditional. Clint got it from a cardboard box factory. So he said. They actually used to sound it to bring the cardboard box-makers back from their fag break. It's all on the site and beautifully filmed.

But that's lost on Hal. He thinks we can go on forever like this. Anyway, you will have seen us this aft over on The Bona Ventura. A pleasant time was had by all, and no, I didn't indulge too much. Always knew I had to help out here, see. Because work instils discipline and self control, even if it involves taking pennies off some beered-up half-wit in whose honour the index of multiple deprivation was specially created. Self control and self esteem, see. But I needed a couple because I woke up feeling weird. Exceedingly weird. Went to make a cuppa and felt like I was walking ahead of myself. No, behind myself. Like I was split in two. Split, split! I was the bad half, the bruised apple. Ahead was the good half, the brimstone buttocked peach. Yeah. In two. By an axe through the middle of the skull. And the headache was the daylight between the twin halves of my brain.

So I needed that drink, the bucket of polecat piss. Sheer poison of course but that's what homeopathy is all about. As to the film, well. Hal, let me assure you, is the spit of Burton in that movie. *Villain*. Seamed, sordid, baggy-eyed. But psychopathic? That's debatable. Capable of the odd psychotic interlude, certainly. He needs to be in his business. Able to turn it on. But he's not mad. Not mad as in insane that is. Not by a long way. But we're an odd assortment these days, I'll give you that.

Take Clint. Hal's halberd. Not the brightest, is he. But toned. He always seems to be shining. Must be the baby oil and the steroids. And not a hair on that golden torso of his. He's been parading it all summer. And have you seen his dog? Bollocks like a pawnbroker's whatsits. Which I suspect is more than you can say for Clint. But of all Hal's enforcers, and they come and they go, believe me, he is the favoured son. The best beloved, Clint's fundament being the repository of the kind old sun's brightest ray. The bad, the badder and the beautiful, that's Clint. Though maybe he's not so important as he used to be. Maybe Clint, even classical Clint has his shelf life. As indubitably have the rest of us.

But that Jocelyn? We're seeing more of Jozz of late. Not my cup of tea, but live and let live. She could do you some damage, could

Jozz. And if she asks you for an arm wrestle, say you've got another appointment. She's the station champion, apparently. Biceps like cannonballs. Or was that the dog? Sorry, they're so alike. Especially when she's wearing leather. Fancy taking her for a walk? I thought not. But maybe we could have her in here, the bull dyke with a bull mastiff making an arrest. Nicking Osama or one of his suicide jockeys. Sorry, yes, sorry. Unforgivable that, but I get carried away when I'm on shift.

D'you know what we had to sit through after the Burton epic? That Stallone effort where he's in the world arm wrestling championships. Las Vegas or somewhere. And of course the odds are stacked, the nasties are conspiring. Talk about muscle-bound. But Hal lapped it up and so did Clint. As for Jozz, well, she never blinked. And maybe Sly's not so bad. Do I or do I not detect an element of welcome self-parody in his later work? Say, after *Rambo 2*? Surely I'm right. Which is more than you could say for Sir Richard this afternoon.

And little Karoona? She made nothing of any of it. I was watching her face and her expression didn't change. But then, she looks inward, doesn't she? To the desert within. Straight over her head it went, all of it. Nuances, see, she hasn't got the nuances. She can't interpret the mumbles and the glances, doesn't get the irony, the thousands of little flavours, the slangy stuff. Our local colour. And please, spare me that business about her being twenty two or twenty five or whatever. That lady won't see thirty again, no matter what the passport will say. Hal gets his enthusiasms and she's one for the present. A touch of the exotic if you like. A little cous-cous in the salad.

Not that Hal's so different. Nice house over the dunes' end, palm trees in the garden, the midnight-blue Jag. Never been there of course, but they tell me it's special inside. Mexican tables and chairs, all those rivets in the wood, the brass studs, the green against the purple. And lots of Spanish things. Dark and muscular. Funny really. Look at the state on The Bona Ventura. Can't shift it now, casino plans scuppered, and there's Admiral Hal walking the deck regardless. Or the plank. Christ knows what kind of thrill he's getting out of it. For some reason I thought of that English actor who played the captain in *Titanic*. But with the prospect of malevolence mixed in. Which is Hal's strength. Exuding, yeah, exuding the possibility that something rather unpleasant might occur. That's a talent.

The captain was an idiot who couldn't see through the fog in his mind. But you haven't seen The Perseverance yet have you? Something else Hal owns and won't give up. It's a pub behind the fair down here on the east end. Closed three years ago because of a fire and never reopened. And it's a derelict disgrace. It makes me sick to look at it. They barbed wired it and everything, but the kids get in, Hal or no Hal, and light their barbecues, have their teenage orgies. And he just sits on it. Does nothing with the site. Would make a lovely club, yes, pretty swish with its location, but it's just a burned out shithole. Which is how he seems to like it. Funny that. I've seen him upstairs in The Perseverance looking out at the sea and the town. Transfixed. You know, kind of catatonic. I don't mean his pupils have disappeared like something in that David Carradine Buddhist martial arts show, but pretty strange. And nobody's dared say anything or lead him away. You just have to wait till the moment's over.

Yeah, The Bona Ventura I can understand. From a distance The Bona Ventura looks surprising. It's there in the sunset like a wedding cake. I've always thought that, so I like The Bona. But The Perseverance's mad. Not mad as in insane but mad every other way.

You see, I love this town. Well, I'm its historian, I'm the chronicler of its present tense. Self-appointed? Certainly. There was a gap in the market and I moved in. The Archive tells all. But The Perseverance's not on, I can't approve of The Perseverance. Pink walls, boarded up windows on the ground floor, graffiti. But as to the rest, it's all very traditional. Mrs Hal runs that part of the show. Blonde piece, a young forty. Her own little silver Porsche and isn't she the bat out of hell all down the prom on a Saturday night, the original Bacardi breeze in her hair. Bit like the looker in *Thelma and Louise*. You know, the Ray-Bans, the headscarf. God, have I a picture of her. In this gold sheath. A sort of pre-Raphaelite goddess, a dress so tight she could hardly walk.

Nah, maybe her face is more Sharon Stone. And her hair done silver for the occasion. Oh she was a candleflame all right, all aquiver in the night. Course I couldn't put it in the Archive. Not yet. But one day perhaps. Yeah, stunner. But a bitch though. Hard as nails. And increasingly fond of the sauce, which is always a good sign for me. A little badge to prove her humanity, no matter how deep it's buried. And that tooth of hers, the gold one at the front. How superb is that? I could look at that mouth all day, I could say...

Hey! for a party of five you get one free! Nice one. Watch out for the zombies, kids. And a quid change.

You see, I'd really like The Kingdom to be up-marketed. But ever so slightly. Give the trogs a thrill to even think about going in. Look at that bunch now. Dad with a roofer's suicidal tan, Mum with a thong, can you believe it, a thong showing above her rhinestone-riddled gunslinger's cartridge belt. Christ, she's garrotted her own arse. Their little girl in the pushchair and already a stud in her ear, and the son and heir who's six, say, with the middle of his hair dyed blonde, yeah, a whiteblonde coxcomb all gelled up in spikes and the rest of it a calamitous ebony. Maybe seven. Why don't they just have the word 'Victim' tattooed on their foreheads?

If I'd had the chance I'd have shot them for the Archive. As yer typicos, yer archetypes, yer trogloditic tendency. Straight out of the arcade where they've all been working the slots and that includes Little Bo Peep in the pushchair, mum and dad serious at it, feeding in tens, in fifties, oh yeah, high rollers, dad on the Cherry Multiple, mum just off the Rio Carnival. And the boy bored and wandering about. With cruelty in his face. I saw it, I identified it, I swear it was there, yes already there. The split second I saw him. And there they go into the darkness and now they are engulfed.

How Hal loves them. His meat and drink. Talking of Sam Rami, which I was, I always like that line in one of the Dead films. You know, *Day of the Dead,* that series. Well the survivors are hiding out in a shopping mall, making a last stand against the zombos. And one of the survivors asks why the dead are coming back to the mall. There's thousands of the bastards hammering on the River Island glass. And the answer comes, and this always kills me – 'because they were happy here once'. They were happy here. And it's the same in the fair. Simple really. Well it has to be simple for Hal to understand.

But careful. He's watching from up above. From this hutch I can't see the office but I know he's there. He sleeps up there sometimes, mansion or no mansion, Mrs Hal undressing on her own, a spindrift of underclothes at her feet, her knickers just a line of asterisks. Such a sweet constellation. But such a haughty bint.

Or maybe he doesn't even sleep. Maybe he stays in the window like he did at the The Perseverance. Looking out. Watching the reflections of the neon that he keeps on all night, the light backwards on the water if there's a high tide and trembling and vanishing and coming back in liquid red letters on the black swell. *The Kingdom of the Damned*. Maybe that's when he feels it most. The sense of empire.

Not that he owns it all. The fair's a warren of petty interests. Might be two bigger players and the rest continually in the process of being bought out. But it's like a medieval field system. Some of the pitches and patches are just a few square yards. Who owns Madam Zeena's spot, for instance? Even she couldn't tell you and she's the fortune teller. And I like it like that, a tangled, historical unravelable mess. So perish the day. Perish the day it gets straightened out and the compulsory purchase orders come in and they drown it all for their marina and their apartment blocks and tapas bars.

China mugs of tea is what this place is. Faggots with vinegar and a scoop of mushy peas. Outstanding. Long live the mush. Perish the day when it's like everywhere else. Because believe me, we're the last of a kind. There's no doubting that. We're the last there is as far as this coast runs. The only reason we're still here is that we're bloody remote. Stuck out here. Out on our own behind our reef. Out on The Caib. Out at the end of our peninsula. In the kaarst and the chaos and the ineluctable limestone where the currents run deadly and our drowned are an unreckonable myriad. Oh yeah, Mr Fish! By the way, one of the last say, thirty words, is in my dictionary on the site. I change that dictionary every three months but keep the local words. Can you guess which one it is? Just look at the Archive. Then you'll know if I'm telling the truth.

Because that's all I'm doing isn't it? Putting you right. In case you start to get the wrong idea. Because there are already enough people knocking around here with the wrong ideas. And we don't want you joining that gang.

Donal

Only out here can you get an idea of what it looks like. The town, I mean, and the peninsula. And okay, it's midnight and you're asking what's to see. Well first of all, surprisingly few lights. Street lamps, of course, and those coloured lights strung along the promenade. But most houses are dark. They go to bed early around here. With relief, most of them. But the seafront pubs are still shining and there'll be a lock-in at a couple.

So what am I, half a mile out? Yeah, you get a good idea of the shape of it all here, the big dunes out west on the tip of the peninsula, then the town, then the fair with the flags and one light burning on the highest ride, then the desert between the fair and the caravans, a quarter mile of blown sand covering the kerbs that lead nowhere, the bulldozed chippies, that place where you could buy anything from a newspaper to decent bait. Pokey little treasure trove that was. Gone. Like a lot of other things. With the sand over everything you'd think it was Babylon out there. A desert all right.

But it's the same with the caravan. If you don't sweep the sand it'll be over the axles. And it can bury the garden overnight. Yeah, all that darkness where the sand is and then caravan city where the tight bastards switch the avenue lights off at eleven so it's like the grave. Then the dunes on the east side which are always especially dark, a total black as if something was missing there, as if something had vanished. Then the hills behind and then the river mouth. Shallow, pretty well unnavigable. All kinds of shoals. In fact a poor excuse for a river.

And that's it. That's us. Stuck out in the ocean. And here I am with the engine off and the lights off just taking it in. What a night. Still? It's flat as a mirror out here. No stars but not too cloudy. No fishing either. But the old hipflask, I've brought that. The best companion to have. It was my father's and I've taken it everywhere I've been. Heart-shaped and almost flat. A silver heart, a lifesaver. And look at this, look at this. The old Prince coming up from the south and lit like a Mississippi riverboat, the Prince steaming back from the other side. Last cruise of the year and guess who's making the most of it. Yeah, all the boys and girls coming back on the midnight full, which strictly speaking is not legal because of the obvious dangers.

Dangers? you ask. Nothing terrible. Well, drunks dropping over the side. And nobody noticing. Hardly the end of the world. But these trips started when I was a kid. They meant you got to see places you'd rarely visit. Resorts of maritime interest, historical sites. But now everybody's mobile, so they're booze cruises, pure and simple. See, in the end, it all comes down to that. Getting out of your head. And I'm a veteran of that war, so I can say it, I'm allowed. Not that I take pride in it. But there's a good choice of bars on The Prince and if you've bought a ticket you can bring your own.

But don't worry. I know their course and it's a safe distance away. And you're right, they can't see me. They haven't a clue I'm here, just ploughing on regardless, so little traffic in this sea now. And look at that main bar. They call it The Ballroom and it's all done up like some grand hotel. Maybe two hundred pissheads in there tonight who've forgotten where they are and that there's only six inches of spar and plate between them and oblivion. One hundred feet of cold and black.

Just look at those reflections on the water. That's what I love to see, the reflections, like gold, like red melting into the black, shivering in that blackness, drowning, coming back. Like a baldaquin from some market, maybe from Zarqa.

Yes, Zarqa. Thought it was just a truck stop. But I was wrong. I bought one there once and it used to hang on the walls wherever I lived. A baldaquin. Kind of a tapestry. Never got the chance to use it in Spain and Christ knows where it is now. All browns and reds and gold, showing a tower with birds around it, and vineyards and gardens at the bottom, and a figure walking up this tower, a tower twisting like a corkscrew, this man climbing away from the gardens towards the top. Which was up in the stars, right up high. It was obvious what it meant. Because it comes to us all. You got to give up the honey and the figs, boss, and opt for a life of contemplation.

Well what do you think I'm doing here? Christ Jesus, they're loud. Tina belting it out, yeah *Simply the Best*. Every miserable mucked-up pissed-in-his-pants mediocrity is simply the best these days. Listen to that. That sound. The sound of people enjoying themselves. People drinking beer and wine and The Prince's champagne in special bottles with its own crest. Because if you don't drink you don't go on the cruises this week, this last week. These are the locals who haven't gone to bed. Who don't use Xanax. Listen to it. Laughing, shouting, people toasting each other. Celebrating being here and now and alive in the dark. Doing it proud.

Okay, just a load of drunks talking as if their lives depended on it and not a word to be remembered tomorrow. But it's the moment they're living in. This moment. And there she goes, the steamer higher than you'd ever think, big as a hotel, and reflections falling over us here below, and you're right, I'm holding on because it's a big vessel and the wake can knock us about a bit.

Yes, a hotel. I didn't finish my story about our bar in Spain, did I? Oh boy, get ready. Well of course the development is chronic all along that south coast. But I thought we'd found a place that had escaped. At least for a while. Not that we were extra specially choosy, me and Marty. But I thought we were winning. Well, one day, these men arrive. Asked why we didn't reply to the letters.

What letters? I said. And that was genuine. Turns out they were letters telling us to sling our bloody hook. Never got them. And I don't believe to this day they were ever sent.

Anyway, a hotel and sports complex were to be built on the headland cliffs above us. There would be roads, restaurants, a swimming pool. A pool, for fuck's sake. We were sitting at one of our outside tables five yards from the ocean. Our feet were in the sand. The black sand. These men were wearing shoes and they were wearing suits. They had briefcases and they were drinking my coffee. I could have knocked their heads together, I could have chased the fuckers off, because there's Marty and me listening and nodding and really we're too scared to say a word. And we're barefoot. Barefoot in the black sand. Marty in her sarong and not much else and me with a stinking hangover after this Dutch couple had stayed till four in the morning.

But it was what I always suspected. Only it was happening sooner than I ever dreamed. I'd thought we'd get a couple of years notice and be nicely paid off. But from then on it was rapid. Oh, incredible. Because they were also talking about the rent we hadn't paid.

The rent? I said at last. What rent? So I showed them the papers I had. The one who must have been the lawyer looked at them for ten seconds. And laughed. He laughed at me without smiling. And I remember a fishermen coming up the beach while we were out there talking. While we were listening. And yeah, did these suits speak good English. Always a bad sign. Well I could see this boy, because he was only a kid, walking along the beach towards us holding this dorado. And he was laughing and joking about it and obviously proud of what he'd caught. It was half as big as himself for Christ's sake. And he comes straight up to the table with it.

Hey Donal, how much you going to give me for this? How much, man?

And there's Marty looking at me, and this kid looking at me, and the suits looking at me, and I swear it, the fucking dorado looking at me. It was a minute dead, that's all, a minute. With its stripey skin and its lovely big eyes with the soul still there. And the boy's teeshirt all wet with it. And I never said a word. I just waved him away and went into El Zorro and opened the brandy.

When I looked out the business types had gone. Up the track to where they'd left their car in the stones and the prickly pear. Yeah, a black Mercedes. How did you guess? And Marty's still at the table and she's gazing out to sea and I could tell exactly how her mind was working.

So I took one out for her, a tumbler full of Soberano, from the bottle I'd just opened. Whose seal I'd broken. The bottle from the case I hadn't paid for. Which I never did pay for. And all I said was sorry. I'm sorry, love. Because it was my fault. It was our money, it was our business but it was my fault. Because the paperwork was my job.

And yeah, there goes The Prince into harbour. Leaving a scar behind it. The Prince all lit up, about to dock, and the booze-cruisers getting ready to totter on to dry land. Better than all the rest. Lucky for them it's a flat night. I've been aboard when everyone round me was puking and moaning and everything that wasn't bolted to the floor was going up and down like in a cocktail shaker. And if the sea was calm before, it's not now. I'll be bucking in this wake till God knows when. In the waves. And yeah, that wave, El Zorro, that people warned their children about? Well I was the one it swallowed, wasn't I? I was the one it snatched off the beach. Funny really. You might even call it ironic. How that bastard wiped me out.

Nia

I came back from the library in Cato Street because I needed stuff from my laptop. There were men in the pub there, The Cato, that's been closed years. Turning it into apartments probably. Mum always asks why not a wine bar? With candlelight and decent music. Jeff Buckley, she said once. And olives in Portuguese bowls. Black not green. Because black have that powerful taste, like medicine. More foreign somehow. Yes, somewhere civilised, she says. Where you can talk over a nice glass of chardonnay. But I came up our street and you know what? She's parked in front of that couple's gate again, five doors down. Shopping's still in it, and all this gardening stuff, a hoe and a bag of tulip bulbs or onions, all a bit dry. She got a ticket for obstructing that entrance about six weeks ago. And a fine. Since she's been on the sleeping pills her head's all over the place. Course, I arranged all the payments after my letter of appeal was turned down. I do all those things now. The things dad did. But those bastards, ratting on their neighbours. They're new see, they don't get it. The cretins called the police. So I was really going to tell her this time but when I got to the door, my key actually in the lock, I could hear them. Mum and dad. Doing the usual. But this one was a proper blow-out so I went to the seafront. There's a big poster up for The Dorrs. Mum's already booked tickets. And I thought, yes, look through the telescope. How's the other side today? You can swing the Owl round and see the hotels, right into some of them. Into the bedrooms. Then the fair, then the empty quarter, well that's what I call it, then the caravans. I can remember dad holding me and explaining how to screw up one eye. What do you see? he kept asking. What's out there? But his hands hurt under my arms and I wriggled too much. And what's he doing home anyway? Okay, they have to talk. But they're both off their heads, though he's the worse. It's the male menopause, Li said down the library last week. Li's great, so hard working, but I was surprised she knew a phrase like that. Do you have it in Mandarin? I asked. Course we do, she said. Chinese men are like... hello? No, Li's brilliant actually. Learning a foreign language, working checkout all hours, saving. Studying. Being funny. Being caring. So I'm getting a job too. Well I have to now, with things like this. So I told Li everything and she shrugged. Men, she said. That's men.

But dad's not men. At least he wasn't. But you hear all these stories in school and you know it's gossip because they've nothing better to do, but some of it's right. Like him and her in the caravan. Yes, off his head. Mad as a snake. And bingo? Who plays bingo? Mum says he'll come back because they always do and boy will he be in for a shock when he tries crawling home. But I don't get it. Okay, I do get it, but what is it with blokes that age and younger women? As if Gil wasn't bad enough. As if that thalidomide bloke in the library wasn't so obvious. Yes, I'd talk to him, I'd be friendly. I would. But he's like one of his waxworks in the House of Pain. Sort of leering. Or maybe that's just the way he is. Verging on the unutterably sad.

When the telescope money ran out I came back to the reading room. Only old Maudline was here. You know, she said, this could be the longest day of my life. And vanished. How weird is that? So I had the place to myself. Still do. And I thought about the first time I met Gil. He came for a meal to the house one Saturday night. They were all teachers, but mum and dad made me stay. Helping serve drinks. Because teachers drink. And when teachers drink they get scary. All blubbery and shapeless like they were made of foam rubber. Kind of spastic. All this muppetry going off. Lost Horizon was there, and Middleton, that creep, and some others who were like joint friends. Their mutual friends. And Gil and some woman from the other school but they weren't together. By the time I was going to bed mum had the silver bag out of the winebox, squeezing this red fountain into her mouth. Like in Spain, they were all saying. They do that there. But with leather bags. With wineskins. And mum's sitting on the floor with this silver bag, and everyone's shouting Siân, Siân down the Autobahn! because that German group was playing in the front room. Kraftwerk. It was Middleton brought the CD. So there's mum, off her head again and showing her knickers. You'll regret it tomorrow, I said, you know you will, and mind the carpet, it's red wine, but dad said to leave her enjoy herself as she was unwinding. Unwinding? Unravelling it looked like to me. Coming apart at the seams. And then there was Gil at the top of the stairs. In that Quiksilver shirt. In those black combats.

Great food, he said.

I did two of those tapas, I said. The courgette flowers and the spicy balls.

Hey, those were my favourites, he said.

And he didn't wink. He didn't grin. That's what I'll always remember. He didn't leer. He just said, yeah, you like food don't you, and I said, yes, I'm getting into cooking a little bit.

Yeah? So am I, he said. Food's important isn't it?

Yes, I said.

So, he said. You and I have a lot in common.

Oh, I said. How could that be?

Oh I just know about stuff like that, he said. I just know.

But dad? He always said he was going to buy one of those camper vans and drive off. Just go. And he'd laugh at mum and put his arm round her and ask if she'd come and she'd laugh too and say he was cracking up, how would they pay for the petrol, what if they were mugged on some lonely track in the north of Scotland or the Australian outback? What if their credit cards were stolen and their throats slit? All those psychos out there. For richer for poorer doesn't mean a lifetime of chemical toilets, she said.

It was a joke, only a joke, but dad took it the wrong way. So he went off to sulk on one of his rambles. Through the fair and God knows where else in the dark. Sometimes I think he went to his room in the school. And okay, I could feel sorry for him then. It's not like he had to be a teacher forever. He used to shout at mum about a life sentence. About doing time. Enough already, he used to say to her. I think it was a quotation. Enough already. But mum hadn't read that book. I understand duty, he used to say. Duty's important. But that stern daughter's no coy mistress. Yes, more quotations. Which, you know, is irritating after a while. And pretty pointless. With dad it's always other people's words.

Well how do you sleep in a camper van? Mum asked once. Those beds are just shelves.

We can work it out, he'd say. School's not everything. It's not some law we can't escape. It's not the law.

I enjoy teaching, she'd say.

No you don't, he'd laugh. You lying bitch.

And she'd laugh too and throw her marking pen at him.

Okay, genius, she'd say, how do we cook?

But when that Rachel went missing and the police asked dad about it, I knew they were wrong. Knew they were desperate. Or just going through the motions. Because he didn't teach her, did he? He didn't have any contact with her. It's a big school. But that was the longest day of my life. And the worst. Because everybody knew he went down the police station. So God knows what Maudline is going through today. But it had nothing to do with him, Rachel vanishing. Or just leaving home. Because she wasn't a child. And everybody in school knew she was seeing people. Every band that came to town she'd be there, back stage in The Ritzy, or biker music nights in The Cat or the art school people with laptops. Siân Siân Siân down the autobahn. Gil, even, I suppose. And there's loads of people doing stuff in their bedrooms now, mixing, recording, demoing. There's a scene here like the surf scene and all Vinny's crowd. And she was always dressed for it too. Like standing out but blending in. Playing the part.

It was only half an hour and then dad was home and he said it was just routine. So why did they never ask Middleton? He was always creeping round the girls, was Middleton, always finding opportunities for a one-to-one. Why didn't they question that sleazo? But it all went crazy after that. I don't remember clearly. Everything got mixed up and mum started the sleeping pills. But like Li says, don't worry, everything will be cool. I love the way she says cool. Cool. Everything will be cool. Li speaks like a cat, and she makes me laugh. Li's like cool incarnate. So, yes, I'm getting a job. I'll ask Maudline if there's anything here. Putting the newspapers out first thing, cleaning in the evening. And Li says she'll try at the Mega. But really, she needs any extra hours herself. Because renting's not cheap. She's got a poxy room in Vainqueur Street, across from the Lady Vain. What a dump that is. Old blokes in overalls leaning on the bar. They're going to knock it down.

So why not come to us? I said last week. Pay us rent. Two birds with one stone.

No, she said. Two cormorants with one fish. A Chinese joke. Ha ha.

But it would be so cool, I said. We could teach each other to cook. Spicy balls, I said to her.

Yes please, she said. And gave this enormous wink. This leer. Dirty girl. God, I love Li. But that stern daughter? I don't think so.

Wednesday

Donal

Those poppies I dug out of shingle. Never thought they'd come because they need a specialised habitat. But they're hardy buggers, with those strange beaks. Or horns, as they're called. There was a colony growing out of the pebbles. I dug down to the sand and took three. And here they are. The old Papa family. Yellow-horned poppy to you. Not rare but worthy of regard. And kind of familiar to this coast. If this town needed an emblem that's what I'd choose, the yellow-horned poppy.

Going over now of course. Couple more weeks and they'll start shrinking back into the gravel. But I love them because they're hardy and they keep coming and they keep coming and not even a hurricane will kill them. Unless it lifts their beach clean away, which has been known to happen. That's it. I like the way they grow so close to the waves. Like a game of dare. Of chicken. Who'd ever think you would find a flower like that growing out of the stones? Where there's never been any soil. Pretty exotic looking thing for this shore too.

Funny, isn't it? I would have always paid attention to something like that. A wild flower growing in a wasteland. But would never have said I loved it. Because I said 'love', didn't I? Jesus. Once it wouldn't have registered, what with everything that was happening. Not in a million years. But when the doctor said I had more of these fucking lesions, yeah, it changed me good and proper. Never had the time see, not even for myself. Always busy with some crap. Making a buck, losing it.

I remember once, we were in Amman for a bit of R&R. There was this restaurant, yeah, a pretty remarkable place. Old stone fortress on the hills above the city. Those hills where the thyme grew. Stone stables, stone apothecary's shop, stone rooms for the old herbalists. And me and the boys are going through the breads they give you there, all flavoured with thyme. They grow thyme because it likes the dry. Great stuff, but we were parched. So we were on the beers too. Nothing drastic, you mustn't come over too strong, but Amman's all right booze-wise.

Well this boy serves us plates of hummus and lemons and more breads. So we had to have a few more bottles of their local brew. Which is not bad, take it from me. And okay, we were noisy. People looking our way. And after a while this old bloke comes round, just to be friendly. Got the whole rig on, the Palestinian scarves and whatever. He knew who we were, course he did. That was a favourite watering hole. Some days half the fucking American embassy was in there. And what a place that is. Like a huge underground car park. Filled with all these spooks who spent their time listening. Just listening. But it was pretty relaxed. That was before all the suicide business. So this old guy's there chirruping away in perfect English, and he looks at me and he's smiling. Then his face darkens.

What's that? he says.

What's what? I say.

And he points to a mark on my throat. Right below the adam's apple.

Sir, he says. See your doctor. See your doctor soon.

It's dry heat out there. You can shrivel up. And I can't say I was ever careful. But then none of the boys were. But I sorted it out and then later I was with Marty and she always told me about covering up. I was going to this clinic pretty regular until it all went tits up. And then Marty's gone, Marty's pissed off, Marty's got a new friend. Younger model too. One of the Dutchies who were always coming down to El Zorro, one of those blond cloggies. Nice bloke. Don't blame her. As for me, I sort of drifted west and ended up in Algercerias. Bit like Amman, but without the swank, without the capital status. Friend got me a room in a back street hotel.

So I stopped thinking about it. Well, the weather changed, it was miserable. Never had my shirt off again. But I tell you, that's the town to meet clients. Oh boy, if you can stomach it, that's the place. It's a mess of languages and a mess of people. And, yes, tell the truth. It's not the slave trade. It really is not. These people want to come. The real slaves, the Africans, were stolen out of their lives.

But these are willing. It's incredible, it really is. So many people wanting to come over. Throwing themselves at you. And think of all those villages. They got satellite now, they're watching Sky, they're watching Snow, they got all this porn coming out of the air, it's all money and fucking and cars. Unbelievable. Do we think they're going to be happy walking behind a mule? Hoeing a row the wind will take away? If you got anything like energy or a brain you'll be under the wire any way you can. And yes, they're exploited. It's painful. But don't ask me to condemn it because I won't.

Just compare them to what's around here is what I say. The trogs. Biggest thing for your average trog is what tattoo to have on your arse. How many Strongbows can you neck before pissing your keks. And yeah, we'd have sorted them out in the service. Taught them a bit of respect. I've stopped bothering to get up when some kid decides to puke his ring up in my garden. Afraid I'll kill the little fucker, see. And you can't compare them. Karoona now, she even speaks English. Though, yes, Karoona's different. A one-off is Karoona. But there's others want to be doctors. Teachers. They want to learn. Appetite, see, they've got this appetite. They're excited.

So I made a few quid and came back. Course I could have stayed but it was the right time. Put down a deposit on the van, which I'll never own now, with property prices like they are. But Hal was good to me there. Of course, he's not the high roller he wants you to think he is. Queer fish is Hal. Can't get out of the small time. Loves the small time too much, see, the closeness of it. Loves The Caib. Because it's not the money with Hal. It's not that. I look at him sometimes when we're on The Bona or around here and I can tell you the clockwork's all in place. He's just ticking differently.

But a caravan with an ocean view? That's significant money. Not that the site will be here much longer. Not enough profit in caravans, is there? So now I grow poppies. Yellow-horned poppies.

Plus a bit of lettuce, some fennel. And peppers. Those I love too. Fierce little things that go green then red then purple. I just reach out the window and pick one, slice an onion, bit of tomato, stewing steak, don't forget your garlic, and I got a chilli con carne going. Fabulous.

So I treat myself to a Dos Equus. Three max. Maybe John'll come over and bring a shiraz or something. And okay, once he brought that girl. Look, nothing surprises me where men and women are concerned. Especially men. I gave him the look, of course, the look that says, what the fuck are you doing, but they seemed happy enough, and Christ, there was nothing in it. Nothing. No touching. Just those bloody camera phones. They never stopped taking each other's pictures. Taking me too, sweating over my special spaghetti sauce in the galley. Where she helped me do the salad.

So we had a chat like. And I asked her, straight out, point blank, what's a kid like you see in an old fucker like Vine? And she looks serious for a sec. With this gorgeous pout. God, I could have kissed her then. Could have grabbed her. And she says, hear this, she says, 'he needs me'.

She was shaking water off the lollo. Drops everywhere.

I grew that, I said. To give me time to think. Because, yes, she was right. He needed her. He needed a bit of fun. A bit of excitement. He needed that aura she had because it was all over her that night. This silver light. I'm not joking. She seemed bathed in it. The girl was radiant.

And John, he's got one big grin on all evening. Because he was lighter. He was treading lightly. I understand because that's what I'm doing too. Treading more lightly. And if everything had been different, he'd have come to El Zorro. He told me that he was ready for the adventure. At last. But it never works out like it should. And for a moment I felt he was blaming me for not keeping the bar going. Because it turns out he'd told this Rachel all about it. The black sand. The bananas.

He gave me this look that meant 'if only'. But I've no time for if onlys. If onlys are for people who do the lottery. But she was a real little sparkler was this Rachel, reciting, mimicking accents off the telly, telling us about what she's hoping to do, the London clubs, busking in Paris. All these plans. Just like Karoona.

Weird that. Only Rachel did it with a big smile. Because Karoona snarls. Or sneers. But then, Karoona's lived, she's lived like none of us have lived. Yes, Rachel had a really wide, genuine smile. A bit spotty, mind, but a nice shape, and yeah, sexy. Can't deny it. Reminded me of the little blue flame in the boiler. The pilot light. Always dancing up and down.

Christ, she was an upfront kid if ever there was one. Liked a drink too, and John obliged. No, he never touched her in my presence, not even a peck. But she had him round her little finger and he loved it. So I poured the wine and watched him watching her. Because he was eating her with his eyes. Couldn't look away. And girls know. They fucking know. Gotcha, they think.

Marty was like that. I just didn't play it tough enough. With her or with those Spanish suits. Not man of the world enough. Not cool enough. Girls like cool. And they like men who look to be in control. Which I never was. And nor was John with his fucking phone and spilling his wine over my table. Which I'd been careful with. Best cutlery. Okay, my only cutlery, but decent glasses. If I have a drink it's always better from a good glass. And a poppy in the middle of the table. One yellow poppy in a vase. They were rare, see. They were precious. And when Rachel asked about it, that said it all.

Glaucium Flavum, I said.

She was alert. Boy, she was curious about her world. That's why John loved her. All this energy coming off her, crackling like cellophane. A rare phenomenon that, though I've seen it before. Saw it round Marty, didn't I? God bless her, wherever she is.

Vine

Vine could smell the change. There was a drabness in the trees, a hungover look. The air carried decay from the mulch of willow leaves underfoot. But there was still green in every direction, pressing in over the path, while the canopy must have been intact because it was darker than twilight in the wood. He stopped and closed his eyes and breathed. Vine had been coming here since childhood, but it was never the same. He smelt the prehistoric smells. Sand and wet bark and the imperceptible riot of moss.

And there wasn't a sound, not a creature alive in that place but him. He could hear his own heart. Behind it was his uneasy breath. Walking didn't aggravate the cough as speech and darkness seemed to do. The steroids were in his pocket, the latest type of medication prescribed to him. They didn't work but he had known they wouldn't. The condition had a natural life and would need to run its course. He had left the inhaler in the caravan because that too had proved useless. The cough was a wound. It had to heal. But the cough was also a companion, usually a dark companion that came to him in dreams or which shook him out of sleep. Terrifying as it was, it broke like sunlight into those subterranean dramas in which he was below the surface of all things, trapped in passageways that grew narrower, hotter, as they took him down into the ground.

He opened his eyes. Here was another passage. The path was a tunnel in the gloom. Around him were the twisted trunks of dead elders, all with that fungus on them, the winey-coloured lobes that felt like wet velvet. Jew's ear they called it, ripped and bloody. It grew in darkness here as something primeval. Vine had never seen it anywhere else.

Now he reached to touch. It was soft. It was alive. But in what way alive he couldn't say. An explosion of cells, perhaps. That was it. Alive as a tumour was alive. One branch was covered, growing from a tree that corkscrewed out of the ground, a misshape, an excuse for a tree but one he had known for years. And often paused beside to think. Or simply to stand and look into the wood. But for what he could never say.

But that was what happened. The straight grew crooked. It happened imperceptibly. Especially in a place like this where there was only light, through the trees, in winter, and then for merely three hours a day, so deep was the cleft into which this wood had crowded itself, a ravine really, a sand-sloped gorge. But the fungus flourished here, red and satiny, yes a child's skin, he thought, a child at bath time towelled until the blood raced. Or a girl wet and split. And he walked on under the honeysuckle vines and the last of their fruit and noticed that riders had used the path, the hoof prints recent in the sand, a strange place for riders to come, he thought, the branches so low, the passage constricted.

Oh, hello, he said.

The nun said hello and Vine stood back in the undergrowth and saw there were other nuns in single file, wanting to go by. Each nun wore a brown habit and each carried a piece of driftwood. Most smiled as they brushed past but they did not speak. There were eleven of them, he counted, stepping silently there. The last one wore red laced Doc Martens.

Vine pressed on and then he was in the open again and making good progress, avoiding the sandy path and walking the grass, and soon there was a view of the sea to his right, the tide starting to edge in, the reef visible, the dredger in its place like some toy ship, spectral in the haze, yet there, indisputably there, and the cliffs on the other side visible, even the field patterns upon them identifiable where the haze had cleared, a bad sign everyone said, because that meant rain.

But no-one believed it. At least Vine didn't. He loved that clarity. The shock of it. The sudden and immense world around him as he stepped out of the wood and breasted a dune and the sea and the sky entered him, head and belly, entered him in an instant, forced their way in, the big and blue and totalitarian world taking possession of him, or so he always said to himself as he reached that spot on the crest when everything opened out, and often he had laughed at it, so shattering was that transformation, laughed outright at the sheer ridiculousness of all that space, because who could ever have imagined it beyond the wood with its narrow path and the internecine lives of its trees, laughed for the joy of it. Though not today.

He walked for a mile and was lost three times. The place changed so quickly. Woods grew, paths became overgrown. Buckthorn especially changed the landscape, blue reefs of buckthorn in places where last year it was bramble or dune grass. From ridges he could look down to see how it spread in irrepressible phalanxes, and how it grew out of some of the old gravel workings and out of sand itself. The fruit was on the thorn, a harvest of yellow grapes. In other years the tree had been hacked down and left in smouldering pyres, but it was winning now. Great areas of the dunes had become unreachable behind its palisades. Familiar tracks proved dead ends, and twice Vine had to turn around, confronted by spiny walls he didn't fancy breaching.

But there was no-one else. That was the surprising thing. Yet that was always the surprising thing. Once summer was officially over he could be pretty sure of having the place to himself. Fifteen hundred acres of south-facing coast and all of it uninhabited. Most of the time.

Within a few yards the land changed. He came upon pine trees that grew only as high as the ridge that protected them from the wind. There were stands of willow and birch, rarely mixed, the willow draped in moss, dusty curtains of it, green and spangled and seemingly dying of thirst, hung from the trees and covering the ground. All of these copses flooded in winter. To Vine as a boy they had been mangrove swamps, icy slacks he had forded barelegged.

Sometimes they had frozen over. How the ice sheets had groaned then as he stepped out towards the dark centre of the pools, the surface clouding white under his wincing toes, the eggshell cracks snaking away from him, the ice speaking as he inched his way to the eyelet that marked the true centre, over the grooved surfaces and dusty bosses of the ice shields, the water visible beneath, the grass waving in that unfrozen water, and flowers sometimes, a late mullein imprisoned there in the television screen-green of the glaciers that might whisper in the hollows of the dunes for weeks at a time.

Not that it had frozen in recent years. Here everything was dry. Vine pushed through head high willow and looked round. Shrugging, he kept west, scrabbling up gravel mounds, squeezing through twenty yards of buckthorn that left him cut on both hands and scagged his jeans. There was another stand of willow ahead, and a few taller pines. But no track and he had to make the best of it, forcing the young branches out of the way, kicking through tussocks, some so high he had to climb across.

He came to a pine tree. On a low branch was a scrap of orange plastic fishing net. Above this was a Tesco carrier bag filled with driftwood. And above this, attached with fishing twine were three or four pale discs.

Vine looked around and listened. Not a bird. Not an aeroplane. He touched the discs. They were cuttle fish, carved roughly into human shape and strung there as a mobile, cuttle carved to its yellow pith, crude figures that would rustle if not ring.

A child's paper chain, he thought. But more than that. An annunciation, there in the thorns. And a warning. The marking of a territory.

He pushed on. After ten yards of undergrowth he could see light through the trees. On another pine he found more cuttle, sculpted into fish shapes, eyes gouged out. There was more netting here and pieces of ship's rope in tarry knots hung from this last trunk. He paused and listened again. His breath sent the cuttle swinging.

Karoona

Late afternoon was usually a quiet time at the fair. Even in the last week, 5 pm was a dead hour. A few people played the machines but most of the rides were grounded. Karoona nodded to The Fish in his hutch and pushed open the blue door between The Kingdom and one of the bigger arcades. Then stepped back. Two men in good suits were coming down the stairs, one behind the other. Both carried briefcases, while under the left arm of the first man was a cardboard cylinder that might have held maps or charts.

They passed without a word and she watched them walk slowly off towards the Firewheel, looking around, laughing at something one of them had said. Behind his perspex she noted The Fish watching them too.

Upstairs was a tiny reception area with a desk and telephone. On the wall was a map of The Caib and a photograph of The Kingdom. She looked at this and saw a younger Hal posing with a young woman in a miniskirt, and an older man. Between them was the hound of hell and upon the hound's back sat a child of about four.

There was nobody in reception so she knocked at the door and was told to come in.

It was a big room. Hal stood at the window staring out, his hands clasped behind his back. A bald and bespectacled man in shirtsleeves sat at a desk covered in blueprints. Hal didn't turn around and the bald man's attention was on the prints.

Karoona waited.

Nothing happened.

Hello, she said.

Come over here.

She stood with Hal looking across the fair. The lights were coming on, red, orange. The view was wider than she would have imagined. Beyond the rides was the beach and then the sea, almost fully in. She could glimpse The Bona Ventura in the distance. Beyond it the rock pools were scattered like broken glass.

What you think?

Think?

Of the view.

Karoona looked down. There was a family passing below, directly under the window, a young couple with a little boy who was crying and would not be comforted. The mother gave the child a slap.

The view is very good.

Hal kept his hands behind his back. She noted the grey in his hair and what looked like a stain of baby drool on the jacket collar.

Yeah. It's very good.

I'll see you tomorrow morning then, said the bald man.

Eight, said Hal.

I'll be here at seven.

The door closed soundlessly. Hal had not yet looked at Karoona.

D'you know? he said. My father told me he used to stand at this window, on this very spot. And you know why? To watch the porpoises out there. Or maybe they were dolphins. He was never quite sure. But they were out there, he said, especially in the morning. Very early in the morning, too early for most people. And earlier than seven, that's for sure.

He put one hand on the glass then took it away.

And once I remember we were up here together and he told me about these porpoises because he was always going on about them, porpoises or dolphins, so I stood on a chair and I waited and I waited, waiting on this very spot. And d'you know what I saw?

What did you see?

Fuck all. Not a trace. Wrong time of year, he told me after. Yeah, wrong time. And this has been my office now for twenty five years and I've stood here almost every day for twenty five years and I've not seen one single porpoise.

Karoona craned towards the sea.

Nor a dolphin.

Karoona stood on tip toe.

And I'm still looking. Funny that, isn't it. You'd think I'd get the message by now, wouldn't you? You'd think I'd have given up years ago. But no, here I am, looking out of the window like David fucking Attenborough, looking out, looking out. And it's still the wrong time, always the wrong time. So today, let me tell you love, and you are privileged to hear this, very privileged indeed, today's the day I finally realised that I'm never going to see one.

Oh.

A porpoise.

No.

Or a dolphin.

Karoona watched the family go into the arcade next door. The little boy was already at one of the Rio Carnivals, jumping to touch the controls.

Yeah, lucky man, my father, sighed Hal. With his porpoises. Said he saw a whale once but he must have been taking the piss. Well he must have been, mustn't he? Worked hard though and built this place up from scratch.

Hal put his hand on the glass again.

You know, when he started there was nothing out there but some poxy sheds and a Punch and Judy man. Oh, tell the truth, Madam Zeena was here too. Same pitch she is now. Always been here has Madam Zeena. In her little hut. You ought to try her out. You might learn something.

Madam Zeena?

Fortune teller. She told mine. Told it to me years ago. And she was right. Oh yeah, that woman was right.

Hal's eyes seemed fixed on the sea.

And my father started right underneath here. Where The Kingdom is. Bought the pitch off this old bloke who was selling teas to bathers. He had this bloody big urn on a gas fire contraption. And these big china mugs. Yeah, he told me all about that as well. Started right below us here. And there were stalls and a market and then word got round and people started bringing their rides. Dodgems, carousels, like. All seasonal then, come and go. So it was a big move, a very big move to build here. But he did it, he took the chance, and yeah, here we are.

Karoona could see the fair was filling up. There were families arriving, and gangs of girls in identical denim skirts. In her blue bandanna the cocklegirl drifted towards the Firewheel. Here in the office she could hear the music that was always played. It was like a theme. John had told her it was *Oxygene*, by Jean Michael Jarre. On and on, it had played all summer. On and on through the night. Sometimes she heard it in her head. Sometimes she dreamed it. One of Karoona's songs used the five main chords of *Oxygene*, but in reverse. That was her revenge, she always said. That was what she would play before she left.

Hard work, see, said Hal. Never had a day off. Not a single day off ever. If I wanted to see my old man I came to the site. Dedicated, see. Took a chance and backed himself. Price of land though, it was cheap then. Specially here. Building on sand, see. Building on a sand dune. Everyone thought it was useless so he got it for a song. Half a song. What's half a song?

Pardon?

A chorus? Forget it.

Hal looked at her then. An appraising study. Then he went to a desk, opened a drawer and returned with an envelope.

Congratulations, he said. You're a British citizen.

Vine

Parting the last willow, Vine stepped into a clearing. It seemed a perfect circle, entirely enclosed, a grass arena seeded with trees that in a year or two would occupy this space. As he moved into the open, a cloud of butterflies rose up, hundreds of them thought Vine, brown butterflies and the small blue ones, the year's last butterflies in this place where the grass was thick and the sun suddenly hot on the back of his neck.

Vine was red and perspiring, his boots covered with grasshoppers, small straw-coloured creatures that ricocheted about his feet like seeds from the leaves. When he moved, they moved, and when he squinted up, the sky was full of butterflies black against the sun. Yes, a slow whirlwind in black and white rotating towards the sun. He had come as quietly as he could but now he caused chaos at every step.

On the far side of the clearing was a shelter made of tarpaulins and driftwood. Around this hut was a litter of wood and netting. Scattered about were plastic bags filled with samphire. Vine made his way across but a rustle in the grass stopped him.

Before he could turn a hand gripped his shoulder.

Heard you coming half a mile away, said Lol. Where's that bushcraft I taught you?

Vine spun and laughed.

No catching you, is there? I expected you to be spark out on that crab-apple poison you call brandy.

They walked to the shelter's entrance and sat on the beaten earth. Hanging over the tarps were burnet roses, scores of them, and clouds of an imperial-looking honeysuckle. The screen was pulled open and in the darkness of the hut Vine could see an Army Stores sleeping bag with a CD player beside it. Now he was closer he could hear harpsichord music, so faint it might have been the goldcrests he'd seen ganged up in these trees the year before. A few pots were scattered about, and tupperware plastic full of leaves. From the willow branches which supported the roof more cuttle was suspended, half moons of it, scalloped and pocked like the polystyrene that blew out of the sea.

Lol was in new-looking denim. A gift, Vine suspected, from his sister. There was a necklace of crab claws around his neck, an iPod's headphones in his hair. His steel-capped walking boots were bleached white by seawater.

Lol poured out two mugs of samphire tea. It was oily, stone cold and tasted of lemon and salt. Vine knocked it back. This was the tea ceremony and had to be endured. Or even enjoyed.

How much this year? he asked.

Samphire? Not a bad crop. As you know it's just going red, but I must have picked five hundred bushels since April.

A bushel was a Tesco's carrier full. Vine knew Lol received a fiver for every ten bushels, paid by a man in town who sold the herb in local markets.

Christ. You're in the pink. How much longer you got here?

Three weeks, say. By then I'll be ready for my bed.

Lol lived in the dunes from April until November. Or, as he put it, from the first orchid to the last gentian. After that, it was back to town, to his sister and their house on the front with its palm trees and tree ferns and missing roof tiles. It was called Mattancheri but everyone knew it as the Taj Mahal, a two storey villa, once maybe a raw opal-white but now indeterminate marine grey. The legend was that the rear garden of the villa had originally been a croquet lawn. Today it was briar.

What were you doing the other night? asked Vine.

Fancied a drink.

Tight bastard. Why not come in The Cat like the rest of us instead of going through the bins.

Maybe I'd rather go through the bins.

Lol looked at Vine.

You're still on the site then?

Yes.

No hope with Siân?

Nothing.

Oh.

Yeah.

Lol brightened. He pulled a carrier across. Have one of these, he said, tipping peaches on to the grass. They were small and red and wizened.

Sis brought them as far as The Bona for me. From those trees in the front garden. Fifty years old and nothing, then two years in a row, a bloody great harvest.

How is the lovely Ceridwen?

Grey as an owl. And still displaying a spinster's ferocious energies, I'm glad to say.

Vine bit into yellow flesh. It was sweet enough.

Fifty six in all, she brought, said Lol. I'm shitting peach stones here.

It's fantastic. Let's have another.

Course it's the weather, said Lol. The new weather.

Once a geography master always a...

Listen and learn, Mr English Department. What about this?

Lol disappeared into the shelter. He came back with what looked like a cricket ball.

Bloody sunfish, isn't it. Caught it yesterday in the pools and smoked it all last night on the fire.

Nothing so weird about that.

Well what about this you bastard? Lol returned to the shelter and brought out a dock leaf. Within it was something that looked like a sprat.

Bloody flying fish, isn't it. Again, in the pools, a group of them dead in the pools. You want to see its wings – they pull out. Like this.

Lol showed how to display the fins.

And you smoked it last night, don't tell me.

New weather, boy. The fish don't lie and nor do the flowers. Strange days ahead, mark my words.

C minus, said Vine, the juice dribbling down his chin. But these are gorgeous. Can I take a few for Karoona?

Jesus.

Hey. You've only seen her once.

I don't have the words for it, John. But she's more than bad news.

Because you don't have the experience.

Okay, I married my sister.

Who keeps you in fruitcake and peaches, and, Vine tugged at Lol's collar, all the technology.

I was listening to Glenn Gould doing the *Goldberg* when you came crashing through.

So what's on in the house?

Well that's Bach too. Music for sunshine. No, with Sis, she can't bear to think of me out in the rain. But this mansion is tight as a nut.

How many years now?

This is the tenth, said Lol.

Any visitors?

Almost no-one. The wood's too deep. The blessed buckthorn and all that.

Ever get scared?

I drink myself to sleep boy. That's what I was up the site for. Put the phones in, trust to God and Morpheus. And if it's warm, lie out and watch the comets. Like bloody fireflies some nights. The sky's a black circle above this camp and there's all manner crossing it.

Lol threw a peachstone into the trees.

Okay, last month, somebody. I heard him a long time before he saw me. Had a mastiff with him. American bulldog. You know the way they deck those dogs – leather harness, studded collar. Christ, you got to pity men like that. We looked at each other and he walked past and kicked a track through the other side. Seemed surprised, fair play. People like that, you're always worried they'll be back. Mob handed as they say. But then you think, why? What's to gain from rolling me over. More tea?

Pour it.

Sis brought a blackberry crumble too.

Just the tea.

Lol laughed.

There was also this couple. Not long ago, can't remember for sure. I could hear voices and stepped back into the trees. They came in, obviously by mistake. Not lost, but sort of. Well I know it was getting dark but they never saw the palace here. Just immediately lay down in the grass and bloody set to it. Christ, I thought, behind my tree, I'm stuck here all night now. But no, two minutes and it was all over and they were brushing themselves down and laughing, not very much, shy like, and off they went the way they came.

So you've seen nobody else?

Lol scowled at Vine.

You think I'm a nutter don't you?

Like I'd be here if I did?

So why are you here?

Vine opened the bag he'd been carrying.

First, he said. And foremost.

He laid a litre of Soberano Spanish brandy on the grass.

Second, he said, and middlemost.

He placed a book beside it. *The Coastline of Great Britain*, by A.V.G. and F.O.L. Fish.

And third and lattermost, he said pulling out two CDs.

Mahler's fifth. Buffalo Springfield's *Expectin to Fly*.

Now that's what I call a guest, said Lol.

I was going through some stuff and found those and thought, well... The rest, I'm sure you'll make a use for.

But you still think I'm losing it. After all I've told you? It's privileged information.

It's a wonderful story.

But it's not a story.

I believe you.

It's the holy truth.

Across the clearing there was a disturbance in the trees. A sparrowhawk had landed with a smaller bird in its beak. Suddenly there was a cloud of crows around it and the hawk was forced to take off, flying north towards the high parts of the dunes and the forest beyond.

I was sitting here once last year, said Lol, and this shitehawk comes over, with something in its talon. Yellowhammer I'm sure. And I kid you not, a drop of that yellowhammer blood fell out of the sky and on to my face. Anointed me, by Christ. Initiated me. I couldn't believe it. And d'you know what I did?

I can guess, said Vine.

I wiped that blood off my face and licked it off my hand. That was yellowhammer blood, all right. Sacred jism.

Hope you didn't tell Sis.

And this year, I couldn't move for yellowhammers. Singing wherever I go. Vanished everywhere else but for me there's chorus after chorus.

That's great.

Yellowhammers everywhere.

Good to hear.

And it's all connected. All of it. But nobody wants to know.

Vine smiled and held up a peach stone he had sucked to the last shred. It was easy to split and he took out the kernal.

Why does a peach have a stone? Why not just a seed?

To protect it, Mr English Department. From pests. Rats and bloody ants. But don't talk to me about ants. They've been everywhere this year. Flying buggers, black as sin. Had to hide in the sea twice the start of last month.

But you've seen nobody else?

Lol threw his tea across the grass.

Ten years earlier, in his last year as a geography teacher at the comprehensive, Lol claimed that one June evening he had been walking through the dunes. Being exam time he was bored and tired so had escaped from marking about 9 pm. The evening was quiet and there had been good light until he had reached the highest ridge. After a rest he had taken a scratch path down into a crater filled with buckthorn and the mullein flowers that could grow taller than a man.

By 10 pm the light had almost gone but the sky was clear. Lol heard a voice. He looked around and saw a child. She was maybe ten years old, dressed in what looked like animal hide. The girl seemed to be singing under her breath and walked past Lol as if she didn't see him. He noted she was carrying a bird's wing, maybe a gull's or a swan's.

Lol said he had crouched down and stayed silent. Then from behind him without making a sound appeared a woman, again dressed in rags of skin. She had long hair and her bare arms showed blue tattoos. She was holding what might have been a leather bag, dripping water. The woman was speaking to the child, who had now reached the rim of the crater.

Lol was hardly breathing now. He stayed put and sensed another presence. He said he never moved a muscle but felt the hairs on the back of his arms and neck standing up. Then once again from behind him another figure came into sight. This was a man, five foot high, Lol estimated, tattooed, dirty, dressed in hide and some kind of cloth. He was carrying bundles of leaves in both hands and seemed to be talking to the woman.

Even when the three figures had reached the crater's edge and turned around to face him, Lol claimed he had felt no fear. He was looking at them and they were looking at him. It was ten o' clock with a half moon over the waves and the sky a dark blue. There was plenty of light left to see clearly, Lol always said, plenty of light to see what happened next.

Because what happened next was always the perplexing thing. It was what had made listeners scoff at Lol when he first told the story. Made them shrug or smile or change the subject. So he never told the story now.

On the crater's edge, the family, because they were a family, Lol sensed that immediately, slowly evaporated. They didn't run away. They didn't slip over the rim. They disappeared, cell by cell, until the evening light was shining through the shapes their bodies made against the sky.

They had become nothing but outlines. Dark outlines on the dune. And then the outlines themselves disappeared. Crumbling away like ash.

First to go was the girl with her gullwing and the insect bites on her arms, the girl with her smile, because Lol swore she was smiling at him. Next the woman with the water held against her breast, the woman slim and tanned to oxblood slowly began to vanish, and as she disappeared the man with his leaves, the father, the leader, Lol, thought, or perhaps the woman was the leader but the man was a magician maybe, a physician with his herbs, he too began to disintegrate, to lose definition as the darkness deepened, and how soon the three became sketches on the dune and then three spectral presences and then nothing at all.

Lol had stayed where he was for thirty minutes. Or so he said. He wasn't frightened. He didn't feel threatened. But he wanted to revere the moment that had been given him. He wanted to honour the family he had met. Because that was it, he said. That was what changed him. He had been wandering in the sand. Heartsick, yes, that was the word, wandering heartsick and wondering what he was doing. Worrying about deadlines. About As and A stars. About Ds and the sad unclassifiable detritus he would have to deal with for the rest of his career.

My career! he had once spat at Vine. A man of fifty walking to work from his mother's house with his father's briefcase to tell children about erosion. About how waves undercut cliffs until they topple into the sea. About the wind that scours every edge until it is as smooth as the rest of the stone, a bright and blasted surface upon which nothing stands out or will ever grow.

The family had looked at him, he said. And although he could not remember one syllable of it, he had heard their language. He had heard them speaking their neolithic language. He had heard the child's song as she brushed the air with her gullwing, heard the woman talking to the child, heard the man's silence. And yes, said Lol, they had turned to him and studied him.

Sometimes the story was embellished. They had saluted Lol. They had waved to him as they disappeared. A kindred spirit, they clearly thought. A dune walker and a lover of June darkness with its cockchafers and crickets before there was a word for June. They had become his friends, Lol said. At that moment he knew he was not alone, not the man in the mac trudging from the Taj Mahal around the corner to the comp. Not the geography teacher in the disco with his galloping knees and his shirt tucked into his underpants. Not the lolloping wing on the rugby field who never got his kit dirty.

All that was over. Ox-bow lakes were over. Ox-bow lakes were definitely over, and all the Year Twelve expeditions to view the nearest ox-bow lake, or those ammonites in the rock, dull as the faces of stopped clocks. And hanging valleys? Those were over too.

No-one knows the despair, Lol had once told Vine over a pint of dark, in a hanging valley. Not an inkling. But I can tell you what.

There's a lot. There's extraordinary despair in every hanging valley in the British islands. And futility. No-one can imagine the futility of a hanging valley. Or maybe it's just the teacher. Hanging in there. Like a fossil. Like the bloody fool he is.

And so Lol was changed. Much to Sis's alarm he resigned his post and began his dune watching. Because he wanted to meet the family again. The family he claimed had adopted him. Soon he was sleeping out. Even in winter he'd stay all night, coming home to Mattancheri for a hot bath and Sis's breakfast kedgeree.

But that was not enough. So for ten years now he had camped in a variety of hideouts, waiting for the next encounter. So far, it had not materialised. But this did not trouble Lol.

They're there, he would say. I know they're there because that June night was no hallucination. But they know where to hide. They've been here four thousand years so they understand how to hide. And they know I'm there too. That's what satisfies.

Lol called his new family 'The Race'. He left gifts for them in the trees. Sometimes he was sure that they returned the favours. Once he had found an oystershell beside a rabbit hole. Others might have said it had been thrown up by rabbits from out of the past. But for Lol it was a family heirloom.

He also knew the story of the amulet. A century earlier, it had been found by a local landowner amongst flowers in the spring turf. A section of dune was cordoned off as the man pursued a leisurely excavation. But nothing else was discovered.

For Lol, the amulet had been a sign. It was a gift. As was the oystershell and a piece of sharp stone that might conceivably be an arrowhead he had come across near the gravel pits. But Lol was changed. Of that there was no doubt. He camped now, sometimes for half the year. He learned to carve cuttle and build wickiups of willow and canvas. He studied the local fauna, which had never been part of his school duties, and claimed to have discovered a shiny blue beetle unknown to science. He could imitate birds, knew where the foxes ran, and what the badgers did when they came out at dusk, the stripes on their faces like black lightning bolts.

This, however, was his last year.

Vine was standing, stretching. Lol had put the Mahler on in the shelter and it was playing softly. Vine had to strain to hear.

Don't want to draw attention, said Lol.

Vine knew he had been affected by his confrontation with the stranger and his dog.

Anyway, said Lol, looking round the camp, Sis isn't so happy. Says she needs me there and I understand. So maybe, just maybe, this will be the last camp.

You're coming out of the desert?

Yeah. Say another three weeks. These willows all go together. One year I woke up and the trees were nearly bare. I'd gone to sleep in a forest and the next morning there were drifts and drifts of these yellow leaves everywhere.

Vine looked around. It was hard to imagine such change. End of the season it might have been, but Lol was right, the weather felt different. These days the trees stayed green. And if there was to be warm weather, it would come in the autumn. Yes, that drabness was there, but it didn't seem to threaten. At least, not here.

Then what?

I'm sixty one, John, with a small pension. That's guaranteed. Me and Sis'll play mah-jong over glasses of samphire tea.

But you'll miss all this.

Oh, they're here. I've no doubt The Race is here. I've turned them into icons, haven't I? Kind of a legend and a legend never dies. But there are more things in our... yeah, well thanks for the book. The fabulous Fish. What a couple. Their work on chitons is absolutely first class.

Lol squinted into the sun.

But how are you John?

Surviving.

That's an interesting little cough you've picked up.

Just like at school.

So do you miss the bloody place? You were there for twenty years after all. And we had ten years together. You in E Block, shouting at the idiots, me in F with that classroom clock that showed only geological time. D'you miss it, man?

Vine plucked a stem of burned grass.

Siân's still there of course, he said. You know, I always thought it would be her that left. It's not as if I didn't encourage her to get out and just take some time. Out. Off. You know, wake up without the cold sweats. Without literally pissing yourself at the thought of 10G. Without loading up on the coffee after the shiraz the night before. But that bloody mortgage on that bloody place we bought was the killer...

Come on, John. Lots of couples work. Face the truth. You had a roving eye and...

Christ, Lol, spat Vine, rubbing his eyes, dry-washing his face.

From the first, John. You were popular. You were young and the kiddos loved you. Specially the smart girls. And it was always the smart ones. In their smart little skirts. So...

We all see people who aren't there, said Vine. Then he put up his hand.

Sorry. That's nothing to do with The Race. To me, the fact that you're here means they're here. The fact that you believe makes it real.

The music was grievous now. Someone's majestic death coming up.

Don't worry, laughed Lol. I'm way past wanting... What? Acceptance? Understanding? Way past.

He paused.

Sis says there's still no news about Rachel. Or who did it. She says it's died down and not even in the local rag. I suppose it's like that. Yesterday's news, one death elbowed out by another. Not that she's dead. Christ, no.

Vine was looking into the dark of the shelter. There were moons of cuttle in its gloom, threaded on fishing lines.

You know they came here?

Vine started.

Police talked to everyone, he said. Surprised they didn't move you off.

Lol grimaced.

Well, I got the treatment if that's what you mean. But you know that night I was with Sis at the house. We'd been meeting that character who wants to buy the plot. For apartments and such like. Retirement with a sea view. So I'd stayed on and spent the night. Lucky really. The local nutter had an alibi. Of sorts.

Vine stepped into the clearing. The butterflies came out of the grass and swirled around him like flakes of burning paper.

That's you sorted out then. Congratulations.

He pointed at the sky, peeled off his shirt.

You know, I think it's warm enough for a swim. Fancy it?

I was in this morning, said Lol. Look at me. Like an old sea bass crackling with salt. You do it.

I think I will.

Vine smacked his friend on the shoulder.

And despite the price that's a pretty smooth brandy.

He turned to go but swung round.

Lol, I think of you sometimes. Here on your own in the dark. Yeah, I know, the stars, the meteors, the bloody big hunter's moon and all the rest of it coming over the crest. I've seen it man, I know. Red as a pheasant's eye. But I think of you lying here on your own in the dark and...

Thanks for the brandy, son. And as you know, I'm not alone. Anyway, three weeks and I can devote myself entirely to Sis's tender mercies. She's mad as a snake but she needs me. She also threatened no more rhubarb wine if I don't quit while I'm ahead, and nobody could put up with that.

Vine waved as he crossed the clearing to the entrance he'd made.

See you before you strike camp.

Yes. I'll have some saucepans to auction off.

Then Lol disappeared into the darkness of the hut. The music seemed to have finished.

Karoona

The hot dog man rose in his plastic seat and stepped away from the umbrella. Karoona saw him stretch and look around and hurry back into his van as a child paused at the menu sellotaped under the serving hatch.

She held the envelope in both hands and opened it and took out the maroon book.

European Community, she read. United Kingdom of Great Britain and Northern Ireland. Passport.

Karoona breathed out.

Good enough? Has to be, love, has to be.

She held it like a mirror.

Funny, isn't it? said Hal. All this fuss. All this money. And there's me who never had one.

Karoona was silent.

I said there's me never had one.

No passport? she asked.

Never had one. Never wanted one. Or should I say, never needed one.

Karoona opened the passport to a blank page.

Why should I?

Karoona turned to another blank page.

I said, why should I?

Why?

Should I need a passport?

Karoona found all the pages were blank. But when she looked at them they weren't empty but filled with red and pink and mauve patterns. They looked like fingerprints.

Because you're happy here, she said at last.

Happy? Yeah. Call it happy. Call it local.

Hal put his hand on the glass.

Yeah. Happy in the sand.

She fanned the pages carefully and at the back of the book

Karoona came to her picture.

Oh no, she said.

What?

Oh no. Do I look like that?

Hal glanced at the page.

Spot on, he said. That's you.

British Citizen, she read. Place of birth, London. Passport number 188878066.

She studied her date of birth.

I'm young, she said.

Yeah, said Hal. We've given you youth. We're magic up here.

Karoona looked at him then.

Magic, he said.

You come from here. This is your home, she said.

Oh yeah. I come from here. Look out there.

Karoona turned to the glass.

Can't see it now, said Hal. Tide's in. But there's an island out there. Only it's not an island. It's a kind of reef.

Yes. I see it every day.

Went out there once, me and the boys. Not this mob. Earlier crew. Good boys too. Mazza, all them. And we took my son. In canoes we were, used to do a bit of that.

To the island?

Yeah. Fucking hot day in July it was. Or August. And we got out and walked around. Flatter than I thought it would be, and slippery with weed. Hey, you fancy a drink?

No. Thank you.

Well I fancy a drink.

Hal took a bottle of Isle of Jura from his desk and poured a measure into a glass inscribed 'greetings from The Caib'.

And we had these folding chairs, see, and we sat around. Well, I sat, and the boy sat. And we had this bloody great bottle of champagne with us. A Jeroboam they call them. Bloody huge green thing it was. And a few paper cups like. And one of the boys had this cassette player and we had this tape.

Hal looked at Karoona.

You do music don't you?

Yes.

D'you like Status Quo?

Status…?

Quo. The Quo. Status fucking Quo. Forget it. Well we had this song, my favourite tune. *Living on an Island*, it's called. You know that one? *Living on an Island*?

Um, no.

Well we played that tune over and over and we drank out of this Jeroboam and we had this pole and we stuck it in the rocks and one of the boys ties a flag to it. Pirate flag. You know that?

No.

Skull and crossbones. The black flag. Just a joke like, seeing we were getting pissed on that champagne. We had it all planned out. Tides and everything.

Outside a crowd was passing under the window. A small queue had formed to enter The Kingdom.

Scorching. I remember that. Sun was beating down. Blinding. And there was this copper boiler wedged in the rocks there. In an inlet there. Huge great thing, off a ship, covered with shells and crap. Size of a room it was. Amazing thing.

Karoona felt the passport cover sticky with her sweat.

What an afternoon. What a place. Even the boy has a drink like, a little snort. Loving it there he was, and everyone singing along with the tape, with The Quo, living on this island, dreaming of this other life. Those are the words, like. Good song. And then the boy goes and touches that boiler thing and it burns his hand. Hot as hell it was in that sun. Must have been ninety on The Caib that day. But I was having a good root round, I can tell you. Every piece of driftwood, every bit of spar, anything that looked like metal. Anything that looked like bone. There was this rock. I touched it. And it was metal. Iron, red iron. And these red iron stains all round it on the reef. Couldn't pick it up, it was fast. But that was a cannonball, I swear. A real cannonball. And then some fucker mentions conger eels. Says there's congers thicker than your arm on this reef.

Hal paused.

Legend, I says.

You're not a fisherman, this character says.

Which is true. So that starts to well, influence our proceedings like.

Six foot bastards, this boy says. Mazza it was. Good boy too. Teeth like a bowsaw, he says. Seen a fella's arm hanging off, he says. Bollocks, I say. Fact, he says. Jesus, I say. Lower the fucking flag. We're casting off. And one of the boys picks up that bottle, which was half his size I tell you, empty it was though, he picks the Jeroboam up and throws it in the sea. *Message in a Bottle*, he says. By The fucking Police.

Christ, we laughed. Pissed and laughing. Come on boys, I say, or they'll have the fucking lifeboat out. So we had a few pictures taken. Got them at home. A record of proceedings, see. And the tide's coming in by then too. Scary that. You see bits of the reef that were there a minute ago vanishing. Seconds ago even. What was like a real island is all separate bits. We were on the biggest, and there's Mazza off on his own little island, and there's George, that's Clint's father, George stuck out on his part of the reef. Waving at us. Well pissed. Living on an island? Not for long.

Hal finished the drink and poured another. Outside it was almost dark. *Oxygene* was playing in the arcades, *Tainted Love* blew in and out of the office.

Sea was calm, though. We knew that. So we pushed off and were back in twenty minutes. Coming in on the tide, no problem, laughing like fools. And the boy loved it. You could tell that, straight off. His mother gave me a roasting though. For giving him champagne and everything. But Mari, I said, and Mari's short for Marianne by the way, Mari, I said, it's his birthright. His birthright, I said.

Birthright?

Yeah. That's right. Birthright. That's why I don't need a passport, love. Because of birthright.

Hal stared with Karoona down at the crowd. She expected someone to look up, to glance back, but nobody did. The hot dog man was doing good business. Davy Dumma was in the line for American donuts.

Listen, said Hal. That reef, that island's in my family's blood.

He paused.

Christ, I think I'll have another drink. You're getting me rat-arsed you are.

Vine

Twenty minutes later Vine was on the beach. Beyond the rocks it lay grey as barley. The tide was coming in but there were no waves, not even a line of surf. He stood on the moraine and looked around. There were whole trees along the sand, white and salt-cured, mostly brought in by a hurricane ten years earlier. No tide was strong enough to move them.

Plants died off quicker here. The sea holly was reduced to thorns, its blue eyes burned out. There were stacks of driftwood, traffic bollards, rusted aerosols. In a tangle of wrack and fishing net lay a gas canister like some missile washed ashore. And shoes. Shoes and sandals. He knew if he walked the beach today there would be hundreds. Why shoes, he couldn't say.

But he looked at one now. A white Nike trainer. Someone had worn that. And what? Thrown it away? Drowned? Lost it while swimming? Probably it had come down the river with the bread trays and the milk crates. Once Vine had found an armchair at the high water mark, a pink and hissing Parker Knoll. It was covered with dead starfish. Maybe there was a lamp standard around, a foot stool, a sherry glass. The beach was a transfer station for rubbish, for life.

Lol picked around here every day. But he was a modern beach-comber, like Davy Dumma, using a metal detector to seek the lost troves. Vine had seen his collection, which was kept at the Taj Mahal: the Victorian pennies, the ship's nails and, in pride of place, part of a ship's nameplate. 'Welvard' it said. Or seemed to. Maybe 'Welyard'. It was screwed to the wall in the villa's front room.

Not far west towards the fair The Bona Ventura lay scuppered in its inlet. More than a hulk, from here it looked almost seaworthy. Vine was always surprised how large it was. The casino plan had fallen through, and when the civic trust proposed it for a marine museum, Hal had laughed the idea away.

He could sell it for scrap, he said. But it was better as it was, a long white splinter in the coast, a dart in the heart of the town. The Fish it probably was who told him The Bona Ventura was art, was an installation, and that's what had seemed to fire Hal's imagination.

Let it rot there, Vine had once heard him say. My big white fucking shark. I might have it painted pink. Or black. Let it stay where it is until I'm ready to use it. I like it as it is.

Vine's shirt lay draped on the sea holly, his jeans were folded over his boots. The only other person in sight was the monk. That's what everyone called him, that brown-skinned man in an orange robe. There he was now, unmistakeable amongst the rock pools, fifty yards away. Cross-legged on a blanket. The monk had appeared a year earlier. Vine thought he lived in a tiny caravan on Avenue S.

But there was no-one else around, not even a dog walker on the mile of sand. Not even Davy Dumma watching the dial. In black Calvins Vine walked round the pools and edges of sandstone reef that either the longshore drift or the dredger was helping to expose, and entered the sea.

It was warmer than he expected. But still cold. Yet he knew he would bear it. The tide was coming in over an afternoon's tempered sand, and the water had had the benefit of a mild summer and autumn.

Vine waded in up to his waist. He felt himself shrink. Then he wet his shoulders because there was no swell at all and pushed himself under.

John Vine was a swimmer who couldn't swim. It was usually impossible for him to make more than a few yards progress. But he could float and this was what he loved, looking back at the beach, the pebble bank, the marram and the dunes behind. And beyond the dunes the hills and then the sky. White today, a white sky, and the dunes a series of broken crests, and the red gas cylinder on the fore-shore, and the monk's orange robe, and suddenly there and suddenly gone, a flock of birds inches above his head, eight of them he thought, a black and white diamond now vanished out to sea.

What he wanted was the sensation that he was flying. Swimming, he reasoned, was flying in water. So he could fly. He could fly as those birds had flown, all with one thought and one movement, the prehistoric instinct that would dazzle for all time, a thought that was faster than flight. So he kept afloat by crabbing and dogging and the seawater held him in its grip and he looked at the sun to the south, starting to turn blue, the scalding blue sun of late afternoon, and the dunes to the north where Lol sat in his camp with Mahler and the butterflies around him, sat and wept, Vine imagined, wept for the ghosts he had allowed to lead him there.

But even without swell there was a current. When Vine pushed himself out of the shallows he was surprised to see how far east he had been taken. The beach was stonier here with larger pools. Wincing over the reef he caught a flash of colour, a yellow that seemed to rear up, then disappear. Vine looked again and there was some disturbance in the water twenty yards off at the lip of the lagoon. The salt was crackling on his back. A breeze he hadn't noticed before felt chilly now.

When he arrived at the pool he saw there was a dogfish marooned there. Left by the last tide, he thought. Strange, but possible.

Going closer, he saw that the yellow was a plastic coating attached to a lead weight, the kind that anglers used. The weight was moored somehow in the lagoon and its line lead to the fish.

Vine waded in. Already the tide had reached the pool, a shock of new water that rose over his knees.

He saw that the dogfish had swallowed the line. Either an angler had caught the fish, then lost the line, or by some chance the fish had swallowed an already abandoned barb. Vine considered his options. It was a big dogfish, about four feet long, mottled like a thrush, captured by ten feet of nylon twine. One end of the line, with its lead weight, vanished into the sand of the lagoon. The other end went into the fish's mouth.

Tugging the line did nothing. Vine gripped it as hard as he could but the nylon would not come out of the sand. Vine pulled again and it cut his palm. Scratching around in the sand he found the place where the line was trapped. He pulled again. Once more it failed to move.

The lagoon by now was part of the sea. Vine noted that the tide had reached behind him. He would have to wade back to the shore. The fish was restless and brushed against his feet. It was a pale creature, desperate now. The tide was throwing it around on its leash. Vine could see alarm in its eye.

Plunging into the water he picked up the dogfish like a child and held it to his chest. Its mouth was open in a silver tunnel. The line disappeared into its throat and Vine pushed his fingers down as far as he could to where he knew the hook must dig in. He could feel the place where the hook entered the ribbed flesh and he pinched there, trying to unlock the line, to lift the barb, to rip it out any way he could, the way he had seen anglers do on the sea wall, a quick flick, and there it was, the hook bright in the air, the fish convulsive on the pissgreen concrete of the esp.

But Vine was no angler. He had never caught a fish in his life. In a seaside resort he had not once held a rod. The hook was embedded in the fish's throat and it would not come out.

The dogfish thrashed but he held it close. Its mouth gaped next to his nipple, its shark's body blotched chocolate brown. The paw of a foxhound, Vine thought. Impaled on barbed wire.

He delved once more into its gullet, his hand almost disappearing. The line was there. Once again he could feel the place where it penetrated the pale throatmeat. Once again he failed to free it.

Carefully he released the fish. Its tail was a creamy feather in the brine. By now the water had reached his chest and was colder than he remembered from the swim. On its short leash, the dogfish was being knocked over by the tide. It would die in minutes, Vine knew.

And no knife of course. He had lost his knife and not thought to replace it. Where had he lost it? A knife would cut that colourless plastic line and free the fish. The hook would still be embedded in its mouth but the fish would be free. To die slowly at sea of starvation instead of from the concussive power of the waves. In this pit. This dark bayou.

So he gave up. The tide seemed to be tearing over the fissures of the sandstone reef where Vine now found himself. Up to his neck in it, he thought. Up to his neck in the griefs of this world. If only Lol had come. Or Donal. Yes Donal would have known how to do it. Donal might have carried his hunting knife, a sword-like thing that had startled Vine the first time he had seen it. And Lol too had a knife. Of course he did. Lol believed in fairies but he carried iron. He was a practical man with a blade for every occasion. Like the others, of course. The others who sported knives. Hal's shiv. Clint's stiletto. Even The Fish carried a blade. But Donal was the best bet. Vine squirmed in the current like the creature had done in his arms before he'd released it to its death.

Well, Mr Sun King, he sneered. Well, Mr Special Boat Squadron who could open up a man like a tin of catfood. Where are you now?

He struggled to shore and felt himself cough.

Fuck this! cried Vine, as he fell on to the sand. All of this.

Each breath was rattling in his chest. His lungs, as he'd once said to Karoona, were a bag of nails. He wheezed and waited for the convulsion to start.

Yet slowly the world was righting itself. The killing world. Behind him he knew the fish was being thrashed against the rocks.

There wouldn't be a fit. Not now. Not yet.

Vine lay in the sand. There was music playing. The Lone Ranger was galloping away, High ho Silver, away.

High ho Silver, Vine thought. The Lone Ranger. What the...?

He took the mobile from the leg pocket of his jeans.

Bloody Id.
Idwal.
Sweet Jesus.
Yes he was fine.
Yes he'd be there on time.
Yes the voice was okay.

When Vine had done that first test session he knew he had the job. Standing there in the empty Shed he hadn't given a damn. He'd slipped in a bit of posh talk, even some French, a couple of soap references, quotes from sixties' pop. Only the political joke had troubled Id.

None of that crap, he'd said. Ever. You can't do that.

And he'd looked hard at Vine.

Why? he had asked then. Why d'you want this job?

I've always wanted to be in show business, Vine had said.

Funny bugger. Money's not great.

That's for me to worry about.

Id liked the idea of a teacher calling the numbers.

But as long as you don't treat them like a class. All they want is a good time. You gotta tease them. This isn't school.

It's a challenge, Vine had said.

Well you'll be different from all the other gobshites who want the work.

Oh, I got that, said Vine.

Id cocked an eyebrow.

The gift of the gob. The gab. The glib, said Vine.

Just as long as you're not too fucking clever.

So it had worked out through the season. Vine learned on the job. But it was the last week with the big finish coming up and no promise of anything extra, though Id had said there were chances in the clubs. And now Id was checking up. Which was decent. The old pro. Vine thought of that face, brown and wrinkled as a walnut. A pickled walnut. And the old man's neck with the cords in it above the velvet dicky-bow, the winged lapels.

Good old Id. Who somehow had survived. Last dinosaur in the dinosaur park. Extinct everywhere else. Seventy if he was a day, Vine thought. Trouper with a toupé and a time-share and a shadow on the lung. He'd worked with some names, had Id. At least, shared the bill. Herman's Hermits, The Merseybeats. He told a story of how he once had to introduce a fifteen-year-old Helen Shapiro to a thousand miners and their wives in the old Bolero Theatre on the site. The MC was paralysed on Johnny Walker and Id who started the night off with a few songs, because he was a singer in those days wasn't he, not bad like, but feeling the pressure from the beat groups even then, Id had been asked to do the honours.

And that started Id thinking. About how he could manage things. Or make them happen. How he could be the link. The Bolero was called something different now, and those signposts that said Hollywood 6000, London Palladium 200 were gone. But when Id had told the story, John Vine smelled the beer in the air, imagined the poxy dressing rooms with their matt of perspiration and slap.

Because Id told a good story. One of his greatest nights was with PJ Proby. The American was touring and making headlines. He'd do *Somewhere* from West Side Story and milk it for every cliché it could muster, his lip curling, sweat dripping. Then when he was doing some rock n roll, Proby would go crazy and his made-to-measure satin trousers split open. Every night, every town. So when he did it at The Bolero and the miners had roared and their wives screamed, Id had run on with a fire blanket and wrapped it round the singer. Who promptly threw it off and kept singing, much to the crowd's delight and the headline writers' outrage. Once again Id had wrapped the singer in the blanket, and helped him from the stage.

Tremendous, was the crowd's verdict. PJ overcome yet again by the power of his own voice and swivelling groin. What a night. That dirty Yank bastard. It was a good scam and never failed to work. The crowds had rolled up. Id told that story every time he could.

And sometimes even in The Shed, Vine could feel the charge. That's what Id called it. The charge, when you sensed the crowd was with you. When it wasn't a battle or a dreary matinée. When you felt your feet an inch off the ground. As if you were flying. Yeah, thought Vine, even bingo callers can fly. Like swimmers do. But he'd always known that. He was a teacher who had levitated across Block E too often to doubt it.

So Vine wasn't sneering when he said he wanted to be in show business. He'd done things himself on stage in a teachers' band. A bit arty, almost always shambolic. Tapes and lights. Sometimes a screen with significant images. Not to mention the school performances, where he'd stage-managed or even directed. A glum bit of Pinter. That stab at Beckett.

And now he was helping Karoona. Who was bloody good. Yes, she was good. Which didn't mean she'd get anywhere, Vine knew. But her voice was a black orchid. Or so said The Fish, who was infatuated with her. Vine could see that. And her songs were pouring out, gypsy songs, Arab-sounding things, bits of folk in them, Joss Stone, Joni Mitchell, jazzy riffs, casbah cool. All mixed up into a style. Karoona style.

But it was too weird for where she was now. On The Caib. Too different. Vine knew that as well as she did. Karoona and he were going to London. Or so said Karoona. She'd always known the litany. Hammersmith, The Fridge, Ronnie's, Shaftsbury Av. And Vine could see her there. The golden pavement. The black orchid. Karoona in the underworld. He wondered whether he could follow her down.

The breeze wasn't too bad here, against the wall of white pebbles. Dressed, he sat on a trunk and looked at his phone. Then pressed for what he knew he shouldn't watch. For Rachel.

It was seven seconds' worth. Vine had seen it a hundred times. There was Rachel upstairs in the Millennium Centre. Behind her were the words of the poem that was emblazoned on the front of the building. In the film they were huge and backwards. But there was Rachel in her black leather jacket and silver scarf. She was holding a drink. Stella, Vine knew. Who had bought it for her. There she was with her long hair up. How different she looked like that. How devastatingly she could change. Simply by twisting that mane into a fist and pinning it back.

How amazing that was, thought Vine. She had become another person. Someone younger, yes, she looked younger like that. With the silver wires of the scarf against her throat. And vulnerable in that leather with its badges. Like seashells, Vine now saw. Lol's bright chitons. A wind power chevron, a CND logo, the Happy Face. Then all the sixties stuff she liked. All the good causes.

She was reciting.

Can there be any part of bliss, in a quickly fleeting kiss, a quickly fleeting kiss?

Then she'd taken a sip.

To art, she said solemnly. Cheers boss.

Cheers darling.

And she'd cocked her head.

Like a yellowhammer does, thought Vine. One of Lol's yellow-hammers.

To one's pleasure, leisures are but waste, the slowest kiss makes too much haste…

And the film finished.

That was her third lager and she was more than merry.

They'd been in The White Hart. Vine had said he'd show her a real dockland pub, even if there were no docks any more.

They had looked in the bar at the framed photos of the smashed hostelries, named after ships and ship owners and mythical creatures.

Maybe it's a shade too self-aware, said Vine.

How could it not be, she'd laughed.

Then they had crossed the square for the performance.

An actor was acting the part of an actor. Vine had asked her to take that in. The stupidity of it. The uselessness.

Someone was pretending to be Richard Burton. The Richard Burton who would never make another film, the Burton who was about to die in Switzerland, who was drinking more moderately now because his illness was catching up. Burton after *The Wild Geese*. After *Villain*. After the return to form as the worldweary totalitarian in *1984*.

Vine had told Rachel that Richard Burton loved vodka. During an operation, the surgeon had found the actor's spine encrusted with alcohol crystals. Vodka literally inhabited him by then. Its pale light. Completely colourless and impossible to cut.

That's what you get for loving a demon, he had said to her in the theatre dark as the monologue went on.

Rachel had laughed and put her head on his shoulder. He could see the silver threads around her neck. He could smell her.

Milky.

Childlike.

That baby smell.

But a perfume mixed in with it.

Rachel's perfume. The one she always used. What was it?

And he could smell her now. But was that smell Rachel's smell?

Maybe it was salt. Maybe the sea's anti-freeze on this sand. Its battery acid on his skin. It was his own wet hair he'd towelled with his shirt. Maybe it was the weed with the last of the sand hoppers crazy about his feet.

There was a gull on the sand. He could look into its seawater-coloured eye. The monk hadn't moved.

She had put her head on his shoulder and held his hand. He had whispered into her ear.

Isn't this madness? he'd said. An actor pretending to be an actor who's stopped acting.

Too many words, she'd whispered.

It's torrential, she'd added. Pleased with herself.

And snuggled up.

But I understand the drinking bit, she hissed. Because I love drinking too.

And giggled.

Let's have another in the interval.

Who had said that? wondered Vine. She had, Rachel had.

Let's have another in the interval. Because Vine who was driving, wasn't drinking. So he would never have said it. Surely.

And so they stood upstairs in the auditorium behind the letters of the poem that shone over the city. Each letter a lighthouse.

And that's where he had filmed her. Held up his phone as people do, and she had performed.

Because Rachel was an actress too. A level Drama that year. Or it should have been. She had done the prac. And that was great, people were saying, that was spot on for a top A.

Thankfully she had never been in his set for English. Vine could not have coped with her essays and projects. Or her chopsiness. And especially her flirtatiousness. That had to be the word. To the rest of the staff it was a guaranteed fact. She was the same with all the young male teachers. High-spirited, foal-like with her long black legs stretched out from the desk, her hands in her hair above her black pullover.

But Vine wasn't a younger teacher. He'd been glad when she smiled at him, but he knew the dangers. Christ, didn't they all. Lol had been right. Vine was a hard nut where that kind of thing was concerned. But it didn't stop him thinking about Rachel. Or noticing.

He'd been by chance her form teacher in Year Seven, but couldn't remember her. Five years later he was taking her to the theatre, whispering critical appreciation so softly his tongue touched the lobe of her ear. The ear with its black stud. Then buying her booze and pouring delirium down her throat. Buying her a pizza and watching her eat. Entranced. By her appetite. The way she chewed her food and talked at the same time and picked an anchovy out and laid it at the side of her plate and drank half a glass of red wine in one gulp and laughed and spluttered and stared out at the world from those huge eyes, big as the letters of the poem, it seemed to Vine, that shone across the city night from the seagreen helmet of the theatre.

Entranced.

By Rachel.

The heartbreaking newness of her skin.

Her black lipstick.

Black, thought Vine, on his driftwood seat. The little Goth who loved Guns N' Roses because they were quaint and before her time and she said she felt sorry for them. Who loved Christina Rossetti because she was brilliant, and Joan of Arc and Emily Brontë and Nico, poor Nico with her harmonium and her smoked out voice and her heroin breakfasts in that buggered up life in a Manchester bedsit. What a role model.

And nuns. Rachel thought nuns were cool. She observed them in town, she told Vine, back and forth from the convent. Scurrying like redwings. But driving too slow. And scratching themselves. Why did nuns scratch? she had asked him once. Did they have sackcloth knickers? Or did they wear thongs? Which were just as bad and she should know.

She had laughed at him then. Laughed and risen up and pecked him on the cheek. A tiny kiss. A yellowhammer's kiss, Vine thought, shifting on the salted trunk, watching the waves approach. Her head cocked to the right. Her eyes closed. It was the most chaste of kisses but the one Vine remembered now. When Rachel kissed she always closed her eyes.

The waves were only a foot away, but that was as far as they would come. And the dogfish was dead already, that shark he had held as if carrying a child out of the sea.

A week after the Burton play Vine had driven Rachel to a pub fifteen miles north. Gil, a friend from Vine's own schooldays, was playing some kind of gig in the back room. When they arrived there were already forty people in, filling the space, as Gil and two others pulled cables around the floor and set up instruments on the tiny stage.

The pub was one of Vine's favourites but he reasoned there would be no-one there who knew him. Or Rachel. As if it mattered. Nothing would happen, he said to himself. Or was meant to. He was introducing her to some live sounds, some ambient noodling, a little taped percussion from tablas and prayer bowls and an Arabian *deff*. With Gil's mad vocals, his own half baked poetry which might well have been improvised on the spot. And the guitarist. So it was performance, Vine told himself. It was his teacherly duty to show such a world to Rachel. Something different for a Thursday night.

On a fine summer evening there could be immense views from the bar window. It was fifteen miles inland but the sea was visible, and then the opposite coast, sometimes with the field patterns clearly sketched. Farther off across the water would be hills and moorland, blue against blue until the world disintegrated.

But this was a winter night. Behind the pub lurked the local church, a thousand years old people said. It always appeared squat and primitive to Vine, dedicated to a saint about whom nothing was known. But what a view of the world. Vine had once sat here in the sun and felt himself blessed. How easy to be a saint in such a place. When the world was bronze and green and the sea easy. Almost asleep. But better to be an innkeeper. Waiting for the pilgrims to arrive.

On those good days the panorama included their peninsula. Vine had pointed south for Rachel in case lights were visible but the night was claustrophobic with mist.

Hiya Rach, Gil had said, and not even given Vine the look. The look that accused or congratulated. Warned or condemned. Applauded. Gil was too busy for that, getting the mixing desk ready. Too cool in his shades on a winter's night.

Then the band had played its set, starting unannounced. Not once did the crowd chatter cease. The five numbers took three quarters of an hour, and as the band increased the volume the crowd increased theirs. A hard core at the front, some of whom Vine recognised, applauded after each piece.

Tough night, Vine had said.

They were all squashed around a corner table. The wall behind them looked a thousand years old.

Thought it went okay, Gil had said over his glass.

Rachel was illuminated. Her eyes were huge.

I liked the tapes, she said. The traffic...

Yeah, that was Paris. Boul' Mich'.

And all that watery stuff... Slapping.

The Turkish baths in Budapest.

Wow, Rachel had flashed. You should be called the Easy Jet Set.

Everyone had laughed at that. Even Gil.

How bright she was, Vine had thought. How brilliant. Holding her own, tossing her hair over that baggy fisherman's jersey. Her hair had been purple then, he thought. The first time he had seen it. An imperial purple that took no prisoners. It clashed with the jersey which was navy blue. Like her eyes, he saw then. And he wondered whether the saint had come there from the sea, from The Caib and over the plain and up the valley to that place with its view. The first of the multitudes. Or whether the saint was a mountain man who yearned for an ocean's implausibility on those few fine days it could be seen from that hill.

Gazing, thought Vine, from his hovel into a greater world of trade and legend and gospel routes. But too terrified to move. Lichen on his own rock.

It had been a good night. Vine had bought one of Gil's home-burned CDs for Rachel, who promised to play it in school.

You'll have to give me your mobile number, she said grinning at Gil. You need all the audience you can get.

And had squeezed out to the toilets.

And then Gil had looked. Finally. Not sly or wry but wearily at Vine. Gil was an art teacher at a school along the coast. He was Vine's age and lived with his mother.

How's Siân then? he had asked.

Fine.

Vine reconsidered.

Overwhelmed. As usual.

Two teachers under one roof, murmured Gil. Christ, I can see your evenings now.

She's head of year and that's huge, said Vine. You wouldn't believe the crap she has to wade through. Okay, you would. But she's the same girl I remember who wanted to save the language. Who went to bloody prison for a weekend. That's the girl who handcuffed herself to the dock in a courtroom.

And everybody just upped and went next door, didn't they? smiled Gil.

Siân's great, said Vine. It's just the house costs a fortune.

She was always a bit…

Sincere you mean?

Stern. Maybe that was for my benefit. Or zealous.

Gil looked pleased with himself.

Yeah, said Vine. Zealous is a word.

Then Gil softened.

But a lovely voice. Still in the choir?

When she can.

Kids okay?

Both with exams coming up.

Your Nia must be the same age as this Rachel.

Just about.

What's Rachel want to do?

Not sure. She talks about journalism. Even teaching. Writing songs, drama. Fame. After a year off. Out. Mind the gap.

And Nia?

Like her mam. She'll stay close and do the language. And I mean do it. Fierce as a Spartan, that kid.

Barry?

Brychan.

Yeah, sorry, smiled Gil. Brychan?

Computers, laughed Vine. The little nerd. Maybe he can get a gig with you some day. How you end up here, anyway?

We needed the practice, said Gil.

His band mates were at the bar with the camp followers. Rachel had joined them, talking, laughing. Her hair was attracting all the looks she needed.

So we paid the landlord fifty quid. Did the publicity ourselves, all the palaver. Yeah, I know, don't tell me. But it's better than staying home and listening to my mother, my mother for Christ's sake, asking if I'm going out. And better than marking a project. Someone else's bloody project. This is my project.

Maybe I can sort out some kind of gig in town.

Great. Do it, said Gil.

Then the band came over.

It had been a good night. Vine drove Rachel back and parked at the dark end of the promenade. He watched her as she ate chips, biting the sachets of tomato sauce and squeezing them into the tray. Five of them, she had ordered, and plenty of salt. There had been sauce on her fingers and sauce on her cheek. Then she had crumpled up the paper and polystyrene, squeezed his knee, and given him a kiss with her salty lips.

He had felt the tip of her tongue then, but the kiss did not linger. And out she had gone. Into the saturated night air.

There's an essay to write for tomorrow, she said.

The door slammed.

A Year Twelve's work is never done, she called back, waving.

Already there were jewels of sea mist upon her.

And Vine had winced.

Year Twelve.

Seventeen years old. Year Twelve.

He prayed Nia was at home. In bed. In bed asleep. And not a dream in her head.

He put the phone back in his pocket. That's all it took, he thought. A word. A word or a line from a song and the memories came back. But sometimes the memories weren't real. Vine knew he remembered things that had never happened. But how could that be?

He looked around. High tide and grey grass. The voice of a gull. That laughing voice, that know-all voice. As if the gull had witnessed everything. Along the beach the water was lapping at the sides of The Bona Ventura. Vine stood up and began to walk back to the caravan. It was darker now but the monk still sat beside the rock pool, his orange robe on fire.

Karoona

Yeah, blood, said Hal, looking out.

Karoona wanted to leave. She had edged away from the glass and Hal had looked at her and she had stepped forward again to resume their watch. The office was dim now. She could smell the whiskey in the air. There was a humming sound under her feet she hadn't noticed at first. Occasionally she heard a siren, then shouting and crying. But from twilight onwards the fair was always full of cries. Sometimes when she went to bed early she would hear shrieks. Lights would sweep over the caravan windows. Music would play that sounded like marching feet. It was impossible to tell whether the cries were real.

See this, said Hal, tilting his glass. This stuff. You can blame this stuff for it. Not that blame's the right word. It's not. But this stuff's responsible. Well, that's what I say. Because you have to be honest in this world. Don't you? I said you have to be honest?

Karoona had placed her passport in a leg pocket of the combat trousers Vine had bought. He said she looked good in them. He liked the buckles, he said. The secret places.

Yes, she said.

Yeah, you learn that. After a while. You learn it's kind of necessary.

Hal placed his left palm against the glass.

And sometimes I'm up here and I can see the weather changing. One minute it's clear, it's blue sky, and the next, there's mist coming in, there's cloud massing. Yeah, massing. And yeah, I think, I'm not bothered by that, it's not bothering me. Because I like it, see. I like it when that happens. When everything closes in. When everything else is hidden. Because you know if the rest is hidden you're fucking hidden too. You can't be seen. Know what I mean. When the mist is in. Because we get a lot of mist round here. Haven't seen it yet, have you?

Er… no.

Thick it gets. Creeping in off the sea. And famous, it's a famous mist.

I know mist, said Karoona. Not porpoises, but I know mist.

Yeah well, like I said, blame this stuff. Scotch mist.

Hal poured himself another.

Normally, I don't. But once in a while I get the taste for it and if I have one I have two and if I have two I have another. You know?

I know. My father, he drinks whiskey.

Christ. Bloody old bugger. Thought your mob didn't touch drink. Renegade eh? Anyway, put it down to the hard stuff. You see, I got this ancestor. This forefather, like. Can trace him all the way back, two hundred years exactly. That's eight generations. Eight. Not that I'm boasting. Done the family tree see, all the way back. On the computer at home. But there was a storm, one hell of a storm. You haven't seen one here have you, a storm, and you're not going to. Haven't seen a mist, either, it's been a good summer. But Christ, we get big storms here. Straight over from America. So there's this ship run aground out there on the island. On the reef. A brigantine it was. A brig, coming from Ireland, and it's got what you call a desirable cargo. Tobacco. And whiskey. Tobacco must have come from the States, and the whiskey from Ireland. And the ship's out there on the reef, stuck fast, high tide, low tide. And a couple of the crew have come ashore and others are washed Christ knows where. And there's the cargo coming in. Bales of tobacco. And these casks, like. Casks of whiskey. The Irish variety. And the locals, well, the locals are going kind of crazy. They're broaching the casks on the beach. They're cutting up the bales and dragging them off with horses. And they're drinking like fools, like fools, like the whiskey is water. Seems like there was hundreds out on the beaches and okay, they might not have been particularly welcoming to the sailors coming ashore. Not too friendly like.

Well, days go by and the casks keep getting washed up and there's hundreds camped out all over The Caib, drinking and partying, getting well gone. So the troops are called out from the local garrison. And there's a kind of stand off. Not so much a battle as a confrontation. So the commanding officer, he reads the Riot Act. Ever heard of that? The Riot Act? Well the commanding officer has the Riot Act nailed to every church door in the area. And yeah, okay that finished it. But on other occasions they actually hung people on The Caib. A bit earlier, like. Hung them for wrecking, for stealing contraband, for smuggling. Because that's the tradition here. As if you hadn't guessed. That's what happens on The Caib.

So it's quietened down, the brig's on the reef, and it turns out that three of the locals have been so reckless as to drink themselves into a state of, well, chronic intoxication. They were dead drunk. In fact they were dead. Drank themselves to death, silly fuckers. And one of them was my great grandfather. That's great eight times. Out on the dunes with his mates, like, and a cask of Irish whiskey and he's gone at it like a schoolboy and he's killed himself. Stone dead. So that's taught me a very important lesson. Oh, very important. D'you know what it is?

Karoona looked from the glass to Hal and back to the view of the fair.

I said do you know what it is?

No, sir, she said.

Always drink Scotch.

Hal waited for her to laugh.

Yes, she said.

Yeah, well, family honour and all that. Seems like great great grandaddy wasn't just some ignorant type. Some labourer who couldn't read like. Who'd never tasted whiskey before. Seems like he was an educated man. A man of standing. So that death kind of rankled. Kind of shamed the whole family. Got this image myself of it, this man about forty, fifty, good boots on him. Nice coat, frock coat. Braid on it, I can see the braid. And stockings like they used to wear. And there's this big earthenware jug that holds gallons. With wicker all round it. And he's pouring pints out of it into pewter mugs or bowls or just cupped hands. And then he's lying down on the sand by this fire and he's in with a mixed bunch, young and old, some women too because there must have been women there, stands to reason. Some young piece he had his eye on. Blowsy, like. And they're singing and partying. And girl or no girl it's the booze that does for him. It's the whiskey that takes over. And in the morning, yeah, the fire's out and people are waking up, hungover, covered in sand. Only he doesn't move. I can see it as clear as day. He doesn't move and he's grey as the fire is grey.

Hal paused.

Good story, eh?

Karoona was looking into the fair.

So, about fifty years later, and I've got the papers to prove it, his grandson is part of the crew of the local lifeboat. The Deliverance it was called. He's part of the crew that go out in another hurricane. Told you we get a lot of storms here. Goes out to some vessel in distress and is lost overboard. Drowned. So he dies doing his duty. Dies trying to save other lives. And I can see that too. In my mind. The rain and the wind so strong you can't stand up. The screaming wind. And the ship out there on the island, the ship he's trying to save. The island just a line where the sea is enormous. Where the surf's huge. What a family eh? What a fucking family.

The Fish

Viney. Or just Vine. Someone called him Vinegar once but it didn't stick. Vinnie didn't either. I think at the end I sometimes called him John. But it was generally Sir. Which is always strange when you meet them afterwards. When you're having a drink and it just pops out.

That happened in The Cat one night, we were all there. Ta Sir, I said, because he'd got a round in. Nobody noticed because they all thought it was ironic. A very insignificant piss-take. But no, it was a genuine mistake. And he knew it because he looked at me and smiled. Which is where my use of the word 'wistful' must now apply. Currently my favourite word. Up on the site dictionary? Betcha.

Yeah, wistful. Because for a split second he looked wistfully at me did John. Did Mr Vine. And then it was lost. But thinking about it, that's what he often was. Possessed by a sense of wistfulness. I only knew him in the last year, for all the exams, and yeah, sometimes I'd catch him with that look. But it's hardly surprising is it? Mid life crisis, male menopause. A restlessness of soul? Course. Call it a seeping awareness of futility. Call it your testosterone level needle dipping into the red. Ha ha.

Doesn't seem to have reached Hal yet and he's sixty. A strange and brutal sixty but there you are. Maybe sixty five. Because what's interesting about Hal are his ideas. No, his hallucinations. Yes! His capacity for the surreal, not that it's a word that's ever been uttered in his presence. As to dad, well, no need to ponder the pointlessness of his existence. He talks about pensions. He talks about teeth and arseholes. Asked me once to look at his haemorrhoids. I told him to bend over between two mirrors and make his own diagnosis. Try The Kingdom after hours, I said. But watch out for the Wolfman.

Yes, dad. Snivels on about the ticker and a liverish spot on his shoulder. Makes futuristic double entry calculations on how long he's got with how much is left in the building society. Might as well be dead already. Yeah, okay, that's harsh. But Christ, he's determined to go with a whimper. He's a driveller is dad, and I know you know the sort. But that's what happens to men. Now some men fight it. They kind of develop a biliousness which reveals their disappointment. But at least they're fighting.

But the others? They buy dogs or have dogs thrust upon them. Not like Clint's bollocky dog but yorkies and westies and those things that look like hairy centipedes. Or they stagger round the golf course. Or do evening classes in cookery and say it's what they always wanted to learn but didn't have the time.

That's always the excuse. That they never had the time. For time of course, read guts. Or spirit. And that's been starting to happen to John Vine. The blight, the male blight, the slow realisation of the pointlessness of it all. And so, inevitably, he's knocking off the girls. The tidy ones. Because that school is just rolling them out on a production line. And he's in quality control. Because, for John, his hormones have entered that desperation stage. They've rung the siren in the cardboard box factory. Last chance, John, they're screaming at him, go out and procreate pronto. Which, frankly, I can sympathise with.

Not that I'll ever experience it. Middle age, that is. And since you're asking, because I know you're asking, because your mind works like that, I see one of the girls from The Ritzy. Once a week, nothing really fancy. Nice massage, all the oils. Coral with her furry mitten's my favourite. Coral's sympathetic if you know what I mean. Lithuanian lady, Coral, very understanding. That glove's got a little face on it too, a little smiley furry face. She can change it if you want. Twenty quid? It's well spent.

But John Vine never had to do that, far as I know. Not until recently that is. Because Princess Karoona hasn't done him much good, that's obvious. Gritting her teeth if it happens at all. Nah, she's well intact and always will be. Far as I'm concerned he's pulled an odd one there. But he liked her from the start. Jesus, didn't he throw his hat in the ring that first night?

We're all well set and he's keeping up to pace and there's this frigid little frightened illegal sipping her water and it all suddenly makes sense. How to take care of Karoona for a while? Put her in with Vine who's already renting. Neat. And she wasn't protesting was she? Could have been worse. Could have been put on the game. But Hal's not like that. No, honestly, he's not. That would be too straightforward. So Karoona is landed. And Vine's always well turned out as they say. Dresses young for his age I'd agree, but there's dad, who's older admittedly, there's the old man in acres of shapeless beige. Or corduroy. Who the hell wears corduroy now?

Yeah, Vine never dressed like a teacher come to think of it. Always the light jackets, your linens, your cottons. And not a pullover in sight. How do you tell a teacher out of school? By the irredeemable sadness of the pullover. Especially vee necks. Round necks are eighty five per cent tragic. Vees have totalled.

But Vine was cool. Always planning trips when I was there, always a sheet of paper up asking for names for Stratford or some place.

And putting it on in town too, fair play. So the locals can see how bright their kids are. But you have to look behind the man.

Now with dad, there's been no-one since my mother. But that means she's still there, a ghost with gin on her breath, puking in the kitchen sink. Hal has the formidable Mrs Hal, dog-common accent in a five hundred quid frock. But built for it, can't deny that. They go back into the mists. And if you want to look at Vine, go no farther than Siân. Who also taught me, that last year.

Boy was she determined. Determined we should all learn what she knew. Which wasn't much. But at least she was genuine with it. Poor Mrs Vine. With her cough sweets and her eye drops. With her hay fever and chronic VPL. Yes Mrs Siân Vine. Whom I bring into our conversation because not two hours ago I was watching her little performance. Oh yes. I saw it all.

Been down at dad's and we saw the news together. God, that house is clean. Unutterably clean. Everything, especially the path and the porch he bleaches every week, so nothing survives. Not a blade of grass and not a wood louse. A litre of Dettol detox and there's not a microbe left. Inside it's the same, with every room smelling of Johnson's beeswax, and the lines visible where he's polished. Sad old git. Round and round you can see those lines. The orbits of fatuity. Christ, I thought men were supposed to go to seed. He might look a codger but boy is he fastidious.

It's unhealthy of course. Me having the arm here, sometimes it's tough to hit the right spot when I'm micturating. Spray it around a bit. So there I am having a slash in the downstairs one, which is saturated already in a pine disinfectant so strong it's bringing tears to the eyes, and dad's outside loitering with his mop. And this almighty aerosol of Glade. Ready to clean up straight after me. Because, like he says, I know you of old, of old, you bugger. That's how he addresses his son. The poor senile tosser, is that all that's left for him? Yeah, well, we had a row about that and I'm coming back towards The Cat and over by the church there are the allotments. And that's where I see her, like I've seen her before. Siân Vine.

And as I'm hidden there like any passer by would be behind the trees, I watch her a minute. Because Christ, she was going mental. Like back in class when nobody'd done the homework. She's there often is Siân and she grows a lot of stuff. And there's this enormous marrow she's grown, it's a white colour. No, a pale gold, a yellowish gold. And it's bloody enormous. And yeah, it's a pumpkin, you're right. A marrow's something else. And this pumpkin has been growing there for months, it must have, and she's been feeding it and watering it and it's grown six foot round. I swear to God, it's that size. But sort of hidden behind the rhubarb and the cabbages.

But now I can see it, and yeah, it's like a spaceship. And bloody Siân Vine has got hold of a metal bar it looks like and she's laying into the pumpkin like it's her old man ha ha and there's bits flying off, bits of gold pumpkin flesh, pumpkin meat being flung around.

And inside it's all orange, a really bright colour like a big Belisha beacon. And she's thumping it and whumping it and giving it what for and these gobbets are going all over and there's a spray all around and an orange mist and she's talking to herself and boy I can hear every word from behind my tree because that plot of hers is close to the road and she's fucking it and she's cunting it and you never heard a woman talking like that, not sober any way, and she's blaspheming like a barbarian and every single word is fuck or cunt or bastard and something else, something like bittern or bitten and I was straining to hear but she was spitting those words and hissing, hissing, and she's using some spike it looked like or crowbar or jemmy and she was hitting hunks out of that thing and I watched her and Christ yeah I felt afraid and soon there was nothing left of that pumpkin but what looked like splinters of broken glass or pieces of pomegranate thrown away in the grass.

Nothing left. Of that gourd. Which it had taken her months to grow. It had swelled right up like a pregnant woman. That great big smooth belly, that dome with blue veins in like a pattern on porcelain. Yeah, like china. Like a toilet bowl. Like my old man's toilet bowl kicked to smithereens. Until it was only a sharp white dust. Or hammered. Which, I wanted to do. I wanted to so bad.

Because what's a piss stain between father and son? What's a wonky slash matter?

Yes, hammered. Because I think now it was a hammer Siân Vine was using. Most probably a hammer. And she must have been soaked in all that water out of it, all the mucus. Yeah, the blood of it, the pumpkin blood, with the bits of membrane. Because that was the colour that poured out through the skin.

Nia

Weeks went by. Might have been months. Everything's a blur these days and I feel confused. As if I wasn't then. But my mobile rang and I didn't recognise the number. I was coming out of school late, thinking about going to the reading room. And it was Gil.

Hiya kid, he said. Remember me?

And I said of course, and he said sorry he hadn't been in touch and I said I didn't know you were going to be in touch. Well you got that wrong then, didn't you? he said. How'd you reach me anyway? I asked, and he said easy, easy as a salsa dip. Easy as cockles in ginger and lime.

Yes, that's pretty easy, I said.

Okay, not as easy as that, he said. It was about as easy as goat's cheese, black peppercorn and rocket roulade, that really spicy rocket that grows in the dunes.

Oh, as difficult as that, I said. Sounds a bit dodgy to me.

And then I looked round and I was in Cato Street. I'd walked all the way there. Automatic pilot, I suppose, but talking to him was so natural I never noticed where I was.

Gil had heard that John Webb's had been taken over and there were new people in doing great food. I'd been over once with some of the girls, for a dare because it was supposed to be a strange place. Hidden away on the other side of the sandhills. Not far if you walked. About three miles. But ten by car. It's at the end of a lane in a cove. All big stone flags on the floor, but the windows done with plastic. Not much to see really, and there's no harbour. Just a slipway that leads to the beach. High tides come right up and there's a couple of boats chained on the bank.

So he said what about a Saturday lunchtime and I knew immediately I was free. But I hung on a bit.

Why John Webb's? I asked.

Changed hands, he said.

Sort of hidden away, I said.

Hadn't thought of that, he said. But they do this mackerel and red mustard thing.

Sounds rank, I said.

Local fish, he said. All local ingredients down the John Webb now. These new people grow their own. They change the blackboard every day.

Like a teacher, I said.

Sharp aren't you? he said. I like that. Very sharp. Yeah, I really enjoyed talking to you that night.

When mum got pissed? I laughed.

Merry, he said. Uninhibited. That's what I like. People casting aside their inhibitions.

You know many people with inhibitions? I asked.

Just about everyone, he said.

What about me? I asked.

Oh, I don't know you do I? I know very little about you in fact. Except that we'd get on.

Would we? I asked.

Yeah, he said.

Why would we get on then?

Two of a kind, he said. Seeing through it all.

All what?

All the crap, he said. We kind of rise over it.

Do we? I laughed.

Yeah, he said. You know what?

What? I said.

We could be sort of…

And he stopped.

Sort of what? I asked.

You know.

I don't.

It's stupid.

What's stupid?

We could be sort of soul mates.

And I remember him saying that as clearly as anything I've ever heard. I was outside the reading room. Maudline would never allow anyone inside to talk on a mobile. I'd hate it too. But it was as if Gil was next to me there on Cato Street. Smiling and pushing back his hair and leaning over in his Quiksilver gear and saying that. And not a touch. We had never touched.

That night of the party I went to bed and I didn't even say good night. Dad called him downstairs, he was looking for him, said he wanted Gil to listen to some old track. Something from way back. I think dad said they were on it themselves, singing, playing instruments. So it can't have been a record. Just a grotty tape. Dad has boxes of them, and then CDs and stuff on his computer. Music and live gigs. He used to film the crowds. And then I remember that one-armed type passing.

All right? he said, in that weird voice. Low, yes, deep. A peculiar voice for a man like that. Kind of sweet growl. I looked at him then and I saw he was older than I'd imagined. And yes, I smiled, but I was really listening to Gil. Only there was silence. Because Gil had gone quiet.

I was quiet too but the hairs on my neck were standing up. Funny, isn't it. You hear that phrase and think it's not real. But it is. The hairs were standing up on the back of my neck. I had goosepimples. I felt sick. I felt I was going to faint. I was trembling all of a sudden and thought that fellow must notice, the bloke from The Kingdom.

Because he looked at me and smiled. As if he had heard what Gil said. As if he could read my mind. As if he knew what was going to happen, like Madam Zeena does. Or is supposed to. Dad went in there, years ago. We'd all go round the fair together once a year. And mum dared him. He had been on the Firewheel with Brychan, right above the town. It was tremendous what you could see from there, you wouldn't believe, he said. But it was hard going against gravity. He felt flattened. Kind of crushed, he said. And yes, we went in the scary scary Kingdom, and I won a plastic coconut. That's right. Like hello, can anything be more exciting? This planet is doomed. And when we weren't looking Brychan bought a ball of candyfloss that made him sick. Then at the end, dad went into that hut Madam Zeena uses. With the moon and stars painted on it and the signs of the zodiac. Because mum dared him. So we waited and waited and Brychan and I wandered off and came back and he still wasn't out. And when he did appear he shrugged and laughed and made this farting noise. Worse than a job interview, he said.

Well? said mum.

I'm going to travel.

Ooo, we said.

A long way.

Ooo

With a companion.

Not in a camper van you're not, said mum.

And if I dig deep enough I'll find treasure.

Ooo, said Brychan.

Digging in sand? laughed mum. Ask Davy Dumma. What's Davy ever found?

You'd be surprised, said dad.

But the phone stayed quiet.

Who knows? I said. With a laugh, this deliberate laugh that must have sounded odd. Like I was choking or something.

Yeah, who knows, Gil said. I hear they do good soups. All fresh ingredients. They grow these butternut squashes apparently. Ever had that? Butternut?

And for a moment I didn't know what he was talking about.

Oh, at John Webb's, I said.

Think they're going to change the name, he said then. Which is probably a good idea. Look, I'll pick you up. About twelve on Saturday?

No, I said.

You're not coming?

No. I'm coming, I said. Because I wanted to. God, I wanted to.

But I'll get there myself, I said.

How? he asked. It's...

Yes, I said. It's hidden away. See you twelve-thirty.

And I switched off.

Wow, I thought. How cool am I? And I went straight, I mean straight, to Mega to catch Li on her break, walking through the fair and across the empty quarter and onto the site. She was standing outside where the smokers go. Only she had her red book with the golden title in her hands, and was sitting on the chair they keep in case a customer feels faint.

How's my little cormorant? I asked. Boy, have I got a fish for you.

Thursday

Donal

Well, *rad* was one.

Rad?

Yeah. Somebody said I was *rad*. Or I'd done something *rad*. Meant it as a compliment and I took it as such.

Rad? repeated Vine.

Short for radical, said Donal. Like it was cool. Which is what they say today. Or just bloody good. Which is what I say. And maybe he was right because I'm nothing if not radical.

They were watching the surfers from the path above the East Side beach, outside the Seagull Room. There were eleven in all together, all without wet suits, all toughing it out and keeping the summer alive. Vine took a coin and put it in the Owl telescope bolted to the sea wall and started scanning the waves.

But I can't remember anything else we used to say. Nothing special, not like the Marines. And not like the boats where it was always a special language. Most of the surf words I know I got from The Beach Boys. And there was this song, Deadman's Curve. Can't remember who sang it but I always thought it was about a bloody big wave. In Hawaii maybe. But it turns out it was just a bend in the road.

It's an industry now, said Vine with his face screwed up. He was gradually pulling the barrel of the Owl towards the caravans.

Tell me about it. Every little fucker in Billabong and Rip Curl crap. That Quiksilver stuff. Like a uniform. Whole shops full of it. Which you know wasn't exactly what it was all about.

Not rad then?

Christ. About as rad as cottage cheese.

Donal kicked a pebble across the path.

Hey. Remind me never to talk like this to those kids out there. They're doing great. You got to be fit to do what they're doing and you got to be brave.

Putting The Caib on the map, said Vine.

Yeah. Who'd have thought it. Just the swell. Just the surf. It was there all the time, been there forever, and, wow, it gets discovered. Like the sea gets discovered? Oh yes it does. Bingo. Oops. Sorry.

No offence, said Vine.

What was it, last month? August? There was a TV crew here. Perched about where we are now. They had some of the lads in, but the swell was two feet max. Just an ordinary day. But it was on the news anyway. Saw it in The Cat. Said it was the future. All clean and healthy and young. The future.

Donal scratched his leg and kicked off his right sandal. His foot was clawed and discoloured.

Bloody gravel.

The money in the Owl expired.

I've seen seagulls with feet like that.

Bloody crap daps.

Blaming on his boots the faults of his feet, laughed Vine.

You what? These sandals have had it.

Ever see that Middleton around who's got my job? He surfs.

Jesus, that's teachers for you, said Donal. Clean up the water and in they come. But you got to draw the map for them first. Listen, when I started there was all sorts of shit in the sea. We used to go and look at the outfall. Not the sewage pipe, the bloody works. Bloody great pipeline a hundred yards long. I tell you, I've seen it red and I've seen it blue, all the dyes pouring out, all the poisons. But nothing to what they let slip in the dark. That's when the real stuff got pumped out. Your mercury, your cadmium. Rip curl yourself through that, you tossers. So who knows what's still out there, coming this way.

Ever catch anything?

Well, the usual, said Donal. Over time. You know, throwing up, sticky ears, bit of a rash sometimes. Which makes me think, which makes me bloody think about you know what.

Vine put another coin in the Owl.

Thought so, he said. Thought so.

Thought what?

Just noticed now, said Vine, his face screwed up once again. You can see my caravan from here.

No way.

You can see my avenue clearly. Or the end of the avenue. As I can see the man on the corner in his garden. There he is now.

Donal took the cold blue barrel of the Owl.

Old bloke?

That's him.

Yeah, that's Glan, said Donal. He's a permanent, been here twenty years. I talk to him sometimes. Knows how to grow things.

Clear as day on Avenue J, said Vine.

Donal looked up and laughed.

What's the matter? Scared somebody's been spying on you?

Vine spun the telescope on its stand.

I've looked at the moon with one of these you know. The one over by the dock. Hunter's moon, low and red. Just climbing over the dunes. Yes, anything's possible round here.

You're getting paranoid.

Oh, said Vine. How about tomorrow? Thought I'd take Karoona out for something to eat. She's getting cabin fever in the van.

You don't want me along.

Yes. We do. We'll make a meal of it.

You don't.

We do.

You're sure?

Sure.

Well all right, smiled Donal. That would be good. Get me out too, stop me singing the blues.

Okay, we'll give you a knock about five. Gives me time before The Shed. We'll walk up town.

Vine

Vine understood that when a man reaches a certain age he must look the other way. The other way when he passes schoolgirls in the street. Schoolgirls with sooty eyes, their legs blackly luminous. So he stared at the pavement when they walked by. But he took their perfume with him and the sound of one's headphones, and the shiny thigh of the third that brushed his leg. And when they laughed he knew they didn't laugh at him but at the secret he used to share. They were from the private school and he didn't know them. Or he didn't think he did.

Vine also knew to look the other way when he met a younger man, or a group of younger men. Because these days younger men were usually angry about something. Here was one coming up now. The muscular type. Say he was twenty five. The man had two-toned hair, blond and black, was wearing a teeshirt and ripped jeans, sporting earrings and tattoos. Vine didn't recognise him either, which was good. A schoolteacher is haunted by his past. Alien faces smiled in greeting or simply stared. Remember me? they asked. As if. But sometimes he did. Yes sometimes he remembered and he and the alien would laugh together, both thinking, yes, what was all that about, that school, that misery, that bloody nonsense we endured together. Because here we are. All grown up. Despite everything we had to withstand. Survivors together on a dirty street.

The man passed Vine and said something under his breath and walked on and Vine walked on and didn't look around. Sometimes, he knew, it was impossible not to antagonise men like that. Vine was wearing a jacket. Jackets often enraged a certain type. Briefcases did it too. Yes, forget smart cars, bags could do it. Bags were effeminate. Yes, something as insignificant as that could unlock the fury that was already there. The fury at the mess they had made of their lives. The fury that had no source and no outlet but pumped its hormones into the blood.

Or maybe the man had been talking to himself, berating whoever had done him down or told him the truth. Cunt he had said. It came like a cough. The man had called Vine a cunt. Yes, a cunt. As clear as day.

Or had he? Perhaps it was can't he said. Almost certainly it was can't. Can't do it. Yes, can't was what the man had said. With his badger hair. His brassy torc. Can't, the terrible can't, and at once Vine felt sorrow for the man. The man in his ripped jeans, his shirt with a meaningless logo. A lost soul. A frustrated life. The man who can't. The man who couldn't. How red his face had been. How useless the bicep. The schoolgirl's perfume had disappeared but his thigh tingled still from where he had touched the third one's leg.

The one with long hair. A kind of auburn. And her face down-turned like an orchid. How modest, Vine had thought. But her cheekbones bright. Ah yes, such bones. Remarkable really. How her face had gleamed up at him, at Vine who was staring at the pavement but understood when and how to lift his eyes. The last moment was the moment to look. Everyone understood that. And surely she had smiled. Vine walked on, his eyes on the tarry street, the broken yellow lines. Causes Death said the silver packet in the gutter. Yes, a smile, the ghost of a smile. And of course, he had smiled back. His own smile hardly a flicker of light in his face.

Or maybe he had smiled first. Yes, possibly. In the infinitesimal spaces of the last moment Vine had smiled first. And had been rewarded. The orchid had turned to the sun. A fraction of a fraction, but that was all it required. Vine felt hot. The third one's smile had passed through him in a parching ray.

And now the man in his teeshirt was walking after the girls. Pursuing them down Jenny Road. A man who would never look away from what he craved to see. The man who can't, a man who couldn't. An angry man whose word had destroyed the third one's smile. Cunt he had called Vine. Vine with his slim black case, his jacket, his open-necked shirt. Vine with the silk of her like a wound in his side. Yes sometimes you had to look away, even if it was only...

IQ.

John.

The man was startled. Vine had reached the corner of Jenny Road and Caib Street. He was outside the Senora del Carman, a grimy green-painted café. This had been converted from an ironmonger's a decade previously and quickly become the town's best restaurant. Tapas, steaks, a wall stacked with Rioja. But the heyday was over. It was a coffee place these days. Lunch time Spanish omelette and chips. The windows hadn't been cleaned for months. Now there was nothing for it, nothing to be done.

Er, I was just popping in, said IQ.

Morning break is it?

Oh, a little ritual. It's not bad upstairs.

So upstairs Vine sat opposite Ian Quentin Jones and waited for his cappucino.

IQ stayed in his tweed overcoat but he did remove his gloves. They were the part leather, part cloth type of gloves. Driver's gloves. As far as Vine knew, the man didn't drive. IQ put the left glove upon the right against the menu at the wall side of the table.

Chilly? smiled Vine. And coughed.

Val's idea. She called me back. I'd almost escaped. And there's a nip you know.

It's mild.

No, a real nip. And it changes so quickly now.

How you keeping?

Very fair, yes very fair. There's so much to do.

Oh yes?

And Christmas will be here soon.

Christmas?

Vine had to laugh.

It's three months away, he said.

Well I'm getting the cards at Oxfam this morning. Val likes it all arranged early.

How's the Gibbon?

Well, the Gibbon, oh yes, well, you know…

IQ had been a history master at the comprehensive. When the chance of early retirement had come up he had jumped at it. Or, as Vine knew, had been told to jump. There had been farewell sherries in the staff room on the last Friday and some bright spark used the whip round money on a second hand *Decline and Fall of the Roman Empire*. All seven green volumes of it.

It was very thoughtful of them all, said IQ. And paused. Well, of you all.

Not my idea, Ian. The English department wanted to buy you an EasyJet weekend to Amsterdam.

Oh dear…

Hotel near the railway station.

Oh no…

Tickets for the Rembrandts.

Oh yes?

And a street guide to the Red Light.

Oh dear. Oh no.

With tickets for the Sex Museum.

Oh John, the Gibbon is, er, the Gibbon is…

Long, Ian. Life is short and Mr Gibbon took the long way round.

It was touching, John. I was touched.

IQ shivered into his tweed.

But, I tell you what, John. It was time to go.

Of course.

You can stay too long.

Certainly.

And it just seems to… go out, doesn't it? It somehow goes out.

What goes out?

Well, what would you call it? Fire?

Appetite?

That's it. English department trumps again. Appetite, John. And of course, there was every, er, incentive…

Wacking great pension, you mean.

Oh I wouldn't say…

They gave you a fabulous deal, Ian. You were the last of the old boys to go, the real old boys who were trained for the grammar schools. How the hell are you spending it all?

Well Val's mother is with us, you see. She's eighty two. Eighty three next week.

You could afford the best for her.

You mean? Oh, Val wouldn't hear of it. A nursing home you mean? I've thought about it, of course. Of course I've thought about it. Alzheimer's is a terrible thing. Terrible, John.

So do you ever get away on your own?

My own? Without Val, you mean?

You used to go to those battles, didn't you? English Civil War things.

Oh no, not now.

You were always a bit of a Cromwellian, as I recall.

Really…

Cromwell came to The Caib, didn't he?

Well so they say.

What about around here? This place could do with a write up. There's plenty to tell.

IQ sipped his coffee and looked out of the window.

Well the Rotary takes up a lot of time these days, you know.

Yes, said Vine. I've seen you collecting on Saturday mornings. So I always walked the other way.

Oh John, yes, you were always a joker. Always the joker, John Vine. But when I can get out, the Rotary dinners are very good. Very good. And there's usually a speaker. No politics mind. Never any politics. We're strict on that.

There were wine stains in the red and white tablecloth. Vine circled one with his finger. Cabernet, probably. High tannin. It blackened the lips and turned the teeth purple. Rachel looked up from her wineglass and smiled with her purple teeth and her face was the face of the private schoolgirl he had passed that morning. He saw again that imaginary smile, the nunlike mystery.

Vine knew that IQ would ask him nothing about his own life. The man was a decent sort, a gentle and unreachable Roundhead who had taught on after his breakdown until the authorities did the decent thing. Boys in and out of windows. Girls flashing their knickers at him. Once Ian had been locked in his own stockroom and had to be rescued by Big Guy. And the hubbub in his classroom sometimes like a weekend pub.

You're a regular here then? asked Vine. He looked around. They were the only customers. There were some bullfighting posters on the far wall. Over the stairs was a picture of David Beckham in a Real Madrid shirt.

Well I like it up here. There's not many come. I read the paper and well, go home by way of the front, past the Sea View. My constitutional, I call it.

IQ lived in the West End. Vine had never been inside the house but he had driven the man home often enough. It was the same street where Vine's grandparents had lived in retirement. He remembered Sunday afternoons there as a child. Cucumber sandwiches with too much salt and a quiver of spills to light the fire. And books locked behind glass cabinets. On every visit he had tried to pull the cabinet doors open but his grandmother had shooed him off and rubbed his fingerprints from the glass.

When you're bigger, she had said. When you're a big boy.

In the garden was a fishpond with a step down into the water. That was another place his grandparents had forbidden. But once Vine had escaped and lain down with his face close to the surface. The water was almost black. Carefully he had pulled away a strand of weed and there it was. The golden fish. Six inches long, the size of a dinner knife. Under the weed, a fish of shocking gold. His hand was in the water and the cold entering him and then something had happened because the memory stopped. Green weed, cold water, the fish. He had been about to touch it. The fish must have been asleep at the bottom of the pool. Vine could see it still. He could see his own finger marks on the glass cabinet and the books in their ranks. On the bottom shelf was a row of HG Wells in red boards. Great thick volumes. One Sunday when he was older his father had opened the cabinet and selected one.

That's good, Richard Vine had said. *The Island of Doctor Moreau*. A very strange tale about strange goings on. You might like that.

The son had gingerly opened the book.

I was really looking for *The Invisible Man*, his father had added. But I can't seem to find it.

Yes, deadpan dad. Richard Vine, straightfaced king of kidology. Where were those books now? Vine's father had not inherited them but the house had been sold, probably with contents, and that was that. And the money had vanished. God knows where. But money had never stuck to the Vines. Especially now. As to Dr Moreau, the boy had persevered, and John Vine owned his own paperback, part of his yard of books in the caravan.

Good doctor, bad doctor. But his creations could live nowhere else but the island. It was their prison. Vine and Siân had seen a film made of the story a few years back. It had been a disappointment. Coming out of the Odeon they found it was too late for a drink. So had glumly driven back to the babysitter. But then, Hollywood had never understood Wells. Only Orson had managed it, Orson Welles, HG's spiritual son. Vine remembered the bearded face embossed on the cover of his grandfather's book. Under the boy's thumb it had felt glassy as an old penny.

The strange thing was, the film had given him a nightmare. He had awoken cold with sweat. Next to him Siân had been a dark island. How far she had removed herself, lying there so quiet that he knew she was awake, remote as a mountain range and dawn not grey in the curtain crack. Or perhaps it was the book getting through at last. Moreau's creatures glimpsing an impossible freedom.

So what'll you do when you get home? he asked IQ.

Well, you know, there's so much.

Such as, though, Ian?

Oh, well, that's a peculiar question. I can't be specific off hand. It's almost lunchtime, isn't it, so Val will have put out a bit of cold meat, and her piccalilli. We share a tomato usually.

Then down to *Decline and Fall* in the hallowed hush of the study?

Oh John…

Or a Stephen King?

Well Val says we need a new rotary washing line but the problem is getting someone to fix it in because the hole wasn't dug deep enough and that metal kind of receiver thing is always loose because the concrete's coming up and the danger is it'll blow over if there's a load on. Her mother's sheets, you know. Val does them all herself. And I haven't got a study, John, or not what you'd call a study. But if Val's got five minutes we sit down to watch *Countdown* together. Very stimulating programme, *Countdown*. Some of the contestants are highly talented.

A waitress was hovering.

I'll get this, said Vine.

Oh no. No no. I insist.

IQ counted out the coins for his coffee. Vine looked at him then smiled and did the same.

Don't forget your gloves, Ian.

Oh no. Could be chilly out now. Nights drawing in, too.

Yeah. Happy Christmas, Ian.

Oh John. Always the joker. Always the joker, John Vine. But happy Christmas to you too because I may not see you, you know. Before, well, before, er, Christmas.

The history teacher walked off, somewhat in the sea's direction, whilst Vine followed Caib Street towards the cluster of banks and their cash machines. Doing Idwal a favour, he had promised to pay the previous night's takings in at HSBC.

Half way up was a small amusement arcade called Las Vegas. It was one of Hal's businesses. On the glass it said *Strictly Over 18* but natives considered this applied only to visitors. Vine watched his son with two other boys push open the entrance door and step in.

Brychan.

The boy had his back to him and Vine saw him wince. Brychan's shoulders dropped and he hung his head. The others stepped away leaving Vine and his son in the aisle between the Cherry Multiples and Dinosaurs Alive.

What?

Thought you might need some change.

You what?

Vine opened the case. Inside were bundles of notes and bags of money.

One hundred and ninety eight pounds fifty five, to be exact. Call it two hundred. Perfect for your system.

My what?

Your system. Don't tell me you haven't got a system. All you high rollers have systems.

We just came in here. It's no big deal.

Well, let's blow it. I'm feeling lucky.

Dad.

I'll change the notes.

Dad.

Be back in a jiff.

Oh fuck. Dad.

You what?

What are you doing here? hissed the boy.

Vine looked around. There were two players that he could see, both women, one old, one young, one skinny, one fat, one headscarved, one with blonde and green hair, one talking to herself, one with a pushchair squeezed into the aisle behind her, baby slumped asleep, Pound World plastic bag on the handle. At the far end was a counter where teas were served and change given. A beverage machine with an 'out of order sign' stood against the wall.

This was all Ma's domain. Ma Baker, as she was known, was an enormously fat woman and a friend of Id. She was often in The Shed, drinking Newcastle Brown from the bottle, shouting at the caller. Once Vine had tried to shut her up and learned his lesson.

Don't tell me about housey, you little arsehole, she'd shouted. I knew Tom Jones when he was playing Sweaty Betty's. I had Frankie fucking Vaughan up against his fucking green door. And the Swinging fucking Blue Jeans. And Wayne Fontana and the fucking Mindbenders. What a scrawny lot of pimply arsed little bastards they were. So why the fucking hell are you calling so fucking fast? How d'you expect us poor fuckers to keep up? And The Searchers. Jesus God, give me fucking strength.

With that she had sat down on Vanno's lap, who screamed her leg was broken.

Vine had looked to Idwal for support but there was no help there. Ma was Ma. The queen of The Caib. Just don't serve her spirits, was Id's only recommendation. And never argue back.

What if she gets violent?

She'd never catch you, boy.

Now Ma was snoring, her black beehive askew. Black was good. Or that was the legend. When Ma Baker donned the black, all things would be well in the world. It was the platinum that alarmed. It had been platinum that night at The Shed. There she had sat, legs in the air, silver wig pulled over her face like a guardsman's bearskin.

Here on the counter she had placed one meaty forearm. In her fist was a key. Behind Ma was her shrine. This consisted of plastic flowers and sellotaped snapshots of approved celebrities. Old pros with ruffled shirts and sideburns. A goddess with a python. Ma grinned with them all. And in pride of place behind glass, the famous one. Ma Baker on the sea front with Margaret Thatcher. Ma in diplomatic black. Mrs Thatcher looking cold in The Caib spring.

There was a ringing noise and a gush of coins. The old woman was winning her money back. The young woman looked round and cheered.

Nice one, love, she said.

The baby and Ma awoke together with a start.

House! said Vine and Ma saluted.

He smiled at Brychan.

Viva Las Vegas, kid.

The boy looked down the arcade. There were tears in his eyes.

Ah, shut up Dad, he had spat between his teeth, and followed his friends on to the street.

He was walking almost as fast as he used to walk. And not coughing. He wasn't coughing even with Karoona by his side although sometimes she lagged a yard and other times pressed ahead. Vine thought he coughed more when he was with Karoona. He certainly coughed with Siân but he was rarely at home now. Maybe it was Nia who brought the worst out in him. But then he saw Nia least of all. So possibly he was getting better. It made a kind of sense.

They had been to the Mega Minimart on Avenue O together. That was where many of the caravanners bought the basics. Vine carried a plastic bag containing milk, coffee, bread. Karoona had her own things, although Vine had paid for them. Karoona ate sardines, usually with cous cous and not much else. There were five tins in her bag and a net of oranges. When John had asked her whether she had enough fish she said yes, it would do for that week, and that was all she was thinking about.

Of course, Karoona never understood his jokes. Who would, he wondered, in their second language. Or it might be her third. But Karoona would never be interested in irony. She'd never get it. Karoona would take everything that was ever said to her at face value. She would consider it and then deliver her response.

Hey, Kar, he'd said, coming out of Mega onto the broken tarmac. There's something fishy about you.

She had paused.

Fishy?

Very fishy.

Because I like sardines? Oh yes. Not that these are sardines of course. These are excuses for sardines.

But Karoona also smelled fishy. Vine had thought so from the beginning. Sometimes he would take her by the waist and she would moan and wriggle free but not before he had kissed her cheek and ruffled her hair and breathed the fishiness of her oily skin, the skin that in her armpits was the colour of sardines, silver-dark and slippery with her Mediterranean sweat.

Once she had let him hold up her arms and taste the salt within those armpits, those deep bells of gooseflesh where the black hair within was tickly and thick as candlewicks. Oh yes, she was the salty one, the salt a rime on her, the rockpools under her arms deep enough for a man to drown. But that was before she had screamed because he had bitten her and she had cried, and yes, he had, he had bitten her, bitten the blue and silver sardine flesh under her arm and he was so sorry, he couldn't say sorry enough until he was forced to go to Mega for a white chocolate Magnum which Karoona slowly and deliciously devoured entirely by herself.

On one side of the avenue the sand had grown into a glacier. It was a crescent shape, with tiny spirals rising from it in the breeze.

Remind you of anywhere? he asked.

Anywhere? No. She scowled. Ah, the desert you mean?

I know you're not from the desert.

If you know I'm not from the desert why do you pretend that I am from the desert?

It's my way of talking. I inherited it.

I might have seen the desert.

What's it like?

And I might have slept in the desert.

So there you are.

But I'm not from the desert.

Well, look, Kar, where exactly are you from?

Vine understood that he hadn't been curious enough. Once he had thought he knew and that had been sufficient. Now maybe it was too late.

Karoona had always been a cool one. A swallow winging over the empty quarter. Now she was growing cooler. She seemed too light footed to be pinned in one place. Identity was not something she dealt in. And even though it said so on a paper he had seen, maybe Karoona was not her name. Karoona al Nazaar. Yes, who was that? Perhaps he'd never know. But her passport? Her passport still hadn't been delivered. Or so she said. Hal hadn't handed it over yet. That's what she'd told him. But maybe he had. Karoona was slipping away, he knew, gaining momentum, silver and trailing musk.

She was also angry with him. Which was better than indifferent. Usually when Vine stopped at Mega he talked to the Chinese girl at the checkout. Mega had one till and several staff, but the Chinese girl was almost always there. Maybe she worked sixty hours a week.

Maybe eighty. Beside her she usually kept a red book with a golden symbol. Vine had inquired what it was.

English, she had smiled.

But your English is very good.

Not so good. I learn.

Ah well, good luck.

After that Vine had always spoken on his visits and the Chinese girl replied. He was disappointed when she wasn't there. Her black hair was a glossy fan. Sometimes she wore it high, pinned with a bodkin. Once he had observed her through the glass. It was early and Mega deserted. She sat at her seat with the book open, mouthing words. Perhaps she was speaking aloud but Vine couldn't tell. Most days he would put his milk and his bread on the conveyor belt that didn't work and the Chinese girl would gather them up and, if the scanner wasn't working, she'd tap the keys and smile and give him his change. Once she corrected his money.

Too much, she laughed.

Her hair had been down that day. Her teeth were the straightest teeth he had ever seen.

That's too much.

At least Vine thought she was Chinese. He didn't like to ask.

In the queue today he had felt Karoona seething behind him. Behind Karoona stood one of his Shed regulars and behind her Clint and one of Clint's friends. Tentpeg, people called him. Both of them were unwrapping chocolate bars.

Okay? beamed Clint.

Okay, said Vine.

Tentpeg dropped the paper on the floor. He was tall with blue hair. Vine had seen him in The Cat. Someone had bet Tentpeg he couldn't eat four pasties straight off. No drink allowed. The Chinese girl already had one eye on him but Vine supposed she had to get used to it.

Now Vine swung his bag, pretended to push Karoona into the littered dune.

Hey.

Next he'd taken her arm.

What?

I'll show you a place you've not been to yet. Just come with me.

She frowned but brightened. And looked almost intrigued.

Where is this place?

Not far.

Where?

Not far at all.

They walked back down Avenue O and turned into D. Here the vans were older and several abandoned. Fires had been lit and there were rings of ash and sofa springs and pools of melted plastic in the grass. A Dormobile parked at the roadside had its windows smashed and driver's door prised open. The owners had scrolled 'We're off to see the World' on the side in red paint but this had been graffitied over and scratched.

The couple walked with the sea behind them and most of the site to the left. The road vanished under sand and reappeared and vanished again as they passed. In the sea holly was an open suitcase spilling clothes, a mound of half burned papers. Down in what people called the Crater a single speedway rider was going round on his bike, accelerating up the sides in clouds of smoke.

On the crest a Tai Chi group was practising. Vine had never seen them there before. He pointed.

That's where the gypsies come. Just turn up. Here for a week or two, then vanish overnight.

Gypsies?

Roma. Or Irish. Maybe Irish Romanies.

I am not that.

Never said you were.

Vine looked at Karoona in her espadrilles and combat trousers. The fleece she was wearing was from his wardrobe.

Had a boy in school once, a talented boy, he said. Turned up when he was thirteen, stayed for three years, on and off. Did a lot of drama, had a real stage presence. Musicals, because he could sing. And *Death of a Salesman* too, or scenes from it. He was a pretty good lead. Seemed to understand it instinctively, which was amazing, considering his life. Though if you thought about it, maybe it's not so strange. Ever bought lavender?

Lavender?

Anyway, he told me he spoke the black language. I asked him what it was but he always refused to say. I wanted him to make a project out of it, speak his black language to the class, but he wouldn't. He just laughed. The black language was the black language he always said, favouring me with his English language.

Maybe I speak the black language, said Karoona.

Maybe you speak many languages.

Not so many.

And he and his family and the other Roma or travellers or whatever would park their vans and lorries in the Crater and sometimes he'd come to school. Which was always a surprise because he could have been working. Scrap metal and scrap cars. That sort of thing. Or fighting, like bloody Brad Pitt in that stupid Cockney Irish film. All that. And he'd come and rehearse *Death of a Salesman*. Or sing *Somewhere*. From *West Side Story*. There's a place for us. All that. Big voice on him too. Which was sort of poignant, considering.

Poignant?

Doesn't matter.

You miss him I think.

Vine turned round on the road of burnt paper.

Hey, he said. I miss everybody.

He led the way and Karoona pattered through the sand in her thin soles and they left the road and the ground began to slope upwards. At the top of this dune was a heap of planks and wire and an evening primrose plant in flower that stood like a sentinel. The ruin once might have been a lookout. Below lay a wood.

Okay, said Vine. Almost there.

They started down and the track led to a place where an entrance had been stamped in a wirenet fence.

This used to be the back way in. Seems I'm not the only one who remembers.

In the wood it was suddenly dark. Vine walked slowly and Karoona came up behind, silent on a bed of pine needles. Around them stretched a wall of evergreen leaves. He advanced and put his hand on a trunk. It was a palm tree, its leaves a yard long and needle-sharp. He looked up and there was a cormorant perched at the top, its wings outstretched like two black palm leaves, its beak long as wirecutters. The bird took off towards the sea.

Nearby there were other palms with pointed leaves and an undergrowth of misshapen exotics. A cedar that stretched its branches overhead in a black reef stood at the centre of the wood. Around it were red-barked pines. There was a metal rail here and what looked like the remains of a walkway. Vine followed this to the far side.

They closed it about ten years ago, he called.

Karoona gazed around. Beercans lay everywhere, crushed and weatherfaded. What looked like a sleeping-bag was thrown over a branch. There were pieces of cardboard and carpet and rolls of foam rubber scattered over the grass.

We used to come here, said John, over his shoulder. Bring the kids with a picnic. It was open to the public of course, but no-one bothered. Or not like us.

She looked at the ash of a recent fire, the silver cigarette packets. A rope with a noose hung from a tree.

Brychan loved it. Really did. Come over here.

Around the fire were pages from a glossy magazine. Girls with open mouths. Girls with their tongues against the roots of the trees.

I was afraid that the palms would be stolen. You know, plant smugglers. Common or garden thieves. But they look all right.

Vine was only a voice now, somewhere ahead.

And they've all matured really well. It used to be a kind of maze. A tropical maze.

Karoona noticed a pair of shoes under a bush.

A sort of Jurassic Park, you know, a prehistoric rainforest. Here on The Caib, a rainforest. We all thought it was great.

One of the shoes moved. Karoona hurried on.

Vine was standing with his hand on the rail. Behind him a black fern spread like a net against the sky.

And these plinths or whatever, these stages, do you know what they were?

She looked at a concrete block.

Platforms. For dinosaurs. Lifesize dinosaurs, including the Tyrannosaurus Rex, which used to lurk just about here. What do you think?

Karoona shrugged.

Give it time. This was a fantastic place. Brychan used to climb up the tail of one of the dinosaurs. Like a flight of steps. I think they were all made of plastic resin because they had to be weighed down. They were pretty light. Hey, come over here.

He walked on.

There was a dip in the concrete.

This was the pond. Used to get frogspawn out of it and tell the kids it was dinosaur eggs.

They stepped round a corner and there were no trees now. Both could see the back wall of the fair. A series of corrugated iron sheets were nailed to the breeze blocks with barbed wire unrolled over the tops. The path here must originally have been crazy-paving because the pieces were scattered and they had to walk on hard core.

Vine stopped and gazed round. Karoona was picking her way across the clinker.

And this is, or was, as you can see, this is the model. Of it all.

He beamed.

Of us.

She looked at what might have once been a map painted over cement.

Well originally there were little houses and whole little streets and the churches and the harbour and even the fair itself. Even the caravans in long white rows. It's this whole coast, minus the awkward bits.

He gestured with his toe at an expanse of flaking blue with a black smear upon it.

And there's the sea. And there's the island. And that's it.

John, she said.

Christ, thought Vine. How seldom she called him John.

There might be robbers coming.

Doubt it.

I saw someone.

Just a local alky. I saw him too.

This is a bad place.

No, it's a mess that's all. Take a few volunteers and they'd have it cleaned up in a day. Just kids drinking.

It's a bad place.

Because it could be fabulous, insisted Vine. These trees are wonderful now. Get the paths cleaned up and the pond filled and you've got the best park in town.

I heard something.

He looked around. A thousand blades pointed towards them.

We'll go out the front way, then. Have to climb over. They've blocked it off but that's no problem.

Vine took her bag and they walked to the gate.

But it could you know, he said. Be good I mean. It could be really great.

He climbed over the fence, holding on to a concrete post, finding footholds in the wire netting loops. He would have helped Karoona but she swarmed up the post and let herself down on to the sandy pavement the other side.

Done that before, haven't you? he laughed.

They found themselves standing under a monkey-puzzle. One of its tentacles reached almost to Vine's head. He touched its black razors.

Hey. What's all this?

Both looked around and saw Clint and Clint's dog and Tentpeg approaching. The men were holding caffeine drinks.

Trespassers will be prosecuted, smiled Clint, coming up close.

The dog sniffed Vine's crotch.

Used to be good in there, said Vine.

Nah, said Clint. Kids mitching off. Fag and a can. Did it myself.

An me, grinned Tentpeg.

And the weirdos, laughed Clint. Some wanking, some watching. Or the other way round.

Yeah, all sorts in there, said Tentpeg.

Willie and the hand jive, said Vine.

You what?

It's a song. Creedance Clearwater Revival.

Who the fuck are they? asked Tentpeg.

Vine looked into the dog's pink eye.

Unique place, he said. With those palm trees.

Yeah, real unique, grinned Tentpeg.

The council should protect it, said Clint.

Yeah, right.

We used to have picnics there.

By order, added Clint.

Tentpeg took a swig from his can.

You heard that story? asked Clint. You must have. It's a legend. You know Mazza? Used to drink in The Cat. Yeah, Mazza. Well he's had a sesh in the afternoon, has a sleep, and a sesh after that. Cider and black he's on, with vodka chasers. Knock out drops for most people. Someone said he had fifteen. So he's going home and he's coming down this way here and he pops in the park for a slash. There was a gate then, never locked. And when he comes out, because Jimmy was with him and Jimmy tells the story, when he comes out he's got one of them fucking great plastic dinosaurs on his shoulder. The ones they used to have here. Twenty feet long, balanced like a plank. Doesn't say a word to Jimmy and Jimmy doesn't say a word to Mazza. Doesn't even blink like. And they're going down here and they turn into the main road and they're walking along like, past The Ferret and this police car just comes up behind. Real quiet. Just pulls up. They never hear it. So the coppers get out and one says, and Jimmy tells this is the God's truth, one copper says to Mazza, excuse me sir, can I ask you where you're going. So Maz stops.

Where I'm going? asks Maz.

Yes, sir, says the copper. Where you're going.

Home, says Maz. All innocent like.

Well, sir, says the officer, and Jimmy tells this bit bloody lovely, could I ask you what you're carrying.

So Maz looks at him.

Not carrying anything, says Maz.

Then sir, says the copper, what is that on your shoulder?

What's what on my shoulder? asks Maz.

That sir, says the copper, and he points to the fucking great plastic dinosaur that Maz is carrying on his shoulder.

And Maz kind of turns his head to look at what's on his shoulder, swivels his eyes like, and he turns and he sees it and he says Oh my God O Jesus Christ, someone get it off.

Clint looked round. Tentpeg clapped Vine on the back. The dog pushed its face between Karoona's legs.

Jimmy nearly pissed himself, said Clint.

Yeah, good one, said Vine.

Get Jimmy to tell it to you because every time Jimmy tells it he remembers something different.

That Maz, said Tentpeg.

Yeah, the pisshead, said Clint. They put him in the loony clinic. He was drinking seawater. Said there was gold in it.

Nia

I was going to ring a taxi. Then I thought, no, walk it. I kind of amazed myself when I thought that. Because where did that thought come from? Who else would do that?

Li said no-one. No-one would be mad enough. You're crazy, she said. You velly clazy girl, she laughed, mocking herself. Li's good at that.

Someone had said it was nice to meet a Japanese person on The

Caib and Li didn't have the heart to tell the truth.

Me velly clazy but you velly velly clazy, she told me in her room. God, it's so beautiful there. And in a street that's falling down. I can't believe what she's done to that flat. All these mobiles carved from shells and cuttlefish.

You make them? I asked.

Yes, she said. I saw this man and he was selling them and I thought I could do that. Whatever that man can do I can do.

And she had twenty tea candles burning, and this music playing that sounded like rain. Like rain falling on water. I love it in the sea when it rains, and that's what the music reminded me of. And then she poured some more wine.

A toast, she said. I ploplose a toast.

To what? I said. I think I was pissed by then.

Death to pandas, she said. And I just laughed at her because she's such a gorgeous little star.

But no, I walked it. You see, what I hate is people thinking that I've tried to look good. Because it's the trying that's sad. Too much trying, not enough doing. I want to look like it's real. Like it's natural. Like I'm real and natural. I just can't stand dressing up, can't credit mum when she tries three, four, ten different things then goes back to the first. So combats and a teeshirt and trainers. The tee with a fair trade logo. And I walked it. That was round about when they'd bought me the MP3 for my birthday. Before everything went crazy. And I was past The Bona, that bloody eyesore, before I realised. I could see people on deck, drinking at that time in the morning, yeah, the usual wasters, the flag they fly sometimes, the skull and crossbones, like on a clothes-line. How pathetic is that? Middle aged hoodies and washed up hard cases. Anyway, I was past The Bona Ventura, well into the walk and Ni, I thought, you must be mad, girl. So I stopped listening immediately. Started paying attention.

Because even when you're high in the dunes you can't tell who's around. Can't make out who's hidden in the willow. Can't see who's looking down at you. There were the usual dog walkers about, and some athletes training. But then nobody. After a while there was no-one. No, it's not eerie. It's not like that. But it is lonely. Oh, it's a lonely place. And old. No, ancient. You can feel it's ancient, you'd have to be a cretin not to sense that. Like time doesn't mean anything there. Or that it passes at a different speed. And we hadn't had rain for ages and the grass was bleached and everything was iron-coloured. Even the willow leaves were made of iron. Everything felt heavy. The air was strange and heavy and there were flying ants, millions of them at one point, like iron splinters, but I just kept on, along the paths that went east, I knew the way but not the paths. Because the tracks change. The ways get overgrown, they get lost, then eventually someone makes a new one. There's a special word for the tracks in the sand. Dad told it me but I can't remember. He said it was a really old word, like it might go back thousands of years. A track in the sand that people make. Hunters and gatherers. Women collecting firewood. In this place. It's precious because it's a local word, he said, and never used anywhere else. It's unique.

So I switched off the Sony. Couldn't have been the MP3 because I was playing a CD I'd found in dad's collection. It was all Gil's stuff, a live set from somewhere, maybe up in the valleys. Weird too, rambling guitar and tape loops and percussion behind it, tabla and tambourine and tiny bells. The usual. But with crowd noise and people talking. There were conversations dad's microphone had picked up. Recorded forever, those people. Just gossiping, just noodling. And now immortal. And as soon as I switched it off I heard this scuffling in the ferns and I looked up and there's this fox going along the ridge. Big dogfox, calm as you like, but noisy. They don't usually make that much racket. And it turned around and looked at me. It did, it stopped and looked into my eyes. And I looked into its eyes. Big rusty iron-coloured fox on the dune. And then it turned round again and went over the crest. But in its own time. It had to show it wasn't scared. That everything was cool. And, it did, it looked right into my eyes. Yes, old man of the willow looked right into my eyes. Right through me, it felt like. As if it was trying to hypnotise me, or at least reading my mind. Then it was gone.

Get a move on, Ni, I thought. Don't lose the way like you've lost the word. The name of the way. God, that's really irritating now. Me forgetting that word. But the fox scared me. It was looking down from above, so it was in control. It had observed me from a distance. And made its own conclusions. It had watched me coming and knew the direction I was going and how far I'd come. Then it was my turn to go over the tops and part of the route was a ridge path where the stone was bare and stuck up through the dune like a backbone. Like the polished knobbly blue knuckly bits in your vertebrae. Showing through the sand. Up where they found that body, the Bronze Age princess, the slave girl that had been executed. Disposed of, ritually slaughtered. Well, that's what they say. I look at the painting of her sometimes and think, there's more left of you madam than there will be of us. Which is a hell of a thought. What had she done? Probably stolen a bottle of wine. Or had a meal with her father's friend. Strangled her, experts think, before they burned the dangerous hussy. Or maybe they were scared of her for some reason. Maybe she had questioned their magic. Or perhaps she came from somewhere else and didn't speak the dialect. Didn't know the word for a path in the sand. Just wandered into the wrong territory.

Then part of the way was through the buckthorn forest and then the willow woods, and then over a gravel plain where nothing grows, and the sand dry and fine in my trainers. I picked up a stone there, green and smooth as if it had been underwater. Green and heart-shaped, a keepsake. And then there were no more ants, no more foxes, I was getting close, and I came down off the dunes and across a field and into a lane and at the end of the lane was John Webb's.

Gil's car was parked on the bank with the lobster pots. Donal was there doing something to his boat but he never saw me, I made sure of that. The Triumph Stag had the roof folded right back. Yes, style, undeniable style. Colour of a good Barolo, Gil says it is. Which is how I felt, all hot from the walk and my bandanna pushed too far back, and my neck red, undoubtedly red as the Triumph, and almost as red as the bottle of soupy almost black cabernet that Li was not exactly force-feeding me that night in her flat.

She had nicked it from Mega. Jesus, I couldn't believe it. A bottle of Jacob's Creek up her jumper. Li pilfering the stock.

But I wanted to surprise you, she said. It's a special present for my special friend.

And all the candles too, Li? Look, young lady, I have to ask, you ungrateful illegal you.

No, no, she laughed. The candles are from Pound World. I only took the wine because it's a discontinued range.

Well, it's discontinued now, I said, waving my empty glass. I've personally discontinued it. So, what else would you do, you little Chinese tart? How bad could you be?

And okay, it went great. I walked straight into the Ladies and when I came out he had ordered me a pint of tap water. Does he know what I'm thinking or does he know what I'm thinking? The man's a genius. And then I ordered the rarebit which the John Webb people make with this rough-grain mustard. And they put a drop of their own beer in it too, this dark mild they're starting to make on the premises. Restoring this old recipe used there hundreds of years ago, when people used to go down to the shore and wave lanterns and sing. Yes, sing in the dark to attract the ships on to the reef. So it's a micro-brewery as well as a gastro-pub. And nothing alcoholic for me. Only more tap water. Gil ordered frizzante for himself, but not San Pellegrino, because they didn't have it. Again, that was cool. He's not exactly a pint of beer man. Not a trace of a gut. In fact, pretty trim, I'd have to say. Gymnasium smooth. And teeth? No wonder he's always smiling. Deep and crisp and even, that's Gil. So I told him about the tape.

John's got loads of things, he said. The bloody bootlegger. Could have been lots of gigs anywhere. What were the tracks?

Long pieces, I said. Some of the words were jokey poems. About drinking.

Oh yes, he laughed. *Dipsomaniac Blues.* Loads of little haiku and things, with a bad case of the DTs in the middle section. Kind of freak out, mostly improv. It's quite an epic. But there's so many versions of that piece even I've lost count. Like The Beatles had a hundred goes at *Not Guilty* and then didn't release it. No wonder Lennon quit, that was hard labour. And there's all these recordings of Miles Davis that people don't have the dates for. Club gigs in Kansas and Zagreb and Christ knows. So it's an industry, trying to fathom this byzantine world of live sound. It's a real industry. You know, Dylan's hotel room opuses, *Great White Wonder* and all that? *VD Blues*, you heard that? It's the new scholarship too. People do degrees in it all. They do doctorates. There's university departments devoted to it in the States. And no, don't tell me, don't tell me. Did it have *I would give my last Rolo for a glass of Barolo* in it?

What's with this Barolo? And that's not a haiku, I said.

Okay, it's a couplet. And it's supposed to be funny in a knowing way. You're bad as your father, you are. A real pedagogue. What about this then, what about 'A bottle of vodka and a ride home in the squad car'?

Hey, I said. I don't know. The whole tape's a wild mess. There's people talking, some girl whispering about who she fancies, the till ringing up a storm.

You're right, Gil laughed. Just like Radio Three.

And I'm not a pedagogue, I said. Don't you start.

What's wrong, squirrel? Can't you take a joke?

With the best of them, I said. The very best. But you know what this place is like. Get a reputation for working hard, for enjoying your work, for wanting to work, and you're a mark one weirdo.

And then we both laughed. And yes, he did have the mackerel.

Bottom feeder, I whispered.

Yes, well, how did you know? Hey, I love mackerel. Colour of a magpie's wings. Ever thought of that? Irreducibly iridescent.

No, I said. I've never even come close.

It was a great afternoon. Simple as that. Then he drove me back to town and I said you can drop me off at Vainquer Street, and he asked why I wanted that God-forsaken and ramshackle *arrondisment*, and he really did use those words, so I said *oui*, it's really Parisian there, and he said *touché* and I said I'll walk to the end and over the empty quarter and through the funfair and go home that way, and he never argued, not once, even though it's a bit dodgy sometimes, which he knew. Treated me seriously. Treated me with respect.

Hey, he called. Almost forgot. And he wound the window down and I bent over the bloody red Stag and he gave me another CD.

New stuff. Done in the studio. No background rubbish this time, no secondhand smoke. I'm really pleased with it and I'd like your opinion. It's got the latest version of *Dipsomaniac Blues* on it. The studio version. And no messing around either. Spotless digital sound, so Uncle Neil Young wouldn't like it would he?

Wouldn't he?

In fact, you ought to come and see it.

See what.

The studio. At home. Hey, I'll ring you. Ciao.

And he turned the car by backing it almost through the front door of the Lady Vain.

But you know the great thing, the really great thing? He didn't ring. He just didn't ring. For a while I thought, yes, cool one, cool bastard, supercool bastard. Then it got as far as phoney fucking charlatan. Then it went up to me asking myself if I had bad breath? Dune walker's crotch? Rambler's armpit? Not that we came close. Nothing like that. It was all too natural for that. Even the squirrel. Three hours passed in three seconds. And then I stopped thinking about him. Because you do. You have to. Even though you're crying and hurting and wondering what the hell it was you did wrong. Because by then it was getting awful with dad and mum.

The Fish

In the east end was Vainquer Street, a three storey terrace. It had once been used by the Social to house its clients – the medicated druggies, the beaten wives. There were still a few bed and breakfast signs but the area had been discovered. Its narrow houses made good apartments. Now there was always scaffolding, a line of skips and usually three or four builders' vans parked on the verges.

Some of the houses had sea views. For developers, that meant gold dust.

It was funny, thought The Fish. Not so long ago the sea had been about as sexy as an acid bath. Grey, rheumatoid, corrosive in its winter damp. These days it was all surfing or sauvignon on the jetty. Perception, see. Change the public's perception. Now young couples were moving in, and vigorous retirees. A decade earlier the profit had been in turning pubs into retirement homes. Or old people farms, as The Fish called them. Today it was apartments for the newly pensioned off or second home owners from the city.

He walked up the street past the palm trees, the newly delivered stacks of breeze blocks and the green-bearded baths thrown into the gardens, and turned in at the last gate.

The Fish lived on the top floor. Up there the landing was uncarpeted and the floorboards tarred black. The light came from an unshaded fifty watt bulb. He unlocked the door and went in and shut the door and chained it.

Welcome. Let me be an estate agent for a while. Pretend I'm selling this to you. So first of all, what's good about the place is what I call the Nook. Okay, it's an alcove or a window bay. But to me it's the Nook. That's where I sit and read and work with my red crystal burning, you know, that rock that radiates negative ions, rugged looking thing nearly two feet high, Brazilian they said. And I keep another lamp on too, nice little anglepoise, and maybe some candles. And the screen of course. Which is on if I'm in. It's never off if I'm in.

Yeah, the Nook. With a mullioned glass window which breaks up the view. Some of those little panes are green and some red. And boy, do they catch fire when the crystal's lit. Think of a stained glass womb. Or maybe not. But that's where I sit when I'm not sleeping. Because it's all in the one room, see. This is a big room but an unusual shape. Twenty five by about twelve. And a ceiling sloping towards the bay so that the Nook actually stands outside the main wall. A tiny room within a room. Oh, it's cosy. It's the real deal in cosiness. Sometimes they offer me one of the bigger places downstairs but no, I say, I like it here. At the top in my eyrie.

Bloke who had it before me, now that's a tale. Cledwyn they called him. And that's a name that always makes me laugh. So this Cledwyn, this Cled was a postman. Worked round town for years and lived on his own up here. Funny isn't it? You never think of a postman having a life. You never imagine a postman after working hours, down the pub or making toast. Like they don't really exist.

Well it turns out the Royal Mail had been getting complaints about missing letters. But specially letters from abroad. And after a long time, years apparently, they decided to do some checking. So they had letters written for delivery all over town. And Cled's letters were the ones that went AWOL. Had him in, sat him down, and he started crying. Cled was about sixty and coming up for his pension. And he just broke down. So when the bosses came up here they found every wall was plastered with air mail letters, those long blue ones, aerogrammes they used to be called, and loads of others with foreign stamps. Every inch of every wall covered with a foreign envelope and a town address.

It was the stamps, he said. He loved the stamps. But Cled wasn't what you'd call a philatelist. He just loved the shapes and the colours and the funny currency. Cents and rupees. Drachmas. That sort of thing. Always wanted to travel, he said. His defence was that he'd never opened the letters. It was the envelopes he wanted. So the mail boys had to unglue all these envelopes and that's about when I took over. So I painted it red. And the ceiling black, because Cled had covered the ceiling too with all those names he loved, Guatemala, Ivory Coast.

You still see him around, old Cled. In his post office overcoat, a long black thing. Lost his pension of course, so he sometimes goes through the wheelies behind the supermarket. But then a lot of those old men do that. There's good stuff to be had. Armfuls of ready-meals, microwave pizzas. Which is a big help when you don't even know how to make a cup of tea for yourself. Oh yeah, the pleasures of retirement. So I just sloshed on the red. No. It's vermilion of course. Which means it's dark in here most times. But I gave it a good scrub with the bleach first because he was a dirty old bugger was old Cled.

And now I love it here. Bloody love it. Not that I can see much. For such a high place I'd have to say the view is a touch disappointing. Let's cut the estate agent crap. Very disappointing. A bit of the fair, a lot of the wasteland between the fair and the east beach, that place where the gypsies sometimes camp and the kids do speedway and where the dunes were smashed and built over and those buildings demolished in their turn. So it looks like some lost city. A flight of steps coming out of the sand and going nowhere. Yeah, that I like. A pavement that's buried both ends. Then something that looks like an air raid shelter. Then the sea. But only a smudge. And then the other side. High cliffs on a clear day and a north facing moor. So they get snow when we don't. Which is good because I hate snow. And the answer's ten years. I've been here ten years, and yes, I'm older than I might have said I was. Can you guess how old I am? Can you believe me?

Okay, I know you can't join in but all the same I'm having a glass of port. Pretty strange, eh? Nobody drinks port now. Well, I do. Cockburn's Fine Ruby port. Under a fiver at Bargain Booze. A mullioned pane, all right. But listen to this. 'Rich, dark and sweet with succulent berry notes'. Notes? Now, I wouldn't have said 'notes'. But note this. 'Making Fine Ruby is a curious marriage of Heaven and Earth.' I love that 'curious marriage' business. Because that's what it all is, isn't it. That's what everything's about. My own curious courtship, betrothal and eventual bigamous relationships with old Cockburn and the rest, Viney's curious marriage to Karoona which is going exactly where we say it will go, Hal with his idea of Hal, his psychotic dream of what the well heeled minor criminal should do with his time, and dad with his dadness, his deadness, his crown green bowls white cap and white shoes, his timetable of tablets pasted to the kitchen wall. So, yeah, I like looking out at the town. At the tides.

Because I love it here. This is where I'm from. And I'm its historian. Up here in my nook I'm writing its chronicles. Like a monk at his illuminated page. Yeah, I haven't told you before but that's my image of myself. Monkish. Bookish. Hardly fashionable yet somehow eternal.

See the screensaver? I change it almost every day. Just now it's a photo of a few wooden ribs in the sand, the idea of a prow. And a big sea beyond, a breast of high pressure swell crowned with a surfer. With that kid Vinny to be exact, who's a bit of a star. Who can do no wrong. Oh can't he? I can see the headlines now. That Vinny won a competition in Sri Lanka, but it's the foreground I like. It's one of our wrecks, and every one of those wrecks is on my list. This one's *The Dunkirk* which broke up exactly two hundred and fifty years ago. One hundred and thirteen capsizings since 1800. And I've listed every name except the one nobody knows. The anonymous ship. So I've put my own name in for that because I'm allowed. I'm bloody allowed. Can you guess what name I've called that ship? I mean, it's obvious isn't it?

So don't tell me it's quiet here. It's a dangerous coast, The Caib. There's always storms, always drownings on The Caib. Because just in case you hadn't understood by now, we're all heading for the rocks. The rocks on The Caib. Our fateful shore.

And no, it's not like other sites, not those personal sites where families give you their news about the kids' careers and their holidays in Thailand. They give me the creeps, those sites. Remind me of the biology lab in school with rabbits in jars. Other jars full of foetuses and weird fish. All preserved in formaldehyde, which, yeah, preserves, it preserves forever. Except it doesn't nourish. But it's what the net allows those sites. To exist. To remain and not to decay. Not to rot away to nothing. But they're dead. They're inert. Because there's no imagination behind them and there's no dream. There's… okay, okay. Yeah, I'm off again.

But look, there's mam, she's on my site. Three clicks and there she is. At her best of course. Young, laughing and a great dress, tight at the waist then billowing out with those chiffon bows. What a looker she was with her hair still dark and her smile and admittedly a glass in her hand, maybe a port, and yes, that's why, that's the reason. But you could imagine her dancing the night the picture was taken, down The Bolero or up The Sea View, laughing and joyful and just delighted to be alive.

How did all this happen? is what that smile says. Don't ask, just dance. And she's dancing there, she's twenty five and she's alive. With Roy Orbison singing *Blue Bayou*, or maybe The Shadows with *Wonderful Land*. Because she could dance to anything. And she's not wrecked yet. Not washed up on the sand. Not with her finger on a tablet chart trying to work out what's keeping her heart beating and her blood from sludging up.

Now look here. Four clicks this time and that's what they want to do with us. That's the developer's plan, the marina, the boulevardiers under the palms. All paid for by the Mall, which they want to put smack on the front, the Mall and the pool and the leisure complex. Which will be located exactly there. That promontory. That outcrop at the tip of our peninsula. Smack on the fair, that prime site. Smack also on the badlands behind the fair. With the syringes in the sea holly. Where the dinosaurs used to roam. Right smack under this window to be exact. You see, it's all here. The history. And the future if we let it happen. Yeah, this site's alive.

And what time's it now? Two, three? The screen says 4.10. Jesus. Black out there. Just the one light on the road through the sand so everything's lit like a pantomime. Because the light doesn't weaken or fade. It stops dead. There's a frontier of light and then immediate blackness until the first rank of the caravans half a mile away. Absolute black. Sometimes I see people walking under that light. If you're on the road you can't escape it. But you're coming from nowhere and going nowhere if you're on that road. So why are you there I ask when I see them. And who are you?

Then they disappear. Just like that. As if they'd walked off the face of the earth. Out of that cone of orange light and into nothingness. Just like mam. Just like that Rachel. Rachel who I never knew about I swear. I don't know any of that. She's just pissed off somewhere.

Girls do that. Why did she want to get away? She was with that arsehole Gil, somebody said, or the guy in his band. Guitarist, I think. He's supposed to be good. Supposed to have taken her for a dirty weekend in London which makes her just another groupie as far as I'm concerned. Or she just fancied the scene. All that music up there. What's wrong with here?

But because I don't know anything doesn't mean I don't have my ideas. And okay maybe I saw her. And maybe I didn't. Well, I saw some girl. Long hair and sloppy jumper under the light and then gone. And yeah, I was doing the ruby, I was well into the ruby and all the stuff I'd had before getting home. So I couldn't even say what night it was, I was that wrecked. But I'd come that way because it's the quickest from The Cat. But you have to be local to know that path. To chance it. Bit spooky, seeing that everything's knocked flat, the chip shops, the caffs. Maybe it's especially hard for locals to get their bearings out there, all the landmarks being gone. But everyone vanishes eventually. And it's usually the good ones first. How long do you think I'm going to be around? Listen, maybe you should consider yourself. Yeah, consider yourself. What about you?

But let's get back to the site. Four clicks and there we are, The Caib in all its geological splendour. Christ, I love this map. That's what we stand on. That's where the salt in our blood and the sand in our eyes comes from. Look at those blues and greens. That's the limestone that made us. And there's nothing so treacherous as limestone. It's a honeycomb under our feet. There are caves and inlets and smugglers' coves all around here and freshwater springs and tiny canyons where you drown if the tide catches you, you have absolutely no chance. And yeah, I like it. Lagoons. Or blue bayous. Which are really black. So when I wake up tomorrow that's what will be in my hair and between my toes. Dust of The Caib. Smell of The Caib. Just look at that, the blues and the greens and the rusty serrated edge of this coast. Like some fisherman's knife. Lost in the sand. Got danger written all over it. Just looking at it tells you how dangerous it is here. But it's where I come from. Born and bred. And born to tell its story.

Okay, cheers. Now listen to this. *We mature our rich, full bodied wines in fine oak barrels, and wait for the magic to happen.* That's old Cockburn again. I love that, see. Because that's what we're doing. He's got it spot on. We're waiting for the magic to happen. As if there was no-one with the brains to understand that it's already happened. That it's already here, all around us on The Caib. And we're living in its afterglow.

So what is that ruby magic? *They're waiting for the raspberry to peak, the plum to amplify.* Which Mr Cockburn, you old bastard, was definitely worth waiting for. Your magic. Because the plum has amplified. And how. It's loud and clear. It's coming over the tannoy, Mr Cockburn. Okay, stuff that. Here's mam dancing again, here's the light in her eye.

I remember dancing with her once. I'd come out of hospital again and I was crying because I would never be like the others. No, not crying. Sobbing. Stop your sobbing, she whispered, holding me round the waist. Stroking my hand. But it was official now. I was always going to be The Fish. And we were in the front room with that rumpled carpet with the *Arabian Nights* design on it and she put a record on the record player and it was, yeah, okay, it was *Wonderful Land* and we were dancing to it slow because that track's not so danceable, but still the carpet was slipping on the block floor like it always did and she was making me dance and I was crying with my face crushed into her because I didn't want her to see me crying but really because I was smelling her scent, all those fantastic things she used to spray around or dab on with that handkerchief that had those flowers embroidered on it. Tansy, she said it was. And I was breathing in that incredible perfume. It just smelt golden. If golden has a smell, that was it. It was her. And the record ended and the arm moved back across the record and it started playing again and I could hear the fuzz on it and the crackling static and it ended again and the arm came over and it slid over the black disc and I was breathing in that golden smell and suddenly she pushed me away and said that's enough now. I've got to go out, got to go.

Do you believe that? Would I lie to you honey? Why would I make things up? Because there she is, mam again, all chiffony and loving it. But that man's arm around her waist. That's all you can see, a man's arm. And it's not dad. As if that man was so proud or so in love with her he had to touch that shining dress. But he's really holding her. He's holding her tight. Such a strong arm. And sometimes when I look at that picture at a time like this, when it isn't one day or the other but when it's the dead zone between times, it seems he's pulling her away. Trying to pull her into the world outside the light.

Friday

Rachel

As usual in the early morning, Vine sat outside the Seagull Room.
The sea was livelier than of late, the marker buoys rocking, their bells
audible across the bay.

The CD had an 'R' scrawled on it in felt pen. Vine couldn't
remember writing that, and didn't think he would have been so
blatant. Or so foolish. But there it was. Now he put the CD into
his laptop and clicked on. There were several files but he went
straight to the movie, kept his eyes closed until he knew it was about
to play.

You could tell it was a hot day. At first the light was blinding. The
camera panned around a deep crater. That had once been John Vine's
favourite dune. He had taken Siân there before they were married.
His children played there while he and Siân laid out their picnic or
sat and drank up the sun and the silence. He had gone there alone
many times in all weathers. From the crest was a view of almost one
hundred and eighty degrees of sea. At the bottom the sky had
seemed a ceiling you might touch.

Now the camera rested on a flower that grew in the bank. It was
a purple orchid, three feet high, an exotic spike. Vine had known
they would find it there. Even with the poor quality film it looked
extraordinary, its leaves like new steel, its head of bronze. There
was something molten about it, as if the orchid glowed. It might
have been a weapon, thought Vine now, something medieval and
barbarous, an instrument of torture. Or maybe worship. There it
stood, livid as an idol. The camera panned round the almost perfect
circle of the crater, through the grass and the thorns and came to

focus on a peacock butterfly that had settled upon Rachel's bare arm. Then it pulled away slowly.

And there she was, laughing. Rachel sitting on a blanket, knees under her chin, Rachel in her red bikini, Rachel whose skin he had always thought of as having an olive tone now revealed as a taut and milky satin, sandy at elbows and thighs, Rachel who had suddenly thrown off her teeshirt and trousers and genuinely shocked him, Rachel with the butterfly, Rachel with a huge half-eaten Californian strawberry as big as a heart between two fingers, Rachel with strawberry juice around her mouth, Rachel whose paper cup of pinot grigio was pushed in a white wedge between her thighs, Rachel with her hair down, Rachel who had writhed on the blanket like a dune viper as she felt the sun upon her, Rachel with her Oxford anthology because they were there to choose poems together weren't they, Rachel who dwelt among the untrodden ways, Rachel as solemn as a nun breathless with adoration as she performed for him, Rachel with a whole smoked salmon sandwich crushed into her mouth, Rachel with her sketch book and pencil, how rapidly she drew, he noted, and there he was on the page, a little grim, Vine thought, and rather like his father, the man who had teased him, teased everybody, as if that might conceal the disappointment of Richard Vine.

Maybe that was the best time, he thought now. How could that ever be improved. The sunshine, the wine, the not-having-to-be-somewhere-else for a whole three hours. Three hours. It had seemed like three minutes. But Vine could conceive nothing better than that afternoon in the dunes. In his secret dune. Where he knew no-one else would come, not a rider, a dogwalker, a naturalist. Not even his own children. Where had they been that day? No. There could be nothing better than the weather that released Rachel's energy. Her wickedness. Her dirty jokes. The sweat on her like salty dew, the sand in her hair and on her brow and over her arms and sand in the pits of her deodourised armpits, the sand that in close up was white as sugar on her arse as they both smacked it off, as she stamped there almost naked inside the rim of what Vine told her was an extinct volcano, her briefs just a crimson string, her voice ricocheting around that sandy coliseum.

Yes, Vine had thought, Rachel the lion and he the Christian. Rachel lion-coloured with sand, he in his muscular Christian's khaki shorts and brindling chest hair.

No, say it, he thought now, greying, greying to irongrey those unlovely tufts.

Like dead grass, she'd said. And plucked two fingers full.

And he'd hopped away. Spilling his wine.

Sadist.

Yes, Rachel the lion. Or panther. A pale panther she had been that day. Not sleek but lithe, not athletic but lissom. Yes. He had said the word to himself.

Lissom.

And white.

Under the sand as white as a lath of sprucewood. But how blue her bones shone when she stretched. How the kisscurls sprouted from her dewy crotch. The rose in her hair was already losing its petals. They lay in a cream spray on the turf. But a panther. That had been Rachel. His friend. His companion. His teenaged heartbreaking soul mate. Or that was what she had seemed. That day. But a panther all the same. And how easily she had devoured him. Everything he knew and had learned and had practised disappeared when he reached out to place his forefinger upon the snake in her belly. Osoboris. The serpent that swallowed itself. And they had clutched at each other and broken away and Vine had hoisted her over his shoulder and she had screamed and again escaped and they had chased one another around the sand and then fallen close together to lie open eyed in that prehistoric place. There had been a buzzard, Vine remembered now, circling overhead, a black speck that he knew was a buzzard and which Rachel didn't see, its cry almost inaudible, a kitten's mewl some said but which Vine always thought was the voice of desolation, but a flaw in that blue porcelain, a predator that Vine could tell was beginning its descent.

Then they had sat up.

Surprised by each other.

It was as if they had slept and dreamed everything that had happened.

Welcome to the Bronze Age, said Vine, gesturing at their camp.

That's funny, she'd replied. And pulled her sunblock out of her satchel. Bronze Age, factor thirty.

He had offered to rub the cream into her shoulders and back. But she had refused and had stretched to do it herself. Vine had thought that strange but said nothing.

He had looked at the wine in his cup and wondered how he might explain its sweetness on his breath. To anyone who cared to wonder.

Then Rachel's mobile had rung. He knew she changed the ring tone every other week but this was new to him. It was sitar music, a sudden cascade of notes. An Indian gourd chiming there on their limestone peninsula. Vine liked to think of the resort as remote from the rest of the country and it was true it attracted no passing traffic. The trains had finished forty years before, and few people discovered the town who did not want to visit. It was miles out of the way for anyone who made that mistake.

Rachel had squealed and chatted for fifteen minutes. After a while, Vine had climbed to the rim and looked around. The tide was out and there were riders on the beach, three dark shapes in the surf, cantering at first but picking up pace, the riders as dark as their mounts and crouched over the horses' stretching necks, holding on for dear life it seemed, the horses' tails streaming behind, the surf beaten black and silver and breaking over their hocks.

That part of the bay was always free from tourists. It was too far from any possible parking. And there were no directions, not an indication that east of the rocks and lagoons lay this immense stretch of sand. It was still a wild beach, Vine had thought then. And a dangerous place. The currents were unpredictable. He turned and looked into their crater. But not so dangerous as the rip tide in the blood.

Down there lay Rachel on her stomach. Listening, laughing, refilling her cup from the wine bottle, shaking out the last drops.

Vine could feel his own skin prickling. He was starting to burn. They'd planned to go to the beach after the picnic, but he sensed it would not happen now. Rachel had brought only sandals, which were no good for the thorny mile they'd have to walk. And he knew that while Rachel swam, he would float or dog around in an untidy circle. She would swim like an otter, he imagined. She had the right shape and energy. He could picture her mane now, dark as dulse down her back, Rachel jack-knifing into the wave and after scary moments emerging as some tipsy Aphrodite while he splashed in the shallows, wet hair thinned out and showing a white scalp. The fifty-year-old novice. Because that was another thing he was doing too late. Something else he should have learned a long time ago.

Who was that? he had asked.

Oh, Vinny.

Vinny was Vincent from Rachel's year.

Everything okay?

It was just about tonight.

Big plans?

We're all sleeping out. You know, barbecue, booze, guitars.

Great.

Some of the boys have started already, picking up driftwood for the fire.

Pack horses.

Yeah.

Get the boys to do it.

Course.

Vinny plays doesn't he?

Vine could see the boy. Lots of floppy hair. Sort of lethargic but always comfortable with himself. Which might have been mistaken for arrogance. Yes Vinny was arrogant, Vine thought. But the arrogance of teenage boys was something he was used to. It bored him. But then most school life bored him. When it wasn't killing him. Vinny's essays were infuriatingly glib but most in the department thought him capable of brilliance. He was a musician and a surfer and all the rest of it. With something in his eye. What was the word? Yes, Vine thought, that was it. Lupine. There was something wolfish about the kid.

Yeah, he's great, said Rachel. They've really got their band together. Nice dude.

And Vine cringed now as he had cringed then. The English teacher betrayed by a word. The treachery of fashion.

Well... Rachel had smiled. Her smile had become a smirk. And for a split second her lip was curled in what Vine felt was a sneer. Which he deserved. He was not multilingual. As a teacher he knew the deathless silences that ensued when staff members tried to prove how contemporary they were. When they pretended to be someone else. That was always the danger. Be out of date, out of touch, out to lunch, they said in the department. But be yourself or they'll kill you. Never be a phoney. Because they'll spot you a mile away. And then you're shark bait.

Brychan used that word and Vine used it to Brychan. But always ironically. Hi dude. What's happening, dude? It's bedtime, dude. Or so Vine thought.

... Yeah. Nice dude, she'd laughed. And looked away. Rachel, for the first time it might have been, regarded her surroundings, looking around the hollow with its sandy walls, the rocks inset with corals, all those lives turned to stone.

Hey, smell that, urged Vine.

He smashed a stone down on a limestone outcrop, and sniffed.

Here you are.

Ah, disgusting, she hissed, her face wrinkling.

Sulphur, he said. The whole place is full of it.

Thanks for that, she said. So are the school toilets.

Vine was abashed.

We've finished the pinot, he said.

Well I can't drink any more if I'm out tonight, said Rachel. Talking of which, I'd better go.

And she had stood up then in her red costume. Hardly bigger than a daisy chain, Vine had thought, and turned away as she pulled the teeshirt with the 'No Logo' logo over her head and stepped into the cotton trousers.

It used to be under the sea, all this, Vine had said. And he recognised desperation's accent in his voice.

Three hundred million years ago it was a tropical ocean.

And he was drowning in it…

Crocodiles the size of buses.

Oh yes.

Rachel put on her sunglasses. They made a black slash across her face.

And all these lilies. Growing everywhere. That's what made the rock under the dunes. Generations of sea lilies decaying. Year after year, dead flowers building up and forming limestone.

How weird.

So they had come down from that high place and taken the tracks through the sand. After a while they met a few walkers but no-one paid attention. Everyone was preoccupied with the temperature, the blinding light. Vine could feel his back stiffening, his shoulders starting to crawl with a nettle's icy rash.

It had been a long walk back to the slipway. Rachel was visibly tired when they reached the car. Around them here were the tinfoil of abandoned barbecues, disposable nappies, carrier bags of empty lager bottles. Trippers had set parasols up and family parties were underway.

The trogs are out in force, said Rachel who seemed to be brightening at last. Talk about a last resort.

Yes, said Vine. The trogs. Like something out of *The Lord of the Rings*. You what?

And the horizon was filled by the trog multitudes waiting to make their final assault on the elves.

Rachel had raised her eyebrows at that.

Where's the party tonight?

Wyndam Beach, she said.

That was a tiny sickle-shaped bay to the west. Vine knew there were always huge amounts of driftwood there.

Good choice. Private.

He reversed over the gravel.

Okay, let's get out of this bloody *twll*.

He used the word deliberately hoping she'd ask what it meant. But perhaps she already knew because she didn't say anything else until he dropped her at the end of her street, a terrace of small cottages and B&Bs. What Vine did in the car was whistle. He remembered that. He had whistled *Brown Eyed Girl*, the old Van Morrison thing. That was their tune. He had always whistled that for her. But hang on. Rachel had blue eyes. So maybe it was that Elton John track he'd whistled. *Blue Eyes*, that was more like it. Considering the mood and the come-down. The anti-climax. Yes, it was *Blue Eyes*, that melancholy lullaby. Siân liked it too. But Christ, he'd never whistle an Elton song for Rachel. How she would have sneered at that. *Blue Eyes*? Got to be joking. Then what colour were her eyes? And how many songs had they shared? It had to be Van the Man surely. That's where the credibility was.

There was a pub, The Lily, on the corner with its door open and a few plastic chairs placed on the pavement. A group of men and young women stood with their backs to the road.

Ta ra, then, they'd said simultaneously, and Rachel was out and gone, disappearing up an alley almost choked by buddleia.

In her bag with the sketchbook was the camera she'd used constantly at the beginning. Vine had wondered about that as he posed for her digital. He was trusting to her discretion. But the light had been wrong. She would probably delete all the pictures she'd taken. Yet Vine had watched her as she crouched beside the orchid. She had taken care then, edging around its brazier of leaves. These were all blotched red. What was the legend? Blood had fallen on them from the sky. No, Christ's blood from the cross.

Some of the drinkers had turned round and were watching him, Vine knew. He'd probably taught some of them. Which was always the problem a teacher faced if he lived in the town where he worked.

Nothing better to do.

Stuff it, Vine had thought. And driven off.

Now he remembered the flowers in Rachel's lane. All had turned brown. Three pint glasses lacy with foam stood on the kerbstone by the pub. And three green bottles.

Vine disliked that time of day when school was off. The last and desultory hour of the afternoon. A child had been crying in an upstairs room. The wine had been singing in his head.

OK? asked a voice.

He looked round and there was Clint, staring at the laptop. But there was nothing on the screen.

Morning, said Vine.

Clint stood bare armed and smiling before him. Self-evidently a weight trainer and Nautilus expert, his vest was black with sweat.

Vine looked at the animal beside him. It was a bulldog whose double leash was attached to a leather harness. There was a studded belt around its belly. Unlike Clint, the dog was panting. A line of drool hung from its jaw. Clearly an albino, its red eyes were buried wounds.

Vine ignored it.

You're up early, he said.

Oh yeah, said Clint, still smiling. It was the smile of a man who seemed to know something that nobody else did.

Best part of the day.

Then Clint crouched down and looked into the dog's face. Its jaw was a wrinkled velvet vice.

Never miss a trick. Do we Kango?

Jesus, thought Vine. What's wrong with Cerberus? He's named the monster after a power tool company. What a prick.

Don't want to disturb you, said Clint, squinting up at the computer.

You're not.

Karoona all right?

Karoona's fine, said Vine.

She's coming to play for us again isn't she?

Not sure.

Oh yeah. She's coming. Maybe upstairs at The Black Lite. Maybe down, just for The Cat. Tomorrow night.

Come to think of it, she told me. Yes.

Nice. I'll be watching.

And me, said Vine.

Tell her to wear that black thing.

What black thing?

Well perhaps you haven't seen it. Kind of see-through.

Clint looked back at the laptop.

School work?

Not exactly.

Oh yeah. It's like hard to forget you're not a school teacher any more.

Comes to us all.

But we had some good times up there didn't we?

Did we?

I did. I always did. Not that I was there often. Watch out for those dinosaurs.

And Clint and the dog walked off towards the fair.

Donal

The nun was coming towards him. Young, he thought. They had taken this one young. Twenty five perhaps. And brown as a thrush. She was carrying a piece of driftwood and walked past him without looking or speaking although he was ready for pleasantries. He noticed her boots. Big things, Army Stores, probably steelies. But with red laces. She walked on into the light and vanished in the glare.

He supposed it all came down to that in the end. Light. This morning it shattered around him on the avenue. The year was turning, there was a sinew in the wind. But that wind was coming from the south west, the wind that was a frost melter, palm nourisher. And occasionally a hurricane. Yes, he'd known them. Lost a boat once, seen it blown one hundred yards inland. The storm had come over from the States. He understood it was on its way and thought he'd done everything. Imagined the boat would be okay. But he was a sloppy sailor. A sloppy man.

Because sometimes there was no trusting the weather on The Caib. The American storm had blown sea walls down and taken the cast iron weathervane off The Sea View. Well, you lived and maybe you learned and maybe you didn't. But this light was a benediction. Yes, that was probably the word. Donal felt it upon his upturned face. He sensed it reach within him. He might even take his shirt off this afternoon. And bask in the garden among poppy leaves.

He remembered the Spanish cats that would lie all day in the sand around the bar and in the evenings jump on to the palm fronds of the roof and hunt lizards. Marty's cats, skinny little scrappers covered in scars and scabs. What had she called them? Ascot, Balmoral, and that ginger fighter was Paddington.

Why the hell? he had asked, but she always had her answers.

Parts of Brisbane, love, she'd laughed. The old town. Why, did you think I'd gone loopy for the royals? You Poms are something else.

I'm no Pommy, he'd retorted.

Well, what are you then? she'd laughed back. Tell me what you are?

That's for me to know and for you to guess, he'd thought. But he had kept quiet and let her stir the soup with the cats at her feet wanting heads and guts and the kitchen floor so slimy with octopus he could hardly stand, and the heat immense, yeah, just immense over their stove where Marty threw in the *pulpitos*, the *chiparones*, his eyes running from the scarf in her hair to the washed-out, worn-out knickers hanging off her scrawny arse, then to her fingers greased with fish oil and her own blood where she'd cut herself with the bone-handled and brass-riveted chopping knife that they'd found in the kitchen.

Little bit extra, she'd whispered, brandishing the blade as her blood dripped into the pot.

And she squeezed more in.

Hey, she'd said, turning round. I once saw this sign in London. It said Lucozade Aids Recovery. I was going past on a big red bus and I thought, yeah, they've found the cure at last.

Hope you're not positive, he'd replied.

I'll bet you do.

Donal had made an effort today. He wore jeans and a shirt and his only good shoes and he carried a package. For a minute he watched the crows on the rocks. They picked up sea snails and flew into the air and dropped the shells and dived after them. Clever bastards. Graceful too. Funny, he thought, you never thought of crows as graceful. No-one ever told you crows were graceful. But they were. They were graceful. And clever. Boy, that was the lesson, he said to himself. You trust to your own eyes and your own judgement and forget what everybody else said. As if he didn't know.

Past the Mega Minimart he walked though the site's last avenues and crossed the expanse of sand and demolished shops and pavements that led nowhere. At the fair's edge he turned right and followed a track for three hundred yards before emerging on the main road. Donal crossed and walked into bungalow land and zigzagged for another half mile before turning left into Narcissus Street. He stopped at number twenty seven. There was a house name on a plate screwed into the redbrick pillar, so rusted as to be almost unreadable: *Twynytywyn*. Above the entrance a larger notice announced *The Sandhurst*.

Donal rang the bell but he always suspected it didn't work and so tapped the door. There was a brass knocker he might have used but Donal imagined the sound this would make inside, his arrival announced and echoing to all, leaving whoever was awake expectant or terrified.

No-one answered and he rapped again and after a while a woman in flipflops and a sweatshirt emblazoned with the word *Friendship* let him in and he stood on the oilcloth of the hall while she disappeared to fetch somebody. Then he turned left up the corridor and opened a door.

This was the dayroom. It was large and the curtains were drawn and the light was hot and brilliant across the mahogany block floor. About ten people sat in chairs, most of them clustered around a television screen as big as any he had seen in pubs.

He recognised Big Eliza and Little Eliza. Big Eliza was blind and by rights should not have been at The Sandhurst because it wasn't equipped. But Little Eliza did everything for her, putting powder and lipstick on for her friend, manicuring her nails, while Big Eliza told stories about working in munitions during the war, going home yellow with the dynamite dust. Better than nylons it was.

So together they got by. In the dayroom, which also served as the games room and television room, were tables scattered with magazines and jigsaws. There was a CD player and two bowls of fruit, and the smell was there too, the smell that was always a part of the room, a sharp and childish odour that reminded Donal of those orange sweets, Spangles, or sherbet with the liquorice fuse.

It was disinfectant with the lemon added, or that tincture you could buy in tiny bottles and was the lemoniest smell you could ever imagine. That was what they used here, one of the girls told him, those phials of fragrant oils they all carried in their apron pockets, only a sprinkle and the room was fresh as an orange grove in sunny Spain, love. But we keep them away from the old dears, she'd told him quickly, don't worry about that. There are warnings on the bottles you see. But they work a treat.

And of course there was something darker beneath that citrussy smell, something more serious, yet hidden, some more mysterious current which Donal knew was no mystery and never had been.

Hello stranger, said a woman behind him.

Thought I'd better.

Yes, well, about time isn't it? she said.

Been busy.

It's a busy world. You're busy, I'm busy. She looked around with a proprietorial eye.

But they're not busy.

No. They're not busy at all.

Everyone okay? she asked the room.

A few of the occupants waved or murmured assent.

Donal closed the door and they stood together in the passageway and he leaned down and kissed her on the mouth. She laughed and pushed him away and they went back along the corridor and up the stairs and came to a door that said 6 and she opened it and they stepped into a magnolia-painted dormitory of two beds. One was empty and Donal's mother Mary lay in the other.

How is she?

Asleep.

But how is she?

The same. Fading used to be the word but fading can take a long time. I'll leave you here.

Thanks, Susan.

There was a wicker armchair by the bed. He sat in this and unwrapped the packet and took the picture out and put it on the bedside cupboard.

A wisp.

That's what she was.

Donal looked at his mother asleep. She was snoring gently. Her hair was unpinned and lay upon her shoulders like bonfire smoke. It was strange, he thought. Hair was supposed to turn grey and then white. That's what happened and that's what was happening to his own hair. But his mother's hair had not remained white. It had changed in streaks and patches to a dirty yellow.

Merely a wisp.

He knew she wouldn't wake and he would not waken her. He sat in the room where the curtains were half drawn and the light flooded in on a narrow ray and spread in hexagons over the floor. Her lips were almost indistinguishable, like the surface line of water in the glass at the bedside. He looked at the water. There were bubbles in it. It was oxidising, which meant it had been there a long time.

The woman's skin was the palest skin he had ever seen. His mother's skin. Chronic anaemia was what they said. One of the complaints she lived with. Exhaustion was the other. He looked at her and knew she was worn out, so worn out that there was no coming back. The woman was drained and used and emptied and no sun would make a difference and no visit this morning rouse her to sit up and take stock. Especially a visit from a stranger.

He looked at her hand that was palm down upon her breast. What would it be like to wake in that home that could never be home and see a whitehaired son at the bedside? His presence would speak to her. Not long now, it would say, it can't be long now. He was an announcement, a death sentence.

Across the room the other bed was stripped. That had been Mrs Evans's bed until when? Yesterday? Last month? Minnie Evans who would soon be replaced by another woman brought to The Sandhurst, Minnie who had died or gone back to her children or been moved to somewhere cheaper. Because The Sandhurst wasn't bottom of the range, oh no. It was decent enough but not the best. It wasn't your Oceanside or Atlantic Rest with their individual rooms and resident medically-qualified staff.

Donal knew that The Sandhurst relied on older schoolchildren or some of those Lithuanian girls for the basic duties such as meals and cleaning or overnight stays. Okay, that was the dicey part, knowing some nights there were only two kids on the premises, double time if they slept over. But it couldn't be helped. And the profit from the sale of the cottage was going, Jesus, that monthly vanishing act out of Mary O'Connell's account. The last time he'd talked to his mother she had rattled on about her will. There was two hundred pounds for the League of Pity, she said. Would he see to it? Well, not now, Mam, he'd thought. We're down to the red cents. But Susan was okay. He could trust Susan. The bastards who owned the place, certainly not. But Susan was a tresh.

A few years back, this had been where the money was, converting pubs and hotels into retirement homes. Now they were being reconverted into apartments for a new population who worked in the city or wanted to enjoy their index-linked with salt in the lungs and a golf course under the feet. Boom time. Which the O'Connells had missed of course. You had to laugh. Mary's cottage had been tiny and its front door opened on to the main road. When the buses stopped people could see right in to the front bedroom.

Donal's sister had arranged the sale and she and Donal had copped a few thousand each and the rest was put into renting Mary a flat in the East End and then a place at The Sandhurst when her health finally failed.

Mary had skivvied and pulled pints and breathed pubsmoke and smoked Woodies herself while bringing up two kids on her own. Because her husband, James O'Connell, was a seaman who never came home, being a legend in the household, then a rumour and finally a missing person. In his twenties Donal had tried tracking his father down but the bastard might have been anywhere, Aden or Argentina, and yes, there were those stories of other women, other children, and perhaps it was better as a mystery, that's what Sis thought, although they both agreed the truth would not be exotic.

And yet they had laughed together that maybe the old man had gone native. Bahia say. With a Brazilian bint. For some time Donal had pictured him as looking like Ronnie Biggs, old Rio Ronnie who'd got clean away with his ill-gotten gains and picked up some classy skirt. With no decent photograph of James O'Connell, because none existed, and that was the hard part, Ronnie Biggs supplied the features. Even when Donal was a middle aged man, that's how he saw his father. With a resemblance to the train robber. Stupid really. Surely the old fucker was already dead, jumped in La Boca or drunk to extinction in a Liverpool dosshouse. There'd once been a story of him knocking around up there, telling his tales, cadging drinks, probably a drop of Jameson's because one of the things he'd left on The Caib was a huge bottle of Jameson's whiskey.

It was tall as a man's arm was long. Empty of course, and green as the waters over the ferry side Donal had seen that time Mary had taken the family over to Cork. There'd been no luck there. Not a trace. But Donal remembered the sea green ahead and the ferry wake a white feather behind. There had been men singing on the boat and drinking. Perhaps it had been a holiday. Then back home they had all decided to save their money in the Jameson's bottle. But it was too big. Or the money too little. It looked foolish there on the sideboard. Two inches of black coins, and so hard to get them out again. And marbles, yes, once he'd kept marbles there, the wall-eyed alleys that were especially precious. But generally the bottle stood on the sideboard as an ornament awaiting its owner.

Until that night when Mary, who'd been bought too many Mackesons at The Lily, came home and threw it down on the stone flags. She'd taken it deliberately out to the back kitchen and hurled the Jameson's to the floor. Held it over her head and smashed it. Donal had seen her. A splinter had caught him under the eye but he hadn't cried. Just looked on cold and amazed. Years later they were still finding green pieces of glass in the strangest places, the curtains, the top shelf, the trunk of an aspidistra that had been struggling for years in its pot in the passage. The wood had grown around the glass. And there was Mary looking up with the pinpricks on her face and forearms that were about to bleed and here was Donal now still with the single scar, the white spot that had never tanned.

A wisp.

He gazed at her hand that lay on her breasts. Or where her breasts had been. Mary had always seemed a skinny one, thin as a Swan Vesta his sister said and when Sis had said no, she couldn't, she couldn't possibly, The Sandhurst had been the only answer. Well, there was always The Zoo. The Zoo specialised in troublemakers, the ranters, the shitters, the hallucinators. Tied them up in The Zoo, didn't they. Fought fire with fire. Well those were the stories. The Zoo was old style. No, they couldn't send her to The Zoo.

It's good here, Mam. I know they're looking after you. And could you see yourself in the caravan with the wind outside so strong the whole thing is rocking and the sand is scouring the paint off and getting in the wardrobe, how the hell I don't know, in the pockets of things I haven't worn in months. In my socks even though the socks are balled up and in the drawer. Yeah, well, I'm not long there either. In the van. That's why I'm here Mam. Got to go, see, nothing for it but to go.

Oh I'll be talking to Hal about the chance of a job or two. But there's not much happening now. All gone quiet on that front. So the boat will have to be, er, dispensed with. There's a couple of boys interested but it'll be a knock down price. It's good enough for me but pretty basic really. Five or six thousand if I'm lucky and when have I been lucky recently? So probably four. And, okay, yes, you've been here a long time, a long time now and it doesn't ever get cheaper in these places, and that's what your money's for, it's for here, Mam. Not that there's much left but that's not for you to worry about is it? Anyway, it's all changing here one way or another. That Casino they've talked about for years, looks like it's coming at last. Yes, I know, been years of planning, but all that waste ground is due for development.

You know, sometimes I think I can remember what it used to be before they built that part of the site. I can see these dunes and these pools between them and the plovers coming down in their flocks in the evenings and then I think, of course not, that was all gone before I was born. So how can I be remembering any of that? And how can I remember the curlews' voices, those weird cries they make just before it gets dark? I'm cracking up. Going crazy in my old age. But then it was you who told me about them. And it was you who said they sounded like ghosts. You'd heard them when you and the old man went for your picnics in the sand hills. So, you used to tell us about it. Tea and bread and butter and yeast cake. That recipe, Mam, I've got it. In your hand writing. Because I make that yeast cake sometimes and it's the best cake you'd ever taste and it's your recipe and everyone who tastes it says the same.

And I know Sis will still come when she can, though I haven't seen her for a bit. We don't talk like we used to and it's my fault and one day I'll put it right, I swear to that, but no, we don't talk like we should. So that's why I've come really and I don't want you to be disturbed. I want you to have good dreams, but I've come to say I have to go away. Most likely. So I've brought you the picture and it'll be here when you wake up and Susan will say I came. But you'll know anyway. And the picture will say it better still. The three of us, me and Viv and Big Billy. All looking good in our whites and me the last one left. Which is hard to credit. Really is, Mam.

You met them both didn't you, and they both slept downstairs and Billy was so tall he lay on the sofa with his feet out the window and then he banged his head twice in the kitchen. You had to go out again for more bacon, they were scoffing so much.

Not smoked, if that's all right, Mrs O'Connell, Billy had called after you, on your way to Jonesey's. Gutsy bugger that he was. Well I warned you, didn't I? So there we are. There I am. What did Sis used to call us? The inseparables. Hardly true, because we had to go where we were told. Overnight sometimes. And once with an hour's notice up to Belfast. Drop everything. And everyone. And yes, maybe you'll be able to go downstairs soon. If you eat the grub, because it's good here, I know it is. Think of Billy, Mam, there at the table. Oh lovely, Mrs O'Connell, that was fantastic, that was just fantastic. Five pieces of yeast cake he had. And what did you say? Full as an egg, you must be, love. Yes, that's what you said. Full as an egg. And he was. So have something, Mam. It's better than these injections. Piece of Weetabix. Nice bit of scrambled egg. And I'll write, I swear. And I'll tell Sis where I am when everything's settled.

Donal looked around. It wasn't so bad. Okay, sharing had its downside, especially if the other person was a bit gaga as a few of them were. Talking to themselves. Talking to the dead. But there were pictures on the walls and a decent wardrobe and a view of the garden which, all right, you'd have thought they'd tidy up and make a decent place to sit in the summer. Could be lovely, and west facing too. Catch the sun. But it was all bramble. Well, as Sis said, it was better than The Zoo. Or The Graig, to give it its proper name. What was that story she'd told him? Some old codger had gone to the toilet and after about two hours they started to wonder where he was. But it was dinner time and some of the staff had popped out to The Ferret, and there were only temps and casuals on shift, doling out the mash and rice pudding. So they track the old man down to the lav and open the door and can't get a word out of him. He looks dead. He smells dead. So surely he is dead. But how do you really tell? So they get one of the cooks out of the kitchen and he comes along, and Sis says, this is God's truth, this cook shakes the old boy and gets no response. So the cook sticks a fork in his leg. A dinner fork off the dinner table. In his thigh because his trousers are down. And when there's still no response, this cook announces to all, yeah, that's it, the old bloke's copped it. Cold meat. Leave him here till the afters are served, then we'll call the doctor. And the cook goes back to the kitchen and puts the fork on the table as he passes.

Jesus, I said. But I had to laugh. And Sis was laughing too. The poor bastard. But think of Viv with a sniper's bullet in him and his head split like a pomegranate in a stinking Belfast lorry park. Think of that Mam. It's laugh or cry in this world.

Nia

Then he rang. That's so typical of Gil, coming out of the blue, always unexpected and talking to you after a month as if it was yesterday.

I was with Li in the reading room and Maudline was hovering and Li made a moony face so I went outside. It had been raining and the sun was setting and Cato Street was silvery and strange. As if I was dreaming. It was the colour of a fish that Donal showed us once. He'd hung it at the slipway like an old suit of armour with scratches along its iron sides. And about as big.

It was a dolphin, he said, and no, he hadn't caught it. The dolphin had been shot and he'd picked it up.

Shot? I remember dad asking. How do you shoot a dolphin? Why the hell? Why?

He was upset and mum had to take him away. I looked over my shoulder at it hanging there, tail up, its head like a helmet. A helm. An iron helm that narrowed to a point.

Down Cato Street I could hear the tide making that bass drum sound under the esp.

It's up, Gil said. Isn't that fantastic?

What's up, Doc? I heard myself saying. As if I was a comedian. As if I was somebody else who didn't feel what I was feeling. Like I was hiding in somebody else's language. Which, yes, is what I do, don't I? Seeing that nobody speaks my language any more.

The site, he said. It's been agony, but I think I've got it right. What with putting that up and the gigging and the rehearsing and bloody bloody school...

Thought you didn't rehearse, I said.

Well, what I mean is I'm never not working, am I? Because when you're a musician and a writer you're always thinking about it, thinking about it twenty-four seven and thought is work, squirrel, thought is work.

I thought you were quitting, I said.

Quitting what?

Wanking, I nearly said. Because I wanted to. There and then. You wanker, I wanted to say. Get off my phone. But I didn't.

Teaching of course.

Of course I'm quitting teaching. But at the right time. There's a rise coming next term too. It'll pay for the site. Look, you've got to log on. You have to see it.

I'm busy too, I said.

Yeah, but see it from this end. I want you to come here. Okay? Okay squirrel? Okay my little squirrely soul mate? Okay my little rarebitty, rabitty...

Soul Mates is a lonely hearts page in *The Guardian*, I said. For sad old gits. Amongst others.

Look, I'll pick you up.

And he named a time and I agreed. Just like that. Tough cookie, aren't I? Hard to win round. So Li and I went for a coffee in that Spanish place with David Beckham looking down our tops.

He lives with his mother, remember that, she said.

So? He's waiting for the right time to move. To give up school and do music full time.

Do you really care about him? she asked.

Listen Li, I said. Gil's interesting. He's at least interesting. There's not many like that. And he told me he's putting nearly fifteen hundred a month into this account he has. For his recording studio and web site and boom box and for just living off if the gigs dry up. Would you rather I hung round with Vinny's crowd, whining about double overheads and who pissed in whose wetsuit?

You have university to come, she said. And what's a boom box?

And we laughed like fools then because I didn't know either, something to do with amplification and all that, but Li was singing boom diddy boom diddy boom diddy boom, I don't know where she gets that stuff, and is it a sonic boom box she asked, or maybe a jack in the boom box, or is it a diddy diddy boom box diddy diddy, and she looked so good with her fantastic hair up and one of those big Chinese pins through it, and she had this killing red lipstick on and a cropped teeshirt, I couldn't believe it of Li, showing this tiny golden waist, such a snakey thing she is, and even Beckham over by the stairs seemed okay in his *Real* kit, much better than those horrible sunglasses he advertises, and you can bet your life he'd have wanted to kiss her, kiss Li then and there on her red mouth. Oh yeah. Working twenty-four seven, see. That's where it gets you.

But I went. The next day. And look, I take it back, the guy is fantastic. The set up he has at home is incredible. He picked me up so it didn't take long. Wow, the house is huge, you could see three storeys as we drove up the drive through the rhododendrons. And so dark inside as we went in. I was too scared to speak. Gil put on these lights but they made hardly any difference. All the hallway was wood panelled and there was a chandelier with these weak little bulbs, three of them not working. I noticed that. And there was this enormous hall stand like antlers with raincoats and overcoats and scarves and hats, which was pretty weird because it was good weather despite that shower. Who was there anyway to wear those coats?

Er, can I ask you to be quiet? he said.

I looked at him then. Fit, much fitter than dad, and no grey hair, none of that thickening that dad's got. That middle aged yoke. Bit of a gut on dad now. Beer in The Cat, chips up at Eddie's, all those takeaways on the front. Dad's the vindaloo king these days. But Gil's kept it together. Mum always goes on about Bryan Ferry and Roxy Music, and how gorgeous he is, how there couldn't possibly be a tribute band to Roxy because no-one could ever match Bryan Ferry. She showed me album covers and yes, I thought then in the hallway, Gil's a bit like Bryan Ferry. And yes, of course. Jesus. Mum must fancy him. Must fancy Gil. Getting pissed at the party like that because he wasn't paying attention. They go way back, all of them. Probably snogged, possibly more. But she doesn't know about any of this. Well, it would hardly help. It's my life. And she's bad enough with the sleepos, which don't even knock her out, just zombify her.

Only yesterday Li said such powerful pills are dangerous. Li's going to get mum some real medicine.

Hey, no rhino horn for Christ sake, I told her. No tiger cock.

We nearly pissed ourselves then. Death to pandas? That girl is velly velly naughty. And she's going places.

Why?

Shush, Gil whispered. You know. Mum.

Your mum?

Asleep. Shush.

I thought we were going upstairs. There was this huge banister with a wooden globe at the bottom. Somehow I thought Gil's studio would be in his bedroom. Which didn't faze me, no way. But we went through a door and along a passage and through another door into what must have been servants' quarters. Or a big larder and pantry.

Okay, we can talk now, he said. It's down here.

There was another flight of steps. We pushed through a third door sealed with felt. Gil put on the light.

That's when everything started to go red. A red glow was growing slowly through this long space.

Takes time, he said. Energy efficient. So efficient it costs next to nothing.

What I first noticed was a gong. At least I think it was a gong. It was a coppery colour and dimpled like a pub table and hung from a stand. Nearby was a quiver of drumsticks, most with furry heads. Beside it was a tray of champagne glasses, each glass with a different amount of liquid. Behind that was a bust on a pedestal, a marble bust of Johann Sebastian Bach. Respect, I thought.

What else? An acoustic guitar and one of those harmoniums you see in chapels, big decrepit wheezy antique with ivory knobs that said 'cello' and 'bass'. And screens, computer screens, and about five laptops and a desk full of winking green and red lights like the console of a plane. And that wasn't everything, because the room wasn't lit properly. Over in the shadows may have been a grand piano, and everywhere there were CDs and tapes and books scattered about and trays of food and winebottles and energy drinks. All that surprised me. It really did. Because until then I thought that Gil was fastidious. I mean well-groomed isn't the word for Gil. He looks blow-dried sometimes. His clothes are just immaculate. I nearly said exquisite but no, they're not perfect, if you know what I mean. That day in the John Webb he wore a Hawaiian-type shirt with red and cream whorls over these cream Chinos. On any one else that could have been a disaster yet it went well enough with the Stag and the food and the attitude. But the shirt had been carefully ironed. Painfully so, if you looked closely. I'm not sure about the sunglasses though, because the pub was well dark, and glasses indoors anywhere is pushing it. In the John Webb it was like, hey, here I am, fans.

Then Gil put this music on.

Listen to this, okay? he said. Listen carefully.

So I started listening. First of all it was Spanish guitar, then electronics.

Hmm, I said.

Now, he said, I want you to scream.

Scream?

Yes, scream over this for me. For this track.

What about your mother?

Oh she won't hear. This is a silent stage. The room's soundproofed. Eight thousand quid, that's what silence costs.

You want me to scream?

Eventually, he said.

Okay, I said. I'll scream for you.

Good, he said.

What's the track?

Oh, it hasn't got a title yet.

And then this bell rang. At least I think it was a bell, and Gil said damn, he had to go upstairs a minute, had to go upstairs. Would I be okay?

No problem.

Back in a jiff. Got to go upstairs.

Then he closed the soundproofed door.

So there I was in the red mist. With this music playing, pretty loud too and it was building to some kind of climax but falling back at the last moment so all you could hear was the guitar being strummed, and then the electronics coming in like the sound of arcades in the fair. Because yes, that's what it was. All the slots and video games squealing and the people clustering there, putting money down, and voices from The Kingdom and the House of Pain and crowds queuing to get on the Firewheel.

It's odd when you hear the fair out of context like that. Especially in a cellar under a mansion. It felt like I was a thousand feet down some shaft, or in the hollow part of the dunes where the springs rise. They say there's a cave system there, the limestone's like a honeycomb. You can get lost forever supposedly.

Boy, what a long track. Dad says *Desolation Row* is the longest decent song there is, but this was taking forever. This was Messien on a mission. After a while I started to wander about. The studio is a bunker, long and low, and there were doors to other rooms, but I didn't try those. And then I was back where I started and so I picked up one of the furry drumsticks. One of the gong-smiters and yes, I joined in. Bang a gong as Marc Bolan would say. Another of mum's heroes. Oh yes, I've seen her jiving round the front room invoking that kohl-eyed archangel. Oops, talking like dad now, but mum more than merry on half a bottle of Tân y Ddraig, cavorting with Marc Bolan in his top hat and electric blue skintights, gorgeous Marc, why'd you have to do that, Marc she'd be crying, you stupid darling, Marc, why d'you have to get in that car?

The electric guitar riff that starts up *Ride a White Swan*? I've danced to that with her myself, nobody can say they couldn't dance to a tune like that. So that's what I did. I danced. And I don't know if the recording tape was rolling or not but I started smoothing that gong very gently, ever so carefully and the sound was like crystal feathers. God, it made me shiver.

But time passed. When Gil didn't come back I started hitting that thing. Yeah, bang a gong, Marc. And I thought, Li, if you could see me now. I'm starving hungry, haven't had a drink for hours, I'm stuck in a dungeon with this creepy music which sounds suspiciously like the fair played backwards, yeah maybe it's that, and I'm knocking seven bells out of the Chinese national instrument. You'd be proud of me.

And that's all that happened. After a while Gil came down and said sorry, I'm sorry but something's come up.

Things are always coming up for Gil.

Your mother?

Well, yes.

She okay?

Yes, yes. But she heard us. You. She heard a different voice.

So?

So, look. I'll take you home, okay?

You don't want me to scream then?

No, he said. Well yes. But maybe not today so I'll take you home.

And that was it and here I am in the reading room and okay, crying a little. Because I've just seen dad. He came in behind me and put his hand on my shoulder.

Hey kid, he said. Got this for you.

And he lay this flower on the opened page. This pink flower, the flower he's been giving me for years. Centuary, it's called, he had brought centuary for me and he gave my shoulder a squeeze and I brushed him off and he tried to kiss my hair, bent over and tried to kiss me, but I turned away, and when I looked around he was gone.

But there was the flower. Dad had disappeared but his gift was there. Centuary's important to dad. One day he'll tell me why. And I closed the book on it, closed *Lucrece*, my copy, not the reading room's, so Maudline won't go spare.

And now I'm going. But I won't go home. Not yet. Mum's pissed. When I left the house she was playing the Stones, stuff like *Wild Horses* and *Angie*, so she'll be well out of it by now. I'll try Li first, God I hope she's home. I'll take her a present like dad brought me one. Yes, I'll take her a green stone and pretend it's jade, pretend it's treasure from The Caib. A prehistoric jewel a squirrel dug up but found for little rarebitty, rabitty me. And then I think I'll ask Li to teach me to scream.

The Fish

Got to be off soon because The Kingdom calls. But I thought I'd have an hour in the Nook. Just doodling, you understand, looking at the news, scanning sites.

Scary isn't it, the net? Like looking inside people's heads. Right into the clockwork that makes them tick. Every sad little tick and tock. Cyber life? It's a landfill where nothing ever rots down. Just layers upon layers of stuff that was brand new, hot gossip, cutting edge research. And then entropy. Law of the universe. But on the net entropy is speeded up. Oh yes, so these things become useless really quick. Or quaint. Or historical. Strange things those dead sites. Like deserted temples.

So this morning I thought, just for a change I'd go down to the reading room. That's in Cato Street. No, not been there yet? Surely you have. It's that little street running parallel to the promenade, but a dead end. Bottom end, which is the open end, is The Cato Hotel. Rough old place, closed now. They're hoping it'll be a wine bar or something. Apartments probably. Windows are boarded up but there's these old Guinness casks inside. And ropes. Lot of ships' rope in there as I remember. The bar's made from the stern of some boat.

And the top end of Cato Street is the Information Centre, tourism and whatever. Got a really nice little reading room with a fire in winter, a real fire, and the newspapers on those wooden spines so they don't get torn. Spindles? Spines? And reading desks too. You stand up at those desks. That old Maudline runs it. She buys the papers, lights the fire, everything.

So, yes, I fancied a change. Interesting to see the clientele too. That bloke with the money sewn into his coat, he was there. Old Spellman, using the photocopier. God knows why. And the Tibetan monk or whatever he is. Must be a Buddhist. In his orange robe, which was wrapped right round him. Looked like a bedsheet but comfy though, I had a good gander. He was at one of the tables reading *The Times*. Nice one, I thought. Sports section, too. Double nice one. Oh, and there was Nia. Vine's kid. Kid? She's filled out well, good figure. I've seen her there before in her school uniform. Apparently she's diligent. Off to university they say, making the great escape. Yes, well remember Steve McQueen is what I reply, Steve McQueen on that motorbike he pinches off the German soldier, then stuck under the barbed wire, captured and slung back in the stalag. The Great Escape? Not for everyone, darlinks.

Well there I was, going through the *Mail*, the *Telegraph*, but not *The Times* of course, due to our Buddhist friend's passion for zen and the art of table tennis, and I've a couple of books on local history up on the desk too, plus two or three magazines. And their OED. And their Latin dictionary. And she comes up behind me, old Maudline does. I never heard her. Made me jump. So old Maudline slips up behind and she whispers over my shoulder, 'Why now, I see you're a deep scholar'. And breath? Breath like a cat's. Because their teeth go bad, cats' teeth, that's why. All that Whiskas tinned abattoir sweepings. Rots the teeth and their breath stinks.

Why now, why not? I said. As I would. Because you get a lot of that with an arm like this. People think you're slow. Or damaged right through. It was as if she was surprised I was there at all. In the reading room and not the day centre next door. Not that I'm knocking it. Roast dinner, rhubarb and custard and a cuppa for two quid in the day centre. That's a bargain. If I ate stuff like that I might pop in. But food's irrelevant to me. I don't do food. Well, I like cucumber sandwiches. White and pale green. And tinned rice pudding, that Ambrosia. For breakfast, cold and white. And I like tea. I drink strong tea. And, seeing as I've started, what else do I like? I like biographies. I like maps. I like charts. I like dates and I like gravestones with names and dates cut into the stone, not stuck on in phoney gold, but cut deep. I like carpets too, with designs of flowers and towers. I like clockwork birds. Had one once, it went round and round on its perch. Mum bought it. And okay, I like waking up and not knowing who I am, that second, that minute when I can't remember anything. When it's all white. An all white empty room. And I like things that glow in the dark. My clock, the green light on the computer that never goes off, the crystal and the red panes in the Nook. Oh yeah, the eyes of my children.

What else do I like? The smell of pub carpets in the morning when George is opening up. The solitaries who come to The Kingdom. I look at them alone in their cars as they smack out through the doors, those kind of saloon doors we got there, painted black but scuffed white by the carriage bumpers, that's a job for off season, as they come out of the tunnel with the screaming ringing in their ears. I look at their eyes. I know exactly what they've seen. But what were they searching for?

You bet your life deep scholar. And how. Silly old bird's never been online, you can be sure of that. But a couple of clicks and she'd see it all. My biography of this place. Here.

Okay, I was in the reading room in Cato Street, which is part of the museum. Follow me now? I'd popped in to reacquaint myself with the extraordinary treasures of this coast. Because, yes, I tend to forget. There's that fossil there. Ram's horn they call it, two feet across, found by some teacher. Like a stone wheel. And oyster shells that were used as drinking cups, and bits of bone and what's left of that girl they discovered in the sand, a human sacrifice they say.

Which seems silly to me because there can't have been many of them in the first place. Those people. Up on the ridge there, eating oysters, murdering their women. There's a painting of how they think she looked. Good figure. Bit like Nia. Tattooed as well. Because the girl in the sand had tattoos and so has Nia.

Yes, surprised me too. I went behind her and she's got some design on her back. On that polished point of the coccyx just above her splendid arse. Pale as a clenched knuckle. It was some blue symbol. Or a name. Couldn't tell really but she was bent over the reading desk and I could see. Yeah, pleasant eyeful. And coincidence in the fact that the painter who painted that girl in the sand painted The Kingdom. The figures inside and the designs outside, like the hound and so forth. Local artist, see, we're helping the locals.

Rest of the stuff in the museum is all ships, which I like best. A ship's wheel that you can actually turn, a couple of compasses and all kinds of logs and inventories. Cargo lists. No order to it either, which is a bit off. It's all jumbled in together. Lot of wine, I'll tell you that. Boy, this has been a thirsty part of the world.

There's a cask of Madeira there, supposed to be full, but no-one wants to open it up and discover it's turned to mud. And this morning there was this bloody stuffed bird too, huge black thing, wings stretched out. Glass eyes, black and red. The cleaner had left her mop and bucket next to it, which tells you what kind of place the museum is. But hold on, I thought. Where did you come from? Don't remember you being here. We could have it in The Kingdom, a bird like that. With those evil eyes. Put an electric bulb in them and wow. Or get the wings to go up and down on a spring. You see, I'm planning all the time. Can't have people thinking that The Kingdom never changes. We're always open to new arrivals.

And all right, I know the question. It's been coming since the start of the week, hasn't it? The question you're dying to ask. What am I going to do when it finishes? Next week? And the week after that? What does The Fish do after the last night?

In a way you'd be right in thinking this town will go to sleep.

That it will subside quietly into its coma. But hold on a minute. Sleep? Some of the fairground people haven't slept for nearly six months. Not me so much, but it takes its toll. That's the season, six months, starting slowly and building, building. Some of the lads working here don't even have rooms. They just roll a sleeping bag under the rides or pitch a tent in the dunes. Up in the morning early for the maintenance check, then full on till as late as possible. We're supposed to stop in the dark but if the crowds are there you'd be stupid to turn money away. Then lock up, quick swill in the camp showers, clean teeshirt, and the boys are out spending their hard earned. Pizza in Pozzo's or grab a takeaway, hour in The Cat, might try The Ferret, then hit The Ritzy.

Yes, what a life. Pulling, fighting, kipping in The Kingdom or in the centrifuge of the Firewheel. It has been known. Off their heads most of the time too, acid being the substance of choice. Can't read or write, some of these boys, but they make a sound living. You see them at the bar flashing the twenties. And that's just the sharp end of the wedge. Some are bad news but I've got to know most of them over the years.

Take Wat. Didn't know his last name for years. A kind of senior figure but only late twenties. Or perhaps not. Perhaps mid thirties by now. Forty? Can't be, but time flies doesn't it? Yes, maybe forty. Wat must have been coming here since he was a kid, and as long as some people can remember. If they had a union Wat would be the shop steward. He's the one people deal with. Hal knows him of old, understands if Wat's happy so are the others. And Wat's usually happy. Because Wat's a man with simple tastes. He's one of those who don't rent rooms, who never take off their moneybelts, who's happy enough with a Rizla and Strongbow-and-black. Just don't look at him twice.

Met him in the Seagull Room once where he was having this gravy dinner. Scorching day too, hot as I can remember. Told me he thought he had five children. Might have been six. There he was out front under this parasol with his shirt off, stuffing himself with Yorkshires and onion gravy.

Hold on, he says, and he took this piece of a newspaper out of his jeans and asked me to read it to him. It was a story about some football game, under fourteens, in Dublin I think it was. Terror Watkin Hits Hat Trick, was the headline. Little Lonnie Watkin, wing wizard, helped himself to a… Yeah, you know the story. Must have been the highlight of his life, poor sod. Apart from screwing those underage tarts under the Firewheel after putting ten away down The Cat. Because, yes, they're magnets, the fairground lads. Girls can't get enough for some reason. All the fun of, all the excitement of… It's romance, honest, it's show business. Well, a shag in the sand. Doesn't do your faith in women much good though.

Since then Wat's got me to read all sorts of things to him. That summer when Ireland were in the World Cup, it was every day. Team news, injuries, he couldn't get enough. Might have been him, he said. Yeah, right, I thought. But you got to humour them, those boys. Short fuses, see, and dangerous. Hard as nails, with a uniform proclivity for the switchblade. And straight after the last week they vanish and just before we start again they turn up. Course, they got mobiles and everything which are always bloody ringing. But they're like animals really, pleasing themselves, doing what they've always done. Working with the seasons. Shitting where they like. They know some stories too. Oh yeah, those dirty bastards could tell some tales.

As for me, I'll take it good and slow. The Kingdom always needs painting after the last week but it's best to leave the outside till the winter's over. The wind strips everything bare here. It can take the enamel off your teeth. This salt air just eats iron. So that's a spring job. Course, if it's anything complicated we get that artist in. Mary Jane, I was telling you about her, she paints the murals in and out. But I'll do the basics inside. Few tins of gloss and take my time. Pressure's off see.

All right, it can be a bit weird because of the silence. After all the season's racket the silence is peculiar. Because it's only when it's quiet that you notice bits of metal banging in the wind. Or a door slamming when no door should be open. And especially all the groaning in the stanchions of the water chute and The Ziggurat. Jesus, that ought to go, The Zig. Should be condemned. Someone's going to cop it soon, surprised it hasn't happened this year. Yes, gradually you realise the whole place is creaking like crazy. It's bloody groaning like a ship on the reef. Every joint, every joist, every rusted sheet of steel or corrugated zinc on the perimeter wall. Place is a scrap yard. You realise that in the off time when there's no-one in but you and maybe Manners doing the books in the office. With Hal looking out the window. Okay, Manners is always there. And I mean always. But it's hardly a comforting thought. Cold fish in a grey suit. Money man is Manners, lines of figures, what's going out, coming in. Grown up and comfortable with Hal. Comfortable. Yeah, that's Nicholas Manners. But Hal's the only one I ever heard call him Nick.

See? You're getting it at last. Manners is the bloke who makes it work. You don't think Hal knows what's going on do you? Or much cares? Hal's your dilettante, your classic dabbler. Hal's an artist, see. No, don't scoff. He is, Hal's an artist. Hal's a romantic. He's curious about stuff. He's got this weird intelligence. But Manners? Not someone to trust. Not that I trust Hal either. Because basically I consider Hal mad as a toad. Mentally erratic. Unpredictable. You'd have to be stupid to trust Hal and I'm not stupid. But Manners is differently untrustworthy. And just now, well, he's extra specially untrustworthy. Came in The Cat last week, looking for Hal. Out of the blue that was. And boy, didn't Hal jump to attention. A couple of us clocked that. Noticed where the power really lay. Something's up, I'd say. Something big.

But until recently he seemed bored to me, did Manners. Still diligent but ready for the fond farewells. You can usually tell. Looking towards his pension? Oh undoubtedly. A life in retirement. Which will not be spent under the frost-buggered palms of The Caib, let me tell you. He's another of these types with property in Spain. Hard to credit, I grant you, Nick Manners on the old hacienda, hiding his bald head in one of those Aussie hats that are all the rage, pair of grey socks on his tootsies. Whew, there's something wrong with that scenario. Me, I just remember the golden rule: it's not where you end up but how you get there. Ending up is nothing. So, it gets creepy in the off. I usually get a carpenter in to look at the walls – they're only plywood after all. And I make sure the cars can run and the electricity's okay and I leave a note for myself to change the tapes. And sweep the sand of course. I come in once a week to sweep the sand away because it builds up. Too right it does, with the wind moving it round. My own private beach.

And that is pretty well that in the fair. But I did have this idea. I thought that Mary Jane might paint a suicide bomber. You know, with the whole rig, the backpack, the apparatus. Scary though, looming at you out of the darkness as you come round the corner and the carriage is bumping on the rail and the passageway gets narrower and the carriage slows and you go past the Wolfman and you go past the creature from *Alien* which Mary did this ace copy of, all dripping teeth and black and silver gloss, you're passing the Ripper and there's this space. Perfect I thought. Kind of a plinth with nothing on. It's where old Frankenstein's monster was, you know, bolt through the neck, diving boots. But he fell to bits. Got the mange. Monster mange. So, I thought, it's perfect. Bring it all up to date with the latest nutter. And you're not sure are you? You're not sure who the hell it is. And then it dawns. A suicide jockey. Yeah, it could work.

Of course the old man thinks I'm mental. Offensive, he says. It'll offend people. Don't you read the papers? he asks me.

Me? Read the papers? I'm more than current, Dad, I said. I'm ahead of the game. That's why it'll be a good draw. Christ, it's The Kingdom of the Damned I said to him. It's supposed to offend people. We got to keep up to date, I said. Even horror has to move with the times.

Offensive, he said again. In his white shoes, because he was going bowling. In his white flat cap. With his bowling balls in that box thing. God help him I thought. That bowls club. Afternoon of the living dead. So I put it to Hal and he just laughed like he always does and I mentioned it to Nick Manners who said it was hardly his department.

Department? This is a fairground. Yeah, why not stick Manners in there on that plinth? Counting the zeros up to oblivion. That's the most frightening thing we'd have. Apart from the bowls team. In their white caps.

So, who knows. But, you're right, it'll be quiet. And that suits me. Because I've still a little money left, from the bequest. Yes, let's call it the bequest. Greatest thing dad ever did and he did it for me. And maybe I've given you the wrong impression. Maybe you think I'm drinking myself into an early grave. Well remember what I said. Don't believe everything you hear on The Caib. Course I drink. But I'm not an alcoholic. Haven't got the yellows yet, have I. Christ no, I ration myself.

Tell you what put the wind up me, that book, *Rummies*, by Peter Benchley. Bloke who wrote *Jaws*. Described this alcoholic's last days. Her last minutes before the liver finally gives up and the blood haemorrhages. Like a chocolate fountain. So there's mayhem in the body, the cells going crazy because they don't know what to do. This young girl drowning in drink and the thousand trillion cells in her body screaming we don't want to die, you bastard. No more bloody vodka for you, lady.

Jesus, I nearly quit there and then. But okay, I like a drink. I like the change it makes in the chemistry. The chemistry of my head. I love that particular moment, the moment you feel the good it does before the moment it starts to do harm. So, evenings at The Cat, and a bit of a laugh upstairs at The Black Lite. And that'll be on a Tuesday because we'll go back to Tuesdays for The Black Lite, that's the night during off season. Just a few films, not many of them too dodgy. Don't need the sickos do we, don't want a weird scene up there.

Used to be stuff from Rotterdam or Soho but these days it's as much DIY as anything else. You know, downloads, shooting the missus with the digicam. People bring phones now, and the quality's getting better fast. So it's not pornography, is it? It can't be porn because porn is Greek for prostitute and most of the stuff we get is just recreational. Well that's what I'd say, your honour.

Though, to tell the truth we've had the odd contribution up there that's been a bit strange. Funny what people get off on isn't it? CCTV some of it. Jozz gets us that. What's to see? I asked her. That Rachel, apparently, on her last night. Last night before you know what. Coming out of The Ferret, that bloody dive. In a line for kebabs on Caib Street. And Christ, there's Clint behind her in the queue. We all had a laugh at that. Small town, see. Never know who you'll meet. Well it did nothing for me. You know those CCTV films, they're a funny light. A stone-coloured light. I'll say it again, what's to see?

But that's The Black Lite. Usually Hal sits there with his arms folded. Half the time he looks catatonic. George is the one though, Clint's dad. It's George who set it up. Odd one, George. Been in Hal's little circus for years. Friendly enough. Happy go lucky even. But questionable tastes, if you know what I mean. For a man that age. And you do, don't you? Know what I mean. Course you do. When a man gets to a certain age there's no way he can get away with stuff like that.

Listen now, if one of those girls on the films they bring, if one of those kids started reading a poem, mid performance say, George would change the film. What's this crap? he'd ask. But Hal? Hal wouldn't even notice. Hal would probably like it better, because he's always backed the idiosyncratic, has Hal. Always supported the underdog. As in Princess Karoona, of course. As in a couple of those Lithuanian ladies. Coral, say, with her furry glove. Yes, sometimes I think Hal's running a charity. Bloody hard to fathom is Hal.

Well, good talking to you. But all this doesn't look much of a life, does it? Rice pudding? Jesus, that's sad. The saddo with the funny arm. But it adds up. So in answer to your question about what I do when The Kingdom closes, I kind of retire to the Nook and compile my history of The Caib. The inventory of everything. A lifetime's task, clearly. Oh, and there's the tutoring. Ah ha, surprised are you? I'll bet. That's why I left it till last. Just a bit of English tuition see, for the local slackers and slumberers. Yes, me a teacher, just think. Not qualified you understand, but a teacher nonetheless. With a good reputation. Oh yes, darlinks, a very good reputation.

Donal

It was half five and the queue impressive. It started at the counter and crossed the floor, then went through the door into the street.

As always, said Donal. He wandered across to the glass-fronted display cabinet where some of the pails of batter were kept with cans of Fanta and Tango. Behind this were the vats. Three women were serving the takeaways, wrapping chips, gesturing at the lines of vinegar bottles and salt cellars for the customers to use themselves.

Got hands, haven't you? cackled the eldest, her hair in a green net. And don't use it all.

Those at the head of the line grinned.

Tell him, Gwlad, said a man in a mac.

Next, Gwladys shouted.

Karoona, hands in pockets, not knowing the protocols, stepped after Donal.

I'll get us a table, said Vine, coming in last. He turned to the right and went up the stairs, feet sticky on the cracked linoleum. At the top a woman paused and started again and paused. She looked at him longer than she needed to, Vine thought. As he finished climbing she hurried down. Yes, she had looked at him hard. Her face pale, as if the blood had been drawn quickly away. Her lips tight and scowling. Cod's mouth, he thought. Well screw her.

It was quieter upstairs in the restaurant but several of the tables were already taken. Luckily there was an empty one by the window, a table with a red plastic tablecloth and six stick-backed chairs set round it. Vine sat down and looked out. He could see the bowls green and the bowlers' pavilion, the clock golf course and the entrance to the rides. A few people were mooching about the hot dog van parked there. Outside The Lily the wooden tables were already taken by visitors, pints and Pepsis arriving on trays. Friday evening. It would be busy everywhere. Perhaps the busiest he would ever be at The Shed.

Apart from tomorrow, that was. The last night. The big night.

Id had already warned him to be in early, Id who was off to his Torremolinos time-share next week. Oh he had put a little bit away, had Id. Learned a few tricks, as he said. Those rainy days, boy, they're getting closer. Bad weather on the horizon. Exit strategy see, always have an exit strategy.

Strange, but he'd miss him. Yes, thought Vine, he'd miss the old bugger. Funny life. Id stayed in a flat in Vainquer Street when he was in town. Lived on his own. Never been talk of a wife, not a whisper. Vine thought of him in the sun. Crossing some scorched but newbuilt plaza to buy the *Daily Mail*, white dust already on those immaculate Clarks. Pint of creamflow in a Brit bar about noon. Afternoon nap, say two hours. Flicking the channels before ironing his shirt and going back out to a different drinking hole. Then meat and two veg. Maybe steak and chips. But a bit tough. A bit dry. Spanish see, can't do the gravy.

Look Id, Vine had once said, you should be writing your memoirs. You've seen it all, man, Kathy Kirby, Gerry and the Pacemakers.

Kathy? Id had huffed then. Loved her, boy, loved her. Once I had a secret love? Too right. And her hair was the blondest hair you've ever seen. And hairspray? Jesus, I was in the dressing room with her and it was like a bloody sea mist coming through the window. Only there was no window, like. I had to leave, get out quick. If you'd struck a match in there the whole place would have gone up. And lipstick? She smacked her lips at me and they were like two bloody pieces of gammon.

You see! Vine had laughed. Get it written. People want to know things like that.

Yeah, well, all in good time, Id had replied. When I'm properly retired. Which isn't yet. Oh no.

There was a gang of boys near the fair's entrance, throwing around a rugby ball. One might have been Brychan. Vine strained to see and willed the child to turn around. He didn't recognise his children's clothes now, and Brychan had grown astonishingly in the last six months.

Moody, thought Vine. But that was typical. Yet he worried about

Brychan. The good times with his son were gone. Maybe that was the hardest part of leaving. And not leaving. Because what might it mean to the kid to bump into his father in town? In front of his school friends? Vine hadn't done the decent thing and skeddadled. Hadn't swanned off with his fancy piece. Vine had stayed to torment his family. To shame his wife and mortify his children.

No, it wasn't Brychan. So when was the last time they had enjoyed each other's company? There was no doubt in Vine's mind. Late last year he had tracked down a DVD of a film he hadn't seen for forty years. He remembered *Jason and the Argonauts* from the old Tryon cinema in Caib Street. It had been closed for decades.

This you have to watch, he'd told Brychan, brandishing the disc. You'll love it. Aw, Dad, had been the response, but Vine had produced a Magnum each from the fridge and they'd shut the curtains on a winter afternoon and settled down. The others were over at Siân's mother's. Perfect.

And yes, Brychan had enjoyed it. Of course he'd respond to *Jason and the Argonauts*, thought Vine now. What boy wouldn't't? The journey into the unknown, the search, the quest. You'd have to be a dullard not to appreciate Jason. Or suffocated by your own cool.

Okay, Vine had said. It's a bit jerky. But these special effects are sheer genius. Bloke called Ray Harryhausen created them. Kind of stop-go animation and camera work.

Yes, Brychan had sat enthralled for most of the time, apart from the odd laugh at the argonauts who seemed to be dressed in nappies for part of the film. But the man of bronze was best, the living statue, one hundred feet high. Delos, Vine thought he was called. Jason disturbed the giant on his island, because that's what the argonauts did, travel from island to island, getting into trouble. The hundred foot statue held up the Argo and shook it like a money box. That Argo was often a wreck. Then the statue seemed about to wipe out the sailors. But Jason discovered a bronze manhole cover in the giant's heel. It was heavy as a bank vault's door, but he forced it open with his spear and the giant's blood ran out. Only it wasn't blood. It was a molten broth that poured like a torrent of new steel.

Surely it was ichor, the liquor of life. The liquid drained into the sand and the giant groaned and cracked like porcelain.

He's like you in the sea, Dad, Brychan had laughed. Can't move his feet!

And there lay the man of bronze. Broken on the beach.

Oh yes, that had been the best part. Ray Harryhausen's greatest moment. Or it was until the end of the film. But then the skeletons arrived.

Get ready for this, Vine had warned. Jason and two companions were marooned on another island. Then out of the ground had sprung the dead; skeletons with swords and spears. The argonauts couldn't defeat them, no matter how many they stabbed and clattered, no matter the skulls they sent spinning. In the end, Jason's companions were dead and Jason was forced to leap from a precipice into the sea to return to the ship. And that was where the film ended. The gods called time on events. Jason was spared death only because they wanted him to undergo further adventures. So it seemed like another Jason film would be made. But as far as Vine knew, that was it. Which was fine because *Jason and the Argonauts* could never be bettered, not with digital animation, not a billion dollar budget.

Whew! he'd said when the credits rolled.

No, the skeletons were best, shouted Brychan, brandishing the Magnum stick like a sword, and to Vine he had seemed a boy again, five years younger, glowing with excitement.

The walking statue was great, grinned his son, but the skeletons were scariest.

Yes, said Vine. It was kind of sex to the skeletons, wasn't it?

Sex? Brychan had shrieked, girlishly. How?

The skeletons were dead people. They wanted to make more dead people. To procreate. The way to do that was to go on a killing spree. To make more skeletons.

I liked it when they stood up out of their graves, said Brychan.

Couldn't be beaten, Vine had said. Too many of them, see. And they just kept on coming. That's why Jason had to jump. There was no other way out. You know what?

What?

We almost called you Jason.

No way.

Yes. Jase. What if we get a boat?

Boat?

And call it The Argo?

And yes, Brychan had liked the idea. But Vine had put it off. Delayed and forgotten and maybe it was too late now.

Donal came up then, and Karoona a little later after visiting the toilet. A teenage waitress arrived promptly with menus and Vine raised his hand.

Okay, leave this to me. It's simple.

Fire away, said Donal. Karoona said nothing.

Cod's off, said the girl. Can't get it now. It's extinct.

Jesus, said Donal.

Okay, laughed Vine. Hake three times, with Eddie's special batter. Chips three times. Big portions. Mushy peas all round. Bread and butter all round and the biggest pot of tea you have.

Laboriously the girl wrote it down.

Mugs or cups? she asked.

Mugs, said Donal.

Tomato sauce is on the table, said the waitress.

Haven't you got a proper squeezy tomato? asked Donal. One of those round red things. Not these sachets. What's this place coming to?

I'll have a look, said the girl.

Hope it's not extinct, grinned Donal.

She left them to it then and put their order on the dumb waiter and it was lowered down to the kitchen. Vine rubbed his hands.

Yes, he said, definitely peckish tonight.

Peckish? asked Karoona.

Hungry.

Yes, she said. But I am not hungry.

We'll eat yours, don't worry, laughed Donal. And he turned to Vine.

What's all this then? What's all this about bad dreams?

Dreams? repeated Vine.

Yeah. All these dreams you're having. Karoona here was telling me about it downstairs while I was showing her round this historic establishment.

Vine looked at Karoona and raised his eyebrows and shrugged. But then he coughed and they looked at him and he coughed again and took out his handkerchief while the others fidgeted and glanced outside at a man walking into The Lily with a white dog the size of a husky.

Couple of nights this week and last, as far as I can remember, said Vine.

John, hissed Karoona. You talk. You talk in your sleep. I hear you. From the other room.

Coughing? Talking? Dreaming? You must be shagged out, laughed Donal. He calls the bingo numbers does he?

He dreams a strange dream, said Karoona. And always the dream is the same.

We all dream, shrugged Donal. What's it about?

Well I suppose what's unusual, said Vine, is that I can remember this one. Because normally they vanish immediately. The trouble is, I'm not sure if I'm making bits of the dream up when I'm awake.

No comprende, said Donal.

You know. You think about something and you embellish it and it all gets added to. And anyway when I'm dreaming these things I know I'm half awake. Not properly asleep. It's always early in the morning. I can see light through the curtain, so I think it's about six. Seven. I can tell the time yet I know I'm not awake.

You got sleeping sickness, said Donal. Which is a true disease. You never get over it, I'm telling you. You're doomed, John, you're bloody doomed. And?

Well, said Vine, I suppose I'd say it's about a wreck.

A ship, hissed Karoona. It's always a ship. You said.

Yes, a ship, a shipwreck. A shipwreck out there on the reef.

Been enough of them, said Donal, examining a sachet of brown sauce. Hey up, here we are.

The waitress had collected the plates from the dumb waiter and now put them down before Karoona and Vine. Then she brought over Donal's plate with a large basket of buttered bread. Next came four white mugs, a brown earthenware teapot, a tartan thermos of hot water, a blue and white jug of milk. Last she brought the red squeezy tomato.

It was on the counter, she said triumphantly. Knew it was about somewhere. Cutlery and napkins on the table, give us a shout if you need anything.

Rad, said Donal. Bloody rad. And he picked up the squeezy and squirted tomato sauce over his chips.

Vine did the same.

What a colour scheme he said, pointing his fork at the peas.

What is that? asked Karoona eyeing her plate.

Peas. *Les Pois*, said Donal. Le Mushy. Talk French, don't you?

Yes. I speak French.

There you are then. Get stuck in. Can't beat Eddie's mushy peas. They are so…

Green? laughed Vine. I'll say. A venomous green. Psychedelic. Used to be record sleeves that colour. Something by Captain Beefheart, if I remember right.

Here, said Donal. And he started to squeeze sauce on to Karoona's plate.

No!

Yes. It's tradition. Compulsory. Now tuck in.

Karoona tried a chip.

Well?

Too many. And what is that? She prodded the battered fish.

Eddie's special, said Vine. He's had this recipe for batter for years. Family secret. Whole place is built on it.

Uses beer, added Donal. Though there's some say there's a splash of the hard stuff in there too. Whiskey.

Karoona grimaced.

And lemon, said Vine. And maybe samphire oil, which tastes of lemon.

Karoona regarded the fish. It resembled a large orange shoe.

And a drop of apple juice, smiled Vine.

Soy sauce, said Donal. Gravy browning.

Spring water. From the ⌐ ·nes.

Dolphin wee.

Cuttle ink.

So dig in, urged Donal, pouring his second mug of tea from the pot.

Vine was making a chip sandwich, the butter melting from the sides of his roll. Spot on, he spluttered.

Look, said Donal. And he cut into Karoona's fish for her. Now taste.

It's breaking, she said doubtfully. It's dry.

Don't complain or Eddie'll be up here. Takes offence easy, does Eddie. Anyway, John, you were saying?

Vine drank his tea.

This dream? It's nothing. Only... okay, there's a storm and a ship is wrecked. At least I think there's a storm. Or maybe not. Maybe the ship just runs aground. Doesn't know the reef's there, it's on the charts but not marked with a buoy. Or maybe the wreckers are out with the lanterns.

Another tradition, laughed Donal. Yeah, they say the women used to go down the beach at night and sing. Kind of a choir. The black choir they called it too. So any ships out there would come closer to shore.

And sometimes it's an old fashioned ship – you know, *Treasure Island*, Long John Silver type ship with cannons and rigging, and sometimes a modern one, some kind of pleasure steamer.

A lot of people dream of that one going down, grinned Donal.

But there's always a cargo, like barrels of wine. Sherry. Bolts of silk washing up, all streaming, all shot through with light, purple and blue, always purple and blue. Washing up and people on the shore taking it in. Unrolling it so it goes on for miles. It's like a harvest, this silk, and people are gathering up this blue silk out of the blue sea. As if they were picking up seawater. And people are rolling the barrels up the beach and putting them on carts or tying them behind horses, even though these people are in modern dress. Though sometimes they're naked. Stark naked on the beach, as if they had nothing. And they're dressing themselves in this silk. They're wrapping themselves up in this blue silk that's come out of the sea. And some of them are wrapped up tight. Like cocoons. And there's others getting merry. There's a party. It's good news, the wreck is great news because it's brought wealth. So the dream has a good feeling. But sometimes the dream has a terrible feeling. Because these bodies are washing up too. These drowned sailors and women and children. These drowned passengers, I can't tell where they were going. All I know is they weren't coming here. They weren't supposed to come here. But they've landed. They've been wrecked on the reef and here they are lying on the beach. Lying on the silk which is spread all over the rocks.

Good hake, said Donal. Nah, sorry. Then what?

Then nothing. That's it. Okay, these feelings that come from the dream. Like they're competitive. Good and bad feelings. Scared feelings, calm feelings. And what's weird is I can see myself dreaming these dreams. I'm half awake and the light is coming through the curtain and I see the light but I'm still dreaming. And by the end the silk isn't blue anymore. It's transparent. And so are these people washed ashore. You can see though them. Like dirty glass. Yes, you can see the other side through them. You can see the people vanishing.

The bread was finished. Donal had appropriated Karoona's peas and squeezed the sauce next to them.

You see, he said, I don't usually remember my dreams. And I'm sorry if you can't sleep or whatever. But, Christ, dreams are dreams. And as dreams go, they don't seem so bad. Not exactly nightmares are they?

Well I don't wake up screaming.

John talks, said Karoona. I don't understand that talk.

I thought the medication I'd been taking was the cause, said Vine.

Yeah. Side effects. There's always side effects. Look at those boys in the Gulf. Got the jab to end all jabs. Supposed to protect them from everything under the sun. Wiped them out it has. Bad hearts, panic attacks, you name it. I might have known some of them.

Doubt it, said Vine. You were before their time.

Yeah, okay. Hey love, you like the food here?

Karoona had managed to finish most of her chips.

You're not keen on the special armour plate round the fish then?

The fish? No. It's too much.

Local delicacy, beamed Donal. Okay, we know, we know. But when in Rome do the mushy. And this is mushy town.

Saturday

Vine

It was 8.30 am and Donal had made tea and toast and was spreading
his bread with supermarket own brand tomato sauce. Vine sat opposite
with his mobile to his ear. It was obviously Siân on the other end.

All right? he asked when Vine had finished. Bit early for a crisis.
Vine sighed.

Siân's always up early. Saturday's another big shop and she usually
wants it done by nine. Nine.

He sipped tea from his mug.

And there's a problem with some standing order. Electric. Letter's
just come. Oh, and Brychan's playing up. As was predicted I suppose. Nicking money out of her purse.

Par for the course. How old now?

Fifteen.

Jesus, when I was his age my mam had to hit me with a belt. Been
camping out all night we had, fags and flagons. I come home and she
gives me this awful clatsh on the leg with the buckle end. She went
spare. I think I cried.

And look at you now.

Yeah, did me good didn't it.

Turned you into an upright citizen.

I like to think so.

With high culinary standards.

Always liked a bit of sauce on the toast. Kind of crostini. How's
Karoona?

Asleep. Won't stir till eleven.

Vine sighed again.

I went in this morning about seven and looked at her and it was pretty dark, but Christ, she's so small. You'd think there was a cat in the bed. She tells me I snore when I'm not coughing and she's right. But she's completely silent. Hardly breathes. Most times I can't tell she's there at all. Only this time the guitar was on the bed with her. She had her arm round it.

How's the chest?

Saw this locum. I said just nuke it, just give me some horrible antibiotics to blast it away. Been going on too long.

Well, it's bronchitis, John, I told you. And pills don't do much against bronchitis. It takes time.

Funny kind of bronchitis.

Trust me.

Thanks, Doc.

So maybe we should forget the swim tonight?

No, said Vine. That's nothing to do with it. And it's the last chance isn't it. The weather's breaking next week and the tide's perfect.

Okay. I'll pull some driftwood together for the fire. Usual place? You know she's playing tonight?

Karoona?

At The Cat. Got the gig herself. Clint being kind again.

Donal laughed.

How much would you really care about that? he asked. I mean, if she and Clint or any other bugger were like, getting close?

Vine drank his tea and looked down the avenue through the caravan window.

You have to remember how strange it is for her here. And taking that into account, she's doing all right.

Yeah. She's brilliant at that. But you got to face up to the fact that she's going to fuck off when it suits her.

We get on okay.

Donal looked up and saw the space where the army picture used to be.

And I'm off too. Pretty soon.

Vine put down his mug.

Got a few options, like. A couple of people owe me favours.

Thought you were settling in, said Vine.

Nah. Too hard. Or it will be. Getting kind of impossible here. It's all change and as far as I'm concerned, not for the better.

There was a silence. Outside a man walked down the avenue with a bag for the wheelie bin. Somewhere it sounded as if a flute was being played.

Thought, yeah, maybe Andaluz again. Or there's this woman I know in Malta.

Nothing to do with the…

Say it, man, sighed Donal.

It's in the past, said Vine.

The dismissal? The dishonourable dismissal? Say it John, say dishonourable.

It doesn't mean…

It means plenty. It means dishonour. Dishonour, John. No pension with dishonour. No pay-off with dishonour. No honour with dishonour.

It was years ago…

But dishonour doesn't go away and there's not a day goes by when I don't remember it.

Donal stood up and put the kettle on again and sat down.

I'm facing up to it, he said. Because it's been crippling my life. Fucking me about. But you, John, you… you're in a dream.

How?

Like tomorrow? And the day after? It's end of season, John, remember. Got any plans?

Vine shrugged. Maybe, he said.

Go back to Siân. And the kids.

Yes. Easy as that.

You both got to go half way. You both got to trust each other.

Well maybe trust is something Siân was never very good at.

As if she didn't have reason. No, you've done your drifting. You showed us you could do it, dropping out and all that. You've had your season.

In hell.

Your choice, brother. And she's rung you up this morning which says a lot.

You don't know how angry she gets.

Course I do. She's torn strips off me enough times.

And jealous.

Jealous?

Possessive. She's always insinuated things.

You're no angel, John.

No. No angel.

Yes, well, I'll get those sticks collected. And bring a few bottles. And maybe get hold of some mackerel. See one of the boys about it. I'm not going out myself. Got this bloke coming along who might want to buy the boat.

Christ, man, that's a big step.

Got to be taken, John. Just like yours has.

Maybe I'm learning to live for the day.

Hey. I'm the master of that. And look at me. Get the electricity sorted out.

Outside the day was warming and the sky clearing from the west. Vine set off towards Avenue J but decided to take the long way round by the beach. Then he heard the sound again. Yes, it was a flute. He stood still and listened. They were high notes that came in a cascade. Vine thought he remembered the tune. Five caravans away he saw a woman on her doorstep. She was playing with the pages of the score fluttering on a stand. He noted she was wearing fluffy pink slippers. Apart from that she was naked. Vine came up slowly and passed her and saluted and the woman raised her face in acknowledgement and went on playing, the flute rising and falling, her right foot in the slipper tapping the step.

Beautiful day, he said.

Again she inclined her head, her grey hair in pigtails tied with two pink ribbons, and she smiled with her eyes and Vine smiled back and he drifted down the avenue to the sea wall and turned left.

Here lorry loads of broken bricks and hard core had been tipped to help shore up the defences. There were tyres and pieces of metal rail on the sandy bank and the rocks at the bottom were slippery with weed. Vine walked with the caravans on his left and after a while he came to a man who sat on a limestone boulder near the path. The man was juggling knives and Vine approached and watched him for a minute. The knives were throwing knives, curved kukris with brightly painted handles. Both the man's hands were bleeding.

Beautiful day, said Vine.

Oh yes, said the man, not stopping. Quite beautiful.

And Vine walked on and looked back once and the man was juggling still and the knives flashing like mirrors as the sun caught them in the air.

The Cat

He was sitting next to the door. It opened suddenly. People looked up to see who had entered. But there was no-one. Only a little sand blew in from the corridor and across the floor. Donal pushed the door shut.

Lol

Twilight he could take. The nights were more difficult. Behind him rose a tall white moon. He came out of the trees and the moon was a face that followed him through the willows. There would be darkness tonight but not the absolute darkness that confronted other walkers. There was no absolute darkness for Lol who understood how to wait until his eyes adapted to the night, and how long to wait until he could see in the dark.

The moon was special in the dunes. Its light was a dark oil that smeared grass and willow leaves. Moonlight in the dunes seemed to be a power that came out of the ground. It was a steely perspiration, a night sweat that oozed from skin and sap and sand. That's what Lol felt as he made his way through the trees. The moon was white again. Last month it had been red, a smokey pink. Climbing a crest one evening that smokey moon had appeared to him so suddenly it had stopped him dead.

A pheasant's eye, he had thought. A bowl of red sand. There was the moon, cratered and round and so close he might have reached out to touch its cold red fire. An enormous red moon on a prehistoric hill.

But that was last month. That had been the hunter's moon. This moon was higher and paler and followed him down a track that was no track to those who did not know their way. Going back would be more difficult, he knew. But that was later. There was no need now to think about later.

Vine

At The Shed Donna put on a CD. Madonna's *Lucky Star*, played loud. Id was pleased. There were fifty in for the first show of the night and nobody won very much. Even Norman Spellman, still in his mac with the moneybags pushed into the inside pockets he'd sewn himself, even Spellman was so far empty-handed. There he was now, mooching about, a stone of coins concealed about his person. Spellman looked grim. Only Vanno had claimed her usual tenner, which she kissed as Vine presented it to her.

All the sixes, eh Van?

That's it, love. You always know when your number's up. Keep my seat warm.

There would now be a break as a new crowd came in. Already

they were queuing outside. From behind the bar where he was serving, Idwal called out.

Good, John. You did well.

Didn't cough you mean?

And you're all ready for the big finish tonight. We'll be packed, boy. You haven't seen it full yet, have you?

Vine stood behind the bar with him and took an order for two gins with tonic plus an orange and soda.

Ice with these love?

The woman smirked.

Well, sorry, but we're out.

Melted have it? Just like me. And she winked.

Hey, you're learning, beamed Id, pulling creamflow. The big finish, eh? I liked the chat tonight. Even the poetry.

Give them something different.

Yeah but don't scare them. You never frighten the punters, remember. They're thin skinned enough about stuff like that. Don't want to think you're looking down on them.

Christ, Id, it's a quotation. And I'm not patronising anybody.

Id scratched round his collar. He was wearing one of his seventies shirts, big wings, pink nylon, under the smoking jacket.

Take it from me, boy. But you'll do. You'll bloody do. And it looks like we'll be here again.

Next season?

Well, there's no closure orders yet. So no news is good news.

Then Donna came back with a box of Britvics and the rush slowly subsided.

Look, said Id. I'll clean up all the mess. Sheets and stuff. You have a spell and rest that golden larynx. Piss off for half an hour and get ready for a full house for a full house.

The Fish

They paid and went in. After a while they came out again. Some giggled, some talked. Most were silent. The Fish gave them his chat while taking the money.

Oldest funfair left, my darlinks. None more venerable.

You what?

Ah, that's my venerable disease. Gift of the gab.

You're right there. Chopsy.

Watch out for Sutcliffe.

Who's that?

Yorkshire Ripper. I tell everyone that can't be a waxwork. That can't be a waxwork, I tell everyone. He's too real.

Oh yeah.

You ought to be here after hours. Dusting the psychos and hoovering between the vampires. That would make you think.

Thinking does my head in.

It's brandy with me.

Why's it called The Kingdom of the Damned then?

Because it's full of the worst things in the world.

You mean my old man's in there?

Is your old man the Demon King?

No. And he's not Zorba the fucking Greek either.

Two pounds each. Um, delicate question.

What's that, smartarse?

You're not virgins are you?

You what?

Because virgins are in demand in there. High demand. On account of all the sacrifices.

Do we look like virgins?

Which take place on the prehistoric altar.

Listen stumpy, do we look like virgins?

Pure as the driven slush.

How're we supposed to sit in a titchy car like that, Stumpy?

In these skirts?

Madam, that's between you and your seamstress. Just keep your knees together.

Is that nutter off Corrie in there? We like him.

The whole malevolent gang.

Two quid?

Last night special price.

Well what's that music playing in there?

That, ladies, is *Jack the Ripper*. Performed by Screaming Lord Sutch.

Kayleigh, hold my bag.

Vine

He walked through the caravans. Under the Welcome sign the neon was hissing on its grid. It shone blue in the twilight like an insectocutor. There was a crowd already in The Cat and they were still coming in. Clint stood behind the bar with his dad. Two girls were also serving.

What the hell are you doing here?

Vine pushed himself behind the counter and put his hand on Nia's wrist.

Working, she hissed, shaking him off. What's it look like?

Since…

Since tonight. Got to start somewhere and Kim's helping me out. She gestured at the other woman.

But it's rough, it's…

It's a job. It'll pay money. Remember money?

Nia turned to the till and made a mess of it. Clint corrected the error and looked at Vine. Then he turned back to the pumps.

And you're dressed like…

A barmaid. Yeah.

She was wearing powder which was not unusual. But the lipstick was. It was black. Her black crop top said 'Staff' on the back. That was new. Her combats were also unfamiliar. Vine recognised the DMs.

It could have been worse.

Or maybe it couldn't.

There was a death metal thrash playing. Everyone was shouting to be heard.

When my number's up, said Vanno in his head.

Jesus, Ni…

Kim got it me. She asked Clint.

But bar work?

It's tonight and tomorrow. Then weekends when Kim's back in college. If I suit.

Ni?

Look, I'm busy. Go away.

You're not old enough.

Of course I'm old enough. And she jammed a pint glass into the tray under the Carling pump and took a towel to wipe the bar and was suddenly talking to a girl her own age. Vine looked round. It was a young crowd tonight. Half the school was in. He'd forgotten that tradition. Last night, big night, with all the town kids around the fair. Shit.

In a corner behind a pillar, Donal was drinking pineapple juice. With a double vodka in it. He was in shorts and an ancient sweatshirt branded with a Greenpeace logo that was peeling away. At the same table sat a middle aged couple. Vine took the last place.

Yeah. I see her.

She's seventeen.

Old enough. You know that.

In this hole?

You left them, John. You pissed off. And yeah, okay, it was a surprise when Nia served me. We had a chat.

But she's not the type.

Donal smiled.

And who is? Look, she's getting six an hour for five hours plus tips. I'd do it.

You know the kind of chat you get over this bar.

Yeah. From dirty old men.

But this stinking place.

They won't have her upstairs, don't worry.

That Hal.

Yeah. That Hal.

They were sitting next to the door. It opened suddenly. People looked up to see who had entered. But there was no-one. Only a little sand blew in from the corridor. Donal pushed the door shut.

Karoona here yet? asked Vine.

Nah.

It's just three songs she told me.

Pity you'll be playing housey.

Might catch the end.

We still on for the swim?

Vine looked at the table.

What's in that glass?

Moscow tap water.

Vine picked it up and drained it.

Yeah, we're on. About twelve. When it's neither in nor out and neither up nor down.

Hal

The aeroplane bumped through the grass, gathering speed for take off. Behind it ran the mercenaries trying to catch up and escape. Some were firing over their shoulders. Others were making a stand so their comrades could escape. But one by one they climbed aboard as the plane rocked through the dust, one by one the wild geese were pulled into the hold to lie panting and bloody, one by one reaching safety until only a single man remained outside.

Richard Harris was running and the plane rolling faster. Behind

Richard Harris the African tribesmen were closing in. They were a tribe famous for killing their victims in exquisite ways. But Richard Harris was injured. He might have been shot. Richard Harris was limping in the dust and yet the aeroplane was so close he might still catch it if he could get up and run. But his enemies were drawing nearer. They were waving terrible knives. Richard Harris shouted to Richard Burton to take care of his son. To take care of…

Emile. Yes, Emile, breathed Hal. His son. His much loved son. Little Emile. Then Richard Harris implored Richard Burton to shoot him. Because the aeroplane was close to taking off now and Richard Harris could never catch up. Because the people behind him were getting closer and if they captured him they would ensure that he did not die even when he prayed for death. That he did not die. So what could Richard Burton do but shoot his friend? What could Alan Faulkner, who was really Richard Burton, do to save his soul mate from torture? He raised the gun.

He raised the gun. He fired. He fired the gun. He raised the gun. There was Richard Harris in the dust. Alan Faulkner raised the gun. He fired the gun. There was Richard Harris in the dust. Alan Faulkner who was really Richey fired the gun.

And Hal cried. Hal cried as he replayed the scene. Hal cried as he fired. As he fired the gun. There was Richard Burton who had killed his friend. With the tears running down his cheeks.

Emile, breathed Hal. For Emile. His son. And there at the end was Richey with Emile, explaining how brave Emile's father had been. What a hero that man was. But of course Richey couldn't let on. He couldn't tell Emile that he had killed his father. Or that his father had begged to die. That his father, tall and gaunt Richard Harris, had been terrified of the knives. The knives coming through the dust as the aeroplane drew away.

Genius, laughed Hal to himself. As the credits rolled again. As the Joan Armatrading song started up again, the theme tune. Classy piece that. What more can we do? Joan sang.

Yeah, what more? breathed Hal and reached for the Jura.

What more? asked George. Not a thing.

Not a fucking thing, said Hal. But Christ, this scene here. Coming up. Forward it on a bit, fast forward it. This bit now, this bit. Look, he's there, in the airport. Richey's in the airport. He's cold, he's tired, he's just off the plane. And he's sitting under the Rabies sign.

Yeah, genius, said George.

Under the Rabies sign. Say it again, George.

Say what?

Say the bit where it starts. In that accent.

Okay, said George. And stood up.

An Evan Lloyd Production of an Andrew V. MacLagan film. *The Wild Geese.*

Beautiful, beamed Hal. *The Wild Geese.* And what else does he say? What does Richey say?

An ineradicable flaw, said George. An unspeakable hotel.

Yeah, said Hal. Genius. An ineradicable flaw. An unspeakable hotel. And he's there for Emile. At the end he's there for Richard Harris's kid. For the boy. Emile.

Yeah, said George. What more can we do?

Oh that's right, said Hal. That's so right. Under the Rabies sign. An ineradicable flaw all right. Alan Faulkner's the part, but Richey it is. It's Richey. Too true, son. What more can we do?

Nia

Nia poured Donal another vodka.

You're not supposed to, you know, she said. So don't lose track.

Of all the things I'm not supposed to do? I lost track of those years ago. Let's see, there was...

Well you haven't got far to go. Have you?

Donal looked at her and smiled.

No. Not far.

Donal?

Nia?

Will you give something to my father for me?

Course.

Nia took an envelope from a pocket of her combats.

It's his. Or it's for him. It's addressed to him.

Yes.

I think he was looking for it.

Oh?

You know.

Yeah. I know.

Donal

When Donal returned to his seat the couple had gone. Two men sat in their places.

He took a sip and the three men glanced at each other.

On tonight, is it? asked the elder of the pair.

Donal stared at them but they wouldn't hold his gaze. The man who had spoken was Donal's age. He wore a black leather jacket and black trousers. His head was shaved. The other could have been his son. Again black leather over a black teeshirt. His hair was thin and green.

Seen you here before, haven't I? said Donal.

The green one giggled. He was drinking Coke.

The music had stopped. Clint's father, George, was clapping his hands. Someone in the corner was tuning a guitar.

Maybe.

The older man raised his bottle to his lips then set it down untasted.

And maybe we've seen you.

Siân

The Dorrs were on at The Ritzy and the doors were closed. Sell out. But a good atmosphere and no trouble. There was never any trouble on the last night. That's what people said. Siân and her two friends were at the far end of one of the twenty tables, immediately under the stage. If they reached up they could have touched the blond organist, the Ray Manzarek character doing the organ piece from *Light My Fire*. And if you looked away, yes, it could have been Manzarek himself, his solo note perfect, but with additions too, improvisations around the riff, the Doors' Hammond organ sound filling the old gin palace of The Ritzy, the notes become neon themselves, shooting, winking like the lights that were flashing in the dance floor, red, green, the lights in glass set under their feet.

The two bouncers at the entrance were rugby club boys, enjoying being wired up. They told each other jokes, smiled at the crowds wandering between the fair and the caravans. The Megablitz and the Firewheel were illuminated like dance floor lights against the night sky, both going round half full, the girls screaming, the kids with eyes tight shut, their parents enduring the pain of the fall as they started another descent and the town with its glow began to vanish, as the badlands beyond the fairground vanished, as did the darkness of the sea.

The Fish

The last night was the big night but it wasn't like it used to be. That's what they said in the queue going into The Shed. That's what The Fish said as he waited for custom, watching the kids come screaming out of The Kingdom. Whether they were frightened or not, the kids were screaming now. Because that's what they did. That's how they played their part.

Nia

Vinny was out with a gang of ten or twelve school friends. They sat at one of the big tables which was covered with Red Bull cans and Pils bottles. When Nia came over to clear up they all cheered. A blond boy grabbed her and she sat on his lap. Nia stroked his hair.

You surf, don't you, butt?

Donal looked up. Vinny was talking to him. A kid from the West End calling him *butt*. *Butt*? *Butty*? A kid who didn't understand the currency of language but who was trying to make the words his own. Yes words were a currency. Sometimes you kept them, sometimes you gave them away.

Always done a bit, smiled Donal.

Longboarder, that's you.

In my time.

Yeah. Longboarder. Mr Santa Cruz.

Wouldn't that be nice.

Respect, said Vinny.

Respect? smiled Donal.

Yeah. There's statues to longboarders over there. Real statues. Yeah, Mr Santa Cruz, that's you. Mr California. Respect.

Bring it on.

I been there, said Vinny.

Where's that?

California.

Oh aye?

Went down on the Amtrak, on the Surfrider train. All the way down from Santa Barbara down to LA.

LA?

Los Angeles. All the way down past the Ventura highway, with the sea about five yards away. Big blue swell. Saw it all.

Must have been great.

Fucking ace is what it was.

Vinny finished off a bottle with a red foil top. A girl was sitting in his lap, tanned and tattooed.

You live on the site don't you?

Caravan site? That's right.

Yeah. I see you. Walking up the beach towards the site.

After a swim, said Donal.

Yeah. I see you. I see you all over, Mr Santa Cruz.

I've seen you too.

Yeah? In the paper might have been. Front page it was.

The tattooed girl was licking Vinny's face.

Maybe, said Donal. Might have been somewhere else though. He emptied his glass. Give me time. It'll come to me.

Siân

On its last night The Ritzy held two hundred souls. Siân sipped her Bacardi Breezer from the bottle and toasted her two friends who laughed back and waved their own bottles in salute, two girls from the choir, two girls who knew when music was sacred and when music was profane, and tonight they were three together who understood the righteousness of music played with heart, played with soul, and if the first wasn't on offer tonight the second definitely was.

But maybe both were. Because when Siân looked up she knew it wasn't Ray Manzarek. How could it be? Not the real Ray. But he was some fantastic player, this boy, this prodigy, this bent and skinny middle aged throwback sitting down to weave that solo, sitting down for God's sake, and who could tell if that white fringe was a wig or his own hair, but he was swinging it, God he was swinging that fringe, but she could still see his face in the light and yes he looked old in that white and merciless beam, like someone caught escaping from somewhere, poor boy he had paid his dues, poor boy with his bad dentures, his watering eyes, but here he was at The Ritzy on the last night and Jim was letting him have his head, letting Ray have this moment, his moment of soul, of heart, because Jim would be back, Jim would be back with *Alabama Song*, Jim would return with *The End*, and just when you thought Jim and Ray and the other three, because The Dorrs were a five piece, just when you were convinced they were done for, when the crowds were sure there could be no other encore, well Ray would start it all over again with the intro to *Light My Fire*.

We can show them, screamed Siân at her mates. We can show them how to party.

Then there he was again. There was Jim Morrison. Jim in his leathers. Jim Morrison writhing like a snake. Scratching his wrinkled crotch.

Vine

It was nearly time to be back at The Shed. Vine took the short cut through the arcade. Last night and it was full. Not that the arcades ever knew a last night. When the fair was shuttered and locked the arcades stayed open. He looked at the gamblers, their faces taut in concentration. Outside the tide was going out and ten yards of beach were already exposed. Figures were moving in the dusk over the sands. He strained to see. They were there in bad weather. They had been there in the dusk of Millennium Eve. He smiled because he liked those people with their metal detectors, sweeping the sand where only minutes before the waves had jostled under the floodlights.

What might he call them if he called them anything at all? Searchers, seekers, fools? But they were not fools. They recognised their territory and had adapted their lives to fit. He knew them all, he had once thought, but now that was untrue. Because he was the odd one out. He was the one who had not made his life fit the shape it needed to fit. The territory of sand. The seekers on the beach were always men and always solitary. They listened to the sand as blackbirds listened to a lawn, patrolling the beach at their own speed, the sea racing away from them and smelling of olives, the sky a ruin. The sea racing towards them covering their tracks. And he knew enough about them to understand he should never ask what they were looking for. Not that they could ever answer. Yes, he knew them well enough to know their search was a form of prayer.

Vanno

Vanno was in the arcade. He looked at her skinny shoulders as she bent down to scoop a jackpot of ten pences from the chute. He looked at the orange peel of her backside, the blue vertebrae.

Golden touch, said Vine.

Some buggers have got it, she said, not looking up. And some buggers haven't. Simple as that.

Don't miss the show.

Don't worry Johnny. We'll be there.

And she turned and laughed at him from her red mouth, her eyes thyroidal. We'll all be there.

Vine hadn't moved two paces before another woman stopped him.

You know every night in here we lose money. But then we think to ourselves, everyone loses money in this arcade. Even her. And she nodded at Vanno. There's no-one winning, Mr Vine. It's the playing, see.

He knew the face. The woman came down on the bus every night. She usually brought her daughter, the daughter who now crouched behind her. Pretty girl, Vine had always thought. Despite that strawberry mark. Or maybe because of it. And that's as far as he wanted to think. The mother, say forty. The daughter eighteen. Playing together in the arcade.

He watched the girl now, feeling the older woman edge closer. She was using three machines at once, baling out coins and pushing the coins away from her, getting rid of money as if it was a curse in her life, ignoring the victories as silver coins gushed back into the room and clattered into the sumps under the machines.

Yes, thought Vine. She was getting rid of it, getting broke, getting down to the simplicities, getting purified. Getting born.

My Molly, said the mother proudly. Though we all call her Moll.

Yes, said Vine. Moll.

And Moll looked up with her hand in front of her face and laughed and returned to her work.

Lol

Even in the biggest arcade it was near closing time. Lol looked at the machines. Monte Carlo or Matrix? He chose the Matrix and fed it a coin. Nothing happened. The last night. The big night. It had always been a carnival night for Lol. He and his sister had usually walked around.

Choc ice or candyfloss? That's what Sis had usually asked, and for Lol it was candyfloss, for tradition's sake, and maybe a drink at one of the bars with the bar girl puzzling over the schooner of sweet sherry for Sis.

And for Sis at the fair the choc ice of course. In its silver paper and that tiny chocolate triangle in the corner of her mouth. But Sis didn't come out so often now. Maybe a Sunday roast at The Sea View. Where they used to do good Yorkshires. Perhaps an aperitif on a July evening outside on the lawn. Once in a blue moon. They used to have musicians there. A harpist, he recalled, as if from another life. The notes like the sunlight itself, he remembered her saying. But they hadn't played for a while. And Sis would never go there again, Lol knew that.

How quickly time passed, he thought. Even when he sat in the willows alone, a Bach harpsichord concerto on his iPod. Even when he listened at the well where the first people had made their camp. And yes, this was the last year for all of that. This was the time to quit.

Because it wasn't the same. Children on motorbikes, being taught by their fathers. Couples screwing. Or seeming to. Right out in the open like that pair a few months back. The girl with her ridiculous hair. And they'd argued, the couple. The boy had stormed off and the girl had sat on an anthill, a velvety green tump that was one of the special places. One of the ancient places. How she'd cried. And her trousers still undone.

He put another coin in the Matrix and examined the machine. It flashed and gasped but no money gushed out. Down the line he was watching a family. The man was red and bursting under a streetmarket CK singlet, his sunrash livid as chilli peppers.

Must have been on holiday, Lol thought. Been where they all go. The weights machine had filled the man out, but what hair he might have possessed had vanished after a Number One, its bristle like a smudge of newsprint. Lol knew the man was bored by the arcade. He knew he was not a gambler. Unlike the woman. She was besotted. An arcade demon shone from her eyes and forced her right thumb against the slots.

But because the man was with the woman the man played too, passing her the plastic money bags, each one emptied in less than a minute and dropped at her feet. Occasionally the man took a swig from a foil-necked bottle and that's when Lol could read his tattoo. The needlework on his left bicep bulged out the woman's name. *Dani.*

Strange name, Dani. But they were all strange names now. Moz and Maz and Mozza and Mazza. Dav and Gav and Jozza and Gazza. No-one remembered Colman or Cewydd. No-one called their sons Tudwg anymore. Which was their loss.

Because names conveyed power, just as names revealed the parents' idiocy. There was power out there that no-one connected with anymore. People had lost the means of reaching it.

The woman was brown. The man was red but the woman was brown. Yet tonight Lol saw she wore the gambler's pallor. He looked at her jaw. How deliberate she was. Truly obsessional. But her belly was dark beneath the croptop, a tiny golden serpent piercing her navel. A rush of coins rattled the shute but the woman did not vary her routine and it was the man who knelt to gather the bounty in two huge hands, the man who laughed for his family's good fortune which was already disappearing into the slots up the line.

On the steamtrain in the corner their son rode around the world. He was shorn like his father, head yellow as an apricot, a darker scalplock braided behind, the little rat-tail twisted with a scarlet thread.

Lol thought of the mother instructing the hairdresser. Maybe tying the thread herself. A mother's love. In the child's right ear was a star. On his forearm a transfer. His mother had fed the train in fifties and as one journey finished another began, taking the boy past the Eiffel Tower and the Taj Mahal, bringing him home through the African sands.

The Cat

The door opened. People looked up to see who had entered. But there was no-one. Only a little sand blew in from the corridor. Once again Donal pushed the door shut.

Lol

Lol looked across the beach at the retreating sea. But it still swept against the breakwater, climbing the wall every thirty seconds, a black escalator that left a ghost of itself behind on the stone.

Maybe, Lol thought, the boy also looked at the sea, and saw the ghosts. If so, he would have thought it strange but no stranger than The Kingdom where he had cried when the siren started and the faces crowded into the darkness that he had filled with the skin and the smell of his father.

On Lol's left was an older woman and a youth in Juventus black and white. The woman owned a driftwood face and Lol thought of the grey, salt-cured implacability of the spars on the tideline. He thought of his camp, littered with the knuckles and femurs of such anonymous wood, but this arcade denizen was made of driftwood, a driftwood idol come to life.

How quickly her careful coins were vanishing. Soon she was drifting away.

The cocklegirl walked through, stiff-backed with her tray of crabsticks and cones of winkles. The family bars were emptying, the final assault on the machines was about to be made by the spent-out, the spent-up, the first come and the last served, and fifty yards distant the sea was a pit where neon figures waved and drowned. Someone had thrown a litter bin into the waves. Tomorrow it would be returned, though a thousand years might not make their mark within that book of tides.

Karoona

Vine had taken money and mobile but left his cards. At the dressing table she sat and looked at them, one by one in the broken plastic wallet. Wine club, out of date. Petrol station bonus card, but Siân had the car. Supermarket loyalty card. Credit card, out of date. School identity card. Library card. Another loyalty card. And there it was at the back. Current credit card, the red one with gold writing. She slipped it out and put the wallet back in the drawer and combed her hair and put on her coat.

Clint was looking at her from the doorway.

Okay, said Karoona. Be careful with those.

He picked up the guitar in one hand and the amp in the other.

Not exactly Pink Floyd, are you?

Pardon?

Forget it. But it's hardly rock and roll.

Karoona looked at him. Clint was smiling his usual smile. The belt on his jeans was fastened with a snake's head.

Rock and roll? Hal was good to pay for them. But I chose.

Oh yeah. Hal's good all right.

But why is he so good?

He wants to hear you sing. His little blackbird he calls you.

I could sing *Blackbird*, she said. By the Beatles. My father liked that song. But I won't. I'm going to sing my songs tonight.

Clint put the amplifier in the back of his Mazda.

Could have carried it there, he said. The amp was a Park G10R, a black cube with controls. The black box, as Vine called it. The black box that told the story of what happens.

Karoona curled up in the front seat.

What time? she asked.

About nine. But be there early. I'll buy you a lemonade.

Of course.

He looked at her.

Nervous?

No.

No, you don't get nervous, do you?

He put his hand on her thigh. You've loads of time.

Karoona closed her eyes.

I've things to do.

Off out again? called the man down the avenue. He and his wife were sitting in their garden.

Karoona might have waved. But it was an imperceptible gesture. She could smell that smell again. Ah, she knew what it was now. John asked her and she couldn't say. But that was it. It was the smell of the market. It was the smell of all that.

She could see her mother pouring water on to the earth and her father striking her mother. She could smell the evening perfume of her mother's tobacco flowers.

Or perhaps she was wrong. Perhaps it was Clint she could smell. Perhaps it was the car that smelled of Clint. The spray in his hair and the oil on his skin.

Then he drove off with such force she heard the gravel spurt against the side of the caravan.

Lol

And some more please.

Like this? asked the man.

And a bit more.

Phew. You like your onions.

And just a bit extra.

The man scattered more fried onions on Lol's hot dog and passed it in its napkin to Lol who covered it in tomato sauce from the squeezy bottle on the aluminium counter of the trailer.

Yes, you really do, he said.

Lol looked at the hot dog in his hand.

I just had this craving. Had it for days. Onions. Fried onions. The smell of onions. Just everything.

That's one fifty.

Lol passed him the change.

I think I know you, said the man. Yes, I do.

Lol bit into the bread.

You're Mr Williams aren't you? Used to teach us Geography.

Lol's cheeks were stuffed, there was tomato sauce on his chin. He nodded vigorously.

Still teaching?

Lol shook his head.

The man looked at him.

You took us on an expedition once, I remember that. We were looking for fossils. Remember?

Lol's eyes were wide. His mouth was full of fried onions. The taste of the Frankfurter was better than Soberano. It was better than smoke. It was impossible to say how good it was. He nodded.

And we found that big wheel-thing in the rocks. With the spokes. Or we thought we'd found it but you knew it was there all along. Didn't you? You knew it was there.

Mm.

That fossil?

Yes, said Lol.

Well that's where I take my kids too, said the hot dog man. We go careful down the track and walk to the cave. And just like you showed us, there it is. Above the mouth of the cave. Like a big wheel in the rock. Only you'd never notice it. Not in a million years. Not unless someone was showing you like you showed us.

Ammonite, spluttered Lol. Or cephalopod, to be precise.

Yeah, I take the little girl on my shoulders. The boy always runs ahead. Going to see the wheel, he says. And I tell them what you said. About the snakes? About how people used to think those fossils were snakes that had been turned to stone?

Yes, well…

I tell my kids that story. Thanks for that Mr Williams.

Thank you, said Lol. That's a great hot dog.

Hey, Mr Williams. Remember Sparky? Sparky Jones.

His mouth was full again.

Copped it didn't he. Last year. But he was there, he was on that expedition too. And I'm Gareth. Gareth Bowen.

Lol swallowed.

Good to see you Gareth. I think I'll have another one.

Karoona

She waited in the queue at the cash machine, Vine's card in her trouser leg pocket, his pin number in her head. It was an easy one and he'd given it her himself.

But that was John, she thought. That was what he was. So open about certain things. Childlike and sweet and good.

I'll try and get over for the set, he'd said. But it's touch and go.

Don't worry.

But I want to see you. Not there especially but I want to see you sing in public.

She had looked at him in his bingo clothes. He didn't wash his shirts often enough but that was nothing to do with her.

Bingo? It was hardly Sudoku. The first time Karoona had visited The Shed she had stayed fifteen minutes. There were thirty people waiting for John to stop coughing.

People were streaming into Main Street. The Ritzy was filling up, the family saloons doing well with tables set outside. Pozzo's Pizzeria and The UFO both had last night special offers. The music blew over her and disappeared and returned and was replaced by another song. Then the first song swirled back on the wind.

One night in heaven, pleaded the singer. One night.

A man with a megaphone was shouting about his famous curry sauce.

The cocklegirl floated through the dusk. Business was very good. Or that's what Llew said. The girl had been back to the van to refill the tray twice already.

Just wait till chucking out time, smiled Llew, doling the crabsticks from the chiller. Everything up a quid, remember. It'll be mayhem. Might even get out there myself.

The cocklegirl said nothing. The scarf around her head was midnight blue. Upon it were the moon and stars.

There were ten people in front of Karoona at the hole in the wall and ten people behind.

Save some for us, they were shouting at the back.

You're buying then? called a tipsy woman at the rear.

Everyone seemed to know one another. They were in it together, weren't they? They were going to the same place. Tentpeg was near the front. Clint had told her Tentpeg's real name was Tim.

And on certain other things John was a bastard. But he was a man of fifty. What did she expect? Where she came from a man that age was old. But John was a boy. Uncertain and afraid. A man that age should understand what was coming next. But John, she guessed, knew nothing. He had his secrets, yes, because all men of fifty had their secrets.

Karoona had replaced the blue wallet in the drawer amongst his socks. He didn't have enough socks either. They were worn out, and some pairs not matched. But that was not her concern. That was where he stored the CDs. That was where he kept his letters and photographs. In an unlocked drawer. As if he wanted her to look at them.

Yes, like a boy. A boy who had found his girl and was telling everyone about it. There she was, laughing, pouting. His girl. His girl on stage in school, his girl with sand on her belly, his girl with men and guitars and a microphone, laughing, drunk.

Always the girls drunk. Didn't they understand? They could not inhabit themselves properly if they were like that. It was men who drank. Some men. Her father held the pot above his head. For women, drink put the soul in chains. Bacardi Breezers, the bottles of wine that turned their teeth black and their tongues black and their necks crimson. With shame. Yes, scarlet women. She knew those words. Then the pot exploded in earth and splinters. There lay the pale tree of the roots. And the smell astounding all around them, the tobacco smell rising from the petals he was treading into the path.

Karoona was fifth from the front now. In a window she watched the chickens turning on the spits.

Donal

He walked through the door marked 'toilets' and went down the corridor. The door at the end said 'private' but he opened that and walked up the stairs. There was another corridor at the top and another door at the end. He opened it.

A walk on the wildside is it? asked Clint. Welcome to The Black Lite.

Hal around? asked Donal.

What's the problem?

Need to talk to him.

What's the problem?

Van.

Come in.

Donal stepped in.

It was a big room with a darkened bar. Its red flock wallpaper bubbled in patches over the damp. There was no power for the pumps so only bottled beer was available. At the far end was a television, a digital projector and a screen on a stand. Around them were gathered about twenty stained and broken-backed chairs. The usual types were milling about. Walter, the accountant Nick, the abattoir boy, the little boozer with the withered arm, some of the faces he'd seen in the pub below. A man who worked in the newsagent's looked up and gave Donal a grin.

He joined Hal at the bar. Two other men backed away.

I need more time, said Donal.

Time?

The van. I can't pay you yet.

Hal was tall in his black Crombie. But not taller than Donal.

So you mean money? You were talking about time. But you mean money.

Okay, money. I can't pay you yet.

No, said Hal. You mean time.

He looked at Donal in his khaki shorts, his faded sweatshirt, his sandals.

Yeah. You mean time. You see, that's what we all run out of first. It's never the money. We never run out of money. It's always, and I mean always, time.

Give me a job.

Job?

Delivering. Picking up. The boat's okay now. Give me some work.

Hal put his hand on the bar, ringed and spattered from ancient spillages. He was holding a teacup.

No jobs. No, there's no jobs now.

No jobs?

No fucking jobs, hissed Hal.

But there's thousands out there who want to come. Millions.

And absolutely nothing to do with me. That's over. All over. I got other plans.

Clint stood there then. Clint with his smile.

Yeah, he smiled. It's over.

Hal sipped his tea.

The Fish edged up.

Ready? he asked.

Yeah, said Clint, looking around. Let's do this thing.

Staying Donal?

With this crowd of weird fuckers?

Hal placed his cup on the counter.

Weird? Where else you going to see such a cross-section? Down below? I don't think so. The Sea View? Hardly. All we're doing is letting people share their enthusiasms. It's fantastic. You know that. Phones, computers, the global democracy. Even I don't know what we're going to see tonight. But I can guess. It's DIYville now. Share and show.

CCTV, smirked the Fish. It's incredible what you can do with those cameras. Digicams. Tapes. DVDs.

And the last time, said Clint. For a while.

Yes, said Hal. The last time here. We've done it on The Bona and done it here. Didn't you know?

He gestured at the room.

These weird fuckers know. Everyone knows. But you were downstairs, Donal. We all saw you. So you felt it didn't you?

Felt what?

You understand, sneered Hal. So don't play me for a fool. It. You could feel it. It. And no, there's no more jobs. No jobbies. Not a single jobby. I want the quarter's money by the end of the month. Or you quit.

It'll clean me out, said Donal. Right out. And it's nothing to you. I thought we were square on that.

Sayonara, said The Fish.

Clint looked around.

All right, he said. Lock the door.

Not me tonight, said Hal. Let them get on with it.

Lol

Well… if you can't beat them, he thought, as he entered The Cat. The place was heaving, mostly it seemed with kids. But there were bikers and groups of older men and a table of women who must have been in their fifties.

The term 'carousing' came to him. What a word. You'd think it was French, but no, he remembered, it was German. *Gar aus*. Right out. Out of it.

Good luck, ladies, he thought. Because tomorrow we die. And he didn't look so bad, he knew. Lol's army parka was an inoffensive green. It's camouflage after all, he said, and noted he was talking to himself. And resolved to stop. But he did it, he did it often now. Everybody did it as they grew older. As they went crazier. As they understood more of the nonsense.

Anyway, he'd shaved and washed in the spring. His hair was cut, he'd done it himself in his fragment of mirror. He wasn't hungry now. And a pint would be perfect, yes ale in a mug, some seaweedy tasting bitter, dark and brackish.

In his coat was a plastic bottle filled with Vine's Soberano. Beer with a brandy chaser. Their mingling skins against his throat, their colour the colour of the spring as it emerged from the pit and formed the pool and flowed into the dunes. The spring that had brought the first people to that place. Yes, a powerful drink. An elixir some might say. And here it was now in the glass. Paler than he'd hoped. Dune grasses. The beach with the setting sun upon it, the light a ruddy lake spreading from the south, the sun beneath the southern horizon and the rock pools filled with wine.

But the taste satisfactory. That willow bark taste of beer. Earth in it and piss and blood. The furious saps of May. Fox shit maybe. The salt in sea-soaked sand. Yes, most satisfactory.

Exorbitant price but it would have to do and the girl brought his change and he removed himself to a corner where he could drink and observe and consider. Oh yes, they were carousing. And the climax some way off. What care they had given to their appearances. How bravely they accosted the younger men who passed the table, how fearless their challenges. With their throats sparkling, their breasts gladiatorial.

Always the same, thought Lol. But these tides were coming in and going out in seconds. A pub was like that. One of the places where he sometimes sat was known as the Rocan. He climbed that great stone and considered the river that flowed beneath. The Rocan stood up from the river bank and announced the river mouth. It was physics he supposed. But something more than that. Where saltwater met sweetwater and how those waters mingled. Beer and brandy. He slipped the plastic back into his pocket. How much of the river was salt and how far the fresh water penetrated. He had led his classes to that very rock and posed the questions. And occasionally the answers had been good.

Does the freshwater flow over the saltwater, sir, because saltwater is heavier?

Ah, an interesting proposition, Jones.

Allwit had been the headmaster then. Silly old duffer, but he had encouraged the visits. Or the expeditions as Mr Gareth Bowen had described them. Lol had put mustard on his second hot dog. So the beer was necessary. Maybe a second pint.

Can't complain, the boy, the man, the man Bowen, Gareth Bowen had shrugged, when Lol asked how he was. It was good to know he had prepared young Bowen so well for life. But at least he appreciated time. Because fossils told the real time.

Truthfully, his classes should not have strayed into geology. But how could you not? Once even his bottom set had stood on that beach outside this pub door and he had talked of the movement of sand.

Contrary to opinion, there is nothing duplicitous in sand, he had boomed over the gale. The girls held their coats over their heads. It always knows where it is going. It is our job to understand why it moves.

Yes, sometimes the answers had made him think, and so the Rocan had become an important place. One of his special places. How often he had sat there and gazed west at the town, deserted and aflame. He took another subversive sip and looked around. Ten minutes earlier he had seen a man with green hair enter the door marked 'toilets'. That man had not come out. Lol smiled. Yes, the tides. He himself was clean and careful as a cat. He buried his stool. He never left a trace.

Karoona

Why did some of them call it a tent? It wasn't a tent. There it was and that was no tent. It was a hut. It was a shed. But it wasn't a tent.

People were streaming past and looking at the sign and slowing down and smiling and stopping and looking again. Then they would walk away.

Karoona paused at the side of the arcade. Above her the Firewheel was going round, its riders holding on to the rails of that burning globe, the two boys who controlled it bare-chested although the summer was spent, their skins black, their arms and backs covered with demons, with birds of paradise, both of them smoking, both thin as sticks.

Part of the tribe, she thought. The tribe that worked the rides. Or the shows as John called them. The earth tilted beneath their feet, horses reared, dragons roared, but the boys were always sure. Of themselves. And of what they did and why they did it. Above them the flames leapt, but they controlled the fire, the boys who never rode because they had already ridden, had already filled themselves with the panorama from the top of the town, seen the beach and the sea and what lay beyond the horizon.

C'mon, love, c'mon, one called to her now. Last night. Last chance. C'mon love.

Two women came out of the hut and closed the door. Karoona looked around. Shirley Bassey was singing. Such a voice, it filled the fair before the breeze took hold and it vanished into the site, into the sand that blew over the badlands, Shirley who had nothing, Shirley, who had no-one, her voice climbing the Firewheel and spinning with its neon and its no-one and its nothing and one of the boys imploring her, his hands and his body on fire, his skin made from mirrors in that spinning midnight, and Shirley who adored him flying back from the dunes, her song swimming through the conflagration of the air.

Karoona knocked and there was no answer and she knocked again and a voice said come in and she opened the door and there was Madam Zeena in a wicker chair at a tiny table.

Lol

The last night and it was dry. He knew the celebrations would continue for hours. Lol walked east along the beach, up the slipway to the lifeguards' station then down the next slipway on to another beach. There was starlight visible away from the fair but he was watching his feet as he crossed an area of flat stones streamered with weed.

Maybe the boots had given him away in the pub. They were Army & Navy Stores metal-tipped oil-resistant Gripfasts. Nothing unusual there except these were bleached white with saltwater. He hadn't cleaned them for a week. Normally, Lol took pleasure in rubbing linseed oil into the leather then smearing in the dubbin and buffing with black polish. That tin of Kiwi had lasted well. He imagined a kiwi in the sand. Hopeless case, of course. Like an ungainly water rail.

Lol had once watched a pair of rails for three hours. Rails were the most circumspect of birds, shy and pernickety. But the seawater permeated the polish and turned his boots grey. Boots were essentials. Boots and the parka with its double hood and detachable lining and countless pockets. Its devious zipcraft.

Sis had bought it for him two years previously, replacing a similar coat. When Lol hung it on a branch it became part of the willow. But he loved his boots. He'd sit in the clearing with the buckthorn blue around him and take the burrs off the bootlaces and the bracken sprigs out of the eyelets. And he would tap the toes to test the metal.

Yes, a man needed steelies in the rocks. He'd tap again. There was a pair of green woodpeckers that came to his part of the dunes. Sometimes he'd hear them exploring the trunk of one of the pine trees that grew out of the thorns. When he tapped they occasionally tapped back. Or so he liked to think. They would not nest there but he listened to their research. Woodpeckers were good guard dogs. They scarpered, shrieking, if disturbed. The pheasants too helped him. The males were especially stupid birds. But they barked louder than corgis when approached or exploded into the air like burst cushions.

Karoona

Sit down, said the woman.

Oh, said Karoona.

Sit down, please. This is no place to stand. Sit down and let me look at you.

Karoona sat in the second wicker chair. The arms were frayed and sharp. She sat with her knees together and her elbows against her sides.

Let me see your right palm, please.

Karoona hesitated, then offered her hand.

You seemed surprised, said the woman.

Yes.

Why?

I thought you were older.

Maybe I am. Older.

No. Very old. I thought you were very old.

Oh no.

And, I've seen you before. I've seen you around here. But I didn't know that, that you were the...

The fortune teller. Yes.

The woman held her hand but she was looking into Karoona's eyes.

You have a strong face, she said. And smiled. Maybe you are a little older too. Older than you look.

Then she studied the hand.

Long fingers, said Madam Zeena. Fine fingers. You must play music, I know you must.

Yes, but...

Don't worry, said the woman, who wore a single ring, whose hair was a dark bushel, whose eyes seemed filled with gold sparks.

Do you have money?

Yes, said Karoona.

Good, said the woman. I can tell you everything you want to know.

The Cat

George clapped his hands and clapped his hands and said ladies and gentlemen please but no-one paid him any heed whatsoever even when the microphone whistled.

Karoona stood behind him with her guitar – small, and powerful the Tanglewood Autumn Leaf, plugged into the Park, turned up to four.

She struck a chord, an A, and some people looked round and then Hal stood in front of the microphone and was telling them to desist, to be quiet, to shuthefuckup because the blackbird was going to sing her songs, Karoona, yes here's Karoona at The Catriona, always the best at The Cat, always the first, and you all know Karoona and if you don't know Karoona you soon will and the mic whistled again and Nia poured away the tray of slops and Donal scratched himself through his shorts.

Then Karoona opened her throat and sang. She sang in English, her own song, and her voice was big in that room, groundglass in a honeypot, that was her voice, deeper than they expected that dangerous voice, and then she had finished and people were clapping although if you had asked them what she had sung about they could not have said.

But they looked at the skin of her and the hair of her and the gold and black top and the black skirt she wore and they were polite.

Donal glanced around for Vine. He couldn't see him.

Behind the bar Clint was whispering to Nia.

Hal had vanished.

Half way through the second song the crowd was talking again but at the end of the third some people clapped and then everybody applauded apart from the bikers at their table in the annexe. One or two people cheered. And yes, there was Hal once again, Hal with his arm round Karoona's shoulders, smiling at her, laughing with her, his lips briefly upon her mouth.

You know how to get there? he asked.

Of course, she said. The taxi's booked.

Siân

Yes! Siân shouted. Yes, yes, yes!

She banged down her empty glass.

One of her friends was dancing on the table.

The music was louder. Maybe it was unbearable. But there was Jim in his leathers, Jim Morrison in his black leathers playing with the zip of his leather trousers, teasing it down and pulling it up as Ray Manzarek urged him on with his Hammond chords, Ray Manzarek biliously pale with white skin behind his white fringe, skin bleached like driftwood, a driftwood man without sap and without blood but if anyone was controlling the crowd it was Ray with his chords as the bassist repeated his three notes and the drummer kept the thunder rolling and the guitarist created an undergrowth of rhythm and the men and women danced between the tables with chicken and chips abandoned, Strongbow spilled and bitter lay in pools on the fag-butted floor and yes Jim Morrison had been arrested in Florida for exposing himself on stage, thirty, forty years before, and if you were a fan of The Doors you might say that was when it all started to go wrong, at least in public because it had been going wrong in private for a long time but Siân was screaming at The Dorrs for Jim to take down that zip how could that be wrong oh how could it and what was he waiting for what was he waiting for behind the microphone which he was using like a whip and then the music had stopped although nobody could tell it had stopped because everyone's ears were ringing but stopped like a knife in the guts it had and Siân was still shouting Jim what are you waiting for but her friend on the tabletop was standing stock still and everyone was silent for an infinitesimal moment as they always were at the climax as Jim held the black cosh of the microphone between his leather legs and Jim, Jim called Siân. I've danced on your grave.

Lol

There was a crowd at the bar and calls of 'Come on love' and 'We're dying of thirst here'. He looked at his glass and stayed put.

How did they stand the crush? Lol was backed into a corner. The sweat stood out on his forehead. Perhaps he should have taken off the parka but that was impossible. Anyway, it was panic not heat. He closed his eyes and breathed deeply. Time to go. The last night for the last time and yes it was very nearly time.

Last orders please! The landlord should be shouting but that voice would not be heard. The man who should be controlling things wasn't there. So the crowd went on drinking. It was pouring oblivion into itself and yet it refused to die. And so many of them now. They were still coming in.

Lol held the glass against his brow. He couldn't tell how deep the water was. The water was cold and black and it should have come to his thighs. But the water had reached his waist and still his bare feet could feel the ground slip away. He had taken off his boots. His boots were in his left hand, his clothes wrapped in his right. The fool he was. He had taken his boots off, the boots that knew the way. Yes, he had been drinking. Under a full moon he had lain on a crest and smelt the sulphurous stones he pulled out of the sand, felt the corals snap into dust between his fingers.

His bottle was empty. The last drop hung on its lip. Lol licked it off. And the quick way back was through the slacks, the seasonal lakes fed by the spring. In a week he'd be home, in his old bed, his old room. Yet he had stripped naked and waded in. The slacks were never more three feet deep. Yes it was cold but he didn't feel it. The moon shone like the bottle he had emptied and yes, he was mad, he was moon-mad that night.

But the water was black. The sky immense. Up to his chest and still his feet told him that there was deeper to follow and when it had reached his neck he was a worried man, yes he had started to panic then. Very slowly he stretched out his right foot. Six inches, that's all he dared. How black the water. A mangrove under the moon. But at last the ground was rising. He had reached the deepest part of the pit. From there on he could climb. And he came out, the water running off him like streaks of a silver crayon, he came out naked with his balls shrivelled like the winter's black damsons, the hairs on his chest in silver filaments and Oh Christ, he looked down and there was no cock at all, where in God's name was it?

But who cared? He didn't care as he struggled up the bank, a merman, an unchronicled darkman of the dunes, sexless and strange, a pale slug he might have been, a great white hermaphrodite at midnight ashiver, the tarn behind with a crease in its darkness and then nothing at all to indicate the road he had come.

Vine

He felt the cough climbing out of his chest and into his throat and filling his mouth. Which was where he kept it for a moment. Until it relented. Until the cough backed down. How like a flower it was, climbing on its stem, a red flower tonight with tiny thorns.

Some days he thought it was poisonous. Sometimes he imagined its seeds in his bones and his veins. And then it had disappeared and he tossed the ball into the air, the white plastic ball that the current had pushed into his hand, the table tennis ball with a number stamped upon it, tossed it up and caught it.

I was angry with my friend, I told my wrath and my wrath did end. Five and one, fifty one.

Behind the bar Id looked up.

Down a bit! called a woman at the front. Give us some thirties.

Up a bit, cackled Vanno.

Keep it down love.

He took the next ball.

I was angry with my foe but I told it not and my wrath did grow.

One and eight, sweet eighteen.

Id pulled at the whiskers in his ear. He looked at Donna.

Never trust a teacher, he breathed.

Donna squeezed out a rag.

Specially English teachers.

He's different, she smiled. I'll give him that.

Lol

He had climbed off the beach and on to the site and waited in the queue for chips. Everyone was boisterous and no-one paid him attention even with his parka zipped to the neck and his hood up. There were so many kids with hoods now. So many hoodies, their eyes unseeable, their heads bowed as if they were thinking, as if they considered one of the great problems, a strange noviciate they seemed to him, brutal in their monasticism.

At the counter he had looked at the white plastic vinegar squeezer. Lol remembered the dimpled glass bulbs they used to have there. The salt rattled on the paper.

Wrapped, he said, and went out. But the chips were good. Chunky chips, all different shapes, not those pipe cleaner things, hand cut chips darker on the sharp sides and paler on the flat. With the oil fresh in that ominous vat.

Lol had peered into the fryer as an old man with chip-oiled hair emptied a bucket of fresh-cut chips into the fat. Lol thought he knew him. Hadn't he worked there for years, worked there all his life that skinny little dwt, all his life with smears on his glasses and hair combed flat? Born on The Caib. A native son. Yes, the ancient race could still make chips.

It was Eddie. Fast Eddie? No, that was the snooker player in the film. Italian Eddie, that's who it was. He had walked with Eddie to school. They had mooched through town and loitered at the sweetshop on Jenny Road, looking at the gobstoppers. A penny each? It seemed incredible. Then they would suck them furiously and take them out and compare colours, the greens, the yellows, and put them back in their mouths and talk and make no sense, so big were those sweets.

Planets they called them. Mine's like Saturn's rings. Mine is Mercury. And Eddie, little Italian Eddie had been working in a chip shop even then. At seven or eight he was peeling spuds. But in the first shop. His family had kept the place behind the seafront. Now they had two, maybe three. And Eddie owned them. With fruit machines and televisions so you could watch while you queued. Yes, they had walked on, spluttering about space travel, cheeks enormous, going to school the roundabout way where the rock pools were and the open air swimming baths that the sea swilled out and once filled with tiny starfish that the policeman swept up with a broom he borrowed from The Sea View.

But Eddie had not seen Lol. He had watched his potatoes slither into the fat, then trudged back to the kitchen while the girls served. Little Italian Eddie with his huge gumboil. Born on The Caib.

A couple were arguing on the slipway, a drunk dragging himself home. After the last van he saw firelight on the beach. In the darkness of the dunes shone another pinpoint. One hawthorn berry. It didn't worry Lol. That fire was a long way from his bivouac. A mile in the other direction Hal's house, The Copper, was illuminated as usual.

Yes tomorrow he would begin striking camp. Have to get Vine or someone organised to help bring out the heavier items. But what were they? The pots, the primus. Everything else would go back to where it came from. The driftwood and ropes to the beach, willow poles to the willow wood, zinc sheeting to the gravel beds.

Or would they? Perhaps he'd have a fire, a last almighty fire and purify the site of himself. He was too old for this now. He'd done his time and served out his shame. He'd seen them once and that was enough, seen the first family, the fair household. The keepers he called them. The keepers were still there and would be there always. The boys on their speedway bikes, the riding school girls so polite under their helmets, they didn't have a clue. They didn't know where they were. Or care.

How often had he stared at the stars through the willow leaves and shivered at the thought. Lol in the prehistoric night. No, it was never loneliness he felt. It was not his singularity. It was that awareness of their presence around him. The woman had looked right through him, the man had stared into his eyes and seen what he needed to see. Seen that Lol understood. That he was one of them, a keeper, someone who was aware of the storm before it arrived.

Yes he had shivered in his sleeping bag. Shivered until the voices in the headphones resumed their canticle. Such music. Sometimes it thundered and yet the owl heard nothing, two yards above his bed. Lol slept under the honeysuckle, under the bryony, their poisons in a garland around his camp. And if Lol shivered it was not from cold or isolation but knowledge of what he had glimpsed.

The little girl with her gullwing. How slowly she had raised it in salute. Her father, the magician, had put a spell on him, on Lol that day wandering alone, thinking of how salt water mixed with fresh, and how it was important, how it was the most crucial thought he had ever owned, Lol lolloping the dunes, geography teacher with a decent MA, cumbersome Lol with a thorn in his sock who had looked up and seen the past and his own future bound together on the crest. And as they had faded away, vanishing before him he knew they had entered his soul. The spirits of that place, grievous and implacable.

There was a taste of Soberano left in the plastic bottle and he sucked it out. He ate the last chips on the tray, scrabbling round for fragments of batter then crumpling the polystyrene in his fist and bundling it up with the paper in a parka pocket. Not a sign. Because he must never leave a trace.

Of course, that's where the girl went. What could be clearer. They had had their revenge and now she was forever one of them. Lol looked at the fire on the beach, The Copper on its hill. She was with the keepers now, her face an oystershell, her skin the mosses on a willow root, that starry moss where sometimes he drank at dawn, his tongue against its tiny hairs, Lol down on all fours with maybe even his throat against the ground, that grass brimful and his thirst so great, lapping at the dew.

Donal

Donal had done most of the work. There was a Mega Minimart plastic bagful of driftwood kindling weighed down with a pebble in one of the buckthorn bushes and a pile of buckthorn sticks and some larger spars, that had previously been used in bonfires, scattered together in the usual spot.

He and Vine had walked half a mile along the beach-head moraine, keeping the dunes on their left. Already there was firelight out in the further darkness, a red spot beyond where they were setting up camp.

How'd it go then?

Bit of a riot, said Vine.

Same all over on the last night.

Bloody Ma Baker shouting the odds as usual. And that Spellman character, well I don't know what happened there.

Old money bags?

Yes. Some of those bags must have burst because when he gets up all these pound coins roll over the floor and he's crying out and down on his knees and of course the others know him of old and they're picking them up and pocketing and the old boy's crying, real tears mind, he's weeping with it all, so we have to hold the session until he stops accusing people of stealing. Which they were.

Less of the old boy, said Donal. I was in school with Spellman.

They were telling me he lives on tinned spuds and mushy peas, said Vine.

At most.

Donal laughed and shivered into the Greenpeace sweatshirt.

You know I seriously thought of going round his place and robbing the useless bastard. When he's up The Shed with you. He's rolling in it. Probably doesn't have a clue how much he's got, either. And it's obviously stashed around the house. You can imagine the places. Behind pictures, under his verminous underwear.

And you'd probably have got away with it, said Vine.

Sure. But it's too late now.

Why? He'll just go up town next week to the Palace.

Well. It's a thought.

Yes. Definitely a thought, said Vine.

The two had been there for thirty minutes when they heard voices and they waited and listened and after a while three Lithuanian girls appeared with Clint and Clint's dog and Tentpeg and everybody said hello.

Don't mind do you? smiled Clint.

Lucky I gathered a lot in, said Donal.

We brought plenty too, said Tentpeg. Drink, I mean.

I can see.

The girls were merry already and were singing together in low voices. They'd been in town for six months, working in old peoples' homes and helping out in the fair and at Mega.

Knew you'd be here, like, said Clint.

Tradition, said Donal. Wouldn't miss. And he started to lay the kindling in the ring of pebbles he'd made and to press balls of newspaper into the salty wood.

You have to see this, Clint said to the girls, who were already sitting down, sharing a bottle. The moonlight was blue on the sand around them and lay in embrasures on the water. The tide had been coming in for an hour.

Master at work, isn't he?

Donal broke more of the tinder, pale as bone, into the smallest possible pieces. He had a matchbox full of touchwood made from dried sea holly and thumbed his lighter in the shelter between the ground and his body and applied the flame and held it to a wisp of the paper which curled and silvered and another piece caught and then another and soon the smallest driftwood twigs thinner than a baby's fingers were starting to catch and the flame from these was red and then blue and more of the driftwood darkened and caught and the smoke rose and Donal pocketed his lighter and sat back on his haunches and complained of being bastard stiff.

The girls cheered. They passed Donal the bottle which he didn't look at before tasting, rinsing the liquor round his mouth.

Ych, he winced.

The girls screamed, delighted.

What's this?

Bajoru, laughed one. We brought it back.

I can feel the enamel coming off my teeth. What's left of them.

Hey, said Clint. See Karoona?

John Vine looked at him.

Not so bad at all.

I saw her, said Donal.

Vine

Vine was looking at the face of one of the Lithuanians. She was stretched out on his coat and drinking from a stubby of Belgian beer and her skin was pale as one of the evening primroses that stood in flower over the dunes.

My village. It is near Kaunas, she said seriously.

Oh yes.

You know Kaunas?

No.

There is an airport there now. Cheap flights. Lots of Kaunas people come.

Mm. I've seen you in the internet café, he said.

Oh yes, she laughed. Seen me?

Yes. I've noticed you.

So now we meet, she said.

I'm glad, said Vine.

Yes. We go online in the café. It is very cheap. We email our friends about how horrible you are over here.

I thought you might.

No. I joke. You will see that I am always joking. We tell our friends to come because there is work here.

Then she smiled at him and took another swig and offered the bottle and Vine accepted it.

Cleaning up, she said. We are always cleaning up. And then she laughed.

You know, in Kaunas, we have the Devil.

Devil?

The Devil has his own museum in Kaunas.

The Devil has a museum? Well, that is interesting.

Yes. His vodka glass is there. A big glass with the Devil's fingerprints burned into it.

She took the bottle back.

And his book. His big book.

Does the Devil have a book?

Of course. With all the names in it.

She winked at him there beside the bonfire out of the smoke of her face.

Maybe your name is in this book, I think.

Oh, I'm sure of that, said Vine. Dead sure.

Donal was cooking the mackerel in silver paper which helped to turn the fire blue. The driftwood burned quickly and Tentpeg had dragged a branch up the beach and placed it over a boulder and jumped on it and broken it in two and had done the same to these halves so there were four more useful pieces to burn.

If you got plenty of fish it's best to dig a pit and build the fire over it, explained Donal. But there's not time for that.

Take it easy, said Clint. We got all night. And he kissed the tallest of the Lithuanian girls who lay beside him on his coat in the sand

and she squealed and pulled away and pretended to spit at him and then kissed him on the mouth.

Hey, laughed Clint. This is Olga. She's very bad. Everybody say hello to Olga.

And everybody did and Olga sat up holding her beer and blinking in the firelight with the shadows of the flames upon her face and said no no she was not so bad. When she had settled back Vine could see the firelight reflected in her throat. It was catching the clasp of her black bra strap.

The girls were racing round the fire. Then they were dancing. There were other people round the fire now and they were laughing and drinking, their faces swimming out of the dark and out of the smoke, and Donal offered Vine a scorched silver parcel of mackerel and opened it for him and rubbed some of the samphire he'd picked earlier between thumb and forefinger and sprinkled it over the charred fish.

Past its best, he said. There's some old rhyme isn't there? About the samphire turning red? Poor man's lemon juice.

Vine lay on his coat nursing a drink. Somebody was playing music now. Christ, he thought. It was Karoona. That was Karoona's voice behind a hubbub of other voices.

What do you think? laughed Clint.

That her? asked Vine.

Karoona live at The Cat, said Clint. Bootlegged already.

He was playing it on his phone. Behind the fire the last crickets were calling.

Donal loomed out of the dark.

She's pissed off, John.

Looking south, Vine could see Sirius blue and pulsing. The heartbeat of a star.

Yes. Yes I thought so. Knew so. But I think she'll come back.

No, man. She won't. Face it. She'll disappear into London and do okay.

A chaste maid in Cheapside. If she busks they'll get her.

No. Karoona's clever. She'll do well. And she's got a passport now.

Jesus, said Vine. She could have said something. Just anything.

She probably did and you didn't notice.

How'd she go?

Caib Cabs to the airport bus, then on to Victoria.

Got no money.

Hal gave her some I think.

Yes. Our benefactor. Another good deed.

I'm sorry, John. I really am. But if you're not going to eat that fish pass it here.

Vine obliged.

I always prefer beer with mackerel, said Donal. Black beer. Dark meat, bottom feeder, see. Any Guinness about?

Stretching, Vine rummaged for a can. He looked at the bodies slumped around him. One of the girls was belly dancing in the smoke and a man swaying on his knees in front of her and somebody else waving a burning branch. The sparks flew in a net around her head. The industrious Tentpeg dragged up another spar.

Everyone's off, muttered Vine.

I'll be here a couple of weeks, said Donal. Got a little business to take care of.

Come in with me?

In the van? You're joking.

If needs must. Tide you over.

You serious?

Yes. Come in with me.

But you'll be back home soon, said Donal. Admit it man.

Vine took a pull of his cider.

What's Hal's game, for Christ's sake? he asked.

Obvious. Helps people out so far as to make it interesting for him. Helps them out to show off his power.

I don't buy that. He's a smalltime crook, said Vine.

Compared with what? laughed Donal. Maybe he's not so small. Maybe not so crooked either.

He bought Karoona's guitar? Why?

Show. Like having a flash suit. And to make things happen.

Why though?

He's bored.

I think he's mad, said Vine.

Yeah. He is. Mad in his own way. Like you're mad in your own way. And I'm going crazy in mine.

Donal gargled Guinness.

Oh, I got this for you, he said. Nia gave it me.

There might have been ten people around the fire now which Tentpeg had built as high as possible, a pyre burning green, the earlier driftwood reduced to ingots of incendiary wood as white as limestone upon a bed of ash. This was the hottest part of the blaze. Donal saw it was going to waste but he was the only one who had brought food. His potatoes in their foil would be ready soon.

Behind their group ran the black ridge of the dunes. Two more fires were visible on that expanse and there was a bigger blaze along the beach closer to town. An occasional shriek came from that direction. The neon in the fairground had been turned off but Vine could see the shapes of the Megablitz and the Firewheel against the sky. Closer to the dunes, there might have been a light on The Bona Ventura, swinging like a lantern or a powerful torch beam. He couldn't be sure. Somebody's phone rang, the theme from *Mission Impossible*, and Clint it was who leapt up and looked for his jacket in the dark and listened to his message without reply.

Donal watched Tentpeg poking the fire.

Leave it, he said. It's fine.

Want it bigger.

Leave it. Put that tree on and it'll collapse. We got all night.

Out of the darkness stalked Clint and he threw himself down in the marram.

Worked in the blast furnace, didn't he, he laughed. Didn't you Tim?

Three days, sniggered Tentpeg.

Till they told him that story. Didn't they, Tent? About this lazy bastard, supervisor or something, feet up in this shed thing, with the paper and a cuppa. Nice work.

Nick, they called him, said Tentpeg.

Well there's a spill. Out of the ladle or fuck knows where and this molten stream of red hot iron or steel comes right by where our boy here was standing. Scared you didn't it?

No.

Well this molten wave is moving along and the boys are screaming and the alarm going like crazy and there's that Nick in the shed with his paper and headphones on and he can't hear a word and this burning stream of lava is getting closer to the shed and they're all screaming at him and it goes straight into the door and through the other side and there's nothing left. Not a trace. Of the shed like. Nor that Nick.

Not a trace, said Tentpeg.

Never found a hair off his head.

Clint was smiling in the firelight.

You'd think there'd be bones. You'd think there'd be his ribs, like. Or the skull. But nothing.

Not a trace, said Tentpeg.

As if he just vanished, grinned Clint, and the salty flames were like pilot lights in his hair. Into thin air, like.

Used to happen a lot, said Donal.

So that was it for this boy here. Quit, didn't you Tim? On the spot.

Too right on the spot.

No way, he said. Didn't you Tent? You said no way.

Yeah. No way.

Lol

Ahead it was all blackness out to sea. There wasn't a pinprick on the other side. But near the town edge of the dunes one light shone. It was familiar to him now. That was The Copper where Hal's family lived. The Copper which was a hill of four dwellings standing above the first flatter section of the burrows. He'd seen their house enlarged haphazardly over the last ten years. There were three storeys now, a rooftop patio and what appeared to be a small turret.

Oh yes, he'd seen it grow, how could he not? There was nothing in front of The Copper but woods, then a mile of duneland, then the beach. Its views must have been startling. Sometimes in the dark he would stand in the gorse and train his binoculars on the house. They never drew the curtains or blinds. From the front there was no other building for twenty miles. Sometimes Hal would be there, Hal who owned so much of the fair, even the beer he had bought tonight.

But mainly it was a woman who must have been Hal's wife. In a bedroom on the top floor was a television screen so big Lol might tell what programme was playing. Some nights he saw six screens flickering. And so many parties. At 4 am they could still be there in all states of undress. The young, the old.

And there was the child of course. The elderly child. Lol, if he pressed himself into the gorse, its flowers pale under the moon and smelling of coconut, could sometimes see the boy. But they never held a party when the child was there. He'd noticed that.

His field glasses were German, Carl Zeiss Dienstglas, lightweight and powerful wartime binocs, serial 1616561 M. Lol had owned them for forty years. They were vital in the dunes. So difficult without them to tell a willow warbler from a chiffchaff. How keenly alive they made everything. A yellowhammer's wing, a black bra thrown aside. The boy looked about eighteen but was probably ten years older. Say he was thirty. Could have been more. That's what people said. Was that possible? Cerebral palsy maybe. He'd never seen him without a comfort blanket. A big boy, trailing his tartan square.

But it was important to observe things. To be attentive, that was the rule. Lol kept a jeweller's glass in a velcroed pocket of his coat or a front pocket of his shorts. He took it everywhere. On the beach he would look at the sand with it and count the grains and notice the teeming mixture. The closer he looked, the more there was to see. That's what he loved. The filth of it. The sand and the shells and the laver and the plastic breaking down ever so slowly, the Piz Buin and all the factor 30s, the Soltan and Bronze Age suncream bottles fading with every tide, and the polystyrene the sea coughed out of itself, those white grains in everything and everywhere, the Fanta and the Coke, their aluminium grown frail, the ship's rope disintegrating into plastic grass, part of the mixture now for as long as he could imagine, yes even the plastic was alive, and the wood worn white as the quills on a gullwing, and through it all the shiver of other life, the sand hoppers and the sand mites and the infinitesimally small creatures only the jeweller's glass could reveal. Busier than the fairground? No, much busier, an invisible carnival between the tides, the eyepiece screwed into Lol's cheek as if he was winking at that world.

One night, Lol had fixed the child fast with the Zeiss. The kid was talking or crying, his big head always on one side, his big pumpkin head, his face pale and green as the underside of a strawberry. But so much went on in that house. So much carousing. The woman ran the show, anyone could see that. Anyone crouched in the sand, that is. Anyone bent and dark as marram.

Lol smiled. He felt warm in the parka, his feet were expert in that treacherous place. The Copper was a theatre. It demanded an audience. Ah, such gatherings he had witnessed, such cruelties. A mirror shattering silently. He could still see its slivers fly, the image of the girl within it vanishing forever.

Vine

Donal said it was warm enough. Stuff it, he was going in. Vine had already changed at The Shed and now took off his jeans and put on the shorts he'd brought in the bag, the shorts he'd worn with Rachel in the dunes. But then he took another pull at the Bajoru which was almost gone and took the shorts off and threw them on the sand where he'd lain. He walked out wincing over the pebbles which were grey in the moonlight.

About two it was now, Donal had said. Maybe a bit after. The sea was a white line fifty yards ahead. He followed Donal who was only a black blur and he expected the girls to come too but they weren't even looking.

Coral was sleeping, curled in someone's coat in the firelight while the others were talking, voices slow and low. Clint might have gone but Tentpeg was slumped in the dune's shadow gazing into the fire as if something was revealed to him, the embers incandescent and the seasalt turning the flames green. Vine didn't know the name of the other figure who sat there. The hood of his fleece hung over his face.

Now Vine crept on towards the surf and then there were no more rocks and he could stand black and silver in the moonlight. He looked back. Already the fire was hardly visible. What had roared in a tunnel of sparks when Tentpeg dropped the branches was now a lobe of mercury. Pale, it pulsed, it breathed. Behind it was the ridge, steeper thought Vine, than he remembered. Because what was that darkness but sand, sand blown against rock, sand that rose in tumuli and tors, sand in craters and caves and those beaches where nothing grew but thorn trees and where until ten years ago a man had dug gravel, a one man operation with a barrow and a shovel and a wide-mouthed rake.

Two hundred years, the man used to say. That permit's been in my family two hundred years. When quarrying was done by hand.

Find anything? Vine had always asked.

Gravel.

Anything in the gravel?

More gravel.

Anything else?

More gravel.

Once the man had considered Vine.

What would be in the bloody gravel?

Rubies? suggested Vine.

Yeah. Plenty of them. And fool's gold. Listen, gravel's good enough for me. Lovely it is. Goes through the hand like silk. Neat as peas. Best you'll ever dig.

Any dinosaur bones, Mr Pye?

Who knows? laughed the man. And Alun to you. It all goes to making screeds. Local builders can't get enough.

But Vine hadn't seen the man for years. Taking the children for walks he had always said they were going to see Mr Pye. Mr Pye on Pye's plot, Mr Pye who filled canvas panniers with gravel and hefted them on to his horse's back to take out of the dunes. Because that was how it had always been done. Transport by horse. That was what the law said.

Evidently Alun Pye was the last of the line. Maybe he was still on The Caib. Drinking in The Lily? A crowd of codgers went there still. More likely beached in The Zoo, but how would a sand miner have afforded even that? Dead, most like, the old magpie. Not that Vine had heard. And the gravel there still, neat as peas, the thorns growing out of it, and the evening primrose that glimmered in the dark, and the smashed glass and the cider cans and the milkcrates and traffic bollards out of the sea and a long piece of driftwood that might have been Alun Pye's rake, thrown up by that stone tide.

Vine remembered he and Siân had walked there once and given eight-year-old Nia a ride on the horse. What was the bloody horse called? Vine couldn't remember. But he remembered Siân's reaction to his musing.

What if I did that? he had asked.

Did what?

Dig gravel. Sell it to builders' merchants. Use a horse.

You're mad, Siân had marvelled.

Might work.

No way would it work. A horse?

Got to be a horse. Can't use a vehicle.

They were walking beside the animal which was docile enough. A big chestnut, Vine recalled. Nia had thrown her arms around its neck.

Just a thought, he'd laughed. Although he remembered now he hadn't felt like laughing. The next day was Monday which meant a particularly difficult Year Ten group. He hadn't marked the Year Sevens either. And there were the reports to write and the departmental meeting after school and something else, something that was lodged at the back of his mind. A questionnaire, that was it. Three weeks late. Simply, he didn't want to go into school. Didn't want to teach. He wanted to dig gravel and smell the horsehide and look into the eyes of the horse which were yellow and mild and without reproach. He wanted to place his hand on the horse's shoulder and feel its heart beat, the blood running in its tide.

It had been a good horse, very old. Its mane was dark and matted and its breath clouded in the cold. Of course, it had been winter. They were on a Sunday walk and the north-facing marram was white with a frosty scrim and there was a black embryo of ice in that old pesticide drum on the gravel bed.

Too chilly for a walk, Siân had said, but he had dragged them out. Nia had cried but she rode with care and then in triumph and they all breathed out in white clouds trying to outdo the steaming horse. For years it had borne the twin baskets back and forth through the dunes. The path was worn deep as a gully in the sand. And working on a Sunday, too.

Please myself, can't I, Pye had muttered when asked about that. Gravel's always there.

But what had been the horse's name?

For some reason, Siân had been offended by Vine's idea. Perhaps, he had thought at the time, she didn't want to be known as the wife of a miner.

Oh yes, she'd said. That'll pay for riding lessons. For ballet. For the shock absorbers and your red wine.

Just a thought. Teaching's not everything.

Well it's not a very educated thought is it?

'If I was a carpenter', he'd sung to her then but Siân didn't see the joke. And that finished it. Vine hadn't wondered about Pye for years. Now he was gone. Last of the line, and the mining rights lapsed?

Revoked? He looked back and somewhere in that darkness was the gravel bed.

Now he walked on and listened to his feet slap the sand. There were pools that hadn't emptied and streams of seawater running back but he knew there were no more rocks and the way was clear.

Donal called from the shallows. It's perfect. Get in.

The Fish

If I didn't know then I know now. But yes I did know then. Well I suppose I knew then. Like I suppose I know now. But I didn't say anything. Because it might have been a rumour. There's always rumours. But nobody told me straight out. There's no straight out here. Things happen but there's no straight out.

And maybe it's my fault because I wasn't paying attention. For that split second I wasn't listening to what I should have been listening. And I missed it. In that split second. Because of this, I suppose. Because of this. Ready, okay, because of *lih, cukr, smes bylin, prirodni, aromatiicke lathy, barvivo E135, E102*. Because of this crap. Because of that crap.

You remember that pedestal I told you about in The Kingdom? The empty plinth? Well tonight I'm sitting on it. This morning I'm sitting in The Kingdom. It's about three, I think. Suicide hour. When you can feel it starting again. Another day beginning though the air is black and the street lamps on, another day although you know it doesn't want to start, it's too painful a birth. You can hear the day crying, not yet, not yet.

It's too soon.

Now, if I'm not mistaken, round about this spot there used to be two coffins. I can just remember that. They fell to bits years ago. But the coffin lids opened on springs and these two people sort of stood up. A girl in one coffin and a boy in the other. And what was strange was that they weren't skeletons. They weren't nasties. Just a young bloke and his girlfriend. Kind of reunited. Hal's dad it was who got hold of them, part of a job lot with a travelling fair. Apparently they were here for a while and the funny thing was that people liked them. Said it was nice. Said it was positive, these coffins opening and the lovers reaching out to each other. But how weird is that?

Anyway, we were over on The Bona and it was supposed to be a party but it never worked out. There was some food and Coral and the girls were there. Hal put *The Wild Geese* on again but no-one was watching and Jozz had to go, thank Christ, and Clint pushed off somewhere, and George got well out of it and I wasn't much better and yeah, maybe I fell asleep for a minute or two, or an hour max, can't have been more than an hour.

Because okay, I told you I don't sleep. Like I said I don't eat. But sometimes, you know, sometimes the eyes have to shut. This last week, boy, it takes its toll, it all mounts up.

And maybe my experiment with this stuff has not been a success. But I'm looking at the bottle now and there's an inch left. Of absinthe, that is. The green fairy. I always wanted to try it and George got hold of this Czech brand. Typical of George. Couldn't be French, could it? Couldn't be the real thing. Had to be the cheap and nasty equivalent from our friends in the Czech Republic. Those are the Czech ingredients I puzzled you with up there. Note those E numbers. We're not talking mountain streams here. But I always wanted to try it see, so I took it along. Started the bottle for the last hour of the last night as a celebration. Wanted a significant toast, see. And Christ, coming in at seventy per cent proof, this stuff seemed the business.

You see, I like the word. I told you I fancy words, and boy do I like that one. *Absinthe*. Absinthe makes the heart grow fonder. The Fish, absinthe from class. *Et cetera*. But, yes, the green fairy is what they call it and I always wanted to try. So, fair play to George. It's the thought that counts. To absinthe friends.

But look at the colour of it. Okay, the light in here is green. Everything in the mirrors is reflected green. I must look green because my hands are green. And there I am in the glass and a godawful green it is. But this stuff was green before I drank it. A curious blue green. A jade maybe. Perhaps a pale turquoise or a barbiturate green. Kind of a mouthwash. Yes, a medicinal green. Because it tastes like medicine, a medicine that's doing you harm. That's pretty plain.

Jesus, said Clint when I gave him a slug. Anaesthetic.

Blame your bloody father, I said to him.

You're mad, said Jozz. It's as bad as meths. Same colour too.

So you see, it packs a punch. And I still have this feeling it gave me. A green feeling. Like a ribbon of green smoke uncoiling upwards from my feet to my head. Like I'm made of the smoke and I can levitate. As if I was under water and I can see the green light above and I'm rising to the surface and my arm is raised as if I'm pointing at the sky. Which is green because the sea is the green colour of the absinthe.

Yeah, it's the colour of a rock pool, this Czech rotgut. And my arm is raised because I'm holding the bottle as if it was a trophy I've won. But what it feels like is that Nicolas Cage, remember him in *Leaving Las Vegas*? He's the character who's determined to drink himself to death. There's a scene in a cinema where he holds up a bottle like it was a religious relic and then he opens his mouth and he tips the whole litre into himself.

Christ, I thought. He should die right on the spot. Immediately. The human body's not meant to cope with a toxic shock like that. With such a poisonous assault.

And okay, fair play to Hal, when he shows us Burton in *Who's Afraid of Virginia Woolf*. You have to say, that's powerful. Yes, that's scary. Bit boring too, mind. But Nic Cage is too bland for the Las Vegas part. Like, where's the despair? The chronic unhappiness that would make a man drink like Cage was drinking? A litre in one swallow. Nah, Cage doesn't cut it in that film. Not that he can't be psychotic. He can, but not in *Leaving Las Vegas*.

Yet that's what I thought about when I was half way through my own bottle. This green light, the colour of cement. Because I was turned to stone. Like my head was in a breeze block. Ever had the feeling that you can't move? That you've been changed into concrete? Yes, you have, I know. We all have. So perhaps I shouldn't have gone on drinking. But we all know drink has a philosophy of its own and a series of rules and protocols.

But I must have been lying down somewhere, maybe it was here because the absinthe tasted of ashes. And something worse than ashes. Yes, wormwood. That's what it's made from. Bitter herbs. Holy water. Absinthe is wormwood which is the sourest taste there is. Like my tongue had licked the floor here in The Kingdom and I could taste the glue and the *papier maché* and the dust on the demons and the hair off the hound and the rust round the Ripper's blade. Yes, as bad as that. I must have come in here and turned on the light. Instinctively. Because I didn't want to walk home across the badlands. Self preservation, see. And why? Because I've got the last night's takings on me. Three hundred quid in notes. Just the notes. Didn't want to bump into any of Wat's mates, did I? Or any of my own last night clientele. Off their heads, most of them. As to the change, it's where it usually is, in the trap door under the demon king. My secret compartment.

Not that the Nook wouldn't have soothed. My room within my room with the crystal and the mullions and the screensaver. Because Jesus, look at this place. It's a disgrace. The dirt is an inch deep and there's chip papers and cider cans between the rails, mainly that black and gold superstrength brew. Which is like drinking sulphuric acid I can tell you. And those polystyrene trays and some bint's knickers and Christ a condom, a pale green durex with the gobbet intact. Yes, the green fairy. Colour of cement. It's a tradition, see, screwing in the carriage as you go through the Kingdom. Specially on the last night. Sort of like the mile high club for your earthbound proletariat, bless them. And somebody's puked of course. Wouldn't be the last night without that.

So yes, I was out of it at the party. Turned to stone as I say. But I was a stone who could hear things.

About time, they were saying. Well, Hal was saying it. And George was there and not liking it. That's the impression I have now. That George didn't like what was being said.

We'll call it *Richey's* they were saying. Yeah, *Richey's*. Or *The Burton*, someone else said, and then there were all these ideas like *Rich*, or *Richard's* and *Gone for a Burton*. I ask you. *Rich*, yes, that seemed the favourite.

But no, I didn't pay that much attention then. Or did I? You see, there's always talk off season. Always plans for development. But they were talking about changing The Cat. New bar and layout, and all this memorabilia like framed film posters and Richey as Mark Anthony or the leader of the Wild Geese and correct, you've guessed it, Hal's specially autographed Allbright beer mat in pride of place. Behind bullet proof glass I suppose.

Because it seems like there's this bid in to develop all this area. Includes The Cat, part of the fairground, and down Sand Alley that leads towards the caravans. But no way will it happen. Take my word. There's always rumours at this time. Once there were even plans for an aquarium that would have held the marine life you get off The Caib. Everything from those tiny transparent shrimps up to sharks. Can you credit it? The types who neck Strongbow in here queuing to look at seaweed?

We get complaints, you understand. From the council and such like. People say we're a disgrace, that the fair is a scrapyard, that there's sex and drugs and runaway kids and illegals and money laundering and that we're a bastion of the black economy. Which is all true. But it's a fair ground I always say. If it offends you, go to Disneyland. Even this August there was a delegation came through. These MPs and councillors and their special advisors wandered in on a Thursday afternoon. And okay, we weren't at our busiest or our best. Five is a bad time, it's an in-between time. Things looked slow.

Roll up, I started shouting. At the delegation. These blokes in their sad linen suits, these women trying to look informal. And nearly every one of them talking on a mobile or whispering into a recorder. One of them even had a lap top. In the fair. Retard.

Yes, Roll up, I shouted. Special rates for party bookings. And did they come in? Did they hell. Smiled as they went past. Oh yes, one kid bought a toffee apple. Just to be cool of course. Took one bite and put it in a bin. About twenty he looked, should have been on the dodgems. Seems like it was health and safety issues, people working while claiming benefits. Well how do they suppose anyone exists in the first place? Jesus.

But Hal's under pressure from Mrs Hal too. Hates the place, she does. And Nick Manners, though what his share is I don't know. But obviously he's ready for off. Christ, come to think of it, Nicolas Cage looked like Manners would do after four pints. Manners who doesn't drink. Cage looked nothing worse than that. Nothing you couldn't disguise with coffee and peppermints.

But I tell you this, what a great feeling it is to shout 'Roll up'. It really is. It's fantastic. Roll up, Roll up. It's therapy for a lot of what ails us. To stand by the hutch and holler that ancient cry. To watch the girls get into the cars and then out again when they're pissing themselves laughing and they've spilled lager over themselves or ice cream, and the boys with their shirts off all pale as lard and scrawny and blue with tattoos, and the middle aged couples doing it because they did it thirty years ago and it'll be gone next year they were saying because The Kingdom's smack in the development area but I don't believe it because it's always the same after the last night and *Rich* or *Richey's* is not going to happen and the memohrahbeeleeyuh's not going to happen either.

And maybe I'm feeling better now. Or perhaps I'm getting worse. But I was paying attention. See, I told you I was paying attention. Or did I? Anyway, I'm the stone who listened and heard it all. A green stone. Who heard it and knows what it's all worth. And you know what it's worth? It's worth *Hazev je advozen ad hlavini chufoue slozhy pelynku* and nothing more and nothing less. Or so it says here. In the green light. Well that's what the man in the mirror says who's gone a God-almighty green.

Vine

Sometimes it was muddy here but now the sand was firm. Vine shivered but he could tell that after a few minutes the water would be bearable. A wave slapped his thighs. It was a black wave he hadn't expected, a wave coming invisibly out of the darkness and breaking behind him, and he winced at the next one that chilled his balls. Yet it released him immediately so that he stood in a stillwater hearing Donal whistling some adenoidal Brian Wilson, and someone else it might have been come wading in although it was hard to tell in the water's electrical hum. He listened to the waves, that shackle-dragging sound they made, approaching, departing, a rattle in the sea's throat, a whisper in its dungeon.

But the smell. Always the sea smell was more powerful at night. And its smell was his smell now. Such a smell. All over him. Sealace and oysters. Mullet shit and samphire tea. And coffee maybe, its bitterest grounds. And school, yes. The sea smelt of school, school's back of the filing-cabinet smell, lost gymkit, the korma the canteen had tried once, the hormonal waft of the corridors in C Block, Lynx and Poison and what were those perfumes called? Jealousy? Terror? Yes all of those, and his old room with the door closed, the door locked, and tequila, of course, especially that brand with the gold sombrero as a bottletop, and the carpet upstairs in The Cat where the damp had risen behind the bar, and Brychan's feet, his son's feet, his perfect son's tiny, petal-like, suppurating feet. And paint slapping under its scab, yes he was forever prising some lid off with a screwdriver, releasing that old paint smell, how often had he thought that, this smells of the sea, and perhaps white spirit on a stinking rag and the white lightning that Gil used to concoct, Gil who was still turning up at 8.30 am, Gil who commuted in that car he loved, Triumph Leopard or Wolf, yes, Gil the predator, the sandwich box on the seat beside him, made up by Gil's mother, Gil who hadn't cracked, Gil who burned his songs into silver discs that hung in the allotment, yeah, the potcheen that triumphant Gil made, it smelt of the sea, the sea that did not make sense, the sea that smouldered like sunflowers when they were blackened and bowed, the marrowflesh-smelling sea, the sulphur in it, the iron, the sea that now tasted of his own blood.

And then there was another of those waves whomping his chest, his chest with its grey hairs, how had that happened, how could that hair have turned grey? And Rachel not asking but he knew what she was thinking, Rachel and her phone, one call after another, sorry she'd say, got to take this, yes, show me the strumpet that began this stir. And Siân. Can't ever, won't ever forget Siân. Never a second without Siân, never a dream, Siân and her marking regime, Siân with her ridiculous ruffled choirgirl uniform. Why didn't they wear something different? Why didn't they sing something else? All those patriotic light operas and stonehearted hymns. What about Bruckner? Now there was a sound the sea might make. That was music that could engulf your life. That was architecture. Yes, nonstop Siân, impossible-to-keep-up-with Siân, for trespass of thine eye, the sire, the son, the dame and daughter die. Yes, the sweat in Siân's groin, that's how the sea smelt, the time he'd licked the tequila off her, it stings she said, you're mad and you're drunk, it's stinging me you fool, but he had poured and licked and hadn't Siân laughed then, her dirty laugh in someone else's dirty bed. Where was that, years ago or last week? Ach, Christ knows where and when.

Now another wave black under Venus caught him in the throat. Vine staggered and laughed and Donal was around somewhere wasn't he, not acting his age, yes that was Donal's trouble, and someone else was moving through the water, maybe Coral, Coral stripped off, yes she would be a conger would Coral, he could see her teeth, he could see them flashing in the water coming towards him, she would be a shark alright, a pale Baltic shark pushing her head between his thighs. Or maybe it was one of the others. Those skinny Lithuanians didn't have an ounce between them. And what did they know anyway? Because they seemed to know something he didn't. Of course, they knew the Devil. The Devil's fingerprints were forever on their glassy breasts, the enamel bosses of their bellies.

Yes if he looked south there was Venus on the water. Jesus how often did you see that? The planet's reflection on the sea was an arrow, its light blue neon, Venus in furs, Mona Lisa with a pony tail. And no further no, mustn't go deeper than this, up to his chest already. But what the hell was that black thing, a black swimmer, a black companion for a second diving beside him then leaping from the sea straight into the night?

It wasn't a fish though they could jump. Vine had seen them. But this was a big one. Maybe it was Donal. But Donal was too clumsy now. So maybe it was Olga. Because Olga would burn like a knife through this current, her arms outstretched. But Olga would have come back for him. Olga would have returned and he would have held her, a dogfish in his arms thrashing him with her tail, Olga's mouth on his nipple sucking the sea out of him while he counted the freckles upon her, the sprockles and moles all over her back.

But it was more like a bird. A diving bird. Blacker than anything else in the night, so black it cut its own shape out of the darkness so there was a black hole in the universe. Olga wouldn't do that. Olga couldn't fly. Instead, Olga would place her hand upon his heart and tell him to relax, John, relax, look at that star, what's that star, John, tell me its name, it's our star John, it's ours.

Then it was calm and Vine glanced around. The sea was a meadow. Or a desert where he was buried to the neck. He came up and floated on his back and the water was warm as Pye's mare, her scarred hide, her seaweed mane. Now it was still. Donal wasn't singing any more. Donal was out ahead, showing off, swimming for the last time that year in his end of season swim.

Something small pittered into the water beside Vine. Perhaps it was rain. He remembered an evening swim with Siân and the kids. There was a storm coming, she'd said, and taken the children out. But Vine stayed to watch the first drops on the sea's skin. What rings they made, like pebbles into the swell. Sweet as peas. Then the rain had started from a sky like brass. The downpour was filled with African sand. In the west the sky was on fire and when the thunder came Vine had felt it in the water. Because the sea had trembled. He would have sworn the sea had been shaken. As if some leviathan had passed out there in the bay. Why not? He had promised whales for his children. He had told them of basking sharks, huge and benign, grazing invisible grass. And the rain was red on the water, each drop a copper nail hammered into that fleece, and the rain dark upon him. Upon his forearm he examined the meniscus of one drop.

Come on, John, Siân had cried. There'll be lightning. And sure enough, she'd pointed and Vine had seen the vein on the horizon.

Come on, John, for God's sake, she'd cried, and yes, he was coming, forcing his way out, the reef's orange and black around him in the sky. But how slowly he stepped from that lagoon.

Oi, come on, Dad, Brychan had screamed. Brychan wore water wings and Vine had crouched before the boy and laughed and said there's nothing to be afraid of, just put your tongue out and taste the rain. It's hot. The rain's hot! What does it remind you of?

How they had danced then. Siân and Nia, the boy and Vine were the last ones on the beach. The last people alive. And they danced in a circle with their faces turned up to the sunset and the rain scalding their mouths. So yes, it was Siân who had written the letter. The letter was from Siân, explaining why he must come home. Why it was time. After exile, after mistakes and recriminations. After the type of problem every adult understood. Typical of Siân, to write like that. With her marking pen, he'd bet. So formal in her high-collared way. The letter would be a sermon. How she would preach to him. And how he would hold her till she laughed and pushed him away.

Yes maybe it was raining now. Or maybe the black bird was coming back. Vine didn't care. He lay in darkness on the shoulders of the sea. Still within his depth. Yes, he was careful about that. If he chose to he might put one foot on the sand. And even with seawater in his mouth he didn't cough. His chest was relaxed. Surely he was getting better. Getting over it. No coughing and no Karoona, gone as he knew she'd go. He had coughed Karoona out of his soul. As if she'd ever been there. And who was she anyway, who was

Karoona? He'd never understand now. A good deed. That's what it was. He'd given her a home, tough little, tight little madam with the sneer and the silences and the whole of the Sahara somewhere inside her. For her to summon. For her to use. Her hinterland, remote and vast, a dune smoking on the horizon. And here he lay in the water he had always known. A child in comparison. A baby in a bath. Because that's what she used to call him. A child.

Oh John, she'd sigh. Oh, John. In that tired voice. Sorry, he'd say. I'm sorry. And the wind chimes at the door would play Karoona's music. Because it was always Karoona's sound they made. It was never his. That music didn't belong to John Vine. Donal was right. The girl would do well, but she wasn't as young as people thought. She wasn't a girl. Oh no, Karoona had experience. There were stretch marks on her belly. That's what they looked like to Vine. On the one occasion he'd seen her naked, that's what they seemed to him. And she'd buckled in half when she saw he was there in the room. Folded herself up, her breasts hanging down, the dark plate of her pelvis with those seams. A scimitar's slashes. Its scars across her. Oh not so young then without her silks. The butterfly without its wings. She was peeing into a pot, which was strange. Not using the caravan toilet but squatting over a saucepan.

Sorry, he'd said. And turned round. Because she had spilled it across the bedroom floor. Spilled her dark green poison. Yes Karoona would do what she needed to do. She would lift her voice in a Greek Street basement and a man would look up. Because that was how it worked, wasn't it? That was how everything worked.

Of course it must be her letter back there in his coat. At the campfire, reduced now to a star. And behind it other stars on the ridge. Once, a cry, far off in the dark. He would open the letter tomorrow. But he could imagine it now. Thank you, John, thank you. I'm sorry, John, I'm sorry. Goodbye, John, goodbye. PS. Fuck you, John.

And Rachel too, how old had Rachel been? Fixing herself in the bedroom mirror, sipping that lighter fluid out of the Vladivar bottle cap. All he was doing was glancing through her CDs scattered across her room, Body Shop bottles and tampons and her little black thong flung away. I hate those, she'd said. God knows why we wear them.

Yes all he had been doing was passing time while she put the piercings in. But he had looked up suddenly and she was staring at him. With her superior smile.

Rachel's dressing table was lit by a white bulb. The rest of the room was dim red.

Not much for you there, she'd said.

What's that? he'd said.

Hey. Why do you do it?

Do what?

You know?

I don't. Do what?

Tuck your shirt into your trousers? That's what? Why do you do that?

What's wrong with it?

It's kind of, kind of uncool.

Oh, he'd said. Uncool. Yes. That's me. Uncool. Never thought of it before.

D'you tuck them into your Y fronts?

You what? Who said I wear Y fronts?

Oh, I don't know, she'd said. And winked. I think you're a Y fronts sort of individual.

And she had warmed to it.

Like you're a sort of 10cc individual.

10cc?

My mother plays them. *I'm not in love.* Real soppy stuff.

Do you know why they called themselves 10cc? he'd asked.

And John Lennon. You know, *Jealous Guy, Watching the Wheels.* She plays all those. Yes, that's you. *I was feeling insecure…*

And that had made him angry. Yes, that had finished it. Not that there was anything to finish. Not with Rachel. Not with her. Jesus, there was nothing. It had burst like a bubble. Like that raindrop in his palm filled with Moroccan sand. A raindrop with a gold bezel. Because if Rachel was anywhere her father would know. The police must have questioned the man. He lived in London and Spain, or so she'd said. Rachel had mentioned him briefly, describing a character she must have seen on television, some genial lowlife, a skunk-dealing joker with a bronze chain and Japanese tattoo. His shirt untucked. His hair grey.

Yes that's what Vine told the police. That day in the caravan with Karoona banished to the fair and the mercies of The Fish who would   show her The Kingdom's history, the House of Pain, the world of wax. Not that she would hear him. Then the next day at the station Vine had seemed to hover above his own body as he spoke. How concise and authoritative he was, a man in a suit and grey tie, the ambitious professional. Vine had shocked himself with the performance.

You should try and trace that man, officer, Vine had said. Because she's gone to follow her father. Find him, find her.

What was the nature of your relationship with Rachel? the detective had asked.

Relationship? She was a friend. But she was also my pupil. At least she was in my school. A highly talented young woman. A certainty to do well.

And from the ceiling John Vine had stared down at himself in the interview room. At John Vine sipping his mug of tea. At John Vine describing what parts Rachel played in the school plays.

Then Vine turned over in the water and struck out. As usual he made little headway. It was better to float. No, it was miraculous to float. To float through the moment upon the sleeping sea. To float there in the darkness, the black bird departed, the night fishing bird vanished from the depths, the water so soothing it might appear impossible to sink, no waves now, or the waves breaking beyond him closer to the beach, the swell holding him high on its cushions and the sky trembling, Venus tipping its torchbeam.

When John Vine stretched out his right foot there was nothing there. He reached as far as he could and maybe his toe touched the seabed but then there was nothing.

The cry came once more. A curlew perhaps, that ghost after curfew.

Then somebody must have poured the Bajoru over the bonfire because a flare shot up and Vine could see the flames bending in the dark. He'd have to swim to shore. He'd never swum so far. Yet at least there was somebody there. Somebody still drinking, somebody talking, holding out. He had thought he was the only one left.

No, he felt too good to drown. He was part of the water now, its smell his smell, his blood its salt. There must be no more death. No more of that. He was the black bird. He was the night fisher. And what had his father told him, his father who had thrown down that book in his grandparents' garden and fished Vine out of the lily pool? The boy was wet and white.

You can drown in a drop, John. Drown in a drop.

Ah, Dad, whispered Vine to the sea. Dad, Dad.

Ahead were the dunes. Ahead was the beach with its black sand.

You never said I might be crushed by a grain.

Acknowledgements

A section of *Sea Holly* first appeared in *New Welsh Review*.

The author wishes to thank the Welsh Books Council
for financial assistance in the writing of this book.

About the Author

Robert Minhinnick was born in 1952. He has twice won the UK's Forward Prize for 'best individual poem', and the Wales Book of the Year in 1993 and 2006 for his collections of essays. His next collection of poetry, *King Driftwood*, is due from Carcanet in 2008.

To Babel and Back
Robert Minhinnick

WINNER OF THE WALES BOOK OF THE YEAR 2006

Join Robert Minhinnick on a journey across a radioactive planet. Researching the use of depleted uranium in modern weapons, the writer follows a deadly trail from the uranium mines of the USA into Saddam Hussein's Iraq. Here, he is led into the temples of a deserted Babylon and to what his guides insist is the site of the Tower of Babel.

Interspersed with these 'radioactive writings' – part-documentary, part-dream – are essays on a host of different places. Berlin, Prague, Buenos Aires, New York, Italy, England, Finland, Canada: this globalised world is simultaneously familiar and bizarre, filled with the background noise of contemporary society yet capable of providing places and moments of silence. Jet-lagged, culture-lagged, Minhinnick returns to his native Wales, its coastline and valleys as extraordinary as anything encountered in a Babel that might be myth or alarmingly real.

Robert Minhinnick's other collections of essays are *Watching the Fire-eater* and *Badlands*.

ISBN:1854114018   £6.99 paperback

www.seren-books.com